WHEN FRANKI SHELTON decided to become friendly with Daye Peters and Rhea Bellon, it was only because she had selected them as the girls from whom she could learn the most. She hadn't counted on growing to love them as she had never loved her very own sisters . . .

Charter Books by Nomi Berger

THE BEST OF FRIENDS
DEVOTIONS
ECHOES OF YESTERDAY

The Best of Friends

NOMI BERGER

CHARTER BOOKS, NEW YORK

THE BEST OF FRIENDS

A Charter Book/published by arrangement with
the author

PRINTING HISTORY
Charter Original/July 1984

ISBN: 0-441-05488-9

Charter Books are published by The Berkley Publishing Group,
200 Madison Avenue, New York, New York 10016.
PRINTED IN THE UNITED STATES OF AMERICA

To my friends, who have always been there for me . . .

. . . With the best of my love

{ *prologue* }

PALM BEACH is a lady.

An elegant dowager, she governs a gilded piece of paradise, an idyllic southern playground burnished by the rays of a topaz sun and licked by the waters of an aqua sea. The aging love child of Henry Morrison Flagler, she is man's elusive Dulcinea, eternally beckoning, forever unattainable, except to a privileged few.

She preens behind box hedges and black wrought-iron gates and nestles contentedly among pastel cushions of oleander and hibiscus and bougainvillea. Hers is the reassuring purr of a Rolls Royce engine, the luxuriant whisper of designer silks, the crystalline sparkle of family jewels and heirloom crystal. While she diets for lunch, she feasts on polo and charity balls, yachting and intimate dinners for twelve.

She is tradition.

She wears the patina of time with regal grace. Serenity is her sacred watchword. With an imperceptible flick of one fine-boned wrist, she waves away whatever inconvenience life may cast her way. She will abide no news but good news, and wherever she walks, the commonplace can have no place, while the harshness of reality wears a gentler face.

And yet today, intrusion, like a silvered serpent, has slithered into her golden Eden: intrusion in the form of change. Youth, with its inherent brashness, is impatiently shredding the tapestry that time had woven for her and then frozen at her bidding. Her supremacy challenged, she rouses herself and prepares for the inevitability of confrontation; for *change* is a word she has never known, and compromise is a way of life she has never understood.

And so she stands, poised and ready, wavering on the borderline drawn between yesterday and tomorrow. Her head raised proudly, the lady arches one delicate golden brow and with a guileless smile, gives change the finger . . .

{ chapter one }

HER FINGERS were trembling as she unfastened her seat belt. Although she was sitting directly behind the first-class cabin and could have disembarked almost immediately, Daye Peters chose to remain seated instead, her hands folded tightly in her lap, just staring out the window of the plane. Beyond the high chain-link fence surrounding the airport, a solitary coconut palm waved its yellowing fronds like the blades of a windmill in the languid November breeze. Not far from the palm stood a brilliant red hibiscus, its trumpet-shaped flowers glowing like stabs of flame against its deep green leaves. Daye sighed softly to herself. Whereas New York had been a somber blur of grayness and frosty drizzle when they had taken off from La Guardia less than three hours ago, Palm Beach was laid out before her like a glorious welcoming carpet of unending sun-licked blue.

Out of the corner of one eye, she could see the ticket, which she had rolled into a tight little cylinder and then stuck in the small metal ashtray in the arm of her seat like a half-smoked cigar. It had already served its purpose, and because Daye had never been a collector of travel mementos, she had no further use for the one-way United Airlines ticket. If she had to, she could always purchase another one-way ticket back again. But only if she had to.

"Is something wrong, miss?"

A young flight attendant was leaning over her, lightly touching Daye on the shoulder. Daye glanced up with a start. All of the other passengers had already disembarked.

"No. Everything's fine, thank you," she replied. As always, her voice was pitched low. Because of its softness, it was a voice that invariably caused others to bend closer to hear her.

"Have you left any personal belongings in the overhead compartment?" asked the stewardess.

"Yes, a tote bag."

The girl immediately reached up to free the spring on the curved door above Daye's seat. The heavy Vuitton bag swung down and hit the carpeted aisle with a muted thud. Daye gave the stewardess an appreciative smile, one that deepened the cleft in her chin, but failed to reach her wide-set hazel eyes. For a moment, the girl appeared flustered, but when Daye made no move to stand up, she hurried back up the aisle to the first-class galley and motioned to one of the other flight attendants to join her there.

Daye leaned back in her seat again. By now Rhea would be convinced that she had changed her mind about coming, and Franki would be upset about keeping the parking meter fed. She smoothed out the creases in her plum silk pants with the palms of her hands and frowned. She would look like a ghost next to them. The very thought of their being together again sent a butterfly of nervous anticipation to hover on delicate wings somewhere between her stomach and her throat. She was almost tempted to get up, but something was still holding her back. For no other reason than to calm herself down, she began to run a checklist of her Manhattan apartment through her head, hoping that the woman who had sublet it from her would remember to keep turning the Boston fern in the bedroom window.

It was not long before her thoughts turned from the apartment she had left behind to the condominium awaiting her now in Boca Raton. A spasm of pain made her wince, and it startled her to think that after eight months the pain was just as acute as ever. It had been eight months since she had buried her parents, or rather what had remained of Lydia and Bennett Peters after the Alitalia jet carrying them and one hundred thirty-seven other passengers had crashed in fog outside Milan. Eight months. Daye gave her head a mournful shake.

Their sudden deaths had found her unprepared for such a tragedy. The nightmare of it had been like a catching in the throat, the sharp intake of breath that triggers a coughing spell, for which there is no other remedy but the simple passage of time. It had spun her from the carousel of her well-ordered life and caused her to take a critical look at that life. And she had found it wanting.

Where Lydia Day and Bennett Peters had been golden halves of a golden couple, the ideal team, the lawyer and the judge, with the ideal marriage, Daye, without brothers or sisters or a partner of her own, was alone. She had always been proud of being alone and being so successful at it. On her own was how she had viewed it. On her own by choice and loving it. But now at thirty-three and with her parents gone, she was not as certain anymore.

She had been forced to admit that time, always her strongest ally, had been transformed into the most formidable of adversaries. Her social life was stagnating; her married friends were involved with their families, her single friends were dedicated to their careers and their independence; and she could hear her own biological clock ticking away her childbearing years. She had peered ahead at her future, and all she could see was Daye Peters, interior designer. Successful. Wealthy. And alone.

Where once "tomorrow" had been her watchword, she began to see it as something of a curse. She had even reserved love for that tomorrow. Until she had opened her own office. Until she had hired assistants and formed Daye Peters and Associates. Until her work took her to Boston and Chicago, to Denver and San Francisco, to Dallas and Miami. Until she was able to afford her own apartment overlooking Central Park, her own mink coat and her own Mercedes 450 SL. Until she had proven that she could make it on her own, relying, not on a man, but on her own talent and energy and her unfailing belief in herself and her own ability. She had been certain that, unlike her mother, she could never successfully combine both career and marriage without her career suffering, and so she had kept pushing tomorrow out of the way. And love with it.

She was now aware of two pairs of professionally cool eyes studying her carefully from the first-class galley. Flushing uncomfortably under their scrutiny, she leaned forward and got a firm grip on the leather handles of her tote bag. Steady now, she cautioned herself as she slowly stood up. This was not an ending, but a chance at a new beginning away from the ghosts of the past, close to the two people with whom she had shared so much of her life. In spite of the fact that both Rhea and Franki had been living in Florida for the past four years, the bond between them had never been broken.

Slinging her purse over her shoulder, she made her way down the aisle to the door, nodding politely to the two flight attendants whose relief was all too transparent despite their smiles. She walked down the ramp from the plane and headed across the carpeted floor of the terminal toward the escalator, striding with long-legged grace, her plum silk shirt outlining the fullness of her breasts as she moved, the heels of her gray snakeskin boots adding another three inches to her lithe five-feet-seven-inch frame. A well-dressed middle-aged man, deeply tanned, lowered his Porsche sunglasses and gazed over the top of them for a better look at Daye as she strode past him. He followed her for one long, appreciative moment, stunned by the beauty of her heart-shaped face, the luxuriant spill of chestnut hair that curved about her shoulders, and the remarkable hazel eyes, richly flecked with green and gold, which seemed so unbearably sad.

Unaware of his perusal of her, Daye continued on to the baggage-claim area and began looking about for a skycap. Her gaze fell on a young girl who was standing at the far end of the luggage carousel, and she found herself smiling. The girl's short, sleek black hair reminded her so much of Rhea's. Daye's heartbeat quickened as she thought of Rhea. Quiet, kittenish, the pampered darling, gliding effortlessly through life on the plush golden carpet provided first by her parents and now by her husband. And then there was Franki. The third side of their contented triangle of deep friendship, which had endured for twenty years. Lusty, raunchy, fiercely competitive Franki, whose husband was the final stepping stone in her long and patient upward climb toward comfort and security.

When two of her four large bags were standing like over-stuffed canvas soldiers at her feet, Daye began glancing around the terminal for some sign of her two friends. She checked the time on her tank watch and frowned. Perhaps Rhea had forgotten to tell Franki. But then, Franki could have gotten involved in a tennis game and forgotten about it herself. She checked the time again. She was just beginning to tap one booted foot in time to the increasingly agitated beating of her heart when she suddenly sucked in her breath. The tapping stopped abruptly. All she could do was stare.

The pitching in her stomach was so much a part of her response to any man with icy blond hair and tanned, chiseled features that she no longer realized she still reacted that way. The arrogant tilt of his head, the navy blue blazer and charcoal gray trousers, the pale blue shirt and striped tie were all so right. But the walk was wrong. It was too casual, too unhurried, whereas *his* walk was all thrust and determination, alive with the sense of already having left today behind in his impatience to plunge into tomorrow.

Their eyes met, and Daye blushed. She hastily looked away, feeling like a complete fool. The glint of appreciation in his own eyes as he walked past her did nothing to assuage her guilt for having felt what she had felt and for having stared so boldly at someone who had been no more than a handsome, disturbingly familiar stranger. It hadn't been Neil. It couldn't have been Neil because Neil was in London. Yet, for one brief, foolish moment, she had been so sure.

She bit down hard on her bottom lip. She had no right to feel as she did, no right at all. But even after all these years, that first glimpse of Neil Howard, whether imagined or real, still had the power to affect her that way. The way it had when she had considered him hers. The same way it did long after she had lost him to Rhea.

FRANKI SHELTON brought the Volvo station wagon to a halt directly in front of the arrivals door and put on the emergency flashers.

"Shouldn't we try to find a parking space?" asked Rhea Howard, nervously scanning the access road for some sign of an approaching police officer.

"Why bother?" Franki was busily angling the rearview mirror for a better look at her newly cropped hair. "Why pay for parking when she'll probably be out here any minute?"

Rhea had to smile. In spite of Brian's money, Franki had never really changed. She was still saving on the little things.

"But what if the plane was delayed or she can't manage her luggage by herself?" persisted Rhea. "You know how impossible it is to find a skycap in this place."

Franki crinkled her nose, and the freckles on its snubbed little tip danced impishly. "Knowing our Daye, she's already got three gorgeous hunks in tow, happily carrying her bags and fighting over who gets to take her to dinner tonight."

"Franki!" Rhea giggled and gave her friend a playful slap on the wrist. Even after twenty years, so many of Franki's spirited, offhand remarks still made her react the same way— with a giggle and a slap. "I still say you should consider parking this thing."

"Thing!" At first Franki's eyes widened in protest, but then her mouth began to droop and the expression in her blue-green eyes changed perceptibly. "Do you think I should have driven Brian's Mercedes instead?" she said, knowing that she had chosen the wagon strictly for practical reasons. "I should have taken the Mercedes," she concluded glumly. "Daye will think this is the best we can do."

"How can you say such a thing?" Rhea's voice was gently chiding. "Daye's interested in seeing *us*, Franki, not Brian's new car."

Franki crinkled her nose again while she considered Rhea's remark, then with a light shrug, she said, "I suppose you're right, Rhee; it shouldn't really matter that much, should it?"

Her rhetorical question was met with silence as Rhea sat beside her with her soft gray eyes now focused on her black alligator handbag. "I think I'll go inside and look for her," she decided, one freshly manicured nail absently tracing the smooth grain of the purse. Then, less certain of her decision, she murmured, "Do you think I should, Franki, or would you prefer me to stay out here with you?"

"Do whatever you want, Rhee," came the nonchalant reply as Franki began tugging at the silk top she had bloused so carefully over her wide suede belt and leather pants. "It's not fair," she complained. "Everything always looks so good in the magazines, but nothing ever stays put on a living, breathing human being." She glanced sideways at Rhea in her tailored black and white tweed Chanel suit with the white silk blouse, the bow perfectly tied, and frowned. Everything always stayed in place on her. But that was because Rhea was a size six and didn't have to go around the way she did draping and hanging and strategically placing things so that her bust looked smaller and her hips narrower. Giving up with a sigh of defeat, she turned her full attention to the troubled expression on Rhea's face. "Go on, Rhee," she urged her gently. "Go inside and look for Daye. In the meantime, I'll simply circle."

"All right," Rhea was quick to agree. Picking up her purse, she reached for the door handle, but with her hand still poised in midair, she turned back to Franki and said, "Do you think Daye's really serious about settling here?"

"Don't you?"

Rhea gave her narrow shoulders a shrug. "I still don't understand why she'd give up a successful career in New York to start all over again in a place like Palm Beach."

"She obviously has her reasons."

Rhea was taken aback by the sudden brusqueness in Franki's voice, and her hurt was immediately reflected in her eyes. Sensing Rhea's withdrawal, Franki hastily gave her friend's small hand a tight squeeze.

"I'm sorry, Rhee, I'm just a little edgy today. It's that time of the month again." Her voice was harsh as she ground out that last word. "I really didn't mean to snap at you."

"I know." Rhea's lips, outlined in the same muted peach as her nails, curved into a forgiving smile. She kissed Franki lightly on the cheek and slid quietly out of the car, leaving the door ajar.

Franki sighed, reached across the seat and pulled the door shut. How many times, she asked herself, have I closed a door for Rhea in the past twenty years?

THE MUGGY atmosphere of the terminal was even more oppressive than the tepid air outside, and Rhea headed directly for the nearest ladies' room to comb her hair. She dug into her purse for her comb and ran it through the straight, thick black hair that needed no combing because it always stayed perfectly in place no matter how high the humidity. Peering at herself in the smudgy glass, she studied each of the features that made up her unremarkable face, and gave silent thanks for the many miracles wrought by the magic of cosmetics.

Leaning even closer to the mirror, she ran the tips of her fingers over the well-concealed circles under her eyes. Does it show? she asked herself. The effects of too many sleepless nights and too many bad dreams on those nights when I *can* fall asleep? Could anyone tell just by looking into my eyes that I feel as if I'm living on a plane far removed from everyone else, looking down at them through a sheet of glass, happy to be where I am and relieved that no one else is up here with me?

She put her comb back in her purse and snapped it shut. Will Daye notice? she wondered. She squeezed her eyes closed and tried to imagine how it might feel if Daye, so remarkably perceptive, could look into her eyes and know the truth. Rhea shuddered. No one must know, especially Daye. And so, before she left the ladies' room, she took the precaution of digging into her purse again and locating her dark glasses and then slipping them on.

FRANKI CIRCLED the airport for the third time, complaining in a progressively louder voice with each elliptical turn she made. She raked her fingers through her frosted silver and gold hair and thought dismally of the tennis games she was missing today. Instead of tennis, she had elected to have her hair cut and her body massaged, her legs waxed, her nails manicured and her makeup applied. That made her smile. Anyone would think she had been getting ready for the most important night of her life, when she was simply going to the airport to meet a girl friend. But then, Daye Peters wasn't just a friend. Daye was one of the two best friends she had ever had.

Before she could stop herself, she was nibbling worriedly on one of her short fingernails, biting away the edges of the freshly applied clear polish. Did she still look as though she was trying too hard? Were the old insecurities and the new frustrations finally beginning to show through the veneer she had perfected over the years in spite of her continued attempts to conceal them? Would Daye see the old Franki surfacing again, the one who still believed she hadn't managed to get it quite right yet?

A horn sounded behind her. Franki scowled into the rear-view mirror at the man with his hand on the horn and careened into the first parking space she could find. Be a sport, she told herself, as she cut the engine and fumbled in her wallet for some change for the meter. She hadn't seen Daye since the funeral, and suddenly she needed to see her more than anything else in the world.

AS HER fourth bag neared her, Daye braced herself to lift it from the carousel. The bag was in midair when she saw Rhea coming toward her. She raised her arm to wave, and the bag thudded back onto the carousel, where it tottered precariously, dangling halfway between the moving ramp and the floor. But Daye had already forgotten about it. All she could see was the loving smile on Rhea's face.

Daye's boots glided across the floor as effortlessly as a pair of wings. Her pulse was racing, and a wonderful heat was surging through her, turning up the corners of her mouth and sending her radiant smile up to her eyes at last. Twin tears stood out in their burnished depths and shimmered there like dewdrops on two golden leaves.

"Daye!"

"Rhea!"

Their voices blended and merged. They reached out, each catching the other around the waist and holding on tightly. They hugged each other close, and Daye breathed in the familiar scent of Rhea's perfume, felt the small bones, so fine and so brittle, and the flesh so warm and dear and strong.

"God, I've missed you," Daye whispered fiercely, hugging her friend even tighter.

"And I've missed you," Rhea answered her. "It feels so good to hold you, Daye, so good."

"Oh, Rhee." Above the hammering of her heart, Daye could hear a small voice chanting, "You're home, Daye Peters, you're home."

"Daye!"

She lifted her head, and through a blaze of tears, she saw Franki bounding toward them.

"Franki!"

Daye extended her right arm, and Rhea raised her left. As Franki ran to them, she opened her own arms wide, prepared to embrace them both. All three of them linked arms and pulled one another into the web of their special closeness and their remembered love. And suddenly, Daye felt safe again. Nothing had changed for them, and if they were lucky, nothing ever would.

THE DRIVE along the winding A1A was much as Daye remembered it from her last visit to Boca shortly before her parents' deaths. To her left was the sea, appearing in silvered flashes between the vertical slabs of concrete and glass reaching high into the cloudless Florida sky. In spite of the surfers riding its waves and the tar balls staining its beaches, the sea, to Daye, remained ever constant, yet always different, restorative, and pure. To her right were clusters of tile-roofed stucco haciendas and rows of stone town houses, all dotted along the narrow Intracoastal Waterway. Behind most of the homes, lashed to their private docks, either gleaming white yachts or smart little sailboats were riding silently at anchor.

At the edge of the dune line, the Carillon rose beside its sister tower, the Trianon, a beige stucco monolith, amoeboid in shape, shimmering with gold-tinted floor-to-ceiling windows, and banded by wide balconies that ran like finely traced lines around its entire circumference. Ten stories high, with only four large condos per floor, it was lovingly and artfully displayed within a man-planted landscape bristling with cabbage palms, sea grapes, red, yellow, and pink hibiscus, and fuchsia and white oleanders. To the west, the view was of the Intracoastal, while to the east lay that glorious expanse of deserted beach and unending sea.

"Well, Daye, you're home," announced Franki, lightly touching Daye on the arm.

Home? Daye started. Could she ever make Florida her home? There were fourteen months remaining on her five-year lease in New York. That left her with eleven months in which to decide whether or not to renew for another three years. If she had made it once in New York, surely she could make it again in Palm Beach. And if she could, then, yes, she would consider making Florida her home.

She smiled at the doorman as he helped her out of the car. Her own car was being driven down from New York for her. Even as a child, she had hated long car rides, and she still looked for ways to avoid them. Her car would fit in well here, that much was certain, but would she ever fit in? Would she ever be able to adjust to all of the contradictions and the clichés of this plastic tropical paradise whose residents had all climbed the magic mountain of success and had been granted full access to all they surveyed?

"The hurricane shutters have been opened and the place aired out just as you asked, Miss Peters."

The voice of the doorman brought Daye back from her thoughts.

"Thank you," she replied somewhat distractedly, glancing down at the name embroidered in gold on the burgundy jacket of his uniform. "Roger," she finished softly, and watched as the man preened in front of her.

While he unloaded her bags from the trunk, Daye turned to Rhea and Franki, her smile sad, her voice apologetic, as she said, "You're sure you don't mind? You promise you won't think I'm rude for rushing off like this to spend some time alone in the condo first?"

"We understand. Truly we do," insisted Rhea, her eyes clouded with worry despite the reassuring tone of her voice.

"We'll have lunch tomorrow, just as we'd planned, all right?" piped up Franki, but her own natural exuberance seemed strangely subdued now.

"All right." Daye swallowed the rising lump in her throat and bent to kiss her friends good-bye. Then before either of them could say anything more, she turned and hurried into the mirrored marble lobby, catching dozens of reflections of herself in the sparkling facets of the glass as she bolted for the elevator.

No footprints marred the plush perfection of the beige carpeted hallway as she followed Roger and the luggage cart he was wheeling. The air conditioning in the corridor barely ruffled the variegated leaves of the croton plants that were grouped in brass buckets outside each of the four gilt-trimmed beige apartment doors. The wallpaper was elegantly striped in beige and gold, and the lighting was provided by intricate globes of translucent glass resembling spiny sea urchins.

When they reached the door of 7-D, Roger stepped away from the cart and with professional ease unlocked the door. With a flourish, he motioned for her to enter ahead of him. Daye drew a deep breath to steady herself and stepped into the marble foyer. The place was a joyous wash of raspberry, lavender, and periwinkle blue, a warm and startling palette that she had created especially for her beloved parents. It was a cozy rainbow world of cheerfully waving stripes and bold, abstract flowers covering both the furniture and the windows. The walls and the carpets were raspberry, the accent pieces white wicker and brass-framed glass. In each room she had used porcelain lamps with broad coolie shades in periwinkle blue.

It was a masterful blend of impossible contradictions that worked together wonderfully and well. Making just such impossible contradictions work for her had long been a Daye Peters tradition. In fact, it was her hallmark. And she had used all of her creativity and all of her skills to make it work for her parents. She had fashioned a peaceful hideaway for them when, for a few stolen weeks each year, they could escape the ruthless demands of their daily lives and hibernate. Daye's bottom lip began to quiver. Her parents had died without having used it even once.

She barely heard Roger closing the front door behind him as he left. Through the open glass doors leading from the living room onto the balcony, she could hear the soft sweep of the waves against the shore. Then, all she could hear was the wrenching sob as it was being torn out of her. Surrounded by the roseate glow of the paradise she had created for someone else, she put her head in her hands and began to cry.

chapter two

THE SUN was melting in a pool of russet and apricot and dripping, bit by luminescent bit, into the indigo waters of the Intracoastal. The moistness of the breeze seeped into Daye's hair as she stood on the balcony overlooking the ocean and pressed the occasional errant strand against her cheek like a lacy curlicue of spindrift. A lone sandpiper skittered around the curve of a foam-capped wave, pecking insistently in the sand as it ran, and a flock of seagulls huddled together at the water's edge, braced against the rising of the evening wind.

Twilight, that briefest of times, when the sky is a smudgy haze of violet and mauve and dusky blue, had always been Daye's favorite time. It was a time for dreaming dreams. Somehow, beneath the gathering mists of night, dreams didn't seem quite as unattainable as they did in the harsher light of morning. Daye had never been one to wish on the first evening star. She had always wished on a bank of clouds in whatever happened to be her favorite color at the time, learning early that even wishes pressed upon a cloud had a chance of coming true.

She leaned against the balcony railing, drawing in a full breath of the tart salt air, and scanned the darkening sky for a cloud, wondering as she did what she should wish for. Peace of mind? Career success? Love? Her fingers tensed on the iron rail. What's wrong with wishing for love? she asked herself. Both love *and* a successful career? She laughed out loud. Impossible. Yet, it hadn't seemed quite so impossible once, a long time ago.

At the age of six, she had wished on a plum-colored cloud that the nine-year-old boy who lived in the same Park Avenue co-op as she did would one day fall in love with her. Neil Howard was the brother she didn't have; the playmate to take the place of Sandy, the imaginary playmate she had invented to keep her company when even the trusted night-light beside her bed failed to keep the night fears at bay; the dream prince who had the power to make all of her other dreams come true. He was tall for his age and slim to the point of thinness. His hair was a startling icy blond, with one thick, straight shock always slanted arrogantly across his forehead like a silken arrow pointing the way to his long-lashed turquoise-blue eyes. Daye always imagined that nothing human had gone into his creation, that the strong planes of his handsome face had been fashioned by some loving fairy godmother, and that his body had been powered by some divine energy force.

Whenever she was with him, she glowed with an incandescence she believed came directly from him. Away from him, she felt that special luminosity dull and disappear. A sensitive child, she was both blessed and cursed by her vivid imagination, while her creativity and her artistic abilities were the assets that her parents nurtured and encouraged most. Some of her most treasured moments were spent painting or writing poetry or designing an elaborate world on large sheets of manila paper with her colored pencils, fashioning a special haven for the people she created with that vivid imagination of hers. The only other person permitted to share that world with her was Neil.

Neil needed her, of that she was certain. Whereas she had two parents who loved her and spent time with her, Neil had only a housekeeper named Maude and a series of maids for companionship. His father, Forbes, was a successful and highly ambitious land developer, who spent his time in almost every other major city in the country but New York. Neil's mother,

Claire, spent most of her time in what was obliquely referred to as a "resort" in Connecticut, one of those luxurious and secluded havens where the lonely wives of successful men continually recuperated from the excesses of their lonely lives. His sister Meredith, who was fourteen when Neil was born, married three years later, and made him an uncle by the time he was four. When his father was not teasingly calling him Uncle Neil, he was cruelly referring to him as "the mistake"— the result of one of those rare occasions when both he and Claire had found themselves in New York at the same time.

When Daye was ten, she and Neil constructed a three-story dollhouse together. He designed and built it for her, and she decorated it. At the official opening of the house, loyally attended by Daye's parents and Maude, Neil's housekeeper, they promised each other that when they grew up, they would work together as a team. He would become an architect, she an interior designer. They would call their firm Howard and Peters, he said, and Daye readily agreed to the name in spite of the tiny twinge of disappointment she felt at his putting his name before hers. Then, to ensure that their dream came true, Daye insisted they seal their agreement by wishing for it on a pale mauve cloud. He laughed at her and called her silly, but he ruffled her hair with his hands and wished with her on her cloud anyway, and then hurried off to play baseball with some of his friends from school. Her dream secure, her future assured, Daye knew that as long as she had Neil, she would have exactly what her parents had. The perfect partnership. Forever.

At twelve, she celebrated the birth of her sexuality with Neil in a game they began to play in the privacy of his father's study. There on the crackly brown leather sofa, surrounded by the books Forbes Howard never read but cherished because of the weight they lent the room, Neil would put down the pipe he had been pretending to smoke as soon as Daye had finished applying the pale pink lipstick she had bought at Woolworth's with some of her weekly allowance, and they would begin to kiss. The touch of his mouth on hers, the warmth of his hands as they cupped her budding breasts aroused sensations in her that overwhelmed and consumed her. As time passed, she realized they were feelings that she could recreate for herself simply by wadding some tissues into a ball, stuffing the ball inside her pajamas, and then getting into bed and grinding her hips against the mattress. In spite of the intensity of the feelings washing over her, however, nothing could rival the excitement she felt at Neil's own hardness as he lay beneath her, fully clothed, his arms locked around her and his body thrusting into hers, and she lived for those special times they shared together.

When her neighbor, Kelly Hathaway, confided to Daye that Neil had groped her in the elevator on her way to school one morning, Daye realized with shocked dismay that she had been betrayed. How many other girls was she sharing Neil with now? she wondered, as she struggled with the pain of Kelly's revelation. Although she longed to confront him with what she knew, she never did. So afraid was she of losing him that she clamped her pride around her pain and thought of new and different ways to please him.

At thirteen, Daye was betrayed again, this time by her own parents when they enrolled her in the exclusive Wilona Danforth School on East Eighty-second Street. Neil was already a junior at the high school she had always assumed she would be attending someday, and she considered her parents' decision a ruthless attempt to separate them. She emerged from one of the pink cubicles in the washroom, after sobbing her way through the entire lunch hour that first day of school, to find two girls standing together in front of the row of white sinks, staring at her.

The taller of the two glanced down at her wristwatch and gave her blond head a shake. "That makes it exactly forty-one minutes," she declared. "I didn't think anyone had that much water in them."

While Daye snuffled and tried not to laugh, the second girl reached into the pocket of her navy blue school blazer and drew out a linen handkerchief, edged in lace with the initial *R* in one corner of it.

"Here," she said to Daye in a quiet voice, "take it. I know it's less practical than Kleenex, but it's certainly softer and much easier on the nose."

As she accepted the handkerchief, Daye gazed into the girl's gray eyes and knew that it was time she made room for someone else in the world she had created exclusively for herself and Neil.

Daye yawned and stretched her arms above her head. Her stomach was growling, reminding her that she hadn't eaten since lunch on the plane and that she still had to stock the refrigerator. She squinted at her watch and saw that it was already seven o'clock. The Grand Union on Spanish River stayed open twenty-four hours a day, so she still had the entire night to shop for her food.

She made her way along the wraparound balcony and stepped through the partially opened sliding glass doors leading off her bedroom. Only one of the bedside lamps was burning, and the entire room was bathed in a soft raspberry glow. She eased off her boots before stretching out on the gaily printed comforter and reaching for the phone. Punching out Rhea's number, she closed her eyes and began to massage the lids with her free hand.

"Are you still at dinner?" she asked when Rhea finally came on the line.

"The children ate at six, and Chloe's just fixing me a salad," replied Rhea, her voice leaden with fatigue. "Are you managing to get settled?"

"Sort of," Daye sighed, visualizing her friend happily curled up on the chaise longue in her bedroom with its spectacular view of the Intracoastal, "although by the looks of this room, you'd swear I hadn't even begun to unpack. I never thought I had that much clothing." Even as she spoke, she pictured Rhea's vast walk-in closet with more clothes in it than most dress shops had on their racks, and she began to grin.

"I can hear you smiling," Rhea said.

Daye laughed. "You know me too well."

"Are you all right?"

"Just feeling a bit nostalgic, I guess."

"Sunsets always do that to you," Rhea reproved her in a gentle voice. "My advice to you would be to stay off your balcony until you've unpacked."

"As a matter of fact, I was just contemplating prowling the aisles of Grand Union and leaving the unpacking for later."

Rhea groaned. "What a bore."

"Feel like prowling with me and making it less of a bore?"

"You know I would, but I'm exhausted."

"Reunions have a tendency to do that to people, I think."

"I think life in general is doing it to me." Rhea yawned. "Why don't I have any energy these days?"

"You obviously aren't doing enough."

"But I'm out every day."

"That might be, but shopping and going out for lunch every day aren't exactly the most stimulating of activities, you know."

"They're fun, though."

"Then continue having fun and stay tired."

Rhea yawned again. "Speaking of fun, where would you like to have lunch tomorrow?"

"I don't know. Do you have any ideas?"

"I'm so bored with all the same old places, I wish I could think of a new place to go."

"How about McDonald's?"

"I'm not *that* bored. Why don't I call Franki and ask her?"

"Good idea," Daye agreed as she struggled to sit up. "Have her call me back, then, and in the meantime, I'll try to put this place in some sort of order."

"Until." Rhea murmured their old familiar parting line.

"Until." Daye repeated it and gently put down the phone.

RHEA HELD on to the receiver a moment longer and then quietly slipped it back into its cradle. Turning onto her side, she drew her knees up to her chin and wrapped her arms around them. Curled into a tight little ball that way, she felt warm and safe and secure, the way Neil had made her feel for a brief time, such a long time ago. She gazed about the master bedroom suite and noted that the rooms with their white Italian furniture and ivory upholstery made no bold or declarative statement; they simply seemed to exist as an inconspicuous and placid background for the lives played out against them. Her entire twelve-room house made no statement either. Awash in ivories and white, it was elegantly unobtrusive, much like Rhea herself.

She yawned again, wondering why the fatigue that usually swept over her at three in the afternoon was now back to claim her again at seven. For years now, her daily ritual had remained constant. At three, she would go into her bedroom, draw the draperies shut around the large four-poster bed, slip on her black eyeshades, and sleep until five. Then she would go downstairs and make certain that her children, Matthew, who was now nine, and Caroline, who was seven, sat down to the supper Chloe had prepared for them. Whenever Neil happened to show up for dinner, she would eat with him on the terrace overlooking the swimming pool, but lately she had begun eating by herself, curled up on her chaise, nibbling with little enthusiasm on one of Chloe's famous salads.

As her eyelids began to droop, she made no attempt to keep them open. Her closing eyes were focused on the small framed pastel hanging over her antique writing desk, and the last thing she saw before her eyes closed completely was the angelic smile on the face of the young boy in the picture, who was standing knee-deep in a field of bright yellow daisies. It was a pastel she herself had done, although no one knew it was hers; and the boy was someone she had known about all her life, yet never seen.

She sighed and shifted slightly on the chaise. She had always thought of herself as an only child, and her parents had done nothing to discourage her. Her father was Gerald Bellon, the prominent Park Avenue obstetrician, and her mother, Margery, was one of Manhattan's most popular hostesses and charity fund-raisers. Rhea's world was a protected and sheltered one, and although she was a pampered child, she grew up lonely, a cautious observer of life rather than an active participant in it. Once a month, her parents would disappear for an entire weekend, leaving Rhea with her nanny and the maid and the terrifying feeling that she had been abandoned. But on Monday morning, her parents would return, their faces strangely sad, the trunk of her father's black Cadillac crammed with gifts for her, with never an explanation as to where they had been.

Then at the age of ten, she was finally told the truth. She had a fifteen-year-old brother named Steven. He was mentally retarded and lived outside the city in a special village with other children just like him. Her curiosity piqued, she fired question after hungry question at her parents, but she was given no satisfying answers. She was strictly forbidden to mention her brother to anyone, and whenever she begged her parents to take her with them on their monthly visits, they refused. It was as if Steven Bellon were a mistake her parents had made and could never erase. Suddenly, Rhea found herself competing with some faceless stranger for her parents' love.

In her naive competition for that love, she tried to become the best possible daughter. She learned to be pleasant and agreeable at all times. She never complained or pouted, and she seldom exerted either her will or herself in any obtrusive or objectionable way. In turn, her parents continued to tiptoe awkwardly around her, treating her as though she might break if they hugged her too tightly or kissed her too soundly. They insulated themselves from her as they isolated her from them through the growing wall of their caution, while at the same time lining the world at her feet with a golden carpet of unending and generous indulgences.

Rhea came to assume that she had only to exist and she would be rewarded. She acted with others the way she behaved with her parents, always pleasant and agreeable, a gentle and unobtrusive presence, a delight to be around. As she grew older, she was not surprised to find that other girls wanted to be her friends while boys battled among themselves for the privilege of acting as her protector. She accepted their attention gracefully and quietly, but she gave little of herself in return. Until she met Daye Peters and Franki Dunn and knew what it meant to have real friends at last.

"Mommy, can you listen to my spelling now?" came the soft voice of her daughter Caroline from the doorway.

Rhea stirred and opened her eyes. "I'm so tired, Caroline," she murmured. "Couldn't Joleen listen to it instead?"

"It's her night off, Mommy, remember?"

"Oh, yes, I keep forgetting that she's taking Wednesdays now instead of Thursdays." Rhea pressed a hand to her forehead, wondering why it felt so warm and was suddenly throbbing with such a hard and insistent beat. "I'm really not feeling very well, sweetheart. Perhaps tomorrow morning before you leave for school."

"But you know you're never up that early, Mommy." Caroline's deep blue eye were gently accusing.

"I'll get up early tomorrow, I promise. Just tell Chloe to ring me when she gets up to make breakfast." Rhea gazed at her daughter's crestfallen face and the sad eyes below the sweep of her black bangs, and she wished she had the strength to do more. "Go tell Chloe now, Caroline, and I promise I'll help you in the morning."

"All right, Mommy," the child conceded with a sigh. "Good night, Mommy, I hope you feel better."

"Thank you, sweetheart, I will." But as Rhea picked up the phone again and dialed Franki's number in Palm Beach, she wasn't so sure. Her eyes met those of the child in the painting. What color would Steven's eyes be? she wondered. What would he look like, this brother of hers, this stranger, this man-child of thirty-eight? This shadow image that haunted her dreams and filled the pastels she painted in secret? This hidden part of her life she herself had never found the courage to face? How strange it was, she mused, that each time she drew him, she drew him not as a man but as a child.

"Hullo." Franki's voice sounded strangely thick.

"I didn't wake you, did I?" Rhea ventured cautiously.

Franki hastily cleared her throat. "I guess I dozed off," she said. "The book I'm reading must have been more boring than I thought."

"I'm sorry, I—"

"Don't apologize, Rhee, it's no big deal. Now, what's the matter?"

"Nothing's the matter. It's just that I was hoping you might be able to think of a special place to take Daye tomorrow."

"What about Café L'Europe in the Esplanade?"

"I hate having to wait in line, and you know they won't take reservations."

"Friday's in the Town Center?"

Rhea made a face. "It's too noisy and far too dark in there."

"Wildflower."

"Not during the day, Franki."

"Well, then, you come up with something."

Rhea's headache was getting worse. "Ta-boo?" It was the best she could do. No one could go wrong choosing the oldest watering hole on Worth Avenue.

"Talk about dark," scoffed Franki, "not to mention your basic chichi."

There was dead silence on the line.

"All right, all right," Franki sighed, "we'll make it Ta-boo. What time?"

"One?"

"One is fine."

"Then would you mind calling Daye and letting her know, while I go take something for this pounding head of mine?"

"Another headache!" demanded Franki.

"Yes," Rhea admitted somewhat sheepishly.

"Haven't you gone to see anyone about them yet?"

Rhea laughed. "You know doctors; everything's tension these days." Then, before Franki had a chance to ask her what she could possibly be tense about, she hung up.

FRANKI SAT cross-legged on the bed and stared dismally at the section of the newspaper she had been reading when Rhea called. Her eyes filled with tears again as she ran down the list of births one more time, beginning with Abbott and finishing eleven names later with Weintraub. She reached for a fresh Kleenex and blew her nose. Why she continued to torture herself this way she would never know. And with Brian away in London with Neil, it was only getting worse. It seemed she was lacerating herself on a daily basis now, scanning the birth announcements in every major south Florida paper and vicariously sharing in the joy of each new arrival with people she didn't even know. Wadding her Kleenex, she dabbed at the brimming corners of her eyes. God, how she envied them, all of them, from the Abbotts right down to the Weintraubs.

She looked up from the paper with tear-reddened eyes to study the blue and white ceramic-framed photograph on the glass-topped, fabric-covered Parsons table at the far end of the bedroom. In spite of her attempt to block it, a bubble of despair broke free from her and burst loudly in the silence of the room. There they were, the entire Dunn family. Poppa Dunn, Momma Dunn, and the three little baby Dunns, with Franki the eldest of the three girls. All of them were posed so precisely and smiling so perfectly for the unseen hand that had snapped the picture all those years ago outside their East Side apartment. The name of the building was clearly visible on the canopy above the double doors leading to the lobby, and the uniformed doorman standing at attention just outside the doors looked properly dignified.

Franki closed her eyes and squeezed down the bitter sting of humiliation clawing at her throat. Poppa and Momma Dunn were Patrick and Louise, the proud proprietors of Dunn Drugs, two shabby drugstores on two equally shabby streets in Queens; and the three little baby Dunns were Franki when she was still called Francine, Diana, and Arliss. At twelve, Franki thought her parents had won a lottery when she was told they were moving to an apartment building on posh East Seventy-third Street in Manhattan. But it wasn't long before she realized that her parents hadn't won anything at all. They had simply traded upward, exchanging a roomy house that they owned outright, among ordinary working people like themselves, for a small one-bedroom apartment they could barely afford, among people who were far too good for them.

Some of their shabby furniture moved with them from Queens, while the rest of it was sold with the house. Franki's parents slept on a hide-a-bed in the living room, and Franki and her two sisters shared the bedroom. Meals were frugal, and treats were few. Nearly every hard-earned penny went to pay for the tuition at the Wilona Danforth School for each of the girls and to buy the uniforms that granted them the same anonymity as the other girls at the prestigious school. Whenever Franki asked her parents why they were pretending to be rich, she always received the same reply. "If you mingle with the rich and act rich, then you yourself have a chance at becoming rich. Watch and learn from them, Francine," they told her over and over again, "and one day, you may have everything we couldn't give you."

And so, while Franki watched and learned, she also began to pretend, just as her parents did. She pretended to be happy. She developed her sense of humor and a saucy tongue, using them as shields to hide her deep humiliation; while she worked out her desperate feelings of inadequacy by going out for school sports and becoming the most valuable player on every team. She trained and honed her body with the same determination with which she was training her mind, grateful for her own natural voluptuousness, which was the only asset she considered honestly and rightfully hers.

She never invited anyone over for slumber parties or socials, and she never introduced any of her friends to her parents. Her dates met her and left her in the lobby of the apartment building, so that all of her earliest kisses were exchanged in front of one of the doormen. When she decided to become friendly with Daye Peters and Rhea Bellon, it was only because she had selected them as the two girls from whom she could learn the most. She hadn't counted on growing to love them as she had never loved her very own sisters.

Franki turned off the brass reading lamp over the bed and got up. Padding over to the windows, she opened the vertical blinds and peered outside. The lights from a yacht slowly navigating Lake Worth were tiny squares of yellow against the blackness of the water. Still watching the boat, she arched her back, placed her hands on her hips, and did fifty fast side bends. Then she touched her toes fifty times and ran in place until she had counted up to one thousand. Panting slightly, she jogged into her blue and white tiled bathroom with the large blue sunken tub and turned on the jets in the stall shower.

She passed the ceramic-framed photograph on her way to the closet for one of her terry robes, and the smile on her mother's face made her stop for a moment and smile back, ruefully and bitterly.

"See, Momma," she whispered, reaching out to touch the faded face beneath the glass, "your little Francine made it, just as you'd hoped she would. She made it all the way up the ladder to a condo high in the sky over Palm Beach, Momma, and God knows you can't get much higher than that."

Slinging her robe over one arm, she walked slowly over to the large Lucite cube she used as a night table on her side of the king-size bed and picked up the telephone. Life is really a bitch, she acknowledged bleakly, with one final glance at her mother's sweet face. Louise Dunn hadn't lived long enough to see her precious daughter make that prestigious climb upward. She had died of cancer just five months after Franki's grand society wedding. Franki was crying again as she stabbed out Daye's number. It wasn't fair, she sobbed; it just wasn't fair for her mother to have died before she could even begin to repay her for having sacrificed so hard and so long.

"Daye?" she sniffed, the moment that familiar, low-pitched voice answered the phone.

"Is that you, Franki?" Daye seemed somewhat dubious.

"S-Sorry," Franki stammered, throwing back her head and rapidly blinking as she stared up at the ceiling. She swallowed hard a number of times and then, in a calmer voice she said, "How does one o'clock at Ta-boo sound to you?"

"It sounds fine. My car's due to arrive first thing in the morning, but if it doesn't, I'll have Rhea stop by and pick me up."

"Lucky you. You can be the first to ride in her new Seville."

"Another new car?"

"Another new car. But then, you know Rhea. As soon as her old car gets dirty, she has Neil buy her a new one."

"Really, Franki!" Daye was smiling, but her tone was slightly reproachful as she said, "She's not that bad, and you know it."

"Said only in jest, Daye," insisted Franki, dabbing at her eyes again, "said only in jest, honest. Well, I'll see you tomorrow, my girl. Sweet dreams."

As soon as Daye put down the phone, she switched off the lamp beside the bed. The groceries would have to wait, she decided, as she closed her eyes. She turned over onto her stomach and wrapped her arms around her pillow. The pillowcase was stiff and smelled of plastic bags and newness, just as everything else in the place smelled of that same strange newness. She felt like a trespasser here, even though her parents had insisted the condo was as much hers as theirs. Time, she cautioned herself, give it some time.

She knew it was still early, far too early even to think about being able to fall asleep, but for the moment, she didn't dare allow herself to think about anything else. There would be plenty of time for thinking tomorrow, especially about the future. Tonight it would take all of her energy just to keep the past at bay.

{ *chapter three* }

WHEN HER car arrived the following morning at nine, Daye immediately handed it over to one of the condo's young car jockeys to wash. Then she unpacked a tin of herbal tea from one of her suitcases, brewed herself a cup, and carried it out onto the balcony. Instead of sitting on one of the cushioned white wrought-iron chairs at the round patio table, she sat down on the green indoor-outdoor carpeting and crossed her long legs in front of her. As she sipped her tea and watched the easy roll of the waves, she began to contemplate what she had refused to think about the night before. Her future.

For the first time in her life, Daye found that she was tired. Tired of being alone, of being responsible for herself, of making all the decisions. Suddenly she wanted to include someone else in the process. She was ready now. Ready to take a chance at finding what she had been denying herself for so long. That special partnership she had believed she could have only with Neil.

Neil. She sighed softly as she gazed off into the distance, remembering. At eighteen, she had graduated from high school, and her parents had thrown her a party to celebrate. She had asked Neil to act as her escort. This was to be their first official date, for even though she was still holding on to their special dream, he seemed to have relegated it to the fantasies of childhood, when wishes pressed upon cloud banks had as little substance as the clouds themselves. Her beloved Neil had been changing, showing far more interest in his father's business ventures than in the architecture he was studying. Dating only college women, he had begun to treat Daye with the same offhanded warmth men usually reserve for their younger sisters.

Whenever she tried to discuss her feelings for Neil with her mother, Lydia would advise her to forget all about him, insisting that her feelings were simply a childhood crush and nothing more. Neil Howard was not for her. How could he not be for her? Daye would demand, close to tears, they had known each other forever. But in spite of her protests, the three years separating them had begun to stand like a barrier between them, driving them farther and farther apart. With Rhea and Franki to fill some of the spaces created by his absences, Daye was seldom lonely, except for those times when she found herself in the arms of another boy. And then, all she could think of was Neil. Neil with his mouth covering hers, his hands caressing her breasts, his hardness pressing against her softness and causing her to melt with desire.

Her love for Neil was the only secret she had kept from her two best friends, but when he strode into her graduation party that night, she was certain that once her friends saw the two of them together, they would know. So, it was with proprietary pride that she finally introduced Rhea and Franki to him, prepared to share her secret with them at last. What she was *not* prepared for was the expression on Neil's face when he was introduced to Rhea; and when he led her into the living room to dance, Daye remained behind in the foyer, too numb to move. While Johnny Mathis was crooning "The Twelfth of Never" on the stereo, all she could hear was Patti Page singing the sad words to "The Tennessee Waltz," and her whole world seemed to shudder and collapse around her.

Without his having to tell her so, she knew that their dream was over. There would be no firm of Howard and Peters now, no merger, business or otherwise, because he had never once looked at her the way he had looked at Rhea. She wished she could hate Rhea for the way Neil looked at her, but she couldn't. Rhea was an innocent; she didn't know how Daye had always felt about him. In the weeks following her party, Daye rehearsed and discarded every speech she considered delivering to Neil along with an open declaration of her love. If he didn't know how she felt about him, she reasoned, how could he ever feel free to express his own feelings about her?

But her pride, coupled with the fear that he might reject her love, prevented her from ever delivering any one of those speeches. Instead, she continued to dissect every sentence he uttered, and examine every moment they spent together in the hope of unearthing some clue as to how he actually felt. But there were no clues, at least not the kind she was looking for. It seemed that, as far as Neil was concerned, she was still sweet little Daye, once his childhood companion and now his friend.

When he confided to her, late one summer afternoon as they were walking through Central Park together, that he was giving up architecture and going to work for his father, Daye was shattered. She thought of his wonderful talent and lamented the fact that none of the ideas he had shared with her over the years would ever be translated from the realm of his imagination to the reality of the drawing board. She mourned his decision as though she were mourning the loss of someone close to her. The dream was truly over for them now, and as she began to cry, not even his arm around her shoulder or his efforts to dry her tears had helped to lessen her pain.

After high school, Rhea and Franki enrolled in NYU, and Daye entered the New York School of Interior Design. Rhea continued to date Neil on a casual basis, protecting herself and her emotions by dating other men as well. Franki moved from man to man, changing them with the same calculated care she used to change her college courses. Chameleonlike, she would learn, absorb, and imitate, and then move on. Daye, meanwhile, dated only occasionally, preferring to concentrate all of her energies on her work instead. In spite of her determination to forget Neil Howard, she knew that she was still looking for him in every other man she met, waiting to feel for someone else what she still felt for him whenever they met—that bolt of equisite pain which had the power to paralyze her momentarily. She was determined to make it on her own now, and if an ideal relationship existed for her somewhere, then it would simply have to wait awhile.

In the summer of their junior year, Rhea left for two months in Europe, Franki worked in a Village boutique, and Daye served her apprenticeship in a design firm. Neil had moved into his own apartment and was making such a name for himself in real estate that his father now referred to him as "the genius." Neil was hardworking, ambitious, and shrewd. With great foresight, he was encouraging investors to sink their investment capital in the Sunbelt—specifically that eastern strip of Florida known as the Gold Coast, a prime piece of real estate that stretched north from Coral Gables to Stuart.

When he called Daye one evening and asked her to go to a movie with him, she was wary, but she wasn't surprised. She wasn't even surprised that he spent most of the evening talking about Rhea. But then something changed. On the subsequent evenings they spent together, he began to speak less about Rhea and to question Daye more about herself, about her apprenticeship, and about her career plans. It was as though, in spite of his own success, he was trying to live vicariously through her creativity and her obvious determination to realize her part of their dream alone. Flattered by his interest, pleased to have earned his respect, she impetuously admitted to him what she had thus far dared to admit only to herself—that she would allow nothing and no one to stand in the way of her becoming one of the city's foremost interior designers. She failed to notice the guarded expression that cloaked his eyes following her declaration, and if his telephone calls were soon spaced farther and farther apart, she was too involved in her work each day and too tired at night to wonder why.

The next telephone call was one she initiated herself, to tell him that she, along with several members of the design firm, would be spending five months, beginning in September, in Mexico City, working on the new Hilton International Hotel, and that the project would be applied as credit toward her degree. To celebrate, he took her out to dinner that evening at the Four Seasons, and after that, his phone calls resumed again. On the night when they finally made love for the first time, there was a bittersweet sense of rightness to it, because while Daye gave herself to him with a yearning bordering on desperation, she knew that, as much as this was a beginning for them, it was to be an ending for them as well.

They shared three more nights of loving together, and then they parted. On the afternoon that Rhea's ship docked in New York harbor, Daye flew to Mexico City. Two months later, Neil's letter arrived, telling her that he had decided to ask Rhea to marry him. She was not at all surprised. What *did* surprise her was why it had taken him so long. With a clarity that astounded her, she realized that Neil had never been hers to have, that she had merely borrowed him for a while, knowing that what the two of them had shared had been no more than mutual curiosity and desire. It was finally time, she told herself, no matter how great the pain, to let him go.

Neil and Rhea were married the following June. When Daye danced with Neil at the reception, the clouded look she had failed to see in his eyes before was all too visible to her now. In their turquoise depths was a confusing mixture of emotions she knew he would never express in words, and in her own returning gaze, she warned him what had happened between them must forever remain their secret. His silent nod told her that he agreed, and he left her at the end of their second dance together to reclaim his bride. It was with an overwhelming sense of helplessness that Daye watched him take Rhea in his arms, for in spite of her determination to let him go, she doubted that she ever really would.

After a three-week honeymoon in the Orient, Rhea returned to New York with the man she had chosen to take the place of her doting parents. With Neil she felt protected, cherished, and secure; and if he was obsessed by his work and spent more time away than he did at home, it didn't really matter. His only demands on her were that she be there whenever he *did* come home, that she look beautiful, and that she entertain for him. In return, she got to spend his money and amuse herself in whatever ways pleased her most.

She was the ideal wife. She gave birth to a son first and then, two years later, she gave birth to a daughter; but she turned both of them over to a nanny to raise because their helplessness terrified her. Needing to fill her quieter moments with something, she began working in pastels. They were tender studies, reminiscent of Renoir and Monet, and her only subject was a small boy whose face was never represented exactly the same way twice. She worked in her bedroom with the door locked, and then she hid each small picture in a trunk. Somehow she needed this secret and she needed to keep it hidden even from her two best friends.

After graduation, Franki continued to move from man to man as she began to move from one job to another. She finally opted for working as a paralegal, taking the appropriate courses, and then going to work for the prestigious criminal law firm of Shelton and Shelton, setting her sights on Brian Shelton, the younger of the two brothers in the firm, simply because his older brother, Eric, was already married. Brian had sandy hair, warm brown eyes, a square, handsome face, and a stocky, athletic build. He was a gentle man, serious and something of a plodder, neither as bright nor as aggressive as his father and older brother, and somewhat intimidated by criminal law. Corporate law was his passion, and he desperately wanted to leave his father's firm. Salvation came in the form of Neil Howard, one of his fraternity brothers from college, who offered him the lucrative position of legal counsel to the Howard Development Corporation, which Neil was now heading due to the crippling stroke his father had recently suffered.

Franki was twenty-six when Brian felt secure enough in his position to marry her. As opposite personalities, they complemented one another perfectly, with Franki meeting all of Brian's needs and Brian meeting most of hers. She was finally able to begin living the kind of life she had been preparing herself for, but she was not prepared to take any chances. From whatever money Brian gave her to spend during their marriage, she intended to invest one third of it and thus build up a nest egg of her own. This would be her way of protecting herself against the possibility of having cast her lot with the wrong man.

When Daye graduated from the New York School of Interior Design, she exploded onto the decorating scene and was soon one of the most sought-after new designers in the city. With very little effort, she could have worked twenty hours a day, seven days a week, but her two closest friends absolutely forbade it. So she learned to take time out from the work she loved to meet with Rhea and Franki at least once a week for lunch, to fill in as the extra woman at many of their dinner parties, and to obligingly date the men they continually directed her way.

On her own, she managed to become engaged twice. Each time she listened carefully to what was being said between the lines of her fiancés' expectations—namely, that she give up her career once there were children, but that she could consider returning to work once they were grown. That understood, she took their diamond rings and their outdated expectations and in the most genteel manner threw them back in their faces.

Although she never admitted it to anyone, Daye knew it was more than just the obsolete demands being made on her that kept her from making a commitment. Something was always missing. It was that special spark, that all-consuming passion which no one but Neil had ever stirred in her. Had he ever cared for her? she kept asking herself. Or had she always been too close for him to really see her? Try as she might to convince herself that it no longer mattered, her female vanity stubbornly insisted on waiting for the answer, an answer that never came. It made being in Neil's presence almost unbearable that first year after his marriage to Rhea, but as time passed, it got easier, until she was finally able to reestablish a semblance of their former casual closeness with him. And yet, during the occasional unguarded moment, she was certain that she could still feel something indefinable lingering in the air between them.

And then Neil's father died, leaving Neil in charge of the Howard Development Corporation. Six months after his father's death, he moved his family and the head offices of the company south to Florida—to Boca Raton, the fastest-rising community on the Gold Coast and one that he had helped create. One month later, Franki and Brian moved to a large condo on South Ocean Boulevard in Palm Beach, overlooking Lake Worth. Daye was devastated by the moves. Her phone bills were enormous, her trips south brief but frequent, and whenever they could, Rhea and Franki came north. But it was never quite the same as it had once been.

A buzzer sounded, and Daye leaped to her feet, spilling some of her cold tea onto the carpet in her surprise. It was the doorman calling from the lobby to tell her that her car was ready. She thanked him and then went into the kitchen to pour the rest of her tea into the sink and to rinse out her cup. As she walked around one of the unpacked suitcases still lying open on the floor of her bedroom, she forced herself to stop and scoop up a handful of sweaters to put away on a shelf inside her closet. Then while she was running the water for a bath, she managed to hang up some of her winter skirts, put away most of her wool suits, and appropriately shelve all of her hats. She gave herself exactly fifteen minutes to luxuriate in the tub before getting out, toweling herself dry, and then trying to decide on something to wear.

She chose a pair of taupe silk pants with a matching blouse topped off with a taupe and brown houndstooth blazer. She knotted a long brown silk scarf around her neck, stepped into a pair of brown alligator pumps, and then began searching through each of her suitcases for her brown alligator bag. She studied her reflection in the bathroom mirror while she sprayed herself with Paco Rabanne Calandre and decided that she liked herself best in muted autumn colors because they brought out the copper in her hair and the gold in her eyes. She left the apartment smiling.

The Mercedes was spotless, its paint, the color of frosted raspberries, shimmering in the noon sun. It was warm enough to have the top down and as Daye headed north, she turned on the radio and settled back to enjoy the drive. It would take her forty-five minutes just to navigate the twenty miles to Worth Avenue along the A1A, but crawling along at twenty-five miles an hour behind a stately Rolls or Bentley was the only way Daye wanted to get to Palm Beach. The slow, leisurely drive enabled her to appreciate Palm Beach's awesome beauty and to prepare herself gradually for the majestic impact of the place.

She drove through Delray and Boynton Beach, past Ocean Ridge and Briny Breezes, and continued on to Manalapan. Above her the boughs of the huge trees lining the road met in a vaulted arch of sun-dappled green, while all around her the landscape was lush and tropical and bursting with exuberant color. The countryside was a strange and exotic blend of forests, golf courses, old frame cottages, new brick town houses, the occasional trailer park, and unbroken lines of stone mansions set back from the road behind high box hedges.

As she approached Palm Beach, the scenery changed

abruptly. Now only estates bordered the widening A1A as it became South Ocean Boulevard. Some of the homes were original Mizener haciendas, vast structures built of beige stucco and roofed in red tile; others were modern and sprawling, built out of great horizontal slabs of wood and smoked glass and gray stone; still others appeared to have been designed with the Mediterranean in mind. These were the neoclassical creations of pastel stucco, boasting triangular pediments supported by fluted plaster columns and roofs decorated with large plaster statues and urns. Behind them, set among landscaped gardens and rockeries, tiny loggias rimmed gleaming tiled swimming pools filled with clear, sparkling water. During the season, most of these homes were inhabited by some of the country's wealthiest families. Others were occupied year-round by members of Europe's moneyed aristocracy who were fleeing high taxes and terrorists in their quest for exclusive seclusion abroad.

Daye turned left off South Ocean Boulevard onto Worth Avenue, Palm Beach's answer to Los Angeles's Rodeo Drive, and began looking for a place to park. Although the season would not officially start for another week, the sidewalks were filled with early Christmas shoppers, all of them lightly tanned, all of them casually dressed in pastels, making it virtually impossible to tell the residents from the tourists.

Worth Avenue was a wide street lined with palm trees and white and gray stucco shops, separated by the occasional bougainvillea-draped archway leading into an enclosed courtyard ringed with even more shops. The names on most of the stores read like a *Who's Who* of the world's most exclusive merchants: Gucci, Hermès, David Webb, Cartier, Martha, Courrèges, Van Cleef & Arpels, and Roberta diCamerino. Saks Fifth Avenue was attached to the newly built Esplanade on the south side of the street, while on the north side flapped the familiar violet-sprigged white awnings of Bonwit Teller.

Daye parked the car in a lot on Hibiscus Avenue and walked the half-block back down the street to Ta-boo, barely managing to suppress a giggle when she noticed a white Fleetwood easing past her. The blond woman driving the car was gripping the wheel with one bejeweled hand while holding a tiny white poodle close to her chest with the other. Daye was still smiling to herself as she tugged open the door to Ta-boo and stepped into a cavern of semidarkness. When her eyes had adjusted to the gloom, she could see that the restaurant was a confused attempt to bring the outdoors inside.

In the middle of the cocktail lounge stood a giant carpet-covered artificial palm tree brandishing several clusters of colored-glass light fixtures in the shapes of various fruits. The tree also served as the focal point for the green cloth canopy fringing the ceiling of the room like a vast spread of palm fronds. As she was shown to a table, Daye noticed that clusters of glass grapes, bananas, and pineapples had been used to light the restaurant as well. The large mirrors on the darkly papered walls reflected the garish colors of the fruit back at her while picking up the glow of candles that flickered inside red glass containers on each of the closely placed tables. How tacky can you get? Daye was thinking as she arrived at the table and found Rhea and Franki already seated and waiting for her.

"Fashionably late as usual," pronounced Franki with a grin, as Daye slid onto the leather banquette beside her.

"You know how it is when you follow the speed limit," Daye retorted, aware that Franki had collected more speeding tickets than anyone she knew.

"Did you manage to get any sleep last night?" asked Rhea, anxiously scanning Daye's face.

"In spite of myself, I actually slept through the night." She laughed and reached across the table to pull off Rhea's dark glasses. "What's your excuse?" she asked.

Rhea shrugged and slipped her glasses back into place. "I don't know. I was exhausted, but for some reason I woke up at three and couldn't get back to sleep."

"Is everyone drinking?" interrupted Franki as their waitress came over and asked if they wanted anything from the bar.

Daye ordered rye and ginger, Rhea a Bloody Caesar, and Franki a vodka martini. When their drinks arrived, they raised their glasses in a toast.

"To us," Daye proposed.

"Together again," murmured Rhea.

"Friends forever," added Franki.

The three of them clinked glasses and drank to their continuing friendship.

"So, now that you're here among the golden people, do you

think you're going to like it, Daye?" Franki asked as she set down her glass.

Daye thought of a flip answer to give her and quickly decided against it. She toyed with her plastic swizzle stick while she considered her response, and then, in spite of her efforts to stop it from happening, her eyes began to fill up.

"Damn," she muttered, reaching for her napkin.

Rhea grabbed hold of Daye's hand and squeezed it hard.

"Sorry," she apologized, giving her head an angry toss. Then she turned to Franki and said, "I really don't have an answer to that question right now. All I know is that I'm tired and that I need a change. Perhaps I'll find what I need here, and then again, I may not. But I intend to try."

"Are you planning to open an office or work directly from the condo?" Franki persisted.

"If anyone's going to know I exist, I suppose I'd better open an office right here in Palm Beach."

"Then we'll have to find you a place on Peruvian Avenue," Rhea said, "and I'll be your first client."

Daye laughed.

"I'm being serious," protested Rhea. "I'm tired of ivory everywhere, and I want you to do something exciting for me. You can start with my bedroom. Then if I like the idea of having color around the place, I might ask you to redecorate the entire house."

"Daye's already licking her lips at the prospect." Franki gave Daye a gentle poke in the ribs. "Stop drooling."

"Well, you must admit that this is one challenge I can hardly refuse," countered Daye, raising her glass to Rhea as she accepted the challenge.

When the waitress returned for their lunch orders, all three of them decided on Caesar salads.

"God, we're predictable," Franki complained. "Couldn't one of us be daring and order something other than hay for a change?"

"No one's twisting your arm," said Daye.

"I know that, but right now I'm trying to be good. I have to lose two more pounds before Rhea's party."

"What party?" asked Daye.

Rhea threw Franki a withering look. "The one I'd planned

for you. It was supposed to have been a surprise."

"Oops, sorry." Franki hastily ducked her head.

"And when is this surprise party going to take place?" Daye inquired.

"Whenever Neil and Brian get back from Europe."

"Which should be any month now," Franki remarked. "Brian cabled me this morning to let me know that they've decided to go on to Amsterdam and Zurich after London."

"Is that true?" Daye asked Rhea.

"It's true," she sighed.

"Not to worry, though," Franki said cheerfully. "The party will be a smash no matter when it's held." She turned to Daye and lowered her voice conspiratorially. "Did you know that our Rhea's turned into one of the top hostesses in Boca?"

Rhea flushed and looked away.

"I'm impressed," Daye told her. "From what I know about the social life down here, that's quite a compliment, Rhee."

Franki chose that very moment to poke Daye in the ribs again, but this time it was far less gentle than before, and Daye looked up with a start.

"Do you see that couple standing in the doorway?" Franki whispered.

Daye glanced toward the entrance, and Rhea swiveled around in her chair.

"Two snakes in the grass," Franki muttered under her breath. "If I were you, Daye, I'd watch myself around them."

"Why?"

"Because they're lethal."

Daye stared at the oddly matched couple who seemed to be attracting the attention of almost everyone in the restaurant. The woman was obviously in her fifties, but remarkably well preserved; tall and striking, with a mane of flaming auburn hair framing her angular face. Her elegantly bony body was draped in a long scarlet tunic, which she was wearing over a pair of royal blue harem pants, belted with a royal blue sash. Sliding her oversized sunglasses onto the top of her head, she swept the room with disdainful coolness and then bent to say something to the young man at her side.

He was deeply tanned and impeccably dressed in what could only have been Giorgio Armani. His black hair was layered and worn close to his shapely head, and as he grasped his companion by the elbow to guide her to the table so obviously reserved for them ahead of time, there was a glittering ripple of gold and diamond chains on one of his narrow wrists.

"All right, who are they?" asked Daye.

"Sybil Barron and Philippe Nadeau," Rhea said.

"So?"

"So, my dearest friend," supplied Franki, "she's Palm Beach's resident bitch and superhostess, living off Daddy's newspaper fortune, and married to David Barron, who was a nothing journalist until he married her. The Barrons tossed the dying *Palm Beach Standard* to him as if they were throwing a bone to a dog, and when David turned it around and made it a paying proposition, the chorus of surprised hallelujahs could be heard around the world. The *Standard* is now the biggest paper in south Florida; but Sybil owns David, which means she also owns the *Standard*. And that means she can make or break anyone on earth by using the almighty power of the press any way she wants."

"And Philippe Nadeau?"

It was Rhea's turn now. "Philippe has been Palm Beach's best known and most successful interior designer for the past fifteen years, and he's been Sybil's pet project for five of those years."

"Uh-oh." Daye pulled a long face and rested her chin in her hand.

"He owns an antique shop on Peruvian Avenue,"continued Rhea, "and Sybil works for him three afternoons a week."

"He doesn't like competition, Daye," Franki warned her, "and no one's been able to beat him yet. The two of them make one hell of an invincible team."

As Daye peered again at the couple now seated across the room from them, watching as they leaned toward each other while they talked, she felt a sudden stirring deep inside her. It was the surge of adrenaline she always felt when she confronted a challenge. One by one, her doubts began to disappear, to be replaced almost immediately by a newer confidence and a stronger sense of commitment and certainty. Suddenly, all she could think of was Philippe Nadeau and how much she wanted to be the one to beat him.

Her golden eyes blazing, she stared across the room at him, daring him to look up and meet her eyes, and to acknowledge the gauntlet that she herself had decided to throw down to him without his even knowing it.

chapter four

"ARE SYBIL and Philippe lovers?" asked Daye, squinting into the sun as they emerged from the dark restaurant an hour later.

"That, my dear, is one of Palm Beach's favorite subjects for speculation," Franki replied, searching in her bag for the keys to her car. "Philippe's as cagey about his age, his origins, and his sexual preferences as the vainest woman going. I suppose he figures it adds to his allure."

Hearing Franki talk about Philippe Nadeau that way made Daye bridle with impatient energy.

"Does anyone feel like walking along Peruvian Avenue with me for a while?" she asked her friends, wondering if either of them had noticed her abrupt change in mood.

"My pedicurist won't be coming to the house until five," said Rhea, "so I have time."

"Franki?"

"Tennis at six, so I'm all yours until then." She dropped the keys back into her purse.

The three women linked arms and headed down Worth to South County Road, where they turned left and continued for another block until they came to that smart little street known as Peruvian. It was an eclectic blend of the residential and the commercial, charmingly set off by rows of palm trees, banks of oleanders and hibiscus, and low box hedges. Antique shops were nestled close to real estate offices, elegant town houses shared common walls with art galleries, and on the corner of Peruvian and Coconut Row stood a tiny building that housed one of Palm Beach's favorite bread and pastry shops, the Little French Bakery. Franki stopped just outside the door to the shop and gazed longingly at a tray of freshly baked croissants.

Daye tugged at her friend's sleeve and said, "Your two pounds, remember?"

"Not fair," moaned Franki as she allowed Daye to lead her away from the shop, "not fair at all." She glanced back over her shoulder just in time to see a young woman in a peacock blue jogging outfit emerge with her arms laden with assorted cardboard boxes. "Bitch," Franki cursed good-naturedly. "Look at her; she's practically anorexic."

They crossed the street, passing a storefront in whose large bay window was displayed an elegant Louis XIV bergère with a bolt of yellow and white striped satin spilling over one corner of it and trailing across the floor. An ornate onyx and ormolu clock was dramatically positioned among the artfully gathered folds of the cloth.

"That's Philippe's place," Franki told Daye, "and as usual, he's heavy into Old Europe."

Rhea, who had been thoughtfully considering the clock, said, "I love it. It would be perfect in Neil's study."

"Traitor," Daye hissed, pulling her away from the window. "I know exactly where those genuine antique clocks are made. I can get you ten more just like it."

"You can?" Rhea's eyes were wide.

"I can."

"Then she certainly doesn't want it, does she?" teased Franki.

Rhea shook her head. "She most certainly doesn't."

Five doors up from Philippe Nadeau's combined antique store and design studio, Daye found what she was looking for: a vacant shop that occupied the entire ground floor of a renovated three-story town house whose two top floors housed a firm of architects. As she walked through the three spacious, sunlit rooms and modern white tile bathroom, she felt a strange pang, and thought back for a moment to her failed childhood dream. She shook off the memory with a toss of her head and walked through the place again, more slowly this time. She opened each cupboard door, inspected the grain of the wood floors and the quality of the paint used on the walls, and studied the view of the street through the new Pella windows.

"I can already visualize how this place will look," she said, turning to her friends with a dreamy expression in her eyes. "Tubs of flowering plants on the windowsills, rattan furniture, pillows and curtains in a bold Marimekko print. Everything has to be airy and light. This is the seashore, not the city, and if Philippe Nadeau wants to confine his clients by giving them only Old Europe, then let him. I intend to offer people the chance to appreciate what's around them—the sky, the ocean, the greenery. And that means giving them a sense of space and of freedom."

Ideas were beginning to bounce off the walls of her mind and float like bubbles in the air, where they burst with excited little pops.

"I can see you climbing back on that carousel again," Rhea said, taking hold of Daye's arm and stroking it gently. "Please don't hide away from us just yet."

Daye was so taken aback by the beseeching look in Rhea's eyes that she bent to kiss the top of her friend's dark head and in as reassuring a tone as possible, said, "I'm just excited, Rhee, that's all. I have no intention of becoming a hermit, honest. But do you know how much it means for me to actually feel excited about something? I've been numb for eight months, Rhea. This is like learning to feel all over again."

Rhea tightened her grip on Daye's arm. "Please forgive me if I sound selfish," she whispered, "but I just can't bear the thought of you locking yourself away again before we have some time together. Does that make any kind of sense at all?"

"Yes, Rhee, it does." Daye smiled. "It makes a great deal of wonderful sense." Reaching for Franki's hand, she said, "I think this calls for a celebration, don't you?"

"What are we celebrating?"

"My new office, of course."

"Then you're taking it? Just like that?"

"Just like that."

"Well, then, what are we waiting for?"

Rhea glanced at her watch and frowned. "My pedicurist will—"

"Forget your feet," ordered Franki. "You treating, Daye?"

Daye laughed. "I'm treating, Franki."

She jotted down the number of the real estate agent before they left. She was determined to take care of the formalities and gain occupancy of the place as soon as possible. Her head was swimming. She could hardly believe it. It was all happening so quickly. But then, she reasoned, perhaps it was better this way.

IT TOOK her less than a week to settle in. She used the two largest rooms as offices, the smallest one as a reception area, and she decorated all three rooms in a striking blaze of fuchsia, green, and white. Tiny green leaves licked bold, stylized fuchsia poppies on the white cotton fabric she had selected, and Rhea's Chloe had proven herself to be as talented with a sewing machine as she was with a recipe, sewing up curtains, tablecloths, and pillow covers according to Daye's specifications. Except for her desk and drafting table, the furniture was rattan that had been sprayed white, with plump print cushions lining the seats of the chairs and the backs of the small sofas. White porcelain lamps stood on inexpensive wooden tables that were covered with floor-length cloths. The windows were swagged by balloon shades, colorful Erté posters dotted the walls, and the windowsills, just as she had originally visualized, were lined with white wicker baskets filled with azaleas and rhododendrons in contrasting shades of white, pink, fuchsia, and red. A discreet brass plaque bolted to the red brick wall of the building on the right side of the front door with the Sheraton fanlight above it, announced that Daye Peters, Interior Designer, was now open for business.

Franki contacted a reporter friend of hers who worked for the *Palm Beach Daily News,* fondly referred to by informed insiders as the Shiny Sheet, and the day after the plaque went up, a glam shot of Daye Peters along with a half-page story about her appeared on the front page of the glossy tabloid, bumping the coverage of a local party for the members of the

Rolls Royce Owners Club to page two. Rhea called the daughter of one of Neil's cousins who was a free-lance journalist, and two days later, the *Sun Sentinel* carried a story about Daye to every community between Fort Lauderdale and Lantana. While Daye waited for some results from the burst of publicity, she began working on sketches for Rhea's bedroom, looking for ways to wean her friend from the safety of ivory to something more exciting, without it being too startling a transition for her.

And then she landed her first clients. Beth and Mark Shopley were a young couple who had just moved to Palm Beach from Cleveland, making this their third move in six years. Their house was a modest seven-room bungalow on a small inland street, with a view of neither Lake Worth nor the ocean, but with an adequate swimming pool set inside a large screened-in Florida room to compensate for it. To celebrate the occasion, Daye took Rhea and Franki back to Ta-boo, in spite of her dislike for the place, because that was where it had all begun again for her.

A photographer from *The Palm Beach Chronicle*, making his daily rounds of Palm Beach's most fashionable restaurants, recognized Daye from having seen her picture in the Shiny Sheet and snapped the three friends together, with Rhea and Franki raising their glasses to Daye in a staged toast to her success. The morning after their picture appeared in the *Chronicle*, the Town Tattler column in *The Palm Beach Standard* devoted one-third of its space to a large photo of Philippe Nadeau shaking hands with Texas multimillionaire Bradley Matheson to signify the closing of their deal in which Philippe was to renovate the three-million-dollar mansion Matheson had recently purchased not far from Mar-A-Lago, the late Marjorie Merriweather Post's deserted seventeen-acre estate.

"HAS IT already been two weeks?" Daye was incredulous. She shifted the phone to her left hand and continued with her sketch of the Shopleys' living room.

"Seventeen days, to be precise," said Rhea, examining the face of the diamond-encrusted Piaget watch Neil had brought from Zurich, "and the party's on for Saturday night. Now if I can only get Laurent to cater on such short notice, everything will be fine. Just pray that darling Sybil hasn't planned anything for Saturday night."

"Why should that matter?" Daye shaded in a sofa and then began to crosshatch an area rug in front of it.

"She and I have been involved in a running battle for the past three years now," explained Rhea. "Every party I plan at the Boca Country Club just happens to coincide with a party she's planned at the Palms Club. She uses the same people I use: the same caterer, the same florist, the same band. It's really exasperating."

"That only shows you both have the same good taste."

"Ha!" snorted Rhea, giving her wrist a flick and watching the tiny diamonds set around the face of the watch catch the light. "Just because she's been one of the main pillars of Palm Beach high society for centuries doesn't give her the right to an exclusive claim on anyone who's good."

"But surely there must be enough good people to go around." Daye began tapping the top of her pen against her front teeth as she considered what she had done so far.

"There are a lot of good people around, but there is only one *best* caterer, one *best*—"

"I think I get the picture." Daye was frowning. The placement of the sofa was not quite right.

"You sound distracted." Rhea's tone was slightly accusatory. "I'm sorry. I suppose I shouldn't have called you at work."

"I *am* a bit preoccupied at the moment," admitted Daye, who was still frowning at the drawing of the sofa. "Can I get back to you later, Rhee?"

"Of course."

Daye was so absorbed in trying to find a more suitable placement for the sofa that it took her several minutes to realize that the dial tone was humming into her left ear.

FRANKI RAISED her head and looked down at her husband. Brian was lying on his back, his eyes closed, his mouth open, his breathing regular and even. She wanted him to make love to her again. Although they had been making love twice a day since his return from Europe, she still couldn't seem to get enough of him. Knowing Brian, in another few days he would be content to slide back into their routine of making love once or twice a week. Even at that, it sometimes seemed too often for him. He was either too tired or too preoccupied, and the excuse was always the same: too much to do and too little time to do it in.

"Bri-an," she crooned, stroking the light covering of hair on his broad chest. She flattened herself against him and flung one leg over his, grinding her hips suggestively into his side. "Bri-an." She blew in his ear and watched his jaw begin to tense.

He groaned slightly as he came awake and reached up with one hand to cup the back of Franki's head.

"Keep that up," he murmured, "and we're never going to make it to the party."

She ran her hand across his belly and down into the thickness of his pubic patch.

"Don't, Franki." He brushed her hand away. "Rhea will be upset if we don't get there before Daye does."

"Daye's so busy working, she's probably forgotten all about the party." Franki wrapped her fingers around him and felt him beginning to stiffen.

"Franki!"

"Yes, Brian?"

With a savage growl, he grabbed hold of her and pulled her down on top of him.

RHEA SWALLOWED two more aspirins, retouched her lipstick, and went downstairs. She walked slowly from room to room, checking the small round tables one by one, rearranging the odd napkin, shifting the occasional plate around, and making certain that the candles in the middle of each floral centerpiece were straight. She was pleased with the way everything looked. Laurent had outdone himself this time. She opened the French doors leading from the dining room to the terrace and the pool and saw that the members of the five-piece band she had hired for the evening were already setting up their stands in front of the cabanas. She closed the doors again and returned to the front hall, pausing for a moment before the large girandole that hung over the marble-topped marquetry console near the door.

Adjusting the strap on the off-the-shoulder cream-colored Halston that clung to her thin frame in its grand silken sweep to the floor, she decided that tonight she looked very much like a dark-haired Marlene Dietrich. Her only accessories were the large square-cut emerald and diamond earrings Neil had given her on their fifth wedding anniversary. And her diamond wedding band, of course. She looked down at it now as she began twisting it around and around on her finger. She and Neil hadn't made love once since he'd returned from Europe. Not that she really minded; but he hadn't even wanted to cuddle. To her, the cuddling had always been more important than the lovemaking.

She peered into the living room at the grandfather clock in one corner of the room and frowned. Neil was late. As usual. Even Saturdays were work days for him, and work had always had a greater claim on his time than she had. With a light shrug, she lifted her trailing skirt and started up the stairs again. Halfway to the landing, she heard the key turning in the lock. She could relax now. He wasn't going to spoil it for her, after all. As she heard the front door opening, she continued up the stairs without so much as a backward glance.

DAYE REDUCED her speed. She was already half an hour late. Everyone else was probably there by now. A thick knot of nervous tension began to tighten inside her stomach. She should have had a glass of milk before leaving the condo. She hadn't eaten since breakfast, and drinking on an empty stomach always got her a little high by the fourth sip. She clenched and unclenched her fingers as she gripped the wheel and tried to force herself to breathe more normally. But her pulse still insisted on racing, while her heart continued to thud uncomfortably against the walls of her chest.

She wished she could turn around and drive back home again. Making a fist, she slammed it against the steering wheel. She had to face it. She dreaded seeing Neil tonight, even though they hadn't seen each other in nearly a year. He had hurt her terribly by not attending her parents' funeral, and she still hadn't forgiven him for that. The wreath he had sent hadn't excused his behavior, and neither had his lengthy letter of condolence. All she knew was that he had left her alone with a grief the two of them could have shared.

Even at the speed she was traveling, it was inevitable that the house would eventually come into view, and it did. It was a massive two-story dwelling, built of white stucco and gray stone, with a high, peaked gray-shingled roof, imposing gray double front doors, and windows gleaming with leaded diamond-shaped panes of glass. The grounds had just been landscaped, and they still looked raw and new, but the pink oleanders and the plump, miniature Norfolk pines planted in front of the house were luxuriant and full.

The moment Daye drove up to the front door and stopped, a young blond car jockey raced up and swung open the car door for her. She sat in the car for another moment and then finally allowed him to help her out. She returned his smile and slung her purse over her shoulder, wincing as the cold metal chain touched her bare skin. In spite of the balminess of the night, she was shivering, and she chided herself for not having brought a shawl with her. But as she started up the broad stone steps, she realized that the cold she was feeling had nothing to do with the metal chain or the cool touch of the long strapless sheath of bronze-colored silk she was wearing. The cold was coming from deep inside her.

She rang the bell and then stepped back just as the door was opened by a uniformed black maid.

"How you doing this evening, Miss Daye?" The shining ebony eyes were smiling as she beckoned Daye inside.

Daye hesitated on the threshold. "I'm fine, Joleen. How have you been?" she asked the Georgia woman who had been working for Rhea ever since her marriage to Neil.

"'Cept for those mosquitoes again, I'm fine, too, Miss Daye."

Daye took a few cautious steps into the front hall and glanced anxiously into the dining room for some sign of Rhea.

"You're looking good, Miss Daye," said Joleen, as she headed back toward the kitchen. "Must be this place's agreeing with you."

"I couldn't agree with you more, Joleen. She *does* look good."

Daye froze. The voice chilled her and then warmed her up

again. It was coming from behind her, sweeping over her in a shuddering wave, and tightening the knot inside her until she found it was becoming difficult to breathe. She arranged her face in a semblance of a smile, and then she slowly turned around to face him.

"Hello, Daye." His voice seemed even deeper than she remembered.

"Neil." She acknowledged him with a slight inclination of her head.

"You're more beautiful than ever," he told her.

"And you're as good a salesman as ever," she returned.

"I tried calling you several times these last few months. Didn't you get any of my messages?"

"Yes, I got them."

"Then why didn't you ever call me back?"

"I've been very busy."

"That's always been your excuse."

"That's because it's always been true."

His smile was knowing as it spread across his handsome face, deepening the tiny lines fanning out from the corners of his eyes and widening the nostrils in his straight, elegant nose. Against the whiteness of his shirt and dinner jacket, his skin was the color of burnished copper, and his eyes were the color of the sea. As always, his physical presence had the power to make her forget that he was still a knife blade embedded deep within her heart. The slightest twist of the handle and the wound, which had never quite completely healed, would tear open again.

"You're shivering," he said. "Are you cold?"

"I'm just not used to air conditioning in December."

He signaled a passing waiter. "It's red, isn't it?" he asked her.

"White," she replied.

"Of course, white." He lifted a glass of white wine from the silver tray, handed it to her, and then raised his own glass. "To you, Daye. Welcome to God's chosen playground. Much success, Button."

Button! Daye recoiled at the pet name he had made up for her when they were children. He hadn't called her that in years. How dare he use it now!

"Daye, about the funeral, I—"

"It's too late for apologies, Neil," she cut him off.

"I tried to explain in my letter how I feel about funerals."

"Too much of an inconvenience?"

He shook his head. "You know that's not why. There are other ways of saying good-bye—"

"Daye!"

She looked up and saw Rhea sweeping toward them, with Franki and Brian following behind her. Daye bent to give her friend a hug.

"I had the most awful feeling that you might still be working," Rhea confided to her in an undertone.

"On a Saturday night?" Daye laughed. "I'm bad, but I'm not that bad. As a matter of fact, I actually left the office at three and went to have my hair done." She fluffed up her long hair with her fingers and struck a dramatic pose for them. "Well, what do you think?"

"How can anyone improve on such perfection?" asked Brian, coming up to Daye and giving her a warm kiss on the mouth. "How are you, sweetness?"

"How else could perfection feel except perfect?" She was grateful for the banter as she gave Brian a hug. She liked Brian. He was gentle and kindly, but more important than that, he adored Franki.

"No bra." He was grinning as he stepped away from her. "Hey, that was nice. How about another hug?"

"Go to Franki like a good boy," she told him. "She has a lot more to offer you than I do."

"And don't he know it?" quipped Franki.

"What does Brian have that I don't have?" inquired Neil, his attempt at levity falling flat as he gazed at Daye. "I didn't get that kind of greeting."

"What makes you think you deserved one?" Brian aimed a playful punch at Neil's shoulder.

A muscle jumped in Neil's jaw. His eyes began to smolder threateningly, and Brian's arm dropped quickly to his side.

Daye turned to Rhea and said with forced lightness, "I thought I was supposed to make my debut tonight. Is someone going to introduce me into high society or do you want me to embarrass all of you by starting to hand out my business cards to everyone?"

Franki rolled her eyes. "Spare us, please."

Rhea linked her arm through Daye's and said softly, "What kind of a hostess would I be if I allowed you to do that? Are you ready, Daye? If you are, there are one hundred and thirty very curious people waiting to meet you."

"Devour would be a better word for it," Franki muttered.

Daye gulped, but in spite of Franki's comment, she signaled to her to take her other arm.

"Why do I get the feeling I've seen something like this in a movie?" Brian asked.

"Chin up, Daye," Franki told her. "How much worse can it be than a trip to the dentist?"

With one friend on either side of her, Daye walked out onto the terrace, knowing that Neil's troubled eyes were following her every slow step of the way.

{ *chapter five* }

THE MORNING is truth time, or so Daye had always believed. The barometer by which she gauged her emotions lay in the way her stomach felt in those first few minutes after waking; and that barometer never lied. The morning after Rhea's spectacularly successful party, Daye woke up with her stomach churning.

Lying in bed and replaying the events of the evening in her head, she knew that what she was feeling was a lingering reaction to Neil's physical beauty. Her eight months of mourning, during which time she had sorted out the twisted strands of her own life, had also been eight months of celibacy. Devastated by her loss, she had found that she couldn't bear to be touched by any of the men she had been dating. Their very nearness repelled and frightened her. The touch of a hand, the pressure of a knee, the brush of a pair of lips and her skin seemed bruised and sore. She felt strangely violated. After a while, all she could do was withdraw completely from everyone she knew in order to nurse herself through her agony alone. Now, after all those months alone, seeing Neil again had reminded her of how it had once felt to be attracted to someone.

She pushed herself out of bed and stumbled into the bathroom to splash cold water on her face. Then she went through the motions of tidying up the apartment and dressing for work. The cramping in her stomach left no room for breakfast, not even a soothing cup of herbal tea, and so she made none. She simply left for the office, grateful for someplace to go on a Sunday, when other people were either in church or at home with their families. Turning up the volume on the car radio, she hoped that the words of the songs would push the dismal thoughts from her mind. But nothing could dissipate the feeling that stubbornly grew stronger with each mile she clocked. It was a feeling of complete and utter loneliness, of missing out on something and not wanting to admit it; and she hated herself for having allowed Neil to stir it up in her again.

As the days passed, however, the feeling gradually subsided, much like the fading of an irritating rash. Thanks to Rhea's party, Daye was given several decorating jobs to do, and although none was of major importance, the assignments kept the work flow constant and kept her creativity sufficiently challenged. To her added surprise, she discovered that she had become something of a celebrated novelty on the social scene; and as the season got under way, she found it increasingly difficult to balance her dedication to her work with her new-found desire to play.

There were openings to attend at the Royal Poinciana Playhouse in Palm Beach, the Parker Playhouse in Fort Lauderdale, and the Burt Reynolds Dinner Theater in Jupiter. There were champagne brunches every Sunday at the Palm Beach Polo & Country Club, followed by polo matches at three; during the week there was polo at the Royal Palm Polo–Sports Club in Boca. There were vernissages at the Society of the Four Arts in Palm Beach and in West Palm at the Norton Gallery of Art. There were tickets to the Fort Lauderdale Symphony Orchestra, the Juilliard String Quartet, a Dionne Warwick concert, and an Evening with the Boston Pops. She danced at several charity balls and attended both the annual Debutante Cotillion & Opera Ball at the venerable Breakers Hotel and the Red Cross Ball at the equally prestigious Boca Raton Hotel. She accepted a number of pre-Christmas party invitations from people she scarcely knew and spent all of her time wandering wide-eyed through some of the most palatial homes she had ever seen, mentally redecorating every one of them.

But in spite of her many evenings out, she always went home alone.

Two days before Christmas, she telephoned Rhea to tell her that she had finally found the perfect lamps for her bedroom. But instead of the enthusiasm she had expected, Daye's announcement was met with a deep sigh.

"Oh, Daye," lamented Rhea, "I'm so busy with the plans for the New Year's Eve party at the club that I don't have time right now for swatches and colors and lamps."

"I see," was all Daye could manage in her disappointment.

"You can still work with Franki, though. Didn't she speak to you about doing something with her den?"

"She did, but since she's decided to teach Matthew and Caroline to play tennis, she doesn't have the time either."

"I wish I could spend more time with the children now that they're out of school for the holidays, but this party . . ." Rhea's voice trailed off.

"What should I do about the lamps?"

"Do you think they can be put aside until after New Year's?"

Daye gritted her teeth. To her chagrin, she had found the lamps at Philippe Nadeau's antique store.

"I'll try," she finally agreed, flipping through her Rolodex for the number of Philippe's shop.

"Am I being awful?" Rhea murmured unhappily.

"No, Rhee"—Daye shook her head—"you're not being awful."

"I'm sorry, I really didn't mean to—"

"Stop apologizing, please. Just make this the best New Year's Eve party in the history of Boca Raton. Okay?"

Rhea gulped. "Okay."

When Daye hung up, she counted to ten and then dialed Philippe's number. At the sound of his smooth, meticulously accented voice, she counted to ten again and then identified herself. This was the first time they had ever spoken to each other, and from the way she was reacting to him, she hoped it would be their last.

"What a supreme pleasure to be speaking to the divine Daye Peters herself," he said, rolling his *r*'s with practiced ease.

Daye swallowed her revulsion and, in her most controlled voice, told him why she was calling.

"I regret, *chérie,* that it has never been a policy of mine to hold any item for longer than three days. Imagine my position if every item in my shop were set aside for an indeterminate length of time. How could I possibly sell anything?"

"I appreciate your position, Philippe," Daye conceded, "but I've asked you to put the lamps aside only until the first of the year. Couldn't you consider it a matter of professional courtesy?"

"All in the spirit of the season?" His snideness made the hackles rise on the back of Daye's neck. *"Ma chère* Daye, I would dearly love to oblige you, but unfortunately, there is little I can do about it."

"Thank you, Philippe," she replied, fighting to keep a tight rein on her rising temper. "I'm sorry to have troubled you."

She put down the receiver and immediately pulled his card out of her Rolodex. Crumpling it into a ball, she tossed it into the wastebasket beside her desk. She would scour all of south Florida, she would even fly up to New York if she had to, but she would never give him the satisfaction of seeing her return to his shop for those lamps.

She glanced at her watch. It was nearly two. She switched on her answering machine, picked up her purse, and set off in search of a new place to have lunch. Torn between Charlie's Crab, Café L'Europe, and Chuck & Harold's, she arbitrarily chose the last one and started walking briskly down South County Road toward Royal Poinciana Way. She considered finding herself a table on the sidewalk terrace and then decided against it, preferring instead to sit indoors out of the sun and the climbing humidity.

The vast restaurant consisted of a double tier of rust and blue chintz-covered tables, with a bandstand dominated by a large white grand piano in one corner of the room. There were Tiffany-style lamps and whirling wooden paddle fans everywhere, and the network of white pipes crisscrossing the high ceiling was partially concealed by a spinnaker of royal blue and canary yellow suspended from it like a giant parachute. She was seated beside a potted palm tree and handed a menu, which she chose to leave closed for the moment. She ordered a white wine spritzer and then sat back in her chair, with her drink in her hand, to simply relax and absorb the impact of her rather unusual surroundings at her leisure.

FRANKI SHOOED the children off the court and hurried into the locker room to shower and change. She adored those children— Matthew, who had Neil's blond hair, but who looked out at the world through the same gentle gray eyes as Rhea; and Caroline, a delicious little bundle, who never seemed to get enough of being hugged and kissed. Didn't Rhea ever hug and kiss her children? she wondered as she turned on the shower and stepped into the narrow tiled stall.

As she soaped herself, she lazily followed each of the lush curves on her muscled body and smiled at the shape she was in. She was built for making babies. Those had been the exact words of her first gynecologist in New York. And she had wanted babies as much as she had wanted the security and comfort of marriage to a man like Brian. Always a bridesmaid, but never a bride. The words of the old taunt came back to her as she pressed the palms of both hands against her flat stomach. Always an auntie, but never a mother. Her two sisters already had five children between them, while she still had none. And then there was Rhea, blessed with two precious children to love and no love to give either of them.

Can't you think of anything but children these days? she lectured herself, battling helpless tears as she turned off the taps. She snatched up her towel and began to dry herself. As usual, Matthew and Caroline would be waiting for her to take them to lunch at some popular Palm Beach restaurant, where they could pretend to be part of the adult world they seemed to find so mysterious and glamorous. Joining them some minutes later in the lounge and seeing how eagerly Caroline reached out for her hand, Franki was again overwhelmed by the unfairness of it all. As always, whenever she was with them, her thoughts began to turn to adoption and then to such absurdities as abduction, thoughts she was suppressing with increasing difficulty these days.

* * *

DAYE SCANNED both sides of the menu and finally decided on linguine, one of the house specialties. She ordered a second white wine spritzer, and when it came, she began to stir her drink with her swizzle stick, watching the bubbles from the soda swirl and rise to the surface. The sounds of childish laughter, so startlingly out of place in a restaurant like Chuck & Harold's made her glance up curiously from her drink. Her eyes darted about the room and came to rest with a bit of a shock on three familiar faces not far from where she herself was sitting.

Both Matthew and Caroline were leaning across the table, their eyes fixed on Franki's face as she talked animatedly to them in a hushed undertone. A moment later, Caroline released a peal of high-pitched laughter and covered her mouth with both hands, while Franki reached out and ruffled the child's dark hair with her fingers. They seemed so natural together, Daye thought, with a sudden pang, so relaxed and so content. Part of her wanted to stand up and wave to them, while another part held her back. It should have been Rhea sitting at that table with her two children, cherishing them and their time together, not Franki. Seeing Franki with them made Daye feel like an intruder, a trespasser, seeing something she was not meant to see and betraying Rhea simply by being there and being a witness to it.

She hastily opened her purse and took out a twenty dollar bill. It would more than compensate for the waiter's bringing a plate of steaming linguine to an empty table. She slipped out of the restaurant undetected, finding herself in the back courtyard of the restaurant facing South County Road and momentarily losing her sense of direction. She was shaking as she started off down the street. Suddenly, all she wanted was to get back to her office and lose herself in her work. It was the only antidote she knew for the pain she felt inside.

chapter six

IT WAS eight o'clock on New Year's Eve, and Daye was late. She had the beginnings of a sore throat, which she attributed to the constant air conditioning, and she was in no mood for a party. Rhea had proudly informed her that she was expecting close to two hundred people at the Boca Country Club that evening, fifty more than Sybil Barron was expecting at the Palms. Daye shuddered at the thought of two hundred people counting down those last ten seconds to midnight, then clinking glasses and kissing whoever happened to be nearest them at the time. As she stood in front of the bathroom mirror, sucking on a throat lozenge and listlessly brushing her hair, she recalled the many New Year's Eves when she had stood, like so many other New Yorkers, with a red nose and a hip flask of brandy, in Times Square, shouting out those last ten seconds as the ball slowly made its descent, and then reaching for the person beside her and welcoming in the New Year with a drunken kiss.

For the first time since leaving New York, Daye felt herself being submerged by a bittersweet wave of nostalgia. She put down her brush and went into the living room to pour herself a brandy and then took it out onto the balcony. The air was balmy, the breeze laden with moisture, and if anyone had told her six months ago that she would be seeing in the New Year in eighty-degree weather, wearing a strapless white chiffon floor-length gown encrusted with silver sequins, instead of her wool jacket and a pair of slacks, she would have laughed.

By the time she had finished her brandy and the remains of the cherry-flavored lozenge, Daye was feeling a bit better. She left her empty snifter in the kitchen sink and returned to her bedroom for the long white chiffon stole that went with the gown. She draped it across her shoulders, flung one tasseled end behind her, and then surveyed the effect in her mirror. In the icy whiteness of the gown, her mother's diamonds at her ears and throat, she looked like the glittering Snow Queen in her favorite childhood fairy tale. Even with her golden tan, she still appeared cold and unapproachable. And that made her sad.

For someone who had thought that she was ready for a serious relationship, she now had to admit that she had done very little since her arrival in Florida to encourage one. She had always detested dating, spending endless evenings with men she didn't want to see again. It was too much of an effort to pretend to be interested in someone when she wasn't, too difficult to keep a smile on her face and her yawns in check when she was bored. She disliked continually repeating the story of her life to some stranger who would forget it the moment he left her at her door, just as she would forget his the moment she closed the door and locked it. It was rare that she met a man she wanted to see again, and in the last five weeks, she had been sparing herself any unnecessary disappointments by keeping her distance, as she had done so often in the recent past.

When the car jockey brought her Mercedes around, she wished him a happy New Year and set out for the club, taking the A1A. As always, she was stunned by the number of houses she passed whose doors were decorated with wreaths of plastic holly, whose windows were trimmed with colored Christmas lights, and whose lush green lawns boasted either a life-sized plastic Santa Claus or a reindeer-drawn sleigh, piled high with gift-wrapped boxes. The only rational explanation she could find for such ludicrous displays was that the houses belonged to transplanted northerners who couldn't imagine Christmas without their Santas and their holly. Why not wreaths of fresh pine branches and fruit? Why not palm trees strung with garlands of flowers instead of plastic pine trees hung with tinsel and plastic icicles and little red felt boots trimmed with cotton batting? She laughed out loud as she recalled her shock at walking into Streb's, a seafood restaurant on Federal Highway in Boca, and finding the entire ceiling strung with large white paper snowflakes.

She parked the car and walked slowly toward the clubhouse, watching as one elegantly attired couple after another swept past without even acknowledging her, causing her to feel even more alone than ever. An elderly man in a black brocade dinner jacket smiled and held the door for her, and she smiled back at him in gratitude and stepped into the carpeted foyer of the newest and most luxurious country club in Boca.

The three main reception rooms on the ground floor of the massive two-story glass and redwood building were ablaze with thousands of tiny white fairy lights, which framed the windows and doors and were wrapped around each potted plant and tree. One room had been cleared for dancing, while the other two were filled with round tables draped in emerald green cloths and ringed by small gilt chairs with green-cushioned seats. A single tall green taper flickered in the middle of each elaborate centerpiece consisting of white roses and carnations, clouds of baby's breath and deep green lemon leaves.

Identical tables had been set up on the stone terrace around the large oval swimming pool whose surface was alive with floating clusters of white carnations and green lemon leaves; and while Daye silently applauded Rhea and her wonderful taste, she also thanked her for not including a single poinsettia plant among the decorations. As she slowly circled the pool, nodding to the few familiar faces she passed, she almost regretted not having accepted Rhea's offer to pair her up for the evening with one of the very eligible and very wealthy single members of the club. But the mood passed quickly, and she was soon castigating herself for falling into the trap of thinking of New Year's Eve as a special night, instead of what it really was—just another night in a year with three hundred sixty-five nights.

She heard her name being called and turned to see Rhea

coming toward her, resplendent in an Oscar de la Renta gown of emerald green satin, with balloon sleeves, a tight-fitting bodice and a full skirt. Behind her was Franki in a two-piece Vollbracht of red, green, blue, and black sequins; both Neil and Brian were in black tie, their pleated white shirts the only stab of lightness against the sleek and somber blackness of their tuxedos.

"Everything looks magnificent," breathed Daye as she and Rhea hugged each other carefully. "You've done a marvelous job, Rhee. You should be proud of yourself."

Rhea was beaming. "I think all those sleepless nights may have been worth it after all," she said, linking her arm through Daye's. "I've found a wonderful new caterer," she whispered. "Now let's hope that dear Sybil hasn't planted one of her spies here tonight."

Daye laughed and gave Rhea's hand an affectionate pat. "Did I tell you that I've just landed my first important account?" she asked, keeping her own voice low.

"No, who?" Rhea's eyes were bright with anticipation.

"Bunny and Jules Adamson."

"The Adamsons from Newport?"

"The very same."

Rhea gestured to Franki. "We need some champagne!"

"One glass or an entire tray?" interrupted Brian as he signaled a passing waiter.

"A tray," Daye said, reaching for two glasses and handing one of them to Rhea.

"What's the occasion?" asked Franki.

"We're toasting Daye," Rhea told her, raising her glass.

"Why?" demanded Neil, who had said nothing at all up to this point.

"Because Daye's just landed a fabulous account," Rhea said. "Bunny and Jules Adamson."

Neil glanced at Daye. "Now, I'd say that deserves something more than a simple toast."

"How much more?" Brian countered.

But Neil ignored Brian as he considered Daye with frank admiration in his eyes. "I think we'd all be well advised to be especially nice to this young lady from now on," he said in a voice that was half teasing, half serious, "because wherever

Jules Adamson goes, millions of dollars happily follow. I understand he's been looking around for some choice real estate down here but he still hasn't linked up with a developer." He moved closer to Daye and chucked her lightly under the chin. "How would you like to introduce your new client to your old friend, Daye?" he asked her.

"I've never known you to need an introduction before, *old* friend," she returned, startling even *her* with the frosty sound of her voice.

"But Jules Adamson is different, he's unapproachable."

"I'm sure you can think of some way to get to him."

Neil's eyes were hard as he said, "A simple no would have done quite nicely, thanks." And with that, he turned and walked off.

Daye was uncomfortably aware of three pairs of baffled eyes regarding her most curiously as she quickly drained her glass and then looked around for some place to set it down. Her sore throat was worse, her body was beginning to ache, and she was afraid that she was coming down with the flu. When Brian and Franki went into the clubhouse a few minutes later and Rhea excused herself to check on the food being prepared in the kitchen, she felt abandoned. Arming herself with a second glass of champagne, she circled the pool one more time and then wandered over to one of the elaborate buffet tables. She put her glass down and picked up a plate, dropping several pimiento-stuffed olives onto it and then moving along to a garnished silver platter of salmon mousse. She spooned some of the mousse onto her plate and then looked around for her glass of champagne. It was gone. She saw one of the waiters disappearing into the crowd, holding a tray of half-empty glasses high above his head, and she wondered dismally which of those glasses was hers.

She was just standing there, contemplating giving up on the buffet in favor of going off in search of more champagne when she became aware of someone watching her. She glanced up and their eyes met, and she felt a sudden searing heat pass from his eyes to hers and run down her body with the tingling force of an electric shock. Flustered, she turned away and tried to focus on the platters of food spread out so temptingly in front of her. She started to lift a silver spoon filled with black caviar, but her fingers couldn't seem to close around the handle, so she let the spoon slide back again into the large chilled crystal bowl.

Nibbling on one of her olives, she slowly moved away from the table and glanced over at the precise spot where their eyes had met. To her dismay, he was no longer standing there. She had difficulty swallowing the olive as she scanned the pool area for some sign of him. Had she imagined the whole thing? She gave her head an impatient shake. She could never have reacted that way to a pair of eyes she had made up. She returned to the buffet table, her legs slightly wobbly and her heart uncomfortably heavy, and cast a baleful look at the caviar.

"I wouldn't pass it up this time if I were you. Beluga's practically a collector's item these days."

She stood there stunned at the sound of the husky voice so close to her ear and watched as a lean suntanned hand deposited a gleaming black mound of the caviar in the middle of her plate.

"Grated egg?"

She numbly nodded her head.

"Chopped onion?"

She shook her head no, and with both hands straining to keep a firm grip on her plate, she turned around to look at him. Her breath caught and lodged in her throat. In the flickering lights surrounding them, she could see that his eyes were deep blue, the same shimmering navy as a pair of sky pebbles cut from the indigo cloth of night, and that his eyelashes were thick and black like his hair, and unusually long. His nose was a straight slash of strength, softened by one tiny freckle near the tip; and as his mouth, so generously molded, began to widen in a slow and appreciative smile, it revealed even white teeth and deepened the dimple creasing his left cheek.

As she continued to study him, Daye could feel her pulse racing and her blood singing with a curious liquid warmth. It was impossible for a man as devastatingly handsome as he was to be at that party alone, she knew; and at that very moment, there had to be either a wife or a girl friend looking for him.

"You're staring." He said it gently, and his voice still had that appealing huskiness to it, as though he had once strained it and changed its timbre forever.

"I'm sorry." She was painfully aware that she was blushing.

"Don't be." There was that lazy, dimpling smile again. "I was doing quite a bit of staring myself for a while. How else would I have known about the caviar?"

As Daye cautiously returned his smile, she was slowly able to relax. "Are you one of the Dragon Lady's spies?" she asked him. "Have you come to sample the food and then report back to her?"

"And if I have?"

"I'll have to turn you in, I'm afraid."

"Then let's keep it to ourselves, shall we?" He eased the plate from her hands.

"My caviar," she moaned, continuing their little game.

"After," he said.

"After what?"

"After we've danced."

He took her by the hand and led her into the room where the ten-piece band was playing "The Way You Look Tonight." She slid easily into his arms, feeling her body being wrapped inside a comforting cloak of gentle strength. She breathed in his cologne, and the smell of Halston's Z-14 became firmly imprinted on her senses. As he led her slowly across the floor, she remembered all the times she had danced with the fathers of her friends at one formal function or another, and how nervous she had felt, being forced to dance with someone she hardly knew. She had tended to babble in an effort to conceal her nervousness, while holding herself like a stick and glancing down at her feet to make certain she was keeping them clear of her partner's shoes.

And yet, here she was, dancing with someone she didn't know at all, and following him as easily as if they had rehearsed their steps together beforehand. He moved with effortless grace, and her body followed willingly, bending and arching with the music, molding itself to his, so that they moved in one smooth, continuous pattern of unbroken rhythm. She was partly aware of the band slipping from tune to tune and vaguely aware of where she was. But with her head resting comfortably against his shoulder and her arms wrapped tightly around his neck, she knew that this was exactly where she wanted to be.

When the band swung into another song, he hummed the

melody for a while and then began singing the words to her in a soft, husky whisper. His breath was warm as it fanned her cheek and the sensitive rim of her ear, and Daye shivered, feeling her nipples beginning to stiffen as his lips moved against her skin:

> Tonight was made for promises
> The dawn will never keep,
> But I'll remember
> How you loved me,
> And dawn won't see me weep . . .

A tongue of fire was spreading outward from where his mouth was grazing her cheek, and soon it was snaking its way down her spine. Daye stirred in his arms as the heat spread to her groin, and she felt herself softening and opening up before him, like the petals of a tightly closed rose. The song was called "How You Loved Me," and it came from the smash Broadway musical *Love on a Shoestring*. She had bought the album after seeing the show for the third time several years ago, and had played it over and over until she knew every song by heart. It had been a long time since she'd played the record and an even longer time since she'd thought of the words to that particular song.

"Jonathan?"

It was a woman's gravelly voice, rich and deep, close to Daye's elbow. It shattered the moment and drove a wedge between the two of them as effectively as if a knife had come down through the air and separated them.

Daye turned and found herself looking up at a tall, rangy woman with an inky spill of heavy black hair cascading down her back. Her deeply tanned face was defined by such broad and sensual planes that Daye felt tiny and brittle by comparison. Wearing a richly embroidered turquoise Indian cotton blouse and skirt, with a fringed shawl wrapped around her waist and a pair of beaded sandals on her feet, she resembled a nineteenth-century Gypsy. Intricate bead earrings dangled from her ears and brushed her shoulders, and when she gave her head an imperious shake, the earrings swung back and forth, making little clacking sounds.

"I must say, darling, I *do* approve of your taste," she growled, her black eyes treating Daye as though she were an object on display in a museum, "but I'm back now, and I'm absolutely ravenous."

Daye needed no further prodding. "If you'll both excuse me," she said in a quiet voice, "I have some food of my own to finish." Refusing to meet his eyes again, she leveled a cool gaze at the woman instead and walked away with her head high and her back straight.

Her face was burning, and her legs were moving as though they belonged to someone else as she crossed the patio. When she reached the buffet table, she leaned against it, bracing herself with both hands while she closed her eyes. Once again, the scent of him enveloped her, the touch of his body lived on in the pores of her own skin, and the sound of his low voice was scorched like a brand on her memory.

"Did I just see you dancing with Jonathan Cort?"

The sound of Rhea's voice made Daye jump. Her head shot up, and her eyes grew wide.

"Jonathan Cort?" she echoed, realizing with a jolt that the song he had been singing was one of his own.

"Didn't you recognize him?" asked Rhea, and Daye shook her head. "Given your interest in the theater, I'm surprised that you never met Broadway's onetime golden boy."

Daye was staring at her friend in shock. She had been dancing with Jonathan Cort and hadn't even known it. Jonathan Cort. One half of the fabled songwriting team of Kerwin and Cort. Nearly ten years had passed since their first hit song, "Stranger to Love," topped the charts and earned them the reputation as the hottest new team since Bacharach and David. During their six years together, Rolf Kerwin and Jonathan Cort had written scores of successful hits and had received a dozen or more Grammys, Tonys, and Oscars for their work. Their three musicals—*Love on a Shoestring, Traveling Light,* and *Sing a Song of Broadway*—had played to sell-out crowds every night, and for a while, all three shows had run concurrently on Broadway. Then, suddenly, it was over. The team split up, and Jonathan Cort mysteriously vanished.

"Daye?" Rhea was staring at her, head cocked to one side, her forehead creased in a thoughtful frown. "If I didn't know you better, I'd say you were smitten."

"Don't be ridiculous," retorted Daye. "All we did was dance."

"You're certain about that?"

"Yes, I'm certain."

"Then wipe that dreamy look out of your eyes. Stop scowling at me, my friend; it's still there."

Daye turned her head away. She was feeling empty again. It was as though someone had pulled a tiny plug somewhere deep inside her and allowed all her feelings to drain out of her.

"He's gorgeous," Rhea said. "I don't blame you for looking that way."

"What way?"

"As if you'd just discovered ice cream."

"I don't like ice cream."

"You'd never know it by looking at you."

"Tell me more about him, Rhea." There was an urgency in Daye's voice that she couldn't suppress.

"Well, he's from a small town in Maine, but he was studying at NYU when he met Rolf Kerwin. The two of them wrote a number of revues for the school and several variety shows for one of the fraternity houses. After they graduated, they began cutting demos and supporting themselves by working in clubs. Some agent took a chance on them and matched them up with a young British singer . . ." Rhea paused, searching for the girl's name.

"Lauren Giles."

"So you *do* know something about the gorgeous Mr. Cort." Rhea's tone was mischievous again.

"A bit."

"He married a free-lance journalist named Andrea Simon, but their marriage was already in trouble when *Love on a Shoestring* went to Broadway. They were divorced just after *Traveling Light* opened. Jonathan built himself a house down here, and both he and Rolf Kerwin commuted between Florida and New York while they were putting together *Sing a Song of Broadway*. After that show began its run, Jonathan Cort dropped out of sight."

"Is he still living here in Florida?"

Rhea nodded. "For the past four years, he's been living in the house he built in Gorham Sound."

"Where's Gorham Sound?" Daye asked.

"It's a tiny fishing village halfway between Boca and Palm Beach."

"And who's the woman with him?" Daye finally worked up the courage to ask.

Rhea rolled her eyes. "That's Maren MacCaul. She's a former Broadway gypsy who never made it out of the chorus line. She came from a very wealthy family, though, and for the past fifteen years, her favorite occupation has been buying failing playhouses, pouring fresh money and fresh life back into them, and then moving on. She's owned the Gorham Sound Playhouse for three years now, and apparently that's a long time for her."

"Is she staying here because of Jonathan Cort?"

"Probably. He's helped her produce a number of shows, and because of his name, the playhouse is always filled. He's even written several very good revues for her; but if what the local gossips say is true, he won't be writing revues very much longer."

"Why not?"

"Because he's supposedly working on a musical that he hopes to take to Broadway very soon."

Cort without Kerwin, Daye mused. Last year it had been Kerwin without Cort; Rolf Kerwin had written a show especially for Lauren Giles, whom he had married shortly after he and Jonathan split up. The show had closed after three nights. She reached for a large purple grape and popped it into her mouth. Chewing on it slowly and purposefully, she casually scanned the area around the pool again. When she finally found what she had been searching for, she stopped, and her heart began pounding wildly. He was looking directly at her, his dark eyes warming her face and sending a flare of melting sweetness through her entire body.

It was with a jarring shock that she realized no man had stirred her this way since . . . She forced herself to form his name in her mind. Since Neil. Their eyes met again, and this time they held until the dark head of Maren MacCaul drifted between them and blocked Daye's view of him. She turned to Rhea, only to find that her friend had slipped away. Strangely dispirited, Daye moved away from the buffet table and wandered back inside the clubhouse. She opened her purse and took out another throat lozenge, wishing at the same time that she had brought some aspirin for the headache that had begun to throb unmercifully behind her eyes.

As the evening wore on, she allowed herself the occasional glimpse of Jonathan Cort, knowing that she was only teasing herself and that brief glimpses were all she would get of him. He wasn't free. He belonged to Maren MacCaul. She danced with Brian several times, but she refused to dance with any of the husbands of Rhea's friends; and every once in a while, she found herself wondering where Neil had gone.

She was on her way back out to the patio after another dance with Brian when someone caught hold of her arm.

"Tell me your name, beautiful lady," he said as she tried to twist her arm free. "Please?"

She wanted to run. She wanted to tell him to leave her alone, that he belonged to someone else and that she didn't want another woman's man.

"Tell me?"

She wrenched her arm from his grasp and broke away from him.

"I'll find out who you are whether you tell me or not," he called out after her.

As she darted around a table, she lost her balance and collided with Neil. His arm shot out to support her, and as she sagged against him, he put both his arms around her waist and held her even tighter.

"Dance with me, Daye?" he asked, their earlier exchange obviously forgotten.

She gave her head a quick nod. "Yes," she told him, panting slightly as she glanced over his shoulder at the dark-haired man who was still standing in the doorway watching her.

Neil looked from Daye to Jonathan Cort and then back at Daye again.

"You're hurting me, Neil," Daye protested, squirming in his arms as they tightened around her like a steely band.

His grip relaxed almost immediately. "Sorry," he apologized, taking her by the elbow and steering her around the tables.

The doorway was empty by the time they reached it, but when Daye caught sight of Jonathan Cort's tall form blending into the rest of the crowd, it took all of her self-control to keep from hurrying after him and to give herself over to Neil instead.

chapter seven

Daye was convinced that if she hadn't developed a fever along with her sore throat, forcing her to take to her bed for the next three days, she might never have thought about Jonathan Cort again. But away from her work, her physical and emotional defenses down, she thrashed about in a state of semidelirium and thought of nothing else. She even went so far as to search through her records for the album of *Love on a Shoestring*. When she found it, she put the record on the stereo in the living room and dropped the stylus at the beginning of the cut "How You Loved Me." Then, clutching a mug of herbal tea laced with brandy and honey, she curled up on the sofa; and as she listened to the words of the song being sung by Larry Kert, she pretended that it was Jonathan Cort singing them instead.

By the fourth day of her self-imposed isolation, she knew every song from *Love on a Shoestring* by heart again. But she was also restless and bored and anxious to return to her office and the work she could rely on to banish all further thoughts of Jonathan Cort from her mind. But as one day ground predictably into the next, she discovered that forgetting Jonathan Cort would not be as easy as she had hoped.

Every dark-haired man she saw had his face, those deep blue eyes, that dimpled left cheek. If a man passed her on the street smelling of Halston Z-14, she would turn and stare after him, certain that it was Jonathan. She found him listed in the directory under Cort, J., 14 Seaside Way, and circled his telephone number with a series of tiny red dots with one of her fine-point felt-tip pens. But even as she committed his number to memory, she knew that she would never use it. It was not hers to use, just as he was not hers to have. Wandering through Saks on Worth Avenue at noon one day, she strolled past the men's colognes, and before she could stop herself, she had sprayed both wrists with Halston Z-14. She left the store without the pantyhose she had intended to buy, sniffing first one wrist and then the other, and wondering why she was torturing herself this way.

When she stopped at her favorite newsstand on Atlantic Avenue to pick up a copy of the Shiny Sheet on her way into work one morning and read that Philippe Nadeau had just been chosen to redecorate the clubhouse of the Lake Worth Beach Club, she wadded the tabloid into a ball and hurled it into the first trash can she could find. She was still fuming when she arrived at her office forty minutes later. The Lake Worth Beach Club was a job she herself had wanted and one for which she had actually forgotten to submit her proposal. She balled her fists and shook them at the ceiling. She had missed the opportunity of bidding on an important commercial project because she had spent all of the ten days since New Year's Eve daydreaming about a man.

She was near tears as she stormed over to her desk and pulled open the middle drawer to get a pen. In her angry haste, she pulled the drawer out too far and sent it crashing to the floor, scattering pens, pencils, boxes of paper clips, and bottles of colored ink everywhere.

"Damn you, Jonathan Cort," she sobbed as she got down on her knees and started gathering everything up again. "Damn you for doing this to me."

But even as she was cursing him, she was blaming herself more. He had done nothing to her. It was she who had permitted her own fantasies to immobilize her and to interfere with her work. As she fitted the drawer back into place, she swore to herself that nothing like this would ever happen again. There was too much at stake right now, and she simply couldn't allow her romantic notions to destroy what she had yet to build.

As RHEA fluttered about the dining room, she stopped to pluck a limp rosebud from the arrangement of roses, irises, and tiger lilies in the center of the table and then lifted one of the Val St. Lambert wineglasses to examine it for water spots. There were eight places set at the oval mahogany table, and this was only the second time that she would be using her new set of Royal Crown Derby Imari dishes. She adjusted the rheostat, dimming the lightbulbs in the crystal chandelier, and backed out of the room with a satisfied smile.

It had worked out well. Maren MacCaul was up north combing Connecticut and New Jersey in an apparent attempt to purchase another playhouse, and Rhea had taken advantage of her absence to invite Jonathan Cort for dinner. His companion for the evening would be Daye, although neither of them knew it. Rhea could scarcely manage to suppress a wistful sigh. What an exquisite couple Daye and Jonathan had made that night. She still remembered how they had looked together on the dance floor, both of them so golden and so beautiful, moving together so well, fitting together so perfectly.

"You look rather pleased with yourself," commented Neil with a wry smile as he came upon Rhea still standing in the doorway.

"I am," she admitted, staring dreamily at the table.

"I don't see why you have to play matchmaker for Daye," he said. "She's a little old for blind dates, don't you think?"

"This is hardly a blind date," countered Rhea. "They danced together at the club, and I know she was attracted to him."

"So?"

"She hasn't done anything about it. She could have called him and—"

"I know she's your idea of today's emancipated woman," Neil interrupted, "but most men still get turned off by women who call and ask them for dates."

"Don't you remember the TV commercial for Harvey's Bristol Cream?" Rhea asked him with a tight little smile. "According to them, it's not only acceptable, it's downright upright."

"Cute, Rhea." His returning smile was as tight as hers.

"Thank you."

"You're meddling, you know." He trailed after her when she went into the kitchen. "He's still involved with Maren MacCaul."

Rhea lifted the lid from the pot of lobster bisque simmering on the stove and sampled it with a silver teaspoon. "That romance won't last much longer," she said.

"So now you're also a fortune teller!"

"Daye's not happy." Rhea turned to him with a stricken expression on her face. "I want her to be happy, Neil."

"And you think Jonathan Cort can make her happy?"

"He might."

For a moment, Neil just stood there saying nothing. Then he took hold of Rhea's chin and said, "You've changed, you know, and I don't particularly like it." With that, he let his hand drop but as he strode out of the kitchen, he gave the door an angry jab with his fist.

Rhea stared after him, startled by his accusation. And yet, as she reached for her bottle of cooking sherry and added another dash of it to the bisque, she knew that nothing he said to her really mattered anymore.

When the door chimes sounded, she jumped. It was Joleen's night off, and as Rhea hurried to answer the door, she hoped she would find Daye standing there, not Jonathan; and that her dearest friend would forgive her for interfering. I love her, she repeated over and over to herself. I love her and I want her to find someone to love her the way she should be loved. To her immense relief, it *was* Daye, and as the two of them embraced, Rhea said, "You look absolutely sensational. That dress is simply superb."

Daye stepped over to the hall mirror and looked at herself in the taupe silk shirtwaist with the dramatic Joan Crawford shoulders and the deeply slashed crossover neckline, and shrugged.

"Not bad," she said.

"Now all you need is that fabulous David Webb choker we saw to go with it."

Daye laughed as she lovingly fingered the ten strands of

white freshwater pearls she had twisted into a thick rope around her neck.

"These will do just fine, thank you, until the right billionaire comes along."

"And I thought all you independent career women insisted on paying for everything yourselves," commented Neil as he joined them in the hall.

"Ignore him," Rhea told her, steering Daye into the living room. "He's cranky because he lost his golf game at the club today."

"We all know how much Neil loves to lose," said Daye with a sage nod.

"A drink, Daye?" Neil asked, heading over to the bar.

"Rye and ginger," she told him. She scooped up a handful of cashew nuts from a silver bowl on the coffee table and started to munch on them.

The door chimes sounded, and Rhea hurried back into the hall. A moment later, Daye could hear her friend speaking to someone in what she had always referred to as Rhea's "hostess voice." It was the tone she reserved for people she barely knew. It was cool, cordial, and very, very polite.

"Daye, I don't believe the two of you have been formally introduced."

Daye spun around, and all the breath went out of her. A cashew seemed to wedge itself firmly in her throat as she looked up and met his deep blue eyes. He reached for her right hand, and like an automaton, she raised it, feeling him grasp it firmly and then continue to hold on to it.

"The mysterious Cinderella of New Year's Eve." He smiled, the huskiness there in his voice just as she remembered it, the same dimple creasing his left cheek. "It's a pleasure to meet you, Daye Peters."

"Jonathan." As she murmured his name, she pulled her hand free of his.

She trained a fierce glance Rhea's way. No doubt Maren MacCaul would make an entrance at any moment. She could see Rhea almost imperceptibly shaking her head as if telling her to wait.

"Has Maren found herself a new playhouse yet?" Rhea was asking Jonathan while her own gaze was directed at Daye.

Jonathan shook his head. "She hasn't found anything suitable in Connecticut so far, but knowing Maren, she'll turn the countryside inside out before giving up and going on to New Jersey."

"Is she actually contemplating moving back up north?" Rhea pressed further.

"For the moment, she's considering the possibility of operating a playhouse up north for six months of the year, while still keeping the one in Gorham Sound open year-round."

So Maren was out of town. Daye's eyes narrowed. She cautioned herself against feeling anything even remotely resembling excitement, because even if Maren was away now, it was only a matter of time before she'd return. She dared another cautious look at Jonathan who was now standing at the bar with Neil. Jonathan was wearing a rust corduroy jacket and tan slacks, and beside him, Neil, in his navy blue blazer and gray trousers, looked surprisingly drab.

She was just about to go over to the two men and join the conversation when the door chimes rang again. Rhea returned a moment later with Franki and Brian and a couple whom Daye had never met before. No sooner was she introduced to Stella and Vernon Joyce than everyone was ushered out onto the terrace for drinks and hors d'oeuvres. After what seemed to Daye to be an interminable length of time, they were finally shown into the dining room where Daye found herself being seated directly across the table from Jonathan.

Numbed by his nearness, she hardly tasted anything she ate or drank. The room seemed to have narrowed until all she could see was the rise and fall of his chest as he breathed, the way his dimple creased when he smiled, and the smooth movement of his right hand whenever he sought to make a point or when he held his wineglass to his lips. She was a spectator and pleased to remain one, so fearful was she of intruding and having the moment disintegrate as it had once before, leaving her empty and more alone than ever.

She was toying with a spear of fresh asparagus, trying to remind herself that it was because of Jonathan Cort that she had lost out on the Lake Worth Beach Club project, when she heard him asking her to pass him the salt. Glancing up with a guilty start, she handed him the sterling silver saltcellar, and then realized that there was a pair of matching salt and pepper shakers in front of each person's place setting. At her look of consternation, he smiled guilelessly and said in a husky undertone, "I apologize for the unoriginal way of finally getting your attention."

She leveled a cool, appraising stare at him. "You could have tried just saying my name."

"I did. Twice."

Mortified, she quickly lowered her gaze and reached for her fork again.

"Rhea tells me that you're an interior designer," he said.

"Yes, I am," she answered, refusing to look up from her plate.

"How are you adapting to Florida after living in New York all your life?"

"Personally or professionally?"

"Both, I guess."

"It's a little too early to tell."

"Do you find you design differently for a home by the ocean than you would for a home in the city?" he persisted.

She set down her fork and gave him a look that told him she thought his questions were legitimate, but she just didn't feel like answering them. Out of the corner of one eye, she could see Rhea watching her carefully. It was a conspiracy, she decided, picking up her glass of wine and gulping it down as if it were water. A conspiracy to force her to be polite to another woman's man whom she already found dangerously attractive. It simply wasn't fair! She set her empty wineglass down with more force than she had intended, flushing uncomfortably as seven pairs of eyes suddenly focused themselves solely on her.

"I need a refill, too," announced Franki in a loud voice, holding up her own empty glass and waving it in Neil's general direction. "If one way doesn't work, I say try another."

There were appreciative snickers of laughter around the table as Neil got up to oblige her, and Daye met Franki's conspiratorial wink with a wobbly smile of thanks.

Over strawberries Romanoff, Jonathan decided to try again.

"Do you like Gerry Mulligan, Daye?"

She swallowed the tip of the berry she had been breaking

into tiny pieces with her spoon and nodded.

"I have tickets for his concert at the West Palm Beach Auditorium tomorrow night. Would you be interested in hearing him?"

Again Daye could feel Rhea's eyes burning into the side of her head.

"I—I don't think so," she said hesitantly. "I've fallen behind in my work, and I'm still trying to catch up."

"You can catch up some other time," he said, leaning forward in his seat and clasping his hands together in front of him on the table. "How often do you get to hear Gerry Mulligan live? Come on, Daye, you can't work every night."

"I'm not working tonight," she retorted.

He made a gesture of acquiescence with one hand. "Why don't we compromise? Go to the concert with me, and stay until intermission. Then I'll escort you back to your office myself."

"It's a good deal, Daye," Brian piped up. "I'd take it if I were you."

Was everyone part of the conspiracy, then? she wondered, studying each of the faces around the table. Neil's contemplative frown convinced her that he was probably the only one who wasn't in on it, but that brought her little comfort. She shifted uneasily in her chair. She felt torn apart by indecision, wretched at the thought of denying herself even one brief evening with Jonathan Cort, but terrified that she might want more. And how many nights could they have together? Two? Five? Ten? It really made no difference how many nights there were; someone would come back to claim him in the end.

"Daye?"

He was still waiting for her answer. So was everyone else, it seemed.

"All right, Jonathan, I'd be pleased to go," she told him, letting her breath out slowly as she said it, "but only until intermission."

All she needed at that moment was for everyone to break into applause and she vowed she would never speak to any of them again. But no one did. They simply smiled and nodded—all except Neil—and continued with their meal.

After dinner, they went into the living room. The four women settled themselves on a pair of facing love seats while the men stood together around the bar. As Daye sat silently beside Franki and sipped on a cognac, she wondered why married couples always drew a line between them after dinner, separating the women into one camp and the men into another. From time to time, she would look up and catch Jonathan watching her. In his eyes was a message which seemed to be telling her that he disliked it as much as she did but that there was very little he could do about changing someone else's rules.

"He's thirty-eight," Daye heard Stella Joyce whisper to Franki.

"Who is?" Daye asked, her curiosity piqued.

"Jonathan Cort," Stella told her, "and Maren MacCaul is forty-three."

"That old!" Franki clapped a hand to her cheek in mock horror.

"She likes to pretend she's still on the sunnier side of forty," Stella continued, "but Vernon's sister was a freshman at City College with her in 'fifty-eight, and Pat's forty-three."

Daye glanced over at Jonathan again. There was a five-year age difference between them just as there was a five-year difference between himself and Maren. Armed with that bit of information, she suddenly felt a little less threatened by Maren MacCaul. As Stella began to describe her sister-in-law Pat's recent face-lift operation in minute detail, Daye stifled a yawn, leaned her head back against the sofa, and closed her eyes.

She imagined herself walking along the beach with her shoes in her hand, feeling the night wind wrestling with her hair and the sand damp and cool between her toes. She started to grin as she saw herself leaving her dress on the shore and wading naked into the water with only a sliver of moon to light her way, while the waves closed in around her like a warm, silken robe.

"You look like someone who's right in the middle of a very enjoyable fantasy."

She opened her eyes and saw Jonathan standing over her. Before she quite realized what was happening, he was taking the glass from her hand and hauling her to her feet.

"If you don't mind, I think I'd better take this overworked

young lady home before she falls asleep," he said to Rhea, bending over her hand with a courtly bow.

Daye barely managed to blurt out a shaky thank you to her friend before she found herself being led by the hand to the front door.

"Your car or mine?" Jonathan asked as he held the door open for her.

She stared at him, at a loss for words.

"You follow me in your car, then," he decided for her. "We'll go to the beach."

As she trailed down the steps behind him, her mind began to clear and she stopped in the middle of the driveway and put her hands on her hips.

"You can follow me," she told him rebelliously. "I know the same beaches."

"Not this one, you don't," he countered, getting into his black BMW and starting the engine. "Coming?"

He turned on the headlights and began backing out of the drive, while Daye continued to stand there, considering the alternatives. Then with a spirited toss of her head, she got into her own car. She refused to think about the consequences of what she was doing. Like the indomitable Scarlett she had imitated as a child, she decided that she would simply think about it tomorrow.

chapter eight

THE BEACH that curved around the sleepy fishing village of Gorham Sound had sand as fine as baby powder. Daye grew tired of carrying her shoes and finally allowed them to drop with a gentle plop into the soft sand. This freed her hands—hands she had purposefully kept filled so that Jonathan couldn't hold either one of them. They had been walking along the deserted shore for nearly an hour, neither of them speaking, content to walk side by side without immediately having to share in each other's thoughts, and Daye had found that somewhat reassuring. It had banished some of the tension between them and allowed a gentle kind of peace to settle over them.

"What we did was pretty daring, don't you think?" she turned to him and asked when she felt it was time to break their lengthy silence.

His smile caused her heart to miss a beat. "If I'd been a bit braver, I'd have done it a lot sooner," he admitted.

They continued for a while in silence again, but when he reached for her hand some minutes later, she was prepared for it. As he threaded his fingers through hers, the skin on her hand began to tingle and throb. He pulled her closer to him, and their hips connected, sending an arc of shivering heat up one side of her body. Her knees began to weaken, and with them her resolve to keep some distance between them. Once more she was reminded of the futility of their pairing, and she fought to harden her slackening resolve again by trying to break away from his ever-tightening grasp.

But Jonathan stopped and turned to face her, refusing to allow her to back off. As she fought him, he caught hold of both of her flailing wrists and pinned her arms gently but firmly behind her back. Then he drew her toward him until the tips of her breasts grazed his chest. She shook her head and squirmed against him, succeeding only in grinding her body deeper into his.

"No, Jonathan, don't."

His lips were hovering just above hers. She looked up to find the moon, but all she could see was his face.

"Jonathan?"

He brushed her mouth with his, no more than a whisper, a delicate butterfly of a kiss, and then he stopped to look at her again. He released her arms and gently clasped the sides of her face with both hands, his eyes searching hers, his mouth lowering slowly, his eyelids gradually closing. She parted her lips and received the sweet pleasure of his mouth against hers with a shuddering sigh. As their kiss deepened, she could feel herself surrendering to him, and she grew frightened again. Stiffening in his embrace, she wavered between a hungry yearning and the need to retreat to safety.

He broke their kiss and held her at arm's length while a tender smile spread slowly across his features.

"That was the New Year's kiss I never had the chance to give you," he told her as he let her go.

She backed away from him and started back along the beach in search of her shoes. Her legs were trembling, her mouth felt bruised by the force of his kiss, and her skin was aglow with the sting of his cologne. When she found her shoes, she picked them up and tapped them together several times to knock the sand off them. He came up behind her as she was standing there and touched her lightly on the shoulder, but she refused to turn around.

"What's wrong?" he asked. Brushing her hair away from her face, he bent to kiss the side of her neck. "Am I going too quickly, Daye?"

She closed her eyes and tilted her head to one side as his lips continued to caress her.

"Tell me, please."

She wanted to tell him to stop, but she knew that she really didn't want him to stop just yet. Her need for him was greater now than her need for caution; and so she turned around slowly, while his mouth traced its way across her skin to the sensitive hollow of her throat. She dropped her shoes again and wrapped her arms around his back. She slid her hands up under his jacket, kneading the smooth, muscled flesh that she could feel through his shirt, with the tips of her fingers. When he kissed her on the mouth again, she returned his kiss with all the pent-up passion she had kept locked away for too long.

It seemed to Daye that they had been standing in each other's arms forever, content just to kiss and learn each contour of the other's body, when Jonathan pulled her down with him onto the sand. It was a soft cushion for her body, warm and dry against the backs of her bare legs, and Daye reached up to bring his mouth down on hers again. He used one hand to gently support her head, while with his other hand, he began to caress the full, round globes of her breasts.

She felt like a virgin being touched and loved for the first time. Moving to the rhythm of his hands as they swept over her body, Daye was transported, lifted outside herself and taken to some distant plateau, where all was heightened sensation and sweet agony. And yet, even while she longed to be re-leased, some small part of her still held back, remembering, protecting her all too vulnerable self from the specter of certain pain.

"No," she cried out, pushing his hands away and drawing her dress down over her knees again.

"What's the matter?" Shaken, he tried to tug her back into his arms. "Daye, for God's sake, what happened?"

"Please let me go. I want to go back right now." Her voice was quavering.

His arms fell away from her. "Can't you at least tell me what's wrong?"

"This is what's wrong," she said, sitting up and shaking out her tumbled hair. "What we were just doing was wrong."

His eyes were clouded, his expression unhappy. "Why was it wrong, Daye?" he murmured. "It felt more than right to me."

And that was the problem, she knew as she struggled to her feet. It *had* felt right, more than right, just as he had said, and that was why it was bothering her. She had wanted him too much, and wanting him could only hurt her. Of all the men she had met in the past two months, why did she have to be attracted to one she couldn't have? Why was she drawn to yet another man who already belonged to someone else?

"We don't even know each other," she offered by way of an explanation for her behavior.

"Now that's an excuse I haven't heard in a long time."

"Don't make fun of me!"

"I'm not," he insisted, getting to his feet beside her and smoothing out his jacket. "It's just that I thought you wanted this to happen as much as I did. But if I was wrong, Daye, then I apologize."

She stood there looking down at her feet, feeling like a child who has just been gently chastened by her father; and suddenly, all she wanted was for him to put his arms around her and tell her that everything was going to be all right.

"Daye?"

It was as if he had divined her thoughts. Reaching out for her, he gathered her into his arms and drew her head down onto his shoulder. He began to stroke her, planting tiny kisses in her hair, while he rocked her back and forth against him.

"What would you like to know about me, Daye?" he asked her.

Nothing. No, everything. She wanted to know everything about him.

"My parents, two sisters, and three brothers still live in the town where I was born. I've been living off the royalties from my songs and my plays for the past four years, and the house in Gorham Sound is mine free and clear." He gave the lobe of one of her ears a little nip and went on. "I love jazz, old movies, pizza with double cheese and no anchovies, and chicken fingers with lots of honey. I don't like punk rock, video games, or discos, but I do like to dance. I enjoy bike riding at sunset, walking the beach at sunrise, and snorkeling whenever I want to shut out the entire world."

So did she. Suddenly, things began to brighten for her again.

"Did you ever see *Marjorie Morningstar*?" she whispered.

"Eight times at last count. How about you?"

"Eleven."

"Casablanca?"

"Fifteen, I think."

"Twenty for me."

"Gone with the Wind?"

"I've already lost track of that one."

"So have I."

"What else could you possibly need to know right now?" he asked her, lifting her chin and making her look at him. "What else do you have to know except that I'm very attracted to you and that I want to make love to you?"

She stiffened. The game had ended, the safety net had been whisked away, and they had come back to the beginning again.

"Let's go," he startled her by saying. "I don't want to spoil what we've shared tonight by talking about it anymore."

"Jonathan, I—"

"Ssh, Daye." He held a finger to her lips. "Not tonight."

She felt something cold enter her body. When, if not tonight? she wanted to ask him. Had she ruined not only tonight but the chance of there being other nights as well? Each step took them farther away from the sea and the sand and nearer to the dark strip of road where they had parked their cars. In a rush of panic, she wanted to hold him back, to keep them exactly as they had been before, and start all over again.

And then she got angry with herself for feeling that way. She was a woman, wasn't she? She wasn't a child, an innocent to be manipulated by a man. Where was she in all of this? What about *her* wishes? She had always respected herself and her body too much to share herself casually simply because that was what someone else wanted. She had as much right to say no to a man as he had to urge her to say yes; and until she was prepared to say yes on her own, no one, not even a man as appealing as Jonathan Cort, was going to blackmail her into feeling guilty about having the right to make up her own mind.

"Why the belligerent look?" he asked her when they had reached their cars. "I thought this was what you wanted."

"It is."

He leaned back against the hood of his car and folded his arms across his chest. "I'm afraid I'm not very good at reading the double messages you women are giving out these days," he said. "No matter what we do, we seem to offend someone. Is that what I did tonight, Daye? Did I offend you by admitting that I wanted you or by stopping when you asked me to?"

"Neither," she answered curtly.

"Well, then?"

She tried to keep her voice even as she replied. "I didn't mean to give you any double messages, Jonathan. I just need time, that's all. I'm not promiscuous; I never have been. I'm not very good at one-night stands."

"And you assumed that's what this was going to be."

Shaking her head slowly, she said, "I don't know what I assumed, but when I said I didn't know you, I wasn't trying to be funny or archaic or prudish. I don't really know you at all, Jonathan, and I'm not prepared to sleep with someone I don't know."

"Fair enough," he nodded. Taking her by the arm, he led her to her car and opened the door. "If you're still interested, the concert is at eight-thirty tonight."

"I'm still interested," she answered in a tiny voice.

"Would you like to have dinner first or would you prefer to meet at the auditorium?"

The romantic part of her yearned to accept his invitation, while her more cautious counterpart made her hesitate. "I have a fairly heavy work schedule today, and that usually means working late," she told him. "Could I call you some time in the afternoon and let you know?"

"Sure," he agreed with an easy smile.

That settled, she slid into the driver's seat, and Jonathan closed the door. She started the car, pressed the button to lower the window on her side, and peered up at him through her lashes.

"Good night, Jonathan."

"Good night, Daye." He bent down and planted a light kiss on the tip of her nose. "Drive carefully."

She headed south, and he went north. She drove slowly, her eyes on the rearview mirror, watching the red taillights on the black BMW growing smaller and smaller. It was only after they had disappeared completely that she finally accelerated, wishing, as she did, that she could magically outrace her thoughts on the lonely ride back home.

"I REALLY don't know how I feel about him," Daye admitted, flipping through a rack of silk slacks on Saks' second floor and pulling out a pair of pleated pants in burgundy for a closer look.

"Too dark," commented Franki, reaching for a pair in dusty pink.

"That's better," Rhea agreed as she drifted over to the blouses.

Daye put the burgundy pants back and took the ones Franki was holding out to her. When they located Rhea again, she was waving two print silk blouses at them for their consideration, neither of which appealed to Daye.

"Well, are you attracted to him or aren't you?" Franki asked Daye for the second time.

"Who wouldn't be?"

"Heaven help us, you haven't changed a bit," Rhea moaned, slipping the two blouses back onto the rack again. "Getting information out of you is just as difficult as ever."

"I'm sorry, Rhee, it's still too early to tell."

"Not that old answer again," muttered Franki.

Franki finally found the silk blouse that went with the slacks while Rhea picked out a long, sleeveless silk tunic with dusty pink, white, and slate gray stripes and insisted that Daye use it to pull the whole outfit together.

"She's obviously interested," Rhea said to Franki as Daye disappeared inside a fitting room. "Why else would she have asked us to help her choose an outfit especially for tonight? That isn't like her at all."

"I heard every word you said," Daye called out to them as she zipped up the slacks.

"Good, I'm glad." Franki located Daye's fitting room, and she and Rhea let themselves in and closed the door behind them. "Now maybe we'll be able to get you to admit that

Jonathan Cort's the best thing that's happened to you since lipstick."

"Let's not exaggerate." Daye laughed as she finished buttoning the blouse.

"Perfect." Rhea applauded. "Now for the tunic."

"Are we doing shoes, purse, the whole accessory number after this?" Franki wanted to know as she looked down at her watch.

"Why, are we keeping you from something?" inquired Daye.

"I have a tennis game at two, and if you think Jonathan Cort is a hunk, you should see the guy I'm playing with these days."

"Who is he?" Daye asked, slipping on the hip-length tunic and studying herself in the three-way mirror.

"Are you ready for this?" Franki paused melodramatically. "Taylor Mead."

Daye looked blank, but Rhea pretended to swoon.

"Doesn't he run the tennis camp in Delray?" Rhea asked.

"The very same."

"I took a lessson from him once. He's gorgeous."

"I didn't think you noticed men," Franki said with a wry smile while she winked at Daye in the mirror.

Rhea actually blushed. "Occasionally I do."

"Well, ladies, what do you think?" asked Daye, turning slowly in front of them. "Yes or no?"

"I say yes." Franki glanced at her watch again.

"Another yes," added Rhea, "and you can borrow my amethysts if you like."

"Thanks, Rhee." Daye smiled at her friend's typically generous offer. "But I think my pearls will be just fine."

"But he's already seen them once," protested Franki with mock seriousness. "Twice in a row? Shame, shame, Daye Peters. You're slipping." She placed a hasty kiss on Rhea's forehead and then Daye's, and picked up her purse. "I'd better go. You know how impatient young men are."

"Just how young is young?" asked Rhea.

"Twenty-seven."

"That's young," said Daye as she began to undress again.

"But he's very mature," argued Franki with a laugh.

"Naturally," Daye concurred.

"He is."

"Cradle snatcher," she called out after Franki's hastily departing back.

"Jealousy will get you nowhere," she sang in reply.

Daye and Rhea exchanged amused glances and then burst into helpless laughter.

"You see, Franki hasn't changed either," Daye said.

Suddenly, Rhea stopped laughing. Turning away from Daye, she pretended to be looking for something in her purse.

"Rhee?"

She fumbled deeper inside her purse as she gave her head a vigorous shake.

"Rhee, what's wrong?" Daye clutched at her friend.

Rhea's head was still lowered. "Nothing," she whispered.

"Nothing doesn't make a person cry."

"I'm just being silly," she sniffed. "I'm sorry, Daye. I guess I really must want things to work out for you and Jonathan." She sniffed again as she pulled a handkerchief out of her purse. Daye smiled to herself. Rhea was the only person she knew who still used handkerchiefs instead of Kleenex.

"Does it have to be Jonathan?" Daye asked.

"No, of course not." Rhea blew her nose softly. "But let it be someone, Daye. You're so alone."

"I'm not so alone," she protested, but her words sounded hollow even to her. "I have my work. I have you and Franki. I've met some very nice people, and I get out quite a bit. I—"

"But don't you ever want to find someone, someone special?"

"Yes, I think I do. But I'm not going to settle for just anyone."

"Jonathan's not just anyone, Daye, I think he's very special."

"And very attached."

Rhea pressed her handkerchief to her reddened nose. "Maren MacCaul's no competition for you," she said. "Be nice to Jonathan, Daye. Give the two of you a chance."

Daye sighed and put her arms around her friend. "All right, Rhee, I'll be nice to him."

While her packages were being wrapped, Daye stood at the sales desk and watched as Rhea restlessly paced the floor. She pulled a dress from one of the racks, held it up against herself, and then put it back again and tried on the jacket of a three-piece Ultrasuede suit. She took the jacket off, hung it up, and started sifting through a shelf of cashmere sweaters, fingering each one lightly as she moved through them. Daye chewed worriedly on the inside of her cheek, knowing for certain now what she had only guessed at earlier. Rhea's tears had had very little to do with her and Jonathan. But as close-mouthed as she was herself, Rhea was even that much more protective of her own innermost feelings. Until she was ready to share whatever was troubling her, there was nothing Daye could do to help her.

She left Rhea in the shoe department on the ground floor and went back to her office. In spite of her promise, she spent the rest of the afternoon resisting the temptation to call Jonathan and accept his dinner invitation. Her work went slowly. She was distracted and edgy. At four o'clock, she finally threw her pencil down in disgust and reached for the telephone. She dialed Jonathan's number, but just as she got to the final digit, she hung up. She gave herself another five minutes to think about it and then dialed his number again. The line was busy. She dropped the receiver back into its cradle and returned to her sketches.

Ten minutes later she dialed his number again. By the fourth ring, she was so nervous that a line of perspiration began to form above her upper lip. By the seventh ring, she was thankful that he hadn't answered. Hanging up, she picked up her pencil again. But instead of drawing a wall unit for the Adamsons' study, she found herself writing out Jonathan's name and then circling it over and over again.

At five o'clock, she picked up the phone and decided that if he wasn't home this time, she wasn't going to keep their date. When he answered on the second ring, she was so unprepared for the sound of his voice that it took her another moment before she could say anything to him.

"I just realized how late it was and thought I'd better call you," she blurted into the phone, hoping he wouldn't see through the lie. "I'm afraid I won't be able to make dinner tonight. Things have been more hectic than I'd anticipated."

She waited for his response with nervous dread, knowing

that only her fear and her pride were stopping her from having dinner with him. That and the fact that she needed the time to drive home to Boca, shower, and change into the new outfit she had just bought, and then drive back up to West Palm.

"I'm disappointed," he admitted, "but I guess I have no choice. How about meeting me on the steps outside the auditorium at eight-fifteen, then?"

"I'll be there," she promised, feeling some of the tension leave her body.

"And, Daye?"

"Yes?"

"I'm glad you called."

"I—well, I said I would, didn't I?" she stammered, caught off guard by his remark.

"But you know how changeable women are." She could see him grinning on the other end. "What's a poor man to do except sit by the phone and wait?"

She felt like wringing his neck, but when she put down the phone, she was grinning too.

chapter nine

DESPITE HER resolve to leave at intermission just on principle, Daye remained for the entire Gerry Mulligan concert, her hand in Jonathan's, her eyes on the stage, while the rest of her body was all too aware of the presence of him in the seat next to hers. When the concert was over, they stopped for liqueurs and coffee at the Banana Boat in Boynton, and then Jonathan insisted on following her in his car all the way back to Boca. Dusting her forehead with a series of light kisses, he left her at the entrance to the covered parking area of her condo with the promise to call her the following day.

She saw him twice more that week. In order to do so, she had to break a dinner date with a lawyer whom she had met the week before at a cocktail party thrown by the Adamsons at the Boca Beach Club, and forgo the opening performance of *Deathtrap* at the Lake Worth Playhouse. She was alarmed by the ease with which she had canceled both commitments; she had never been one to alter her previous plans for the sake of a date, as so many of her friends did. She was starting to break her own rules, and she realized with some trepidation that for Jonathan Cort, such rules were meant to be broken. She was discovering him the way one discovers a gift hidden away between many layers of carefully folded tissue paper. With each protective layer she peeled away, a bit more of him was revealed to her, and she found herself looking forward to the removal of each layer with mounting anticipation.

He had been badly bruised by the breakup of his marriage to Andrea Simon, who had worked her way up from a job as a reporter for a small Milwaukee newspaper to a prestigious staff position with *Ms.* magazine. A dedicated feminist and a vocal participant in the women's movement, she had apparently warred long and hard with herself before finally opting for life without a husband or any of the restrictions of marriage. As liberated as Jonathan had thought himself to be, he had discovered, much to his chagrin, that he was really a rather conventional man after all. A man who wanted a wife and children and a home to serve as a refuge from the turbulence of his everyday world. His four years alone in Gorham Sound had provided him with the refuge he had been seeking, but now after four years, he admitted candidly to Daye that a refuge was no longer quite enough.

The morning following their fourth evening together, Daye found it impossible to concentrate on her work. Plans skittered in and out of her head, eluding her like so many teasing shadows and vanishing before she could capture them with her pencil. Jonathan had told her that he would probably call her around eleven. He would have put in three hours at the piano by then and would be breaking for his noon swim and a quick lunch before sitting down at the piano again.

By three o'clock, her stomach had looped itself into one solid knot of discomfort. Unable to sit at her desk any longer and pretend that she could work, she got up and began to pace the floor. She had just taken on two new clients, who had given her a large condominium in Palm Beach and a town house in Delray to decorate, and for the last few days she had been considering hiring an assistant. She gazed up at the ceiling as if the answer to her dilemma lay there, and then she glared over at the telephone. Clear thinking was all but impossible right now as her agitation continued to mount.

He's busy, she told herself. He has an entire play to write on his own. He doesn't have the time to think about me right now. He said he would call and he will. As soon as he has time. Time! She looked at her watch, but instead of the time, she saw the pages of a calendar being torn off and discarded with alarming speed. Two months down and only nine months to go on the New York lease. She peered outside at the pink oleanders beneath her window and at the bougainvillea climbing the porch of the house directly across the street, but she could see nothing except snow-covered rooftops and slushy streets and frosty breath hanging in the air. And what she saw made her shiver. She couldn't go back up north again; she simply couldn't.

The jangling of the phone sent her dashing across the room to answer it. But when the woman's voice on the other end asked to speak to Peggy, Daye barely managed to tell her that she had the wrong number before she hung up with a whimper of frustration. Why was it always like that? she asked herself. A wrong number whenever you were waiting for that one special call?

Suddenly, she needed to speak to one of her friends. Picking up the phone again, she dialed Rhea's number, only to be informed by Chloe that Rhea was attending a benefit luncheon on behalf of the Boca Symphony at the Boca Beach Hotel. She immediately tried Franki's line and was just about to hang up after the seventh ring when a drowsy voice whispered a weak hello in her ear. When Daye apologized for so obviously waking her up, Franki brushed her apologies aside.

"I played tennis all morning without a hat and crawled home with this roaring headache," she explained with a low moan of pain. "Dumb, Daye, really dumb of me, and now I'm dying."

"Have you taken anything for it?"

"Only four extra-strength God-knows-what; they're all the same. I was just about to get up and take two more. That ought to kill me."

"Or cure you."

"Ow, I think I'd prefer death right now." There was a slight pause, a rustling of sheets, and then Franki said, "Is something wrong? You sound a little uptight."

"I think it's called panic."

"What, may I ask, are you panicking about?"

"He hasn't called."

"Who hasn't called?"

"Jonathan."

"Oh. But you saw him last night, didn't you?"

"Yes."

"Well, how did you leave it? Did you make another date? Did he say he'd call?"

"He said he'd call me around eleven. It's now three-thirty."

"Maybe he's dead."

"Thanks a lot."

"Well, if he hasn't called by now, he's obviously dead, isn't he?"

"Oh, Franki." Daye sighed, putting her chin in her hand. As always, Franki was able to make her see the absurdity in her panicking. She took a deep breath and let it out slowly, repeating the exercise until the feelings weren't quite as strong as they had been before.

"Daye, why don't you pick up the phone and give *him* a call?" Franki suggested. "Why sit around and torture yourself?"

"I'm not exactly torturing myself," she protested. "I just hate myself for feeling this way. I don't like these feelings of dependency, this notion that somehow my day isn't complete unless I hear from him, that everything else I do is now secondary. I haven't felt this way since I was a teenager, for heaven's sake, and I'm too old to start feeling that way now. Henry Higgins was right when he said, 'Why can't a woman be more like a man?'"

"What would be the advantage in that?"

"For one thing, we'd be spared a lot of unnecessary aggravation. Men don't sit around analyzing everything the way women do. Can you imagine two bankers in three-piece business suits moping over their martinis, while one of them asks the other what he thought she really meant when she said this or did that, and what will he do if he doesn't hear from her again? Never! That's why I sometimes wish we were more like men."

"But then, think of all the good loving we'd be missing," Franki reminded her. "And speaking of loving, I think I could use some of that myself right now."

Daye began to laugh. "Why don't you call Brian and suggest a late afternoon rendezvous?"

"And interrupt his working day? You must be kidding. Didn't you know that some men were put on this earth just to work?"

"Franki"—Daye's voice was troubled—"you sound so bitter. I've never heard you talk this way before."

Franki hastily retreated, saying, "It's only my headache talking. I'm sorry. Let me take two more of those pills and I'll be just fine. Now you'd better hang up and keep your line clear for a while. Call me and tell me what happens, okay?"

"Okay," Daye agreed, putting the receiver down with a dispirited sigh.

Something was wrong. Something was happening to her two best friends while she, like a naive and hopeful fool, had been so certain that nothing had or ever would change between them. Rhea was growing more and more withdrawn, and Franki was becoming restless again. Why? She put her head in her hands and began massaging her temples with her fingertips. Around and around she worked the pads of her fingers while she tried to find a reason for the way her friends were behaving. She found three. Too much money, too much free time, and not enough attention from their men.

She lunged for the phone and dialed Franki's number again. The line was busy. She tried Rhea again. Chloe told her that Rhea had just come in but that she had gone upstairs to take her nap. After trying Franki's number three more times, Daye gave up in frustration and slumped forward in her chair, folding her arms on the top of her desk and resting her head on them. After a while, she knew that it was useless to try to work anymore that afternoon. She had already lost the entire day, and nothing could bring those wasted hours back. She switched on her answering machine and went into the bathroom to fill up her watering can. Her azaleas were looking rather limp; she was now two days behind in her regular watering schedule.

The phone was ringing as she came back into her office, the plastic watering can trailing drops of water on the floor behind her. The volume was turned up on her answering machine, and she listened with her heart pounding while Jonathan apologized for calling so late. He had worked through the day without a break and had just now gotten up from the piano and realized what time it was. If she was free later, he hoped they could have dinner together. He would wait for her call.

She set the watering can down on the edge of the desk and ran the tape over from the beginning. A tremor of excitement shook her body at the sound of his husky voice. She felt weak with relief, but that feeling passed all too quickly, to be replaced instead by resentment. She left the watering can where it was, snatched up her purse, and left the office. She was angrier with herself than she was with him. Not only had she wasted an entire working day worrying about when he was going to call, but she had been so grateful for his call that she had been prepared to make herself available to accept his last-minute invitation, no matter what it was.

She roared out of her parking spot and headed south. Then she changed her mind, executed an illegal U-turn on South Ocean Boulevard, and headed north again. She drove aimlessly up and down a number of hushed residential streets before making up her mind and pulling into a parking space across from Chuck & Harold's. She ran a brush through her hair, touched up her lipstick, and sprayed herself with Calandre from her purse atomizer. Getting out of the car, she strode across the street, searching from behind dark glasses for a table on the sidewalk terrace of the restaurant. As soon as she located one, she moved toward it purposefully, aware of several appreciative glances being thrown her way.

She decided on a piña colada for a change, and while she sipped her drink slowly through a single straw, she settled back in her chair and tried to convince herself that this was where she wanted to be. Just as she was starting on her second piña colada, her waiter came back over to the table, leaned down, and in a low voice, said, "The gentleman over there would like to buy you your next drink."

Daye looked at the man in question seated three tables away from her. He was in his early forties, very fit looking, lightly tanned, and quite handsome. He met her glance with a slight nod of his head and then raised his highball glass to her and smiled. Daye hesitated for a moment and then nodded to the waiter. No sooner had her fresh drink been set down in front of her than the man got up and sauntered over to join her. The moment he sat down across from her and introduced himself, she regretted having accepted the drink.

* * *

"I HAVE tickets for *Morning's at Seven* at the Caldwell Playhouse in Boca this evening, and I thought you might like to join me," she said.

Daye held her breath and waited. It was eight o'clock in the morning, and she had been up since five, alternating between pacing the floor and sitting out on the balcony as she forced herself to wait until a civilized hour before calling him.

"I'd like that very much." Jonathan's answer came readily, easily, and she began letting out her breath bit by bit. "What time is the performance?"

"Eight."

They agreed that he would come for her at seven-thirty, and they hung up without either of them mentioning the fact that she hadn't called him back the night before. Daye dialed Rhea's number, hoping that she still had those spare tickets, and shuddered at the memory of the hour she had spent at Chuck & Harold's being bored by a man whose name she had forgotten as soon as he had said it. She vowed never to do anything like that again.

The play was delightful but far too long, so that by the time they emerged from the theater, Daye was so tired of sitting down that all she wanted to do was take a walk on the beach. Jonathan concurred, and they drove back to the condo, left their shoes in the car, and headed for the beach hand in hand. As they walked along the water's edge, allowing the waves to swirl around their bare ankles, they stopped every couple of yards just to hold each other and kiss.

But in spite of their growing closeness and her hunger for him, which flared brighter and hotter with each embrace, Daye knew that she was not going to invite him back to her place after their walk. It would be far too easy then, too tempting. She had only to think of Maren MacCaul, although Jonathan never mentioned her at all, and she could feel her ardor begin to cool. As much as she wanted Jonathan to make love to her, she didn't want to act as a stand-in for his permanent partner.

"Let me take you upstairs," he murmured some time later, his lips warm against her cheek, his hands buried deep in her hair.

"No." She shook her head.

"I won't stay," he promised. "I just want to hold you in my arms for a while."

"Not tonight, Jonathan. Please?"

He cupped her face in his hands and looked deep into her eyes. "You're so incredibly beautiful, Daye, and so very loving. Why are you so frightened? What are you afraid of?"

She tried to turn her head away, but he wouldn't let her.

"Daye, who bruised you so badly that you won't trust anyone anymore?"

She closed her eyes and watched as dozens of faces blurred together and then merged into one.

"Daye, my beautiful Daye, I wish I could be the one to teach you how to trust again."

"Oh, Jonathan." She buried her face in his chest and clung to him, her fingers digging into his back.

How could she explain about Neil? What right did she have to ask about his relationship with Maren? How could she make him understand that as much as she wanted him, she was afraid of wanting him, afraid of diluting her creative energies and her ambition by losing herself to the intense emotions required for any new relationship? When a woman became too needy, she tended to forget how good it had once felt to be independent, and Daye didn't dare become that needy now. Not when she had already seen how vulnerable it could make her. Not while Jonathan still belonged to someone else. And not until she was completely convinced that she could combine both love and a career and do it successfully.

"Come," he finally said to her. "Let me at least walk you to your door."

They got their shoes from the car. Jonathan slipped his on, but Daye chose to carry hers with her into the elevator. When they reached her door, she took out her keys and toyed with them for a moment before determinedly fitting the house key into the lock. Pushing the door open a crack, she effectively blocked the entrance with her body as she turned around and looked back up at Jonathan. He tugged her into his arms, and she responded with a yearning bordering on urgency.

He kissed her hungrily, scalding the tender flesh of her mouth and stroking her back with hands forged from liquid steel. She began to weaken, the heat of her own desire surging through her, making her giddy and robbing her of her self-control. And then he was pushing her away from him, a combination of pain and desire contorting the features of his handsome face.

"Good night, Daye," he whispered. He kissed the tip of his index finger and pressed it to her lips. Then he turned and walked briskly down the corridor to the elevator without looking back at her.

She leaned against the door frame for support. He hadn't said anything about calling her again. But then, she could hardly blame him. He had been playing the game according to her rules, and she couldn't blame him for tiring of that game and the frustration that went along with it.

"Damn, damn, damn," she muttered, her hazel eyes bright with tears as she watched the doors of the elevator closing behind him. "What a fool you are, Daye Peters. What a stupid, stupid fool. If he's just walked out of your life for good, you deserve it."

Without turning on the lights, she made her way through the darkened apartment to the kitchen and stared bleakly out of the window. She could see the guest parking lot from there, and a few minutes later, she saw him hurrying through the lot to his car. When he glanced back up at the building, she flattened herself against the wall, hoping that he hadn't seen her there, gazing after him and wishing she had the nerve to run out onto the balcony and call him back.

But she didn't have the nerve, and she didn't call him back. She simply stood alone in the dark and watched as he slowly drove away.

chapter ten

MAREN MACCAUL had come home.

Daye stared dismally at the photo of a smiling Maren and a serious Jonathan dancing together at the annual dinner dance sponsored by the Palm Beach County Playwrights Society, which had been held recently at the Colony Hotel. She read the caption under the photograph and thought back to the night of the dinner, trying to recall what she had been doing that evening. She grimaced when she remembered the movie she had seen with a business associate of Neil's from Chicago whom Rhea had insisted she meet.

"Just to take your mind off Jonathan," Rhea had assured her when she had called her at work that morning.

"I seem to recall you begging me to do just the opposite a few weeks ago," said Daye.

"Well, perhaps if you'd listened to me then, we wouldn't be going through this now."

"I was nice to him, Rhea," Daye insisted, tiring of everyone's concern over her and Jonathan, "but obviously being nice to him just wasn't good enough."

"And I had such hopes for you two."

Daye decided to change the subject. "Rhee, do you want to talk about what's been troubling you lately? And don't you dare tell me that you were worried about my relationship with Jonathan Cort."

There was silence at the other end of the line.

"Rhea Bellon Howard, this is Daye Peters you're talking to, and I don't accept silence as an answer, so speak up."

"I really don't have anything to speak up about."

"Rhea, please." Daye softened her voice. "I can sense that you're troubled. Don't think I'm prying, because I'm not. I'm concerned, that's all."

"I love you, Daye, and I thank you for your concern, but nothing's wrong. I'm fine."

"Then, if that's true, I suppose nothing's wrong with Franki either."

"Franki?" Rhea laughed. "Franki's been playing tennis nearly every day for the past three weeks with gorgeous Taylor Mead. What could possibly be wrong with her?"

"That's precisely what I'd like to find out."

"Oh, Daye, think about yourself for once," Rhea pleaded in her gentle voice. "Save some of your concern for you. You're the one Franki and I worry about."

Daye watched as a single teardrop splattered onto the social page of *The Palm Beach Standard*, blurring Maren's smile and reducing her features to a damp gray smudge. She tore out the page and crumpled it in her hand before tossing it into the wastebasket next to her desk. As she sat slumped forward in her chair, she wanted to believe that her tears were the result of having recalled her recent conversation with Rhea and not because she hadn't heard from Jonathan Cort once in the last eight days.

She gave her shoulders a vigorous shake as if to throw off all lingering thoughts of him and unrolled the set of plans she had nearly completed for the Adamsons' condo. They were good, she decided, even better than good. They were superb. The happy result of having channeled her deepening feelings for Jonathan away from the man himself and into her work instead. She had buried her preoccupation with their faltering relationship deep inside her consciousness and then summoned all of her creative energy to the surface in its place. In the very act of creating lay her rebirth, and she had felt restored and renewed and content within herself once more.

She had even hired an assistant, a twenty-four-year-old arts major with a degree from Florida Atlantic University named Connie Chase, who had been working for the same design firm in Miami for three years. She was extremely enthusiastic about Daye's projects, faultless in her own taste and judgment, and capable of conceptualizing with ease. As soon as a drafting table was installed in the second office, she immediately took over a number of Daye's smaller accounts with a competence and an eagerness that Daye found most reassuring.

This freed her to devote the bulk of her time to her major accounts and to catch up on the professional journals that had been accumulating on a shelf in her office. To her increasing chagrin, Philippe Nadeau's name was mentioned at least once in each of the journals, and she was forced to admit that as old-fashioned and ostentatious as she considered much of his work, he was obviously designing precisely what the wealthy older Palm Beachers wanted. He was still considered the undisputed czar of interior design in south Florida. More and more she was coming to realize that if she wanted to compete successfully with him, she would have to focus her attention on the younger crowd, the children of the old guard, with their careers and their active sports lives and their natural impatience with things past.

When the telephone rang, she was so immersed in her work that its intrusive jangling didn't register until the fifth ring. At the sound of that familiar husky voice on the line, the blue felt marker she had been using slipped out of her hand and rolled across the paper, leaving a trail of tiny blue dots.

"How are you, Daye?" he asked as she sat there too numb to respond.

You're very photogenic, Jonathan, she wanted to tell him, but all she was able to force through her lips was a raspy, "I'm fine, thank you, Jonathan."

"I've been thinking about you, Daye. I would have called sooner, but my work took over for a while. You know how that can be sometimes."

Do you regard Maren as your work, Jonathan? she asked silently. "Yes, yes I do," she said aloud.

"Daye, will you have dinner with me this evening?"

His invitation so unnerved her that all she could do was hold the receiver away from her ear and stare at it as if she had no idea what it was.

"Daye, are you still there?"

How could he? she wondered, her chest heaving, her own breath hot on her face. She's back again, and he's asking me out for dinner as if the last eight days of silence meant absolutely nothing!

"Daye?"

She put the phone back to her ear. "Tonight's impossible, Jonathan. I'll be working late."

"Well, if it isn't *my* work, I suppose it's bound to be yours," he said with a slight chuckle. "Would tomorrow night be better?"

"I'm afraid not. I'll be working late tomorrow as well."

"Whatever happened to those occasional nights off?"

I could ask you the very same thing, she wanted to counter, but she bit down hard on her pride and simply said, "I'm busier now than I was before."

"All work and no play." He sighed. "It sounds as though you've decided to give up on fun altogether."

"Not really."

"Just fun with me, then."

She said nothing, but she began to squirm in her chair.

"You can be honest with me, Daye. If you'd prefer not to see me again, just tell me. You don't have to use your work as an excuse."

"It's not an excuse." Her voice was growing testy now.

"All right, then, how about having lunch with me tomorrow?"

"Why, Jonathan?"

"I'm not sure I understand."

"Why lunch?"

"I thought that if you wanted to keep your evenings for your work, you might like to take a break during the day instead."

"What I meant was, why do you want to see me at all?" She picked up her blue marker and began chewing on the end of it. "You're still involved with Maren, aren't you?"

There was a slight pause, and then in a voice resembling that of a parent explaining the facts of life to a child, he said quietly, "Maren and I are very good friends, Daye. We respect and like each other very much, but we've made no commitment, nor do we intend to. I'd hardly be inviting you out for lunch if it were otherwise. I'd probably suggest we go to a motel instead."

She smiled at that, but in spite of his assurances, the picture of Jonathan and Maren together was too firmly etched in her mind.

"Daye?"

"Yes, Jonathan."

"How about lunch tomorrow at the Café L'Europe? Have you eaten there yet?"

"No," she answered, her throat suddenly tight.

"Shall we say one o'clock, then?"

Again she hesitated. "All right."

"Good. Then I'll see you tomorrow."

"Yes." Her voice trailed off weakly. "Tomorrow."

When she hung up, she was shaking, and the only antidote for the renewed turmoil she felt was work. She worked until midnight, completing the plans for the Adamsons and beginning her preliminary sketches for the town house in Delray. Then she drove home, made herself a tuna sandwich, and ate it in front of the TV in her bedroom, half-dozing while Humphrey Bogart smoked and snarled his way through *The Petrified Forest*. At two, she switched off the TV and collapsed into bed.

She was still awake at four. Her mind was alive with images. Images of her and Jonathan, their bodies locked together in tender combat, his fingers in her hair, his lips on hers, his legs holding her prisoner. Aching for him and for a release from her terrible need, she rolled over onto her back and began running her hands along her body. As she continued to caress herself, she closed her eyes and imagined they were his hands touching her instead of hers. Her skin was soon tingling, and her nipples grew taut and full and tight.

She touched herself between her legs, where she was warm and moist and more than ready. Her rapid breathing filled the silence around her as she stroked herself faster and faster. Her tender nub, swelling and dancing beneath her teasing fingertip, stiffened and broadened as she began to peak. A low, whimpering moan escaped from her parted lips when she neared her climax. Wave after wave of delicious feeling swept over her, and her body arched and fell rhythmically with the intensity of her pleasure, until she drifted to the end of the feeling and was able to open her eyes once again.

At what point had the images become confused? she wondered as she lay there with only the sounds of the sea and the wind in her ears. When had the inky eyes lightened to turquoise blue and the black hair paled to blond? She turned onto her stomach and wrapped her arms around her pillow. With a sob of despair, she buried her face deep in her pillow, convinced that the present would never be strong enough to vanquish her past finally and forever. Perhaps Jonathan Cort wasn't even the one to try, especially since she seemed to be fighting him as strenuously as she was still fighting the image she carried of Neil.

She gave up in her attempts to sleep after that, spending the remaining hours until dawn sitting on the balcony, waiting for the sun to rise. At seven, she telephoned Jonathan and broke their lunch date.

FRANKI HUMMED softly to herself as she adjusted the white terry-cloth sweatband around her forehead. She picked up her racquet and left the locker room, heading for the number three court where she knew Taylor would be waiting for her. The former California phys. ed. teacher was undoubtedly the best partner she had ever played with, and she looked forward to their times together as much as she had once looked forward to making love to Brian. Catching herself in mid-thought, she suddenly frowned. *To* Brian. When had it stopped being *with* Brian?

Brian was out of the country again, following after Neil like the loyal puppy he was, always pleased to be able to serve his master. Don't complain, she scolded herself. It was because of Brian's loyalty to Neil that he had gotten where he was, taking her along with him; and it was due to both men that her own nest egg was continuing to grow. She no longer thought of her portfolio of stocks and bonds as just a security blanket; she had come to consider it her reward for being Brian's faithful and supportive wife, and the perfect, uncomplaining corporate spouse.

"How ya doin'?" Taylor Mead—tall and sandy-haired, his green eyes flashing—gave her a light kiss on the tip of her nose and a friendly whack on the behind with the head of his racquet.

Franki's acknowledgment of his customary greeting was to give one firm cheek of his own tight behind a good, solid pinch. Then she crossed the court to stand with her back to the sun, crouching low while she waited for him to get ready. He tossed two bright yellow balls onto the court, hit both of them several times with his racquet, and then pocketed one of them.

She watched closely as he went up on his toes to serve, left arm flexed, ready to flip the ball into the air; right arm taut as he drew his racquet back. It was as if she were seeing him for the first time. Suddenly all she could see was the way his white shorts strained across his crotch as he tensed his body to serve. She was so unsettled by the effect it was having on her that when the ball finally careened over the net and landed in her court, she missed the shot completely.

"Fifteen—love," he called out as he trotted across the back of the court and positioned himself for his next serve. "You awake over there?"

Franki signaled him with her racquet. "I'm awake," she assured him.

Bracing herself, she followed this serve more carefully, returning it easily when it came and then racing up to the net to counter his next shot. As they continued to play, she divided her time between following the ball and gazing longingly at his suntanned legs and dark, powerful arms. Brian was so pale. Even when he wasn't working, he seldom took the sun. He wasn't a sportsman either. His idea of activity was sitting on the balcony with a drink in his hand, the stereo tuned to some classical music station, and *The Wall Street Journal* in his lap.

"You're not concentrating, babe," shouted Taylor as she missed an easy backhand. "Must be all that heavy socializing of yours. Too many late nights."

"Just the opposite," she shouted back, "not enough."

"Hubby out of town again?"

"What do *you* think?"

"Ah, another sad tale of yet another abandoned wife." Tucking his racquet between his knees, he pulled a sad face and began to bow an imaginary violin.

She gave him the finger and went on to win the next three games and the set.

"Not bad." Taylor gave her an approving nod. "Insults seem to work better with you than praise. I'll have to remember that."

They were more evenly matched at the start of the second set, but Franki found it increasingly difficult to concentrate as the set progressed. She tracked each of Taylor's movements with mounting greed, watching the way his white polo shirt stuck to his broad chest and how his entire body was now slick and golden with sweat. She could almost smell his skin and the musky warmth that had to be there between his legs; and as her desire grew, it flamed into a hunger she could taste on her tongue.

"Franki, you're dreaming again, babe. C'mon, get back down here."

She was in agony. She threw away the last two games to him just to put an end to the way she was feeling. But as they walked off the court together, she made certain that their bodies brushed together several times before they reached the clubhouse. As he held the door for her, his green eyes met her blue ones squarely. The quizzical look in his was instantly replaced by a knowing gleam.

"You're wicked. You know that, don't you?" he teased her, running the index finger of his right hand down along the damp valley between her breasts. "Yeah, damned right you know it."

She pretended she didn't know what he was talking about. Her eyes were wide and guileless as she slipped past him through the open door. But just as he was about to follow her, she caught him unprepared by making a quick grab for his crotch and then racing down the corridor to the women's locker room, her whoop of girlish laughter rippling behind her.

chapter eleven

WHEN RHEA put down the phone, she was frowning. She couldn't understand Franki. Not only was she playing tennis with Taylor Mead nearly every day, but according to the Town Tattler column in the *Standard*, the two of them were now being seen dashing from one Palm Beach watering hole to another "like teenagers who have not only discovered that holding hands is fun, but that the more people who catch you at it the better." Poor Brian, she thought as she curled up on the chaise in her bedroom and tucked her legs under her. According to Franki, though, it wasn't poor Brian at all. He didn't seem to resent her public hand-holding one single bit.

"At least I've finally made the Tattler column," Franki had joked over the phone a moment ago. "It's harmless, Rhea. It means absolutely nothing, but Brian's like a new man. This whole thing has been fantastic for our sex life. I should have done something like this sooner."

Rhea wondered how Neil would react if she ever did what Franki was doing. Knowing Neil, he would undoubtedly slap a libel suit on every paper that reported her activities. His Rhea just wasn't capable of such behavior. She allowed herself a

115

vague semblance of a smile. *Wanton* was the appropriate word for such behavior, she believed. As she straightened her legs and raised her arms above her head in one long, luxurious stretch, she thought she might like to try being wanton for a change.

"Take me, Neil, darling," she purred, arching her back and lifting her arms to her imaginary lover. "Take me, I'm yours."

She began to giggle as her arms dropped to her sides again. How many women had used that kind of line on her husband? she wondered, trying to calculate the number of times Neil had been out of town during their twelve years of marriage. She had known from the beginning that Neil was not a man created for fidelity, but then, fidelity was not something she had ever expected or demanded from him. She had always considered sharing her husband with some faceless woman to be a minimal price to pay for a life of security and comfort.

She didn't remember dozing off, but what she *did* remember was the intensity of her dream and how vivid the images were when she woke up. By now it was such a familiar dream that she couldn't recall a time when it hadn't haunted her sleep.

She was rocking a cradle and singing a lullaby to the infant who was sleeping under his pale blue wool blanket. When she reached the end of the lullaby, she sat back in her chair and watched as the cradle continued to rock by itself. Suddenly it began to rock more quickly, making loud banging sounds on the floor as it rocked and swayed, moving harder and faster. She put out a foot to stop it, but it only rocked back and forth across her shoe with increasing momentum. Getting down on her knees, she used both hands and the weight of her slender body to try to stop it. The cradle rebounded off her chest and tipped over on its side with a violent thud, pitching the sleeping infant onto the floor.

The baby awoke with a whimpering howl and scurried off across the floor on his hands and knees. She crawled after him, calling his name and begging him to come back. With a shrill giggle of mischievous glee, he stopped abruptly and looked back over his shoulder at her. She covered her mouth with her hands and started to scream. The face staring back at her was the face of a grown man.

"Mom, there's a man downstairs to see you."

Rhea jumped. Matthew was tugging on the sleeve of her quilted dressing gown and trying to get her to open her eyes. The first thing she saw when she finally opened them was the pastel that hung over her desk. Then she saw the concerned gray eyes and the serious face of her son.

"A man?" she repeated, raising herself on one elbow and brushing the sleep from her eyes. "What kind of a man?"

"He says he's helping you with the party at the country club. What party?"

For a moment, Rhea was at a loss, but then she remembered. "The Easter party, sweetheart," she told him with a smile as she got up from the chaise and tightened the sash on her robe.

Matthew's eyes brightened. "Can Caroline and I go to the party, too?"

Rhea shook her head. "It's just for the grown-ups, sweetie."

His face fell. "Everything's always for the grown-ups," he complained.

"Now, that's not true." She bent down to touch his cheek and frowned when he pulled away from her.

"Yes, it is," he insisted, backing toward the door.

"Matthew, please." She went after him. "Where are you going?"

"Aunt Franki's taking us to a movie."

"Oh." Her voice was small. "I'd forgotten about that."

"If we didn't have Aunt Franki, we wouldn't have any fun at all."

"Matthew!"

"Well, it's true." Tears of hurt stood out in his large gray eyes. "You're always painting your silly pictures, and Daddy's always working. It's lucky for us that Aunt Franki loves us."

"But we love you, too," she protested, feeling a terrible longing begin to pluck at her as her son twisted free of her grasp and scampered out of her room and down the hall.

Rhea stood where she was, staring at the spot where her son had been a moment ago. A sense of bleakness settled around her, worming its way inside her and making her feel weak and faint. She should never have been a mother. She should never have taken on the responsibility of raising two other human beings without first making certain that she could do the job properly. Not only had she failed at it, but her very own son had just told her as much. She moved on trembling legs to her dressing room and began to change her clothes.

As she descended the semicircular grand staircase, she suddenly felt dwarfed by everything around her. There were too many steps for her to take. The ceiling was too high, and the chandelier suspended from the ceiling was too large and too bright. She was shrinking, growing smaller and smaller with each step she took. The hand that had been trailing lightly behind her on the mahogany banister was beginning to shake, and as she stumbled, nearly missing one carpeted step completely, her heartbeats became erratic, and her forehead broke out in tiny beads of perspiration.

"Mrs. Howard, how good it is to see you again." The young man with the brown mustache and trim goatee rose from one of the sofas in the living room and took her hand. "I must admit we're in a bit of a bind, you and I, and rather than discuss the matter with you over the phone, I thought it best if I spoke with you directly."

Rhea sank weakly into a wing chair facing the sofa and dug her fingers into its upholstered arms.

"What seems to be the problem?" she asked him, her voice slightly tremulous.

"Unfortunately, there appears to be a conflict in our dates, Mrs. Howard," he said with his clipped British accent punctuating every word. "I had thought your party was scheduled for the ninth of April and subsequently booked another party for the second. Then to my horror, I realized that your party was not scheduled for the ninth at all but for the second as well. And now I simply don't know what to do."

"Why not tell the other people that you made a mistake and that you're already booked for the second?"

"I wish it were that simple, but you see, Mrs. Barron is one of my oldest clients, and it would be unthinkable of me to disappoint her. I had thought that perhaps you and I could make some other arrangement instead." He made a palms-up gesture with his hands.

Rhea sighed. Sybil was doing it again, making certain that no one in Boca used her precious Nigel Amery. The other members of Rhea's social committee had been skeptical when she had announced that she'd actually booked Palm Beach's highly popular caterer for the Easter party, and with good reason. She should have known Sybil would find some way to keep Nigel Amery from sullying his sterling reputation by catering a party in upstart Boca Raton.

She clasped her hands together in an effort to control their violent trembling. "I don't think you're being particularly fair, Nigel. We had an agreement, the date was clearly understood, and when you and I discussed the party, there was never any doubt about what night it was to be held. I'm afraid you'll just have to tell Mrs. Barron that you're already booked for the second and that she'd better find someone else to cater her party."

All the time Rhea was speaking, Nigel Amery had been growing increasingly agitated. Now he began tugging at his mustache and stroking his goatee while he glanced nervously about the room and refused to meet her eyes.

"I don't think you fully appreciate my position, Mrs. Howard," he said, staring down at his shoes. "Mrs. Barron has sent me more clients than I could ever hope to thank her for. You know yourself what a persuasive woman she can be and how well connected she is. One word from her and—"

"We have a contract, Nigel," Rhea cut him off sharply, "and I suggest you abide by the terms of that contract. You can tell Mrs. Barron either to hold her party on another night or to hire someone else to do her catering." And with that, she got to her feet. "Now, if you'll excuse me, I have things to do."

She was proud of the way she had dealt with him and even prouder of the way she kept her back straight and her head high as she walked from the house out to the little white latticework gazebo set behind a bank of pink oleanders in the farthest corner of the garden. It was here, with the wooden door carefully locked, that she painted now. She had recently made the transition from pastels to watercolors, and as her collection grew, so did her need for complete privacy and seclusion. Locking the door behind her, she slipped on her paint-smudged smock and went over to her easel. There was just enough natural light still filtering into the tiny structure to enable her to complete the watercolor she had begun the day before.

As soon as her brush touched the canvas, sweeping a pale blue streak of color across the misty spread of a blue and mauve sky, she forgot all about the Easter party and Sybil Barron and Nigel Amery. Released from the unpleasantness of it all and growing calmer within herself once more, all she could think of now was how to paint the face of the young boy who was sitting on the large brown swing.

DAYE WAS impatiently tapping one end of her rolled program against the palm of her hand as she continued to scan the red-carpeted lobby of the Royal Poinciana Playhouse for some sign of her friends. It was nearly curtain time, and neither the Howards nor the Sheltons had arrived yet. She glanced up at the ornate crystal chandelier above her head, noticed that two of the lightbulbs were burned out, and mentally chided the playhouse management for allowing such a thing to go unattended. In one of the large gilt-framed mirrors hanging on the red-flocked wall directly across from where she was standing, she caught a glimpse of herself scowling and hastily reset her mouth in a less discontented line. The man beside her squeezed her arm, gave her a broad wink, and then continued his discussion with the two men standing on his right.

At fifty-one, Blake Jeffreys was a striking man, a Stewart Granger type, a recent divorcé, who had consulted Daye on the redecorating of his yacht some weeks before. They had had dinner twice since then, and she had found him an interesting and attentive companion. But tonight, for some reason, she felt that he had invited her to the theater strictly as a decorative ornament he could show off to his friends.

As if to confirm her suspicions, the moment the two men had returned to their wives who were waiting for them in front of the cloakroom, Blake turned to her with a smile and whispered, "You're quite the attraction tonight, my dear. You have half of Palm Beach wondering what I did to deserve such a gorgeous creature."

"And the other half?" she teased him.

"Only one half counts," he told her. "Why worry about what the peasants think?"

Her attempt at a smile to acknowledge the cleverness of his

remark more closely resembled a grimace. What a snob he was! At that moment, she would have given anything to have made up some excuse to leave. But Blake Jeffreys was an important contact, and one she didn't dare alienate, and so she continued to smile at his poor jokes and nod politely to the various people he introduced her to, while she prayed for her friends to arrive and save her.

When Franki and Brian finally entered the lobby, Daye was so relieved that she began waving her program like a banner to direct them over to where she and Blake were standing. Even before she could introduce them to Blake, Franki said, "Rhea has a bug or something, but Neil decided to come anyway. He's parking the car."

Daye felt a tiny tug at her insides as she made the introductions, wishing that Rhea had chosen any night but that particular one to be sick. Just as the lights were being blinked off and on to signal the start of the performance, Neil came rushing into the lobby.

"Sorry," he apologized, brushing the hair out of his eyes. Eyes he kept trained directly on Daye's flushed face even while she was introducing him to Blake.

As the five of them were starting down the aisle, Blake suddenly stopped, pulled away from Daye, and reached out to clasp the hand of a man walking alongside them.

"Will you excuse me for a moment, Daye?" Blake said to her, handing her the tickets before drawing the man back into the lobby with him.

Daye stared after them dumbfounded, but Neil took her by the arm and propelled her down the aisle to their seats before she could protest.

"That's Blake's seat," she whispered as Neil slid into the seat beside her.

"Not anymore."

"But—"

"Ssh." Neil held a finger to her lips. "If I know Blake Jeffreys, he'll be out in the lobby talking stock options until intermission."

"Do you know Blake?" she asked.

"Let's just say I know *of* him. With him, business comes first; the rest is just marking time."

"That sounds like someone else I know."

"You mean me?"

"How perceptive of you."

"Why so hostile tonight?"

Daye got a firmer grip on her program. "How many times has Rhea had to sit through plays by herself while you were off doing exactly what Blake's doing now?" she demanded.

"Has it been that bad?"

"Worse."

"Now you really *are* hostile."

"Not hostile, just truthful."

"And if I'd married you, Daye?" he asked, reaching up to ruffle her hair. "You'd have understood, wouldn't you?"

"What makes you think so?" she retorted as she smoothed her hair back into place.

"Because you and I are two of a kind; we have the same kind of drive. I always thought yours would work against mine, but I was wrong. You'd have understood, because you've done exactly what you've accused me of doing, only in a slightly different way. You told me once that you'd never let anything stand between you and what you wanted, and you never have."

The curtain had gone up, but Daye was so stunned by what Neil had said that she found it impossible to concentrate on the play. She ran his words over and over again in her mind, effectively blocking out the dialogue on the stage and trapping herself instead inside her own private drama. Were they really so similar after all? she wondered, stealing a furtive glance at him out of the corner of her eye. Would it have made any difference in their lives if he had felt less threatened by her career and her independence all those years ago when the choice had been his to make? She was suddenly reminded of Jonathan Cort, and her chest constricted in pain. Neil had been wrong about one thing: she had been letting *every*thing stand in the way of her and Jonathan. She hadn't heard from him again after she broke their lunch date exactly five weeks and two days ago.

How she despised herself for knowing precisely how long it had been. She had managed to lose track of everything else— everything, that is, but her work. She had lost track of the number of men she had dated once and sometimes twice since then. She no longer remembered how many dinner parties and gallery openings and plays she had attended or how many polo games and jai-alai matches she had watched. She had even lost count of the number of times her name had appeared in the columns linking her romantically with one eligible man after another. What she *did* know was that photos of Jonathan and Maren together had appeared twice in the Shiny Sheet, three times in the *Chronicle,* and five times in the *Standard.*

At intermission, they located Blake in the bar just off the lobby. He signaled to them with his highball glass, and from the way he swayed as he walked over to them, it was obvious that he had drunk his way through the entire first act. He planted a scotch-soaked kiss on Daye's cheek, and she tried not to be too obvious about turning her head away, but she was deeply embarrassed in front of her friends.

"Sorry about that"—he aimed a lopsided grin at all of them— "but business is business, I'm afraid. I assume everyone is drinking?"

"You assume correctly," replied Franki, slipping her arm around Brian's waist and steering him over to the bar. She turned and managed to throw Daye a look of sympathy complete with a thumbs-down signal before Brian grabbed hold of her hand and playfully pinned her arm behind her back.

Daye glanced over at Neil, but he was staring intently over her shoulder while a smile began spreading across his face. She turned her head to see what he was looking at and immediately turned around again.

"Here to check out the competition, Cort?" Neil said as he reached out to shake Jonathan's hand.

"A revival is never exactly competition, Neil," came the smooth reply in that low, husky voice of his, "but this play stands fairly well on its own merits."

He was now directly in front of Daye, but when he only favored her with a curt nod, the jelly in her knees turned to stone.

"I understand you're in the market for a playhouse," he said, focusing all of his attention on Blake Jeffreys.

"So Miss MacCaul's been talking out of school, has she?"

Jonathan smiled. "All I know is that some people from the Llewelyn Corporation have been coming around and asking her some interesting questions."

"She's sitting on a prime piece of real estate, Jonathan," admitted the older man, "and anyone on prime real estate is of particular interest to us."

Daye was devastated. Stung by Jonathan's dismissal of her, she tried to ignore him by moving closer to Neil and talking to him instead, but it didn't help much.

"Would you like a drink?" Neil asked, touching her lightly on the shoulder.

She declined his offer with a shake of her head while she kept her eyes trained on his face. Was it true? she asked herself. Was Maren really thinking of selling the playhouse? Had she found a place up north, then? There had been no mention of such a move in any of the recent newspaper items about her.

"How about getting some air?" Neil suggested, toying with a strand of Daye's long chestnut hair.

"They'll be dimming the lights in a few minutes," she said as she flicked his hand away.

"We'll be back in time."

She looked down at her program and wondered what to do.

"Come on, Daye," Neil urged her in a muted undertone. "He's ignoring you."

Her cheeks flamed. "Shut up, Neil," she warned him from behind clenched teeth.

"Well, he is! The smart thing for you to do would be to leave right now. Show him that you don't give a damn."

"I really don't think I need your advice on this!"

"You're absolutely right." His hand was on her elbow. "What you need is some fresh air. Excuse me, gentlemen," he announced grandly as he steered Daye through the lobby and out the front doors of the theater.

They stood for a while on the lawn in front of the building. Then they crossed the drive and began strolling through the Royal Poinciana Plaza, stopping in front of the various store windows they passed.

"Would you like to head over to Capriccio for coffee instead of going back for the second act?" Neil asked when Daye stopped to study the furniture on display in one of the windows of Worrells.

"I *did* have a date this evening," she reminded him somewhat caustically, wondering if Maren had come with Jonathan or if he was there alone.

"Some date," Neil snorted. "If he's not talking shop, he's boozing."

"Don't, please." She felt the beginnings of a headache, and she had no energy to spar with him.

"I'm sorry, Daye." Neil placed both hands on her shoulders and rested his forehead against hers, as he had done so often when they were young. "It's just that I hate seeing you waste your time with guys like Blake Jeffreys. The man's a user."

Her head came up sharply. "Is he so different from the rest of you men?"

"Hey, don't take it out on me," he protested. "I'm on your side, remember?"

Now it was her turn to apologize. They continued walking awhile in silence, and as they walked she allowed him to take her hand. The gesture was strangely comforting, and for one impetuous moment, Daye almost believed that if she wished for it hard enough, time would stop for them. They could be children again, innocents starting from the beginning again, but making different choices this time around. Could it really have been different? she asked herself for the second time that evening. Or was it better not to know and only to pretend that it could have been?

"Daye?"

Neil had stopped and was drawing her closer to him. Startled, she looked up to see his eyes fastened on hers and his lips just inches from her face. Instinctively she began to pull back.

"Neil, don't."

But he wasn't listening to her as he tugged her toward him. His chest was hard and unyielding against the softness of her breasts, and as his mouth grazed her forehead, she flinched.

"Neil, please!"

"Please what?" he murmured, brushing one corner of her mouth with his tongue.

She was shivering as she fought both the magnetic pull of him and that weakness within herself that could still be so stirred by him. Jonathan Cort was the one man with the power to break Neil's hold on her, and yet she had run from him before he could do so. With a sobbing cry, she finally managed to wrench herself free and start across the street, signaling frantically to one of the taxis waiting at the curb for the show to end. Hurling herself into the back seat, she gave the driver her address while she began locking the doors.

She turned in her seat at the sound of Neil rapping on the window on her side of the cab. He motioned for her to roll the window down, but she shook her head.

"I was just trying to help," he shouted to her, his hands cupped around his mouth. "Let's talk, Daye. Dammit, we're friends, aren't we?"

Friends! As the cab pulled away from the curb, Daye pressed a fist to her mouth to check the sound of the bitter laughter curdling deep inside her.

{ chapter twelve }

RHEA'S EXPLANATION the following morning for having missed the performance at the Royal Poinciana Playhouse was the twenty-four-hour flu, and Daye would have accepted her explanation without question had it not been for the distracted quality of Rhea's voice. The distance Daye had been sensing in Rhea over the weeks was now more pronounced than ever. Her thoughts seemed dispersed, her sentences disjointed, and she reminded Daye of a bird flying back and forth in search of a safe resting place, repeatedly touching down and then just as quickly taking flight again.

Daye was sitting at her desk staring blankly at the drooping leaves of one of the rhododendrons on the windowsill in her office and absently chewing on the cap of a green felt-tip pen. She had been sitting that way for more than an hour, doing nothing but fixing her gaze on one object after another while she sifted through her troubled thoughts. Bits of Jonathan were jumbled together with snippets of Neil. Fragments of Rhea were tangled up with pieces of Franki, who appeared first with Brian and then with Taylor Mead. With her mind so cluttered, work was virtually impossible, and all Daye had managed to accomplish since her conversation with Rhea was to leave a trail of teeth marks in the plastic caps of three different felt-tip pens.

There was a knock at the door, and Daye whirled around in her chair. A woman's arm brandishing a thick, glossy magazine was slowly being extended across the open doorway. After the arm had waved the magazine up and down a few times like a one-sided semaphore, the flushed and smiling face of Connie Chase peeked around the door frame. As usual, her glasses were perched on top of her head, lost somewhere in her nest of cropped brown curls, while her brown eyes squinted somewhat myopically at Daye.

"Ta-*da!*" she sang, flapping the magazine so that it made a loud, whirring noise. "Behold, O creative one, the magnificent wonders thou hast wrought!"

Daye burst out laughing and eagerly extended both arms as Connie advanced step by measured step into the room.

"You're killing me," groaned Daye, greedily flexing her fingers and pretending to pant. "Con-nie, please!"

"Patience, O impetuous one," Connie teased as she drew closer to the desk.

"Aha!" Daye's cry was triumphant as she grabbed at the magazine only to miss it.

Connie dangled it high above Daye's head and simply smiled at her.

"Cruel," Daye moaned, "you're cruel, Connie Chase." Leaping up, she reached out, snatched the magazine from Connie's hand, and hugged it to her chest with a satisfied grin. "All right, where is it?" she asked, her voice sounding slightly breathless.

"Pages twelve through fifteen."

"Four whole pages?" Daye was gleeful as she turned to page twelve of the April issue of *Condominium* magazine. "My God, you're right, Con, four marvelous, beautiful, delicious pages, and each one in glorious color."

Nothing can compare with this, she thought as she scanned the text of the article. *Nothing.* The sweet flush of triumph spread through her, scattering her tangled thoughts like the filaments of a tattered spider's web, and filling her with a wonderful sense of accomplishment, validating her as nothing and no one had ever been able to do in quite the same way. Three of the condos she had been working on, including the Adamsons', were highlighted in the article, and as she examined each of the photographs accompanying the story detail by detail, she was reminded once again of just how good a designer she really was.

"Everything looks sensational, Daye," said Connie, leaning over Daye's shoulder and pointing out the various touches she thought worked especially well. "You're something, you know that? You really are." Straightening up again, she made a fist and thrust it high in the air, crying, "Philippe Nadeau, watch your ass! Your crown's slipping, baby, and whether you know it or not, you're about to be dethroned."

Daye shot her assistant a skeptical look and set the magazine down on her desk. "I think you're being a bit premature, Connie my dear," she said. "He's still way ahead of me, especially commercially. But if I could just land one major commercial account, *then* we might be able to talk about deposing kings."

"In the meantime, though, how about you and I getting out of here?" proposed Connie. "Come on, we'll celebrate. In a few minutes, that phone's going to start ringing madly, and I think you'd better be slightly bombed when you begin accepting everyone's accolades. Otherwise you're going to be impossible to live with. Come! The champagne's on me."

"Am I paying you that well?" One eyebrow arched quizzically.

"Speaking of paying—"

"Chàmpagne's a wonderful idea." Daye jumped up from her chair and clapped an affectionate arm around Connie's shoulder. "Tell you what."

"What?"

"We'll go fifty-fifty on this one. Deal?"

"Deal."

They shook on it. Then Daye switched on the answering machine, and they left the office arm in arm and grinning happily.

They had champagne cocktails at Ta-boo and then decided to splurge by heading over to the popular Two-Sixty-Four restaurant on South County Road and ordering a bottle of Dom Perignon. By the time she had started on her second glass,

Daye's head was spinning and her stomach was growing queasy. As usual, she had forgotten to eat breakfast, and now that it was just past noon, she was beginning to feel the disastrous effects of her oversight. When their waiter stopped by the table to pour them each their third and final glass, Daye placed her hand across the top of hers and shook her head.

"I think I'd better eat something or I could be in a lot of trouble," she whispered to Connie, conscious of how several of her words had run together.

In answer to that, Connie raised her own full glass and then proceeded to drain most of it while Daye stared at her in rapt fascination. Another sip and Connie's glass was empty again.

"Well, I suppose someone should be in the office to start accepting those accolades," she said, rummaging through her canvas bag and coming up with two crumpled ten dollar bills. "Here," she laid the bills on the table in front of Daye, "if I owe you more, let me know. I'll see you later. Now eat!" She wagged a stern finger at Daye and got up to leave.

As Daye picked her way slowly through a large seafood salad, she was continually interrupted by people who stopped by the table to congratulate her. If she was slightly inebriated from the champagne, the praise took her even higher, and she was perilously close to bursting when she sensed rather than saw someone pull out the chair facing her and sit down.

"Neil?" Her eyes widened in surprise. "What are you doing here?"

"This *is* a restaurant, isn't it?"

She looked down at her plate and tried to focus on a large pink shrimp instead of on his face.

"Your assistant told me I could find you here, and I quote, 'either draped around a chair or propped up against the wall and giggling.' She's got some sense of humor."

Daye chuckled in spite of herself. "She's a good kid," she said. "We make a good team."

She missed the brief clouding of his eyes as she continued to stare down at her half-eaten salad.

"Daye, I want to apologize for last night." He kept his voice low as he leaned across the table toward her. "I meant it when I said we were friends. I wasn't trying to come on to you. You looked so unhappy that I thought if I just held you for a while it might have helped."

She considered what he was telling her and asked herself how much of it to believe. But her mind was floating so blissfully above all negative feeling that nothing seemed quite as serious now as it had a few hours ago.

"Let's not discuss it anymore," she decided. "I'm celebrating today."

"So I understand." His smile was genuine as the tension eased from around his mouth. "Congratulations," he said, giving her hand a tight squeeze. "I'm damned proud of you, Daye."

She met his eyes then, and smiled back at him. "Thank you, Neil," she whispered. Yet even as she thanked him, she wondered if Jonathan would ever see the article. She was frowning again as she picked up her glass and took a small sip of the champagne, which was slowly going flat. Of course she could always send him a copy of the magazine anonymously in the mail. She shook her head. Far too obvious.

"I got here a bit late for the celebration," Neil said, interrupting her train of thought. "Should I order another bottle for us?"

"I can't even finish what I have here," she told him.

"Then would you mind if I ordered myself some lunch?"

She shook her head, watching with some amusement as he signaled her waiter with an imperious flick of his wrist. As soon as his meal arrived, she began to nibble at her salad again, while he tore into his steak. Throughout the meal, he alternated between looking at her and scrutinizing the various people who came up to congratulate her, and it was soon obvious to Daye that he was enjoying the attention she was receiving just as much as she was.

Her head was clearer as they sipped their coffee, and she decided to take advantage of their time alone together to ask him about Rhea.

"Rhea?" Neil looked as though he wasn't quite sure who Rhea was.

"I'm worried about her," Daye told him. "She's been so distracted lately, so unreachable. Yet whenever I ask her about it, she denies there's anything wrong."

"What do *you* think is wrong?" His eyes were carefully monitoring her expression.

Daye thought for a moment. "Well, for one thing, she's started to disappear every day for hours at a time. Chloe won't tell me where she goes, and neither will Rhea."

Neil laughed as he leaned back in his chair. "She doesn't go anywhere. She's out painting in the gazebo."

Daye's eyebrows rose. "Painting?"

"Didn't she tell you about it?"

"No." Some of the worry began to dissipate.

"I thought you girls told each other everything."

"Obviously not," she replied somewhat curtly. But a moment later, she leaned across the table and asked eagerly, "Tell me, Neil, is she good? Is she painting seriously?"

"Who knows?" He shrugged. "She keeps the place locked and refuses to let anyone see what she's done. I'm not knocking it, Daye, believe me. It sure as hell saves on the credit card bills every month."

"Tsk, tsk," she chided him, "are you turning stingy in your old age, Neil?"

He met her teasing remark with a scowl.

"Oh, Neil, where's your sense of humor?"

"You know damned well Capricorns don't like being teased, especially about themselves."

"Being a Capricorn has nothing to do with it." She playfully flicked her napkin at him. "Admit it."

He responded by catching hold of a corner of the napkin and yanking on it. She was pulled partway out of her seat, and he narrowed the distance between them by thrusting his face closer to hers.

"Brat!" he hissed, although his eyes were laughing.

"Double brat!" It was a name-calling game straight out of their childhood.

A sudden flare of white light made Daye blink and glance up with a start. There was a second flash and then a third, and as Neil dropped his end of the napkin and scraped back his chair to get to his feet, the photographer from the *Standard* snapped him a mock salute and dashed out of the restaurant through a side door. Daye's face was flaming as heads began to turn and a buzz of excited conversation started up all around them.

"Great, just great," Neil muttered, pulling in his chair again. "That bitch is really out for blood this time."

"Do you mean Sybil?"

"Who else!" His eyes were darkening, his expression turning stormy.

"But why?" Daye began chewing nervously on the knuckle of her thumb.

"She and Rhea are at it again. Christ, you'd think there would be enough caterers to go around in a place like this."

Daye was still baffled, but as soon as Neil explained to her about Nigel Amery, the reason for Sybil's vindictiveness became all too clear to her.

"Obviously Nigel is more ethical than Sybil if he's honoring his obligation to cater the party for Rhea," she observed, dreading the effect those photos would have on Rhea when they appeared, as she knew they would, in the Town Tattler column of the paper.

"I'll sue the bastards," Neil threatened. "Come on, let's get out of here."

Although she tried to insist on paying for her meal and the champagne, Neil refused to take her money.

"Some celebration this turned out to be," he grumbled as they left the restaurant.

At that moment, Daye didn't know whom she felt sorrier for—Neil, Rhea, or herself. But she laid a comforting hand on his arm and said as gently as she could, "Don't worry, Neil, there'll be other celebrations."

THE PHOTO the *Standard* ran in the Tattler column was as suggestive and provocative as any picture could possibly be. The napkin they were holding between them was barely visible. Daye and Neil were shown leaning toward each other in a pose that could only be interpreted as a kiss about to happen. Tears filled her eyes at the sight of the two of them caught in such a compromising situation, and when she reached for the phone on her desk, Daye was shaking so badly that it took several false starts before she was finally able to punch out all the digits in Rhea's number.

"Neil explained it all to me last night," Rhea told her before Daye could get a word out. Her voice was so calm and her tone so even that Daye was momentarily stunned. "I know why Sybil did this," Rhea continued, "but if she intended it to hurt me, she failed. Daye, we've been friends too long for me to ever doubt you."

Daye could feel the tears coursing down her cheeks as she strained to keep her grip on the receiver. "Oh, Rhee, I'm sick about this." Her voice broke. "Just sick."

"That photograph means nothing," insisted Rhea. "Please believe me, Daye, it means absolutely nothing."

"Thank you," she gulped, wiping at her tears with the back of her hand. "Rhee, I've been so worried about you lately but Neil told me that you've started painting and that—"

"He told you!"

Daye sucked in her breath. "You mean you didn't want me to know?" Her anguish began to intensify again. "Rhea?"

"No, it's just that I . . . I suppose it's been so private and so special for me that I haven't wanted to share it with anyone."

"Even us?"

Rhea's sigh was heavy. "I guess so."

"I'm sorry." Daye squeezed her eyes shut against what she believed to be the second betrayal of her friend in a matter of hours. "I wish to God he'd never told me."

"Would you mind if we didn't talk about it right now?" asked Rhea. "It's just too personal, Daye. Please try to understand."

"I do understand, but I also want *you* to understand that I never meant to pry. I was concerned."

"I know that."

Daye was desolate when she put down the phone. She immediately switched on her answering machine and told Connie she was going out for a walk.

"Take a raincoat," Connie advised without looking up from her drawing board. "It's another one of those dismal, drizzly mornings."

The weather suited her mood perfectly, Daye decided, as she slipped into her trench coat and took her traveling umbrella out of the bottom drawer of her desk. She tucked the umbrella under one arm and headed out of the building with her collar turned up, her shoulders hunched, and her hands buried deep inside the pockets of her coat. She found it curious that there were no drains and no sewers in south Florida. After fifteen minutes of a steady downpour, the roads flooded and travel became a challenge capable of thwarting even the most seasoned Floridian. As she stepped into an ankle-deep puddle, she made a mental note to ask someone about it some day.

She walked west along Worth Avenue to the end of the street, passing the supremely snobbish Everglades Club where several members dressed in tennis whites were standing in the doorway, waiting for the rain to stop. She crossed the street and headed east, coming to South Ocean Boulevard and following it south for a while. Then she turned around and swung back up toward Peruvian again. As she neared Philippe Nadeau's shop, she saw a familiar figure emerge and start across the sidewalk for the black Lincoln limousine drawn up to the curb. She slowed her steps, hoping that Sybil Barron wouldn't see her, but she did.

With a haughty toss of her auburn mane, Sybil fixed Daye with a pointed stare, making it clear that she intended to remain where she was until Daye passed. They had never talked to each other before, and yet Daye knew exactly how the woman's voice would sound when she spoke. She wasn't wrong. The voice was icy, as cold and as smooth as Sybil herself, with a glittering edge to it that promised a deadly thrust.

With her catlike green eyes holding Daye's she said, "You're to be congratulated, my dear Miss Peters, on the rather generous coverage you received in *Condominium* magazine."

Daye thanked the woman with a slight inclination of her head.

"I must also commend you on your excellent taste in luncheon companions," Sybil continued. "You both take a marvelous picture. I trust, of course, that his sweet little wife doesn't object to your meeting this way."

Daye refused to be baited. "We're all very old friends," she answered, keeping her voice calm and pitched especially low.

"How cozy." Sybil's smile was now a suggestive leer as she purred, "And how wonderfully incestuous."

"If you'll excuse me!" Daye started around the woman.

The tip of Sybil's beige umbrella embedded itself firmly in the middle of Daye's chest.

"Did you know that I've asked Philippe to redecorate my home for me, my dear?" Without waiting for Daye to reply, she went on, "When he decorated the place for us three years ago, he did such a superb job that we found it impossible to keep the photographers away. Philippe won several awards for the house, you know, and I see absolutely no reason why he shouldn't do so again, do you?"

Daye was fuming as she brushed Sybil's umbrella aside, but she strode off down the street with her shoulders squared and her head high, refusing to dignify the woman's question with a response of any kind. As she approached her office, her feet suddenly began to drag and her shoulders started to slump. Sybil Barron was the undisputed arbiter of all things social in Palm Beach, and if she intended to use her home as a showcase for Philippe again, then it wouldn't be long before the rest of Palm Beach society began to claw and elbow its way onto the Philippe Nadeau bandwagon. In the face of such potential competition, her own recent triumph receded into insignificance, and so it was with mounting frustration that she watched as another page was ripped from the monthly calendar she kept in her mind.

chapter thirteen

PHILIPPE'S NEW project was the talk of the town. Within a few days of her unpleasant encounter with Sybil Barron, Daye picked up the copy of the *Standard* that Connie had left for her on her desk and saw that the entire front page of the Better Living section had been devoted exclusively to the Barrons' Lake Worth home. Full-color photographs showed Sybil and Philippe taking a walking tour through her home—a twenty-five-room mansion built by Addison Mizner—with its tennis court, swimming pool, and private marina, while the text of the article described the changes the two of them were contemplating. Included in the article as well was a brief itinerary of the buying trip that would take Philippe to the major auction houses in New York, London, Paris, and Rome. When Daye put the paper down, she felt sick to her stomach and wondered just how soon the doors would start slamming in her face.

It began almost immediately. Before noon, one client called to cancel a project Daye had already started for her. Then two potential clients phoned to inform her that, after some serious deliberation, they found her preliminary sketches far too extreme for their decidedly conservative tastes. When Franki called her from the tennis club at one, Daye was so upset she could barely form a cohesive sentence.

"Did you know that Addison Mizner, that brilliant mastermind behind bastardized Spanish baroque in Palm Beach wasn't even a licensed architect?" she barked into the phone, and heard Franki react with an exaggerated yelp of pain. "But I think I've finally discovered what the problem is," Daye continued.

"And what's that?"

"They're just not ready for me down here. I'm obviously way ahead of my time."

"Feel like going back to New York and then trying it down here again when you're fifty?" asked Franki.

That thought sobered Daye immediately. "No," she admitted in a tiny voice.

"Then forget about the blue-haired crowd and keep pitching to the jogging set."

"I am, but what I really need is what Philippe has—a patron with a showcase home for me to redesign."

"You could do our place over," offered Franki with a wry laugh, "but I doubt it would do you much good. Compared with most of the other condos around here, ours is a tenement."

"Franki!"

"It's true," she insisted. "Have you taken a good look at Breakers Row or Worden House or Old Port Cove lately? Hell, Daye, those are *condos;* what we've got could be used as their servants' quarters."

"Please have lunch with me," Daye blurted out, cutting Franki off. She couldn't bear the bitterness in her friend's voice, and her own mood was rapidly plummeting toward complete despair. "I think I'm in desperate need of a friendly face right now."

"I don't know." Franki hesitated uncertainly for a moment. "I've already . . . Let me see if I can make some changes, and I'll call you right back. Oh, what the hell, okay. How about Café L'Europe at two?"

"Thanks, Franki," Daye said gratefully. "I'll see you at two, then."

Climbing the flight of inlaid tiled stairs to the second floor of the Esplanade shopping promenade on Worth Avenue at precisely two o'clock, Daye hoped that the usual line of patrons waiting for tables at Palm Beach's newest and most popular restaurant would have thinned out by this time. She was in too bleak a mood to have to endure standing in the crowded bistro area while she waited for a table to open up on the restaurant side. Stepping inside the door to the sounds of noisy chatter and piped-in classical music, she grimaced. There were eight women in line ahead of her, standing two by two in the doorway alongside the bar and patiently waiting their turn.

Daye gave her name to Norbert, the restaurant's Bavarian owner and maître d', and then stood with her back against a brick wall and her arms folded across her chest, watching as he escorted two elderly blondes in Chanel suits and gold Bulgari chains to their table. She smiled knowingly to herself, certain that the two women—both identifiable as widows by the telltale gold men's watches they were wearing—were among those numerous women of indeterminate age and unlimited means who could be found dining and dancing every Saturday night at the Colony Hotel with handsome young men whose services for the evening had been more than generously paid for.

She was now first in line and hungrily eyeing the elaborate sweet table, draped in a long peach-colored cloth and banked with pink and fuchsia azaleas, when Norbert crooked his finger at her and gestured to the phone on the bar. Her heart sank as she picked it up and heard Franki breathlessly apologizing for having kept her waiting, but that something had come up.

"Nothing of Taylor's, I hope," cracked Daye in spite of her disappointment.

She was rewarded by a rich burst of typically Franki laughter, deep and deliciously bawdy. "Don't I just wish! No, I'm afraid it's something a lot more mundane. The girl I was practicing with all morning twisted her ankle, and I've spent the past half-hour applying ice packs to it. She came with me in my car, so I have to drive her home again, and who knows, she might even need an X-ray. I'm sorry, Daye, I really am. How about a drink later, though—say around five?"

"I don't think so," Daye decided. "I'll probably just head home and go for a nice long swim in the pool. You know, for the first time since I opened my business here, the office is the last place I want to be right now."

"Why don't you give Rhea a call, then? Catch her before

her three o'clock siesta and you might get lucky."

Daye hadn't spoken to Rhea since the morning that photo had appeared in the *Standard,* and the more she thought about Franki's suggestion, the more she realized that what she really wanted most was to be alone for a while. She left the restaurant, walked back to the office for her car, and drove over to Publix to pick up some groceries. If she waited until she got back to Boca to do her shopping, she knew she wouldn't bother, and her refrigerator was now down to a slice of brick cheese, two oranges, and a quart of skim milk.

She pushed her empty shopping cart up one aisle and down the other, trying to find something even remotely tempting to buy. She had no appetite whatsoever at the moment, and nothing she saw seemed worth the effort of reaching up or bending down to lift it off the shelf. A tin of smoked oysters finally caught her eye. She plucked it from the top shelf and dropped it with a metallic clang into the bottom of the wagon, only to change her mind a moment later and put it back again. Moving slowly past the frozen foods, she stopped to consider just how many different kinds of frozen vegetables in varying combinations there were. Curiously studying the list of ingredients on a box of frozen mushrooms, peas, and rice, she was almost tempted to take it, but one look at the number of chemicals mixed in with the vegetables and back it went.

She was dawdling near the meat counter when she saw him. Wheeling a wagon half filled with groceries, Jonathan Cort was briskly swinging her way. With her heart in her mouth, Daye abandoned her cart and fled down the aisle containing all of the crackers and cookies, condensed soups, rice, and pasta. She stopped, panting for breath, and tiptoed cautiously around to the next aisle, pausing for a moment in front of the jams and jellies.

"What goes better with lamb, mint sauce or mint jelly?"

She froze, feeling her cheeks redden in embarrassment as she straightened up to face him. Passing a dry tongue over her equally dry lips, she said hoarsely, "I've always preferred mint sauce."

"Mint sauce it is, then." One dark hand closed around the jar of Lea & Perrins mint sauce and casually dropped it into the cart. "How've you been, Daye?" he asked her, all the bantering gone now from his dusky voice.

She hated herself for shrugging in answer to his question, but she did. The tug of his deep blue eyes made her feel that her body was swaying toward him in spite of her best efforts to stand still. Dressed in burgundy cords, a powder blue V-neck, and cordovan loafers, he looked more like a preppy college kid than a successful songwriter and playwright turned modified hermit, and that brought a touch of a smile to her lips.

"I've missed you, Daye, and I—"

"How is your play—"

They had both started to speak at the same time. Now they both stopped, each glancing down with anxious eyes at the contents of his shopping cart, as if neutral territory lay somewhere among the mint sauce, a bunch of large green grapes, and two nearly ripe avocados.

"Dammit, I haven't been able to get through a single day without wanting to pick up the phone and call you." He stabbed her again with his piercing blue eyes.

"Then why didn't you?" It was out before she could stop it.

She tensed as a mischievous smile broke across his dark face. "And speak to your answering machine?" he said. "Or worse still, speak to you and have you tell me you were too busy to see me?"

She met his eyes squarely then and asked, "How's Maren?"

His gaze never faltered. "The same," he replied offhandedly. "Working on a new production, thinking about the merits of either keeping or selling the playhouse, and buying one in New Jersey." He shrugged. "I guess she's fine."

That wasn't what Daye had meant, and Jonathan knew it. So it had been narrowed down to just New Jersey, then. Daye suddenly became very interested in a jar of orange marmalade while she pondered the significance of his remarks.

"Robertson's is better," Jonathan said.

"What?" She looked up at him, startled.

"Robertson's." He indicated the jar she was holding and shook his head. "It's much better than that one."

"Oh." She almost dropped the jar in her haste to put it back on the shelf.

"Feel like celebrating with me tonight?" He threw the invitation out so casually that she was convinced she hadn't heard him correctly.

"Celebrating?" She was beginning to feel like a foolish echo.

"Yes, celebrating." He leaned his elbows on the handle of the wagon and grinned up at her. "I've nearly finished the play, and my agent in New York is trying to get Everett Rakwell to produce it."

"Everett Rakwell?"

As Jonathan nodded, Daye gulped. Everett Rakwell was Broadway's hottest new producer, a thirty-seven-year-old failed actor who was already threatening to supplant both David Merrick and Joe Papp by staging one major hit show after another.

"Jonathan, that's wonderful," she said, smiling and feeling genuinely thrilled for him.

"The play's good, Daye." Again his tone was serious, making her feel somehow that he hadn't yet shared this news with anyone else. "The songs work, the story line's believable, and it has just enough pathos to make it at least a two-hanky show."

"I'm glad," she told him, feeling a tightening in her throat as she gazed at him. "I'm really very glad for you. Do you have a title for it yet?"

"The working title is *Arpeggio in Blue*," he told her, "but titles can change at least a dozen times before they ever make it to the marquee."

"*Arpeggio in Blue*," she repeated it, enjoying the way it slid so lyrically off her tongue. "I like it, Jonathan. It's a beautiful title."

"So, now that we've agreed on something, how about celebrating with me?"

She turned away and refused to meet his questioning gaze.

"Daye?"

He was waiting, much like an excited, impatient child, with his hands clasped together expectantly, for the answer she wanted to give him but didn't dare.

"I can't, Jonathan." She finally managed to force the words past her stubborn lips.

His smile began to fade. "Why not?"

Because you just can't come bounding back into my life after so many weeks of silence and expect me to welcome you with open arms and no questions asked, she thought to herself.

Her words were slow and measured as she said aloud, "Judging from the coldness of your greeting the other night at the Poinciana Playhouse, can you blame me for being just a little surprised by your sudden invitation?"

He spread the fingers of both hands wide and bent his head as though studying them very carefully. "I suppose I *was* less than courteous," he admitted, dropping his voice, "but then I didn't think you'd care whether I said hello to you or not. You'd already made it fairly clear to me that you had your priorities arranged and that I wasn't one of them."

"Then why are you inviting me out again?"

"Because I want to be with you and because the fates decided to send us shopping for groceries in the same place at the same time. Obviously, we were meant to take advantage of the situation, and I am. But if you don't feel like celebrating tonight, we could just go out for a quiet dinner instead and save the celebration for another time."

Another time. How easily a man threw out that line. How many times were supposed to have been one of those "another times" in her life? She stood there in front of him, shifting uneasily from one foot to the other.

He took her by surprise when he said, "You've got to stop running away from this, Daye."

"I'm not running away from anything," she retorted.

"Call it what you will—self-defense, self-preservation, maintaining your independence, whatever; it doesn't change what you're doing. You're still running away."

"Don't!"

"Please, Daye." He reached for her hands, but she tucked them behind her back. "Daye, you're not the only one involved here. I'm in this, too. Like it or not, you and I have been dancing around each other for over two months now, and I'm tired of it. I'm tired of the fencing, the cool greetings, the pretending you don't exist when you're standing three feet away from me and pretending, too. Daye, I want to spend time with you. I want to get to know you and share things with you. I think we could have something very special if you'd just give it a chance."

"I don't have time," she told him. "I don't have time both

for you and for my career right now."

"Is it really that difficult?" he asked. "God, you'd think you were the first woman who ever held down a job. There are millions of women out there, Daye, with full-time careers who actually manage to handle a marriage *and* children at the same time. Now how do you like that revelation?"

"It's nothing I didn't already know," she retaliated. "I just don't happen to be one of those women. I'm me."

"And being you means being a one-sided woman, is that it? Work and nothing else, or a man and nothing else. Why not both?"

"Because as much as I might like to believe I could do it, I really don't believe I can. Something would suffer, and it would probably be my work. I can't allow that to happen, Jonathan. I need my work too much."

"Need, Daye?" he queried. "What about your other needs? What about the part of you that might want to share things with someone, the kinds of things only companionship can provide? Wouldn't it be worth sacrificing a few hours a day of your precious work to find that out?"

"And I suppose you're the one who's going to provide me with just the companionship I need." Her voice had a mocking edge to it.

"I might be, if you'd give me half a chance to get to know you."

She looked down at her feet and said nothing, while deep inside, her conflicting emotions somersaulted like so many pratfalling tumblers.

"You still haven't told me when you'll have some time for me, Daye."

"Don't push me, Jonathan. I just don't know right now."

His voice was bristling with impatience. "Will you have time after you get all the jobs Philippe Nadeau wants? After Palm Beach declares you the official winner of the race the two of you are entered in?"

"Stop it, Jonathan," she hissed, glancing uncomfortably around her, but he refused to give up.

"I think I have a right to know how much longer I'm supposed to wait, don't you?"

"I never asked you to wait. We saw each other only a few

times, and that was it. You have no claim on either me or my time, Jonathan, and you have no right even to speak to me this way. We weren't an item; we weren't even a couple. We were nothing more than two people who went out on a few casual dates!"

"*You* are a liar, Daye Peters, and you know it!"

"Damn you, Jonathan Cort, why can't you just go away and leave me alone?" She was shaking as she spoke.

"Because I'm still waiting for an answer to my question."

"The only answer I have is the one I already gave you."

"You can't see me because you're too busy working." One black eyebrow arched cynically. "You seem to be able to make time for Neil Howard."

Her own eyes began to narrow. "And what should I say to that, Jonathan, that you and Maren make a most photogenic twosome?"

"Don't throw that up to me all the time, Daye. What happens between Maren and me has nothing whatsoever to do with us."

"Doesn't it?"

"No, because we're friends, Daye, nothing more." His voice was almost pleading as he said, "Why can't you believe that?"

She stood there glaring at him, wishing with all her heart that she *could* believe him. She nearly laughed out loud when she thought about the excuse she had given him. Her work. Would there even be any work for her when she returned to her office in the morning? The fear of seeing her business collapse after so short a time made her wince.

"Daye?" The tips of his fingers were caressing her cheek. "Daye, please say you'll have dinner with me tonight."

He continued to stroke her face gently, as though she were a wild animal he was attempting to tame. Suddenly, she was exhausted, worn out by the events of the day, tired of battling, with no one to urge her on. And so she capitulated. With a tentative nod, she agreed to have dinner with him.

"And you won't call at the last minute to cancel out on me again?" His eyes were twinkling, the dimple creasing his cheek as he grinned at her.

She found herself grinning back at him. "No," she promised him, "not this time."

He took her to La Vielle Maison, the renowned Mizner

house in Boca, which had been converted into a maze of small, flower-filled, antique-accented dining rooms in March of 1976. Sprawling behind a high wall, ringed with trees lit by ropes of white fairy lights and perched on the edge of the Intracoastal, it was a two-story beige stucco hacienda with a red tile roof and an inner courtyard complete with an ornamental fish pond. The courtyard was flooded with azaleas, ferns, and Persian violets and set with small square tables. They dined alone on the tiny covered porch leading off one of the larger upstairs rooms, ordering from the fixed menu and enjoying some of the finest French cuisine in south Florida.

They scarcely spoke during the meal. Daye barely tasted the exquisite dishes set before her. Her eyes were riveted to Jonathan's face, her left hand rested on the table with his right hand covering it, and her body tingled with a thousand pinpricks of heightened sensation as they moved from *escargots aux petits légumes* to *faisan fumé* to a tossed green salad and finally to an assortment of French cheeses. Neither of them wanted dessert, but they both ordered a cognac and coffee; and then, when the unspoken feelings passing back and forth between them grew too intense for either of them to contain, Jonathan paid the bill and they left.

While they waited under the protective canopy of a huge banyan tree in the courtyard for Jonathan's car to be brought around, Jonathan massaged Daye's back with his hand and nuzzled the side of her neck with his lips. Then he turned her around and, cupping her face in his hands, gently brushed his mouth across hers. Daye shivered and closed her eyes while the last bit of resistance drained out of her. She reached up to wrap her arms around his neck, and she returned his kiss with a joyous yearning that increased as their kiss deepened. Clinging to him, her body shaping itself to his, she knew what it was to have been thirsty and hungry and suddenly to have both appetites appeased.

And so, when he drove her home and asked if he could come upstairs with her, she was finally ready to say yes.

chapter fourteen

SHE UNLOCKED the front door of the condo, and he followed her inside. As they stood together in the marble foyer, it struck her that this was the first time a man had crossed that threshold to enter the space she had cherished as hers and hers alone for over four months. She felt strangely violated by the simple act of having invited Jonathan into that space, but as she slowly walked him through each room, the feeling gradually began to dissipate. How ironic it was, she mused, watching Jonathan devour her home with his remarkable eyes, that he should be the first man to see where she lived and not— You can say his name, she told herself, everything's different now—Neil. There, she had said it. Suddenly, it was almost impossible to remember who Neil was, and that what he had once stirred in her, Jonathan now stirred.

"It's exquisite," he exclaimed as he took her in his arms, "but then with you living here and that distinctive Daye Peters touch everywhere, how could it be otherwise?"

"Flatterer," she murmured, nestling closer to him. She was pleased that he approved, because his approval was very important to her now.

"I never had a chance to compliment you on that excellent spread in *Condominium* magazine," he said.

"You saw it?"

"I most certainly did. You're an extremely talented designer, Daye. Your work is unique."

She warmed to his praise, smiling when he planted a light kiss on her mouth.

"If I ever decide to do my place over, I think I know just the person for the job," he told her.

Her sigh was wistful as she said, "The way things are going for me at the moment, I hope it's soon. I need the work."

"Patience, my sweet Daye, patience," he counseled her. "Give yourself some time and give Florida the time to get to know you."

Time again, always time. She stepped out of his embrace, a worried frown replacing the smile that had been there a moment ago, and walked over to the bar in one corner of the living room. She suddenly felt nervous about being there alone with him. She needed something to keep her hands busy and to keep her mind off what was bound to happen between them tonight.

"Cognac?" She kept her back to him as she anxiously fingered the cut-glass knob on the crystal decanter of Courvoisier V.S.O.P.

"That'll be fine."

He came up behind her and locked his arms around her waist. With some difficulty, she managed to pour the cognac into two Baccarat snifters, and after handing him his, she suggested they take their drinks out onto the balcony.

The crescent moon was riding high in the clear ebony sky; the ocean was no more than a gentle, swishing whisper as it rolled shoreward; and the lights from the distant yachts winked like dozens of fireflies through the night. Daye took a long, warming sip of her cognac, swallowing it bit by burning bit, and felt its heat spiral through her. She leaned against the balcony railing, both hands cupped around the bowl of her glass and gazed up at the constellation of Orion, which was perched above the building. Then she sought out the Pleiades.

Jonathan bent over her, running a hand through the coppery spill of her hair and pressing his lips to the rapidly beating pulse point in her throat. She threw back her head as if to discourage him, but his lips followed after her. A moment later, his tongue was tracing teasing circles across her throat, moving slowly toward the sensitive rim of her ear.

A spark of tremulous feeling began to flame inside her. The glass she was holding seemed magically to disappear from her hands, freeing her to wrap her arms around his neck while he whispered her name and gathered her close to him. The very nearness of him was both reassuring and bewildering, exciting and terrifying. He was both the threat and the promise. With their bodies melded together, Daye felt herself growing weak, her strength flowing from her into him, and leaving her to smolder with unquenched desire.

"Let's go back inside." It was part question, part command.

"Yes," she told him, taking his hand and leading him from the balcony to her darkened bedroom.

In the lambent spill of moonlight reflected off the waves and into her room, they began to undress. He lowered her zipper in one long, smooth metallic sigh, and when he slipped her dress off her shoulders, it slid easily over the rounded curves of her body to fall in a pool of silken ripples at her feet. She stepped out of the dress and kicked off her shoes, her eyes never leaving his face as his own eyes swept her body with awed and gentle reverence.

"My God, you're beautiful, Daye," he breathed, his gaze slowly returning to her face.

His words were caresses to her deprived senses, his appreciation of her a soothing balm for the scars that were still so fresh. She helped him undress, and when their clothing was no longer a barrier between them, he pulled her up against him and their naked flesh met and touched for the first time. His hands on her body were like fiery tendrils, curling around her and shaping her to their will, awakening all that had lain sleeping within her for too long.

He eased her onto the bed, laying her down slowly and gently, and then he lowered himself beside her. She was a rush of warmth against the coolness of the cotton coverlet. He was thrusting hardness against her pouting softness. Together they were loving adversaries pitted one against the other. She lay spread before him like a moistened flower, each velvet petal opening at his touch. His mouth took possession of hers and his tongue laid siege to hers, while she kindled a pathway of desire down the length of his back with the fingers of both hands.

Her eyes were closed, but she used the sensitive pads of her fingertips to trace the muscled contours of his body and commit them to memory. Never before had she been so aroused by the touch of a man's skin against hers or the scent of his maleness as it enveloped her in its musky cocoon. Arching her back, she offered him her breasts, and his mouth released hers to claim the twin orbs of golden flesh that had peaked so temptingly for his pleasure. His gentle suckling coaxed whimpers of surprised delight from her parted lips, while her fingers, deep in his dark hair, urged him to taste more of her. As though possessed of a will all its own, her body began to undulate, challenging his to meet her rhythmic movements, and where she led, he quickly followed.

He cradled her head with one hand while his other hand smoothed a sinuous path across her belly and down to that precious part of her which impatiently awaited the command of his nearing touch. Spreading her legs, she beckoned him inside, moaning as his fingers banked the fires of her unleashed passion with every gentle but persistent stroke.

"Jonathan," she gasped, straining against him, writhing beneath him. "Oh, Jonathan, Jonathan."

He answered her urgency by raising himself above her for one brief moment, and then, gathering her close to him, he entered her at last. With their desires evenly matched and their bodies locked in loving combat, they circled each other warily and curiously until they finally set aside all caution and plunged together eagerly. They searched and probed, exploring and learning each other's secrets, knowing that for them, this first glorious time would never come again. His yearning sweetness as he took her was met equally by her own yielding gentleness, and she gave herself to him in tearful gratitude for being released at last from the solitary prison of her aloneness.

She was the first to stir. Propping herself up on one elbow, she brushed the hair out of her eyes and peered down at him while he drifted languorously somewhere between sleeping and waking. She used the index finger of her left hand to trace the contours of his face, which was etched in silver by the moon. He flinched, and his eyes opened slowly. When he looked up and saw her leaning over him, he began to smile a slow, lazy smile of sheer contentment. Cupping the back of her head with both hands, he brought her face just close enough to his for their lips to touch and finally hold in a warm and tender kiss.

"Hi," he whispered up to her.

"Hi," she whispered back.

He pulled her down beside him, and she snuggled against him, noticing how well they fit together, how easily the planes and angles of their bodies matched. But as she continued to lie there in the circle of his arms, her own contentment began to give way to fear. She had surrendered herself to him with an abandon that frightened her. It had also allowed him to see how very great her need for him had been. She felt exposed now, open to bruising, and that both saddened and angered her.

Need and want warred within her for control of her emotions. Wanting was one thing, a feeling easily dealt with; but needing was something entirely different. She knew only too well that need made you vulnerable, threatened your independence, and diluted your drive and ambition. As much as she wanted Jonathan Cort, she knew that she couldn't allow herself to need him. For in her neediness lay her potential downfall.

When he began to make love to her again, she tried to force her doubts aside, but they persisted nonetheless.

She awoke to an early morning spread with buttery sunshine and slipped out of bed to take a hasty shower before Jonathan woke up. Binding her hair in a lavender bath towel and wrapping it turban fashion around her head, she stepped into the stall shower and stretched and preened under the cascade of hot, steamy water. The blurred shadow on the other side of the translucent glass doors alerted her to his presence there, and when he slid back the door and asked if he could join her, she impulsively held out her arms to him.

They soaped each other with their hands, each following the contours of the other's body as though they were anointing one another as part of some mystical ritual of cleansing. Then they rinsed themselves off and began again. Some time later, they emerged from the shower, flushed and warm, and toweled each other dry. Slipping into a long periwinkle blue silk dressing gown, Daye brushed out her damp hair and watched in the mirror while Jonathan wrapped his towel around his waist and then borrowed one of her combs to slick his own hair into place.

"I'm starving," she told him, leading him toward the kitchen.

"Lovemaking will do it every time," he said, his dark eyes glowing as he held the refrigerator door open for her.

"Then I'd better not indulge myself too often. I could wind up looking like the Goodyear blimp."

"You? Never. I'll make certain that you burn off everything you eat."

"And how do you intend to do that?" she asked, glancing up at him through veiled eyes.

"By simply making love to you after every meal you eat."

She laughed. "Promise?"

He held up his right hand. "I promise."

A moment later he was eagerly rubbing his hands together as he bent down beside her to peer into the refrigerator. "You obviously hate eating," he observed dryly, noting its scanty contents.

"Does that mean the deal's off?"

For a moment he seemed confused. Then he began to laugh, reaching up and tugging playfully on a handful of her hair. "On the contrary, you little schemer; it means that I'll either have to stock up your refrigerator for you or take you out for dinner a lot."

"What's this, no return invitation to your place?" she said. "Don't you ever cook for yourself?" Even as she asked the question, she was aware of treading on potentially dangerous ground.

"Oh, I can make the usual bachelor dishes," he conceded, counting them off on his fingers, "steaks, hamburgers, salads, eggs—"

"Lamb chops."

"Lamb chops, of course."

His look was so completely guileless that she hated herself for what she was doing, and so she stopped it before it could go any further. Jonathan was a good sport. Together they settled for toast, since she always kept a loaf of six-grain bread in the freezer, a sectioned orange for each of them, and herbal tea with honey. While he carried the wicker tray out onto the balcony, she hastily set the table with lavender and raspberry striped place mats, matching napkins, and appropriate cutlery. When they sat down to their meager fare, they pretended they were about to enjoy an elaborately catered banquet instead.

"I must say, Miss Peters, you brew an excellent cup of tea." Jonathan's voice was haughty as he raised his cup in tribute to her prowess.

"And you, Mr. Cort, slice a most elegant orange." She picked one neatly divided section clean and then licked her lips appreciatively.

"Then there's the toast, of course." He considered the plain, unbuttered toast with a skeptical eye, and the two of them burst out laughing. Both of them ate the toast anyway.

She had just poured them each a second cup of tea when he suddenly set his cup down and leaned across the table. "I'd like to show you my play when I finish it, Daye," he told her. "I think I can trust you to tell me whether it's good or not."

What he was saying took her completely by surprise, but the shock quickly gave way to a little trill of pleasure. She was flattered by his apparent faith in her judgment, and she was elated that he had chosen her rather than Maren MacCaul to read it.

"I'd be delighted, Jonathan." She took his hand and lightly kissed the back of it. "Delighted and honored."

"I'm really excited about this play," he said. "I feel good about what I've done with it. And you know, Daye, it's been more than four years since I've felt that good about anything."

She pulled back with a slight gasp of surprise. It could have been her talking instead of him.

He seemed unaware of her reaction, because a moment later he said, "Four years ago, I was played out, fed up with writing in the same mold and giving people what they'd come to expect from Kerwin and Cort. We didn't dare deviate from the successful formula we'd devised, and I came to hate what we were doing. I've always despised formulas, Daye, and I never thought I'd fall into that kind of a trap. I felt my creativity starting to dry up, and I truly believed that I'd sold out my talent just to keep pulling in the crowds and the big money that came with them."

"Is that why you and Rolf Kerwin split up?"

"That wasn't the precise reason four years ago, but when I look back on it now, I realize that it was probably behind my decision to break up the team all along." He leaned back and locked his fingers behind his head. "You see, I'd built the house in Gorham Sound for Andrea and myself, but I stopped work on it just before our divorce. Afterward, I altered the design so that it had two separate bedroom suites, each with its own bathroom and sitting room, situated at either end of the house with the living room, dining room, library, and kitchen between them. I desperately wanted to get out of New York, and I had the crazy idea that Rolf and I could share the place. We did, and the arrangement worked well for a while. We each went our own way, and we got together only to work on *Sing a Song of Broadway*—but Rolf has always been a city person, and it wasn't long before he was commuting between Gorham Sound and New York. He was soon spending more time in New York than he was in Florida, and we began drifting apart. It got harder and harder for us to agree on anything we did. Everything became a sacrifice, whereas in the past we'd always considered whatever we did in terms of its being a compromise. And then he wrote a song for Lauren, which she recorded for a new label. That was the one thing we both swore we wouldn't do without first asking the other's permission; and that's what finally tore it for me. As soon as *Sing a Song of Broadway* opened, we officially dissolved the partnership." He sat forward in his chair again and studied her solemnly. "Well, he continued to use the formula, but that didn't prevent his show from closing last year, so let's just hope that my attempt to deviate from the formula won't end up the same way."

"It won't, Jonathan. It's going to be a hit; I just know it." Daye's eyes were bright with the force of her conviction. "Your excitement is palpable; it's something I can feel, and it must be there in the play, too. It has to be."

"Sweet Daye," he murmured, taking her hands and giving them both a tight, grateful squeeze. "We both have a dream, don't we? And that's something very vital that we have in common. Only someone else with a dream could possibly understand what I've been talking about and feel it the way you say you do. That's one of the reasons I'm so attracted to you, Daye. You know just how I feel and that's rare."

Oh, Jonathan, Jonathan. Her mind repeated his name over and over again like a litany, and she wanted to slide onto his lap and press herself against his chest, feel his hands burrow deep in her hair while she dug her own fingers into his. She wanted to be held awhile longer before the demands of the outside world claimed them again. But he was glancing down at his watch, a slight frown creasing his forehead. She was shaken by a cold spasm of fear. He was getting ready to leave, and she was suddenly afraid of not being able to handle it as well as she should.

She wanted to feel nothing when he left. She needed to show him that his leaving meant nothing at all to her. She knew she mustn't appear anxious or seem concerned about when they would see each other again. She had to appear calm and self-contained in spite of how she really felt, but the longer she looked at him sitting across the table from her, the harder she knew that would be.

He got up from the table at last and pulled her to her feet beside him. Brushing the heavy fall of her hair back from her neck with both hands, he said in a whispery voice, "I wish I could spend the rest of the morning just holding you, but we both have work to do, and the faster we get to it, the sooner we'll be able to reward ourselves with something special this evening."

She could feel her heart beginning to lift. "What kind of a reward did you have in mind?" she asked, keeping her own voice soft and low.

"How about some jazz at the Beowulf in Pompano?"

"Uh-huh."

"Followed by some good loving?"

"Even better," she murmured. "I think I like that reward." She hugged him then, and as she did, she hoped that she didn't appear either too grateful or too relieved.

"I'll call you around six," he said, giving her a quick kiss on the mouth before going back inside to get dressed.

She walked with him to the elevator, and when she returned to the apartment, she glanced at the clock on the kitchen stove and wondered just how she was going to last the nine hours and twelve minutes until she heard from him again.

"RHEA, FOR God's sake, Rhea, wake up!"

She fought off the hands trying to hold her down and continued to scream.

"Rhea! Rhea, you're having a nightmare again. Do you hear me? A nightmare. Wake up, Rhea. It's Neil."

Some of the fight went out of her at the sound of his name, and when she finally managed to open her eyes, she could see that he had only been trying to shake her awake, not hold her down. Her black hair was plastered to the sides of her face, and her thin silk nightgown was stuck to her moist skin. She passed a shaky hand over her eyes and struggled to sit up, leaning back against the brass headboard and gasping as her back touched the cold metal bars.

Neil got up from the bed and went to stand over by the windows. Keeping his back turned to her, he said, "Don't you think it's time you thought of going to see someone about those nightmares of yours?"

"You mean a psychiatrist?" Her voice came out in a hoarse, dry croak.

"Why not? They're fashionable these days, and it might even do you some good."

What she had first perceived as concern in his voice was immediately nullified by the snideness of that last remark, and so she decided to ignore both Neil *and* his suggestion. She pulled the covers up to her chin and burrowed under them like a small, frightened animal seeking shelter.

"If I could hear you all the way down the hall, the children must have heard you too, Rhea."

His voice came to her through a thickening barrier of self-protection as she drew the covers up over her head. It had been two weeks now since Neil had moved into one of the guest rooms, saying that her tossing and turning kept him awake and that her dreams, which she steadfastly refused to discuss with him, were too frequent for him to cope with any longer.

"I can't go on like this," he had complained. "I have to get up and go to work in the morning, and you don't. You can nap in the afternoon and catch up on the sleep you miss at night. Unfortunately, I don't have that luxury."

She had tried to be placating, even teasing, when she had said, "I know the real reason you don't want to sleep in here anymore."

"Oh?" His eyes had narrowed suspiciously.

"Ever since we had the room redecorated, you've been complaining that it's too feminine."

He had smiled at that, but he had moved out of the bedroom anyway.

She really didn't mind sleeping alone at all now. The dreams came whether he was beside her in bed or not. And she loved her room. Daye had papered it in beige silk with a delicate Chinese motif of gray pussy willows and tiny copper-colored marigolds. She had used the same material for the canopy, comforter, and dust ruffle as well as for the Roman shades on each of the room's four large windows. All the other furniture had been reupholstered in gray silk with throw cushions in copper and beige silk to compliment the paper.

"Rhea!" With a swipe of his hand, he ripped the covers off her. "Rhea, you've got to do something about the way you're feeling."

The eyes she turned on him were studiously blank. "How would you even begin to know how I'm feeling?" she asked him.

"I don't have to know. I can give it a good guess."

"Can you, Neil?" Her laugh was short and bitter.

"Ever since Daye moved down here, you've been acting different, and I—"

"Daye has nothing to do with this," she snapped. "None of my friends do."

"Then who is it? Sybil Barron and her rich-bitch Palm Beach crowd?" he snarled. "You feel you can't compete with them, is that it?"

She turned onto her side and covered her ears with her hands. No, she wanted to shout at him, it has nothing to do with Sybil Barron. It has to do with us, you and me, and the charade we've carried off so successfully for nearly thirteen years, and a faceless man I still don't have the courage to see and . . .

"Rhea?" Neil gently pulled one hand away from her ear.

"Rhea, what is it you want? Do you want to move to another house? Do you want a new car? A trip to a health spa or a cruise somewhere? Name it and I'll see that you get it. Please, Rhea."

Tears filmed her eyes and began to spill, one by one, down her face. She had never known how to ask for what she wanted before. How was she supposed to ask for it now, when she herself didn't even know what she really wanted?

chapter fifteen

THE EASTER gala that Nigel Amery catered for the Boca Country Club on April second worked with the precision smoothness of a dance number choreographed by Bob Fosse. The Englishman had obviously decided that there was less of a class difference between snobbish Palm Beach and upstart Boca Raton than Sybil Barron believed there to be, and he had provided the newer Boca club with as opulent a setting as any he had heretofore provided for the long-established Palms Club. He had transformed the clubhouse and the terrace around the swimming pool into a veritable floral bower, using only spring flowers ranging from palest lilac to deep purple and accenting them with lilies of the valley and white calla lilies. The floor-length tablecloths, the napkins, and the cushioned seats on the small gilt chairs arranged around the tables that had been set up for the midnight dinner were in a floral print of lilacs and mauves, while clusters of mauve, lavender, and lilac candles of varying heights and thicknesses lit up the night like an iridescent pastel rainbow. A local rock band providing dance music for the younger members of the club alternated throughout the evening with a nine-piece combo playing standards for the older mem-

159

bers; but as the evening progressed, the line between the two generations began to blur until it finally vanished altogether.

All of the Palm Beach newspapers had sent a reporter and a photographer to chronicle the much-heralded social event that threatened to eclipse the legendary annual Easter gala at the Palms Club. All of them, that is, except the *Standard*. In her determination not to be outdone, Sybil Barron had managed to upstage the Boca affair by holding her spectacular party the night before, and then using the entire four-page High Society section in the Saturday edition of the *Standard* to feature the event and the scores of luminaries—among them, a number of billionaire industrialists, some congressional leaders and their wives, and several members of Europe's few remaining royal families—attending it.

But tonight Sybil Barron's spiteful bid for social supremacy was the furthest thing from the minds of the one hundred and forty partying members of the Boca Country Club and their guests. What interested them most was having a good time. As their official hostess for the evening, Rhea felt it was her duty to ensure that they *did* have a good time. But she floated through the festivities like a disembodied spirit. She exchanged the requisite number of pleasantries with everyone, conferred on occasion with Nigel, and spent the time in between sweeping from room to room wearing a fixed smile, her gown of tiered gray chiffon billowing about her in gossamer waves.

Daye and Franki had spoken to her only briefly when they first arrived, and for the next few hours, they continued to exchange worried glances and voice concerns over their friend's puzzling behavior. The word *breakdown* seemed to hover unspoken in the air between them, casting a lengthening shadow across the evening they had both been determined from the outset to enjoy, in spite of their worry. Nestled contentedly in Jonathan's arms, her head resting against his shoulder, her own arms draped around his neck, Daye felt slightly guilty about being so happy when her dearest friend was so obviously *un*happy. Unaware of her mounting concern, Jonathan began to nuzzle Daye's ear with his mouth, making her shiver. She moved even closer to him, tightening her hold on him and struggling to banish all thoughts of Rhea from her mind.

As much as she kept trying to deny it, the advent of Jonathan

Cort into her life had given her a new sense of completeness. Although her days remained filled with her work, they were now bordered and defined by the times she spent with him, making any day that began and ended with him a far better day than one without him. In spite of the article on Philippe Nadeau in the *Standard*, the article that had appeared in *Condominium* magazine had finally brought her a number of new accounts, and Jonathan liked to tease her by insisting that *he* and not the article was responsible for the upturn in her career.

"Keep me around, Daye," he had advised her after she had told him the good news, "and I'll bring you even more luck."

"Luck had nothing at all to do with it," she had retorted with an exaggerated toss of her head. "It was talent, Jonathan, pure and simple. *My* talent."

"You mean you don't believe in wishing on stars or keeping four-leaf clovers or tossing pennies into fountains?"

Her voice was markedly subdued when she answered, "I most certainly do." And she had gone on to tell him about her childhood habit of wishing on a cloud, a secret she had never shared with anyone but Neil.

"Do you mind?"

It was Neil asking Jonathan if he could cut in. Daye watched with some dismay as Jonathan relinquished her and then wove a determined path through the crowd in the direction of the bar.

"Don't look so sad, Button; he'll be back."

Neil's strong, deep voice was something of a shock after Jonathan's mellow huskiness, and Daye found being in his arms somewhat disconcerting.

"You look radiant, Daye," he said, holding her away from him for a moment while he studied her in her long, backless halter dress of ivory and gold pleated crepe. "Could it be love?"

"Stop it, Neil." Her voice was snappish as he pulled her in against his chest again.

"Can't you accept it as a compliment and just say thank you?"

"Thank you."

"You *are* radiant, you know."

She felt as though his eyes were compelling her to respond to him, but she refused to be seduced by their persuasive pull.

Anxious to deflect the conversation away from the two of them, she said, "Don't you think Rhea's done a superb job here tonight?"

"Nigel Amery did it, my pet, not Rhea. Let's give credit where credit is due."

"Still, if she hadn't convinced him to—"

"You still babble when you're nervous, don't you, Daye?" He cut her off with a knowing smile.

"I—"

"See? You're doing it again." His smile widened as he said it, and that succeeded in disarming her completely.

"Brat!" She aimed a playful punch at his shoulder.

"Double brat!"

They danced awhile in silence after that, until Daye simply had to say, "I'm still worried about Rhea, Neil."

He rolled his eyes in obvious impatience with her, but his own voice showed his concern when he replied, "I've tried to reach her, but I can't. She refuses to admit that something's wrong."

"Can I do anything to help?"

He shrugged and got a firmer grip on her waist. "I doubt it. I think she's actually enjoying this, whatever it is. She's off on a cloud of her own somewhere, and she seems to be quite happy to stay there."

Daye began to move leadenly in his arms, her thoughts now more distracted than ever.

"Ouch!"

"Did I step on your toe?" she asked him.

"Damned right you did."

She laughed. "You're lucky you never danced with me at those awful classes I took when I was eleven. I had the dubious honor of dancing with the shortest boys in the class, and to pay them back for having to rest my chin on top of their heads, I would step on their toes as often as I could."

"Nice girl," he commented, dipping her with a grand flourish at the end of a slow tune and hearing her squeal with fright. "That's on behalf of all the short boys whose toes you stepped on," he told her when he lifted her back up again.

Her head was spinning, and she stumbled as she straightened up, nearly tripping over the hem of her gown. "God, I hate being dipped," she gasped, recovering slowly from the shock of his surprise maneuver. "I'm always convinced I'm going to be dropped."

His eyes were twinkling mischievously. "Care to try it a second time?" he asked.

"No, thank you." She held both hands out in front of her as she backed away from him.

He lunged after her, and she burst out laughing. Turning around, she bolted across the floor, slamming into Jonathan on his way back from the bar and stopping short at the sight of the thunderous look on his face.

"Well, you certainly seemed to be enjoying yourself out there with Mr. Howard," he remarked coldly. "I had to change my mind three times about interrupting the two of you."

"Were we dancing that long?" she asked him, aware of how rapidly her heart had begun to beat.

"I counted five dances, but then again it could have been six. At one point the band was playing a medley of—"

"Jonathan, we were only dancing!"

"So I noticed, but then, so did everyone else in the place. Very Arthur Murray of him, that dip. You should be thankful that no one from the *Standard* was here to capture it on film for posterity."

"I've never seen you like this." She put her hands on her hips and glared at him. "Are you drunk?"

"Drunk?" His blue eyes had darkened until they seemed more black than blue. "Don't be ridiculous."

"Then you're jealous." She watched with some amusement as his eyes lightened again. "Why, Jonathan Cort, you *are* jealous." She clamped both hands around one of his arms and snuggled up close to him. "I'm flattered."

He remained stony-faced as she continued in her attempts to pacify him.

"Jonathan?" she whispered up to him. "Jonathan, I'm cold."

"No wonder," he grunted. "You're half naked."

"That's not true," she pouted, "but I could be . . ." She allowed her voice to trail off suggestively.

"Do we have to discuss this in the middle of the dance floor?" He scowled, seizing her by the hand and hauling her after him.

"Leaving so soon?"

Daye groaned inwardly. Of all the times for Neil to intrude!

"Don't you have a wife around here someplace?" Jonathan demanded as the two men faced each other with Daye caught between them.

"I thought I did," answered Neil in a voice as silken as Jonathan's was rough, "but she's busy playing hostess tonight."

"Jonathan." Daye laid a placating hand on his arm again. "Why don't we go for a walk around the grounds?"

He responded by pulling his arm free and saying, "Perhaps Neil would like to come along, since he obviously has no one to keep him company at the moment."

"Jonathan!" Embarrassed now, she turned helpless eyes on Neil.

"Well, I hate to see two people having such a good time together, so if you'll both excuse me," he said, giving Daye a brisk peck on the cheek and nodding curtly to Jonathan before heading back across the floor again.

"That was very rude—"

"He certainly managed to—"

They both broke off in mid-sentence and stared at each other.

"There's something between you and Neil Howard, Daye," said Jonathan after a lengthy pause. "I sensed it the first time all of us were together, and nothing's happened since to change that impression."

She was not prepared to face this kind of accusation from Jonathan, so certain was she that nothing remained to even hint at what she had once felt for Neil. Evidently, she had been wrong. The hurt and accusing look in Jonathan's eyes was making a lie out of the best of her intentions. Reaching up to stroke his cheek, she said softly, "There's absolutely nothing between us, Jonathan. We're friends, old friends, and that's all we are."

"I don't believe you, Daye."

"I swear it's true."

"He's got the kind of hold on you that old friends simply don't have on each other. Either you're unaware of it or you're putting on a good act for my benefit."

"That's not fair!" she cried. "He *has* no hold on me. We've known each other for over twenty-five years, and maybe twenty-five years *does* give a person some kind of hold on the other. But he's not a Svengali, if that's what you're implying, and I'm not under any kind of hypnotic spell."

"Then perhaps I was wrong. Perhaps you're the one with the hold on *him*."

"Jonathan!" She was bristling with impatience now. "If you want me to accept the fact that you and Maren MacCaul are only friends, why can't you accept the same of Neil and me?"

His grin was almost sheepish as he replied, "For the same reason you're still not quite convinced about Maren MacCaul and me. You and I don't know each other well enough yet to really trust one another."

She was just about to respond to his remark when she caught sight of Franki and Brian heading their way. Brian was busily patting his damp forehead with his handkerchief while Franki was fanning her cleavage with her blue satin evening bag.

"It's definitely a sign of old age when you start collapsing after two disco numbers," she complained, leaning up against Brian while she eased off one of her shoes. "Whew, could I use some of Nigel's delicacies right about now."

"You're in luck, my sweet," replied Brian, as he squinted at his watch. "In precisely three minutes, you'll be able to sit down to dinner without looking either too plebeian or too unfashionably hungry."

Franki looked from Daye to Jonathan and then back at Daye. "Did we interrupt something here?"

Both Daye and Jonathan shook their heads.

"Not much," Franki scowled, slipping her shoe back on again and linking her arm through Brian's. "Come on, husband of mine, let's go act plebeian."

She blew Daye a parting kiss, and Daye gave her a halfhearted wave in return.

"Are you hungry?" asked Jonathan as soon as they were alone again.

Daye shook her head. She was far too upset to be hungry.

"Would you like to dance?"

Again she shook her head.

"What *do* you want, then?"

"I don't know," she admitted. "I think I'd just like to go home."

"Alone?"

She studied him for a moment while she considered the alternatives. She didn't really want to be alone, and yet, after the scene he had just caused, she wasn't sure she wanted to be with him either.

"Could you hold me for a moment?" she asked him, her eyes filling up with tears of confusion as she reached out to him.

He pulled her up against him and hugged her, brushing his lips back and forth across her forehead while he caressed her bare back with his hands.

"My beautiful Daye," he murmured, "there's still so much of the little girl in you, isn't there? Come, let me take you home."

He left her at the door of the condo with a good night kiss and nothing more. As she watched him leave, a wave of desolation washed over her, and she was convinced that she was never going to see him again. She lay awake for the rest of the night, leaving the house at six to go for a long walk on the beach. Alone with the seagulls, the incoming tide, and the rising sun, she didn't feel quite as despairing as she had a few hours earlier. She had a full day of work ahead of her with precious little time to waste dwelling on the follies of the night before. She still had her career, whether Jonathan Cort was in her life or not.

FRANKI SHIFTED nervously from one foot to the other while she waited for Daye to answer the door. Her heart was beating so wildly that she raised her brown alligator clutch a bit higher to cover her heart's telltale pulsing against her thin cashmere sweater. "Come on, come on," she chanted impatiently, tapping her fingers against the door frame. What was taking her so long? She was just about to ring again when a sleepy-looking Daye, her hair tousled, her dressing gown loosely sashed, opened the door and yawned apologetically as she motioned for her to come inside.

"My God, what took you so long?" Franki burst out before she could stop herself.

"Long?" Daye's bleary eyes began to widen. "I practically ran."

Franki glanced suspiciously at her friend. "You're alone, aren't you?"

"I'm alone."

"What's wrong?"

"Nothing, why?"

"You look terrible."

"Thank you."

"And you slept in," Franki pressed on. "I've never known you to sleep in on a work day."

"I didn't sleep in," Daye retorted, heading for the living room with Franki trailing after her. "I was already awake when you phoned, and all I did was lie down again for a while."

"Okay, okay, don't bite my head off. I suppose even the inexhaustible Daye Peters is allowed to sleep in without feeling guilty about it."

"Thank you again." Daye tried unsuccessfully to block another yawn as she sank onto one of the sofas and patted the place beside her. "Sit! I'm too tired to watch you pace."

Franki obliged her by perching on the edge of the sofa, both hands gripping her purse.

"You haven't heard from Jonathan, have you?" she asked.

Daye blinked. "How did you know?"

"I just know *you*, that's all."

"You're right, I haven't heard from him."

"It's only been two days."

"It feels more like two years."

"Let him sulk; he'll get over it. A little jealousy never hurt anyone."

"And you're speaking from experience, of course."

There was a provocative glimmer in Franki's eyes. "Of course."

Daye leaned her head back against the sofa, stretched out her legs, and crossed her arms over her chest. Staring down at her bare feet, she said, "Relationships are just too difficult, Franki. Why can't two people who like each other simply come together and enjoy themselves without there being confrontations all the time?"

"Because only clones don't have confrontations."

"You see? If that's true, then how can two very different people with their own personalities, their own private pasts, and their own way of doing things ever expect to get along?"

"The word is *work*."

"I work, but I consider it fun!"

"Not the same thing. Loving is hard work, Daye. Falling in love is the easy part; making it work is what's hard."

"And I'm not even in love," she sighed, covering her face with her hands, "and I don't think I want to be either. There's just too much hurt involved, too many ups and downs to play havoc with a person's equilibrium."

Franki took a deep breath. "How would you like to try another word?" she said.

Daye glanced over at her sharply.

"The word is *affair*," Franki said.

"You're having an affair."

Franki shook her head.

"You're thinking about having an affair."

This time Franki nodded.

"And?"

"And I hate to ask you this, but I need your help."

"What kind of help?"

Franki cleared her throat and met Daye's eyes squarely. "Could I borrow your place once or twice a week for an hour or two at a time? Daye, I'm desperate. I can't risk sneaking around to a motel or anything. I can't take the chance of having someone see us, and...Oh, damn, I'm not doing this very well." She stopped for a moment and drew several more deep breaths before continuing. "This will be the first affair I've had in all the years I've been married to Brian. I can't explain why it's happened now, but it has. Oh, Daye, I've been so restless, so bored and—"

"I don't want to hear any more," Daye said, getting up from the sofa and walking over to the sliding glass doors leading onto the balcony. "Give me a few minutes to think." She opened the door and stepped outside into the fresh sea air.

She shook out her hair and tried to clear her mind of everything but what Franki had just told her. At first, all she could think of was poor Brian. But then she thought about Franki and Taylor Mead, and she wondered why it had taken them so long. She nibbled worriedly at her bottom lip. She didn't want to judge Franki and what she intended to do, but she didn't know if she wanted to become involved in it either. To be an accomplice. To condone it. How would she ever be able to face Brian again if she agreed to help his wife sleep with another man?

She closed her eyes and rubbed the swollen lids with the tips of her fingers. Poor Franki. She had never looked more embarrassed or more uncomfortable than she had a moment ago. If she and Taylor used the condo, where would they make love? Daye found herself wondering. Her bedroom was out of the question, and it seemed almost sacrilegious to allow them to use the room that would have been her parents'.

She leaned against the balcony railing and dug her hands inside the pockets of her dressing gown. Seeing Franki still sitting on the edge of the sofa, her shoulders stooped, her head bowed as she clutched her purse to her chest, finally made up Daye's mind for her. Aching for her friend, she walked back into the living room and laid her hand gently on the top of Franki's blond head.

"All right, Franki," she said, "you can use the place."

Franki shuddered convulsively as the tension drained out of her body.

"Thank you, Daye," she whispered, looking up with her eyes brimming with tears.

"Once or twice a week, then?"

"Yes."

"Mornings or afternoons?"

"Afternoons."

"Will you let me know the morning before you plan to use the place?"

"Always."

Daye looked down at the floor, feeling awkward as she said, "If you don't mind, could you use the hide-a-bed in the den? I'd feel strange if you used my par . . . the guest room."

"The hide-a-bed?" Something flickered in Franki's eyes for a moment and then was gone. "Of course I don't mind. And Daye, you won't tell anyone, will you? Not even Rhea. It's just so chancy, I—"

"I won't tell anyone, I swear it. Now come, I'll give you a key."

"All keys look alike to me," Franki declared as Daye pressed the key into the palm of her hand. "I'm always using the house key to try to unlock the car door and breaking the car key trying to get it to open my locker at the club. So this time, I think I'll be clever about it. Do you have any nail polish?"

"Of course I do, why?"

"You'll see."

Daye led the way into the bathroom where she opened a drawer and withdrew a small plastic tray containing her various bottles of nail polish.

"Take your pick," she said, indicating the choice with a sweep of her hand.

Franki studied each bottle carefully and finally settled on Indian Red by Dior.

"I guess this is the closest I'll get to scarlet." She laughed as she began to coat the head of the key with the polish. "There's no way I'll ever get confused now."

Daye was laughing, too, in spite of herself. "Thank God for your sense of humor," she told her friend, giving her a hug. "Now I think I could use either a Valium or a drink."

"Make that a drink and I'll join you," said Franki, waving the key in the air to dry it, "and make it a double while you're at it. This is celebration time, you know. Your friend is about to earn herself a scarlet letter."

chapter sixteen

WHEN JONATHAN called her the following afternoon, he didn't mention the night of the Easter party, and neither did Daye. She kept waiting for him to tell her why he hadn't called since then, but when he made no attempt either to apologize or to explain, she decided against bringing it up and risking an answer she might not want to hear. She was so preoccupied with keeping the anxious edge out of her voice and her heart beating at a normal rate that his parting question caught her completely by surprise.

"Do you mean I'm actually being invited to the illustrious playwright's ocean retreat?" She tried to aim for a note of gaiety, but her voice sounded strained even to *her* ears.

"Can you think of a better place to read the illustrious playwright's latest masterpiece?"

"You finished the play!"

"I did."

"And you want me to read it?"

"I do."

For a moment, her giddy relief swept every clever response from her mind.

"I thought I'd throw in a tour of the premises as part of the deal," he continued, "and as an added feature, a home-cooked meal."

As soon as she recovered her voice, she quipped, "One of your many renowned bachelor dishes, no doubt?"

"No, as a matter of fact, it's a departure of sorts—lobster."

"Lob-ster," she repeated, sliding the word slowly off her tongue and following it with a long sigh of feigned ecstasy. "What time *is* this feast?" she asked.

"Come over right after work," he said.

That made her laugh. "Open-ended invitations like that are dangerous, Jonathan. You know that could mean midnight as easily as either six or seven."

"Well, whenever."

She found his nonchalance somewhat unsettling, as though he didn't care one way or the other what time she got there. But she immediately chided herself for reading her own doubts into his reply, and brushed her doubts aside.

"I'll get there as close to six as I can," she told him, "and I'll bring the wine."

She arrived at 14 Seaside Way in Gorham Sound at five minutes past six, a chilled bottle of B & G Chablis in one hand and in the other, as a result of a last-minute impulse, a long white florist's box containing an assortment of anthurium lilies, calla lilies, and birds-of-paradise. She was wearing an ivory raw silk tunic over a pair of matching slacks, and a heavy rope of large coral, ivory, and tiger-eye beads was wrapped twice around her neck. It was an outfit she usually found very comfortable, but now that she was standing on the porch outside his house, shaking with nervous anticipation, she could feel her top beginning to stick to her back and her necklace cutting off the air supply to her lungs.

"Daye!"

He was standing there in the open doorway in black cords and a pale yellow crewneck sweater, wearing only one black loafer while the other dangled in his hand.

"You sound surprised," she remarked, instantly on the defensive. "It was *your* invitation, remember?"

His eyes crinkled as he laughed at her brusqueness. "How could I not remember? It's just that I didn't expect you to tear yourself away from your work so soon." He gave her a quick kiss on the mouth. "I'm the one who's flattered now."

She flushed at his veiled reference to the remark she had made the other night and held out the wine and the flowers to him as though they were peace offerings. He slid his left foot into his shoe and accepted her gifts as he motioned for her to come inside.

"I thank you for these," he said, leading her toward the kitchen. "Let me put the wine on ice and the flowers in some water, and I'll take you on that tour I promised you."

The house was laid out just as he had described it to her. It was a large, comfortable one-story sprawl of gray fieldstone, glass, and cedar, nestled among towering Norfolk pines, dense clumps of seagrapes, and clusters of pink and white oleanders. Furnished in corduroys and suedes in a palette of beige, slate gray, and pale blue, it was restful and yet surprisingly dynamic at the same time. The beige walls were hung with bold geometric prints and large, dramatic wool tapestries, and the vast living room, with its cathedral ceiling and back wall of floor-to-ceiling glass overlooking the ocean, was dominated by two black Steinway grand pianos, set facing each other, so that they were interlocking.

"I always liked the effect of having the pianos linked together that way," explained Jonathan, giving the one nearest him a loving pat. "The two of them combined to form a very special kind of wood sculpture, and so when Rolf and I split up, I bought his piano from him and kept them just as they were."

She was moved by his tender sentimentality, and a lump of sadness rose inside her throat. Going up to him, she slipped her arms around his waist and hugged him, hoping that by this simple gesture, she could show him that she understood.

They ate their dinner at a long redwood table on the flagstone terrace off the living room. The terrace itself extended out to the dune line, and after a narrow strip of sandy beach came the sea, which was calmly rolling breaker after breaker up to the shore and then greedily drawing each one of them back again. Crickets chirped in the long grasses of the dunes, a tree frog croaked in a nearby banyan, and the occasional moth fluttered up to one of the hurricane lamps positioned around the terrace, as if to investigate the candle flickering inside its fat glass globe.

"It's so peaceful here," sighed Daye, draining the last of her wine and gazing thoughtfully at the shells of the four lobsters they had eaten, piled high inside the wooden bowl in the center of the table. "I can see why you chose to leave New York and live here instead."

"You can?" His dark eyes were skeptical, but she rose swiftly to meet the challenge she read in them.

"Of course I can. Most people see New York as a cannibal. It devours life, while a place like this is restorative; it gives life back. You're very fortunate, Jonathan. If you wanted to, you could have the best of each of these two very different worlds. With Gorham Sound to come home to, you could cope much more easily with the demands of a city like New York. This place would always be the safety valve, the security blanket, the stop you would make to recharge your energy force before stepping out to do battle again."

Jonathan put down the fork he had been toying with and reached out for her hand. "You're quite a remarkable woman, Daye Peters," he said, "quite remarkable." He took each of her fingers in turn and kissed them gently before laying her hand back down on the table again and covering it with his.

With his eyes so warm on her face, Daye retreated inside her own head for a moment, admitting to herself what she would never dare admit to him. That his house was ideally suited to the kind of relationship she had come to envisage for herself one day. It was a relationship that would enable two people to live equally but separately together. With each one's physical space so clearly defined, they could live with a maximum of emotional and creative freedom, coming together only when it was mutually agreed on by both of them. That way neither one would suffocate or risk being suffocated by the other. Love could flourish without being stifled by overcrowding of any kind. Love. The very word brought her up short, and she began timidly backing away from her own romantic fantasy.

After coffee, Jonathan led her into the library, sat her down on the slate gray corduroy sofa, and thrust a bound manuscript into her hands.

"Enough fun," he said with a wry chuckle. "Now, down to work. While you read, I'm going to go outside and pace like an expectant father." Even while he was talking, he was edging his way to the door. "Don't be afraid to use a mental blue pencil on it, Daye. I'm counting on you to be honest with me."

When she opened the typed manuscript and saw the title *Arpeggio in Blue* with the name Jonathan Cort under it, a tremor of excitement rippled through her. God, she prayed, please let it be good. Please let me love it. She was plunged into the emotional drama and loyally bound to the two principal characters and their bittersweet love by the time she reached the bottom of the second page. Each of the fourteen songs, which Jonathan had promised to play for her once she had read through the entire script, smoldered with the yearning beauty of that love, and in the middle of the song entitled "Turn Away from Loving," Daye began to cry. She wept off and on through the next three songs, but when she finally reached the end of the play, she was smiling again, laughing in fact, as much from relief as from satisfaction. Not only was she silently applauding the two principal characters, but she was also applauding Jonathan. *Arpeggio in Blue* couldn't be anything less than a smash hit!

Sitting next to him on the piano bench, hearing him sing the lyrics she had just finished reading, Daye was doubly affected by their strong yet whimsical beauty. When he played the final song for her, she threw her arms around his neck and just managed to choke out, "The play is magnificent, Jonathan," before bursting into fresh tears all over again.

"No blue pencil?" he asked while he gently stroked her hair.

"No blue pencil," she sniffed.

She heard him sigh and felt his shoulders sag for a moment before he straightened up again. Then, without saying another word, he got up from the bench and held his hand out to her. She took it and let him pull her to her feet. Lifting her into his arms, he carried her into his bedroom and made love to her until the sun reminded them that it was time for her to leave.

She drove home in a state of numbed exhilaration. Her body was one muted, stinging sensation, her skin was a tissue of bruised contentment, while her mind was balanced somewhere between dreaming and reality, unable to decide in which of

the two realms it belonged. It was only after she had closed
the door to the apartment and was hurrying into her bedroom
to change her clothes that she was shaken out of her state of
glorious bewilderment at last. The Lalique crystal vase filled
with pink roses, blue irises, and mauve and purple lilacs and
standing on top of one of the stylish white Formica dressers
wasn't hers. And then she remembered. Franki had used the
condo for the first time the previous afternoon.

She immediately set off on a hasty inspection of each room.
Her eyes darted about, looking for some sign of intrusion, but
she found none. She sniffed the air for some lingering trace of
either his cologne or her perfume or for the telltale scent of
their lovemaking. There was none. She felt slightly foolish for
making such a search, but she was more than a little relieved
to find the house exactly as she had left it. Except, of course,
for the stunning vase and the flowers so thoughtfully chosen
to match their surroundings.

She felt herself humming as she ran the water for a bath,
and she wondered if she would be haunted forever by the
melody and the words to the song from *Arpeggio in Blue* that
had touched her most: "Turn Away from Loving." Even as she
was humming it, she could feel her eyes starting to burn. She
angrily brushed the tears away before they could slip past her
lashes. She had nothing to cry about, absolutely nothing at all.

RHEA LAID the heavy book down on her writing table and leaned
back in her chair, rubbing her tired eyes with both hands. The
technical terms Dr. Henri Bauer had used in his final chapter
of *The Child in the Mind's Eye* swam around and around inside
her brain like a school of maddened fish. Pressing her fingertips
to her throbbing temples, she tried to put into her own words
what the eminent Swiss psychiatrist had expressed succinctly
but clinically in this, his fifth book on the subject of mental
illness in children.

Of all the books she had read over the past few weeks,
including several by Robert Coles and Bruno Bettelheim, she
found Dr. Bauer's the most helpful. Little by little she was
coming to know the boy in the pastel hanging above her writing
table, piecing together for herself a composite of the man he

probably was today. She checked the date on the white slip glued on the last page of the book and saw that it, along with the others, was due back at the Delray Beach Public Library in two days. Stacking the books on the dresser beside her purse, she congratulated herself for having taken only five days to read all three of them.

Driven by her growing compulsion to know her brother Steven, Rhea had continued to withdraw from her own familiar world in order to lose herself in his. It had shocked her to discover that the two of them had been leading almost frighteningly parallel lives. Both of them had been sheltered and protected by others, with most of life's major decisions being made for them, while they themselves had done little more than simply exist.

"I'm considering doing some volunteer work at the hospital in Boca," she announced that evening during one of her infrequent dinners with Neil.

As he glanced up from his poached salmon, his look was one of complete disbelief. "What brought this on?" he inquired. "You've never shown the slightest interest in volunteer work before. Don't you remember all the times you were asked to join the Women's Auxiliary at the hospital and you refused? Hospitals made you nervous, you said. Why the sudden change?"

Rhea straightened out the napkin in her lap and lowered her eyes. "It isn't exactly sudden, Neil," she murmured. She felt like a child having to explain herself to her teacher. "I've been thinking about it for some time now."

He nodded his head in sudden understanding. "So that explains all the books lying around the place," he said. "But for God's sake, Rhea, if you have to choose something, couldn't you at least pick something a little less depressing than the psycho ward?"

She could feel herself stiffening. "They don't call them psycho wards anymore," she snapped. "There's been more progress in the field of mental health than in most other fields combined."

"You sound like an authority on the subject."

"I'm getting to be," she muttered more to herself than to him.

Neil's laugh was harsh as he said, "To tell you the truth,

Rhea, I never pictured you as the Florence Nightingale type.
But what I'd like to know is whether you get to wear designer
uniforms or will just any old uniform do?"

The heat was rising in her cheeks. How dare he mock her!
She balled her napkin and threw it down on the table. Then
she got up and walked quickly out of the room. Charging up
the stairs, her hand gripping the banister for support, she bit
down hard on her trembling bottom lip to keep from crying.
In spite of his remarks, she could hardly blame Neil for reacting
as he had. He didn't know about Steven.

She glanced at her wristwatch, and when she saw that she
still had time to get to the library before it closed, she scooped
up her purse along with the three books and started back down
the stairs.

"Rhea?"

She heard Neil call out to her from the dining room, but
she only quickened her steps.

"Rhea, where the hell are you going?"

She paused at the front door and called back to him the
answer he had come to expect from her. "I'm going shopping!"
Then she ran out of the house and slammed the door behind
her.

DAYE'S THIRTY-FOURTH birthday was ten days away. She read
the date, May 10, on the front page of the *Sun Sentinel* and
automatically checked off on her fingers the months already
gone. It now required both hands to count them. She was
incredulous. Nearly six months had passed, leaving her with
the feeling that professionally, she was still treading water. Of
course there was enough work to keep both herself and Connie
busy, but that one major project still eluded her, and she remained convinced that without it, she would never become
established in Palm Beach. Philippe's progress on the
redecoration of Sybil Barron's home, so faithfully charted and
photographed in the Better Living section of the *Standard* each
Saturday, had become a chronic irritant she had learned to
ignore. But on those days when she was feeling particularly
frustrated, it reminded her of how far behind she really was.

"More toast?"

She had almost forgotten Jonathan was there. With an apologetic smile, she looked up at him and shook her head. The slice of toast she had buttered ten minutes ago was still lying untouched on her plate. Jonathan. Repeating his name to herself made her smile widen. After he had sent his play off to his agent in New York, they had fallen into the comfortable pattern of seeing each other two or three times a week, alternating their nights between his house and hers. They often began and ended those nights by riding their bicycles along one of the many bike paths at sunset and walking the beach at sunrise, while filling the hours in between with the sweetness of their lovemaking.

She should have been content, but she had been growing increasingly lonelier as one week slid into the next. She missed her two closest friends, and the fact that the three of them had been drifting apart left her deflated and sad. She had finally abandoned her attempts to remain in daily contact with Rhea, whom she hadn't seen since the Easter party, and their telephone calls had dwindled down to a brief and unsatisfying chat once a week. Although she spoke to Franki more often, she seldom saw her. Franki was now practicing with Taylor every day for the annual tennis tournament to be held at the Palms Club in August, and using the condo two afternoons a week.

"I think I'll throw myself a birthday party," she suddenly decided, announcing it to Jonathan and feeling somewhat hopeful again.

"With balloons and a birthday cake and presents, the works?" he teased her, setting his part of the paper down and giving her a wink.

"I'll settle for just the presents," she tossed back at him. "It'll be small, only the six of us. Maybe if we're all together again, even for a few hours, we . . ." her voice began to fade until it died away completely.

Glaring up at her from the Goings On column of the *Sentinel* was a photograph of Jonathan with one arm draped around Maren MacCaul's shoulder. Daye's stomach heaved. She felt herself being gripped by a spasm resembling a wave of seasickness, which pitched her upward and then slammed her back down again, while she remained rigid and unmoving in her chair. Through a gathering cloud of tears, she studied the man seated across from her at the table on the balcony of her home. Cursing him for being an intruder at that moment, she wished she could find the strength to tell him to leave.

"Is something wrong?"

Daye ignored him and looked down at the photograph again. The caption underneath it explained that the two of them had been attending a party to celebrate the four years that Maren had now owned the Gorham Sound Playhouse.

"Daye, what's the matter?"

He got up and went over to her. Putting both hands on her shoulders, he leaned down to plant a kiss on the side of her neck. One of her trembling fingers pointed to the photo, and she could feel him tense.

"When was this taken?" she asked him, her voice cracking.

"The night before last."

"You look very cozy together."

"We all had something very special to celebrate, Daye. Everyone at that party looked just as cozy together."

"I don't think I care for the tone you're using, Jonathan," she said, shrugging him away from her.

"And I don't particularly care for yours."

He sat down in his chair again, folded his arms across his chest, and proceeded to stare out at the ocean.

"Why couldn't you have taken me to the party, Jonathan?" she asked him.

"Because it was Maren's party and—"

"And Maren wouldn't have approved!"

"And it was only for members of the cast and crew and their families."

"I see."

"Daye, don't be jealous," he pleaded, finally turning to look at her again. "I wasn't excluding you from anything that vital. The playhouse has meant a great deal to me these past four years, and at one time Maren was very important to me as well. But that was over long before I met you, Daye, long before *us*." Although he had emphasized the word *us*, Daye refused to be mollified.

"She's still in love with you, isn't she, Jonathan?"

He let his breath out slowly and shrugged. "I really don't know," he said.

"Are you sure you're not still in love with her?"

"No!" He was emphatic as he shook his head. "I love her the way one will always love a dear and special friend, but no, Daye, I'm not still in love with her."

He scraped back his chair and stood up again. "It's late," he said. "I'd better let you get to work."

She found little solace in her work that morning. All she seemed capable of doing was leaning back in her chair with her legs stretched out and her hands locked behind her head while she stared up at the ceiling. Why was it, she asked herself, that whenever things were running smoothly, something always happened to shake you up again, to keep you from getting too comfortable or feeling too confident? She hated being jealous. She despised possessiveness in anyone but especially in herself. And yet, the slightest doubt was like an itch, starting small and then spreading until it was *all* you could feel.

Connie's curly head popped up in the doorway. "Neil Howard's on the line. It's the second time he's called this morning."

Daye lunged for the phone, her heart pounding, bracing herself for some grim news about Rhea.

"What's wrong?" she immediately blurted out to a startled and silent Neil.

"Why does there have to be something wrong?" he asked her after a moment's hesitation.

"You're not calling about Rhea?"

"Rhea? Why would I be calling you about Rhea? Sorry to disappoint you, my pet, but I'm calling about some work I'd like you to do for me."

"Work?" Now it was her turn to be surprised.

"I'm considering redecorating my offices," he explained. "How would you like the job?"

She was so relieved that nothing had happened to Rhea that she had missed most of what he was saying.

"Daye, are you interested in the work or not?"

She blinked and tried to concentrate. "Yes, I think so. I mean—"

"I'm talking about redoing eleven executive suites, two

waiting rooms, four washrooms, and a boardroom. In other words, the entire top floor of the Tolbert Building on Federal Highway."

"Are you offering me this job out of pity, Neil Howard?" she demanded. "You just moved into the Tolbert Building two years ago."

"Pity is hardly the way I operate," he said with a chuckle. "I have an image to maintain, Daye. Money attracts money, success attracts success; you know that. No signs of tarnishing allowed on the mighty Gold Coast. Too many hungry climbers trying to knock you down from the top, and I intend to stay on top. But you not only have to be the best, you have to look the best. And that means no fraying upholstery, no stained carpets, and no cigarette burns on the tables. So, yes or no?"

"Give me a few minutes to think it over, and I'll get back to you."

"How many minutes is a few?"

"Neil!"

"Okay, okay. Good-bye."

She sat back in her chair again, tapping the end of a green felt-tip pen against her front teeth, and tried to think clearly. Did Neil really have to redecorate his offices or was he just being kind? Neil, kind? Devious, perhaps, but kind? Hardly. Why now, though? She tossed her pen down in disgust. Why did there have to be an ulterior motive behind what he was doing? She hadn't seen the offices since he first moved into them. Perhaps they *were* shabby and in need of a complete change. She would go over to the Tolbert Building and have a look at them for herself. And *then* she would decide. Still, she mused, as she picked up her pen again, it *was* a good commercial account and one she would be a fool to turn down.

She was still agitated a half-hour later. On impulse, she picked up the phone and dialed Jonathan's number. She was restless, and she was hungry. She would take him to lunch if he was free. She needed to speak to him, to be with him, if for no other reason than to reassure herself that everything was still good between them.

"Hello?"

Daye froze. There was no mistaking that gravelly voice.

"Hello!"

It was Maren.

Daye hung up and put her head in her hands. They're friends, she repeated over and over to herself. They're only friends, working friends. She knew they were putting together another revue for the playhouse. Maren had every right to be there with Jonathan.

Before she quite realized what she was doing, Daye had grabbed the phone again and was dialing Neil's private number. As soon as he answered, she said, "Mr. Howard, you've just hired yourself a designer. Now, how about taking me to lunch so that we can discuss exactly what you want."

chapter seventeen

OVER THE next few weeks, Daye devoted most of her time to Neil's project while entrusting Connie with much of the work for her other clients. Because of Neil's numerous press contacts, lengthy articles describing the refurbishing of one of south Florida's most sumptuously elegant real estate development offices dutifully appeared in the major Miami, Ft. Lauderdale, and Palm Beach newspapers. Partway into the project, Daye was featured in prestigious *Office Style* magazine and given a lavish three-page spread in *Boca Life*. It didn't take the business community long to respond to the flurry of favorable publicity. Suddenly Daye Peters was someone in whom a number of major corporations were interested. There was a Lear jet to be decorated for one of them, a yacht for another, an executive suite for a third, the penthouse of a vice-president for a fourth. Daye delightedly accepted all assignments and then quickly hired a second assistant.

"You, my darling Neil, may have just turned out to be the opportunity I've been waiting for," she bubbled excitedly as they left Worrells in the Royal Poinciana Plaza where they had finally selected sofas for three of the executive suites she was currently working on.

"So now it's darling Neil, is it?" He pretended to glower at her while he tucked her hand through his arm and gave it a couple of light pats. "To think that it's taken you all these years to appreciate me again." He sighed and balefully rolled his eyes for her. "Ah, Daye, Daye," he murmured, "it breaks my heart when I think of all the time we've wasted."

She slapped at him with her free hand and laughed. "Don't think of it as wasted, silly, consider it as merely preparation."

There was a wicked gleam in his eye as he turned and leered at her, and a sudden tightening in her throat convinced her that he had misinterpreted what she had just said. In a hasty bid to clarify herself, she added, "Professionally speaking, of course."

"Of course," he agreed, giving her hand another friendly pat.

They arrived at her car, and he held the door open for her. "It's already five," he said. "Why don't we stop someplace for a drink? I have an eight o'clock flight to New York, and my bag's already in the trunk of my car, so I'm all set to go."

"But won't Rhea be expecting you for dinner?"

"Rhea's never expected me for dinner."

Daye flushed and looked away.

"Didn't I tell you," he continued, "that your friend and my wife is now working as a volunteer three mornings a week at the hospital in Boca? In the psychiatric ward, no less."

"She is?" Daye reacted with the same mixture of surprise and pleasure she had felt when she learned of Rhea's painting, only this time there was a wistful sadness attached to it.

"I can see the two of you are as close as ever."

She hung her head, hoping he wouldn't see the hurt in her eyes.

"Sorry, Button, that wasn't very kind of me."

His hand ruffled the hair spilling forward over her face, and his voice was gentle. "Come on, Daye. Let me buy you a drink."

Happy hour was well under way by the time they arrived at Elephant Walk in the Glades Plaza in Boca. There was the usual bottleneck of people blocking the narrow entrance as they fought their way toward the bar, and it seemed that the paddle fans suspended from the ceiling had already lost out in their bid to stir the smoke-laden air that hung over the bar like a thick gray cloud.

"Whose idea was this anyway?" Daye called up to Neil above the blare of the Eagles singing "Hotel California."

"You were the one who said Ta-boo was for old people, remember?"

"But this place goes too far in the opposite direction. It's for teenyboppers."

"Think young, Daye, just think young."

She watched him eyeing one of the nubile young bartenders in her skimpy black leotard covered by a six-inch draping of black material that passed for a skirt.

"But not quite that young," she admonished him, tugging at the sleeve of his jacket.

"Spoilsport," he grumbled, but he was laughing as he said, "let's find ourselves a table, shall we?"

The hostess seated them at a corner table with matching high wicker peacock chairs and an unobstructed view of the lushly planted tropical garden outside the restaurant's glass walls. They ordered banana daiquiris and then decided on a basket of fried chicken fingers to snack on.

"Did your friend Jonathan tell you that I've been trying to persuade Maren MacCaul to sell me the playhouse in Gorham Sound?"

Neil had posed the question so casually that Daye almost choked on her drink.

"No, he didn't," she gasped as she tried to catch her breath.

"In back of the playhouse she's got five acres of land that aren't being used, and I know exactly what should be done with them. I intend to build twelve exclusive town houses on that land along with a clubhouse and two tennis courts. I've already had an architect draw me up some preliminary sketches, and they're superb. Think of it, Daye. You'd have a couple of models to decorate. Does the idea appeal to you at all?"

"Of course it does. It sounds wonderful," she admitted, "but aren't you being a bit premature? I thought the Llewelyn Corporation was interested in that land."

"They are, but I'm offering her more than they are."

"Then what seems to be the problem?"

"Dear Miss MacCaul doesn't want me to tear down the playhouse. If she agrees to sell me the land, she wants me to guarantee that I'll keep the playhouse and build everything else around it. She's crazy."

"Perhaps it isn't as farfetched as it seems," Daye commented after a moment's consideration. "Clubhouses and tennis courts are so conventional these days, but how many exclusive enclaves can boast having their own theater on the premises?"

"Whose side are you on anyway, hers or mine?"

"Neither. I'm just trying to play devil's advocate here."

She jumped as Neil startled her by leaning across the table and seizing her hand. "It's team time again, my dear Miss Peters," he said, lowering his voice to a conspiratorial whisper. "I want you to work on Jonathan Cort, convince him to get Maren to sell out to me. Then once the deal's concluded, she'll undoubtedly move away from here. She'll have her money, I'll have the land, and you'll have Jonathan. All of us end up getting exactly what we want."

"Ever the devious schemer, aren't you, Mr. Howard?" Her tone was slightly teasing, but the prospect of Maren MacCaul leaving Gorham Sound was most appealing to her.

"Well?" he prodded her. "Are we a team or aren't we?"

The way he was looking at her, the pressure of his hand on hers, and his use of the word *team* all conspired to send a rush of painful memories spilling into the space between them. She swallowed hard, as though the simple act of swallowing could force those feelings down again and return them to the place in her past where they rightfully belonged. She had no answer for him at that moment, and in a muted voice she told him so.

"Oh, Christ, not again!"

His outraged snarl brought her head up sharply, just in time for the flashbulbs to catch her full in the face. Neil was out of his seat and lunging for the photographer before Daye even realized that he had let go of her hand. But the man was small and wiry and obviously well practiced in the art of scrambling away from irate subjects. He slipped out of Neil's grasp with infuriating ease and melted into the throng standing like a human wave between the tables, the bar, and the door.

Still fuming, Neil straightened his tie, pushed his hair back out of his eyes, and scraped his chair up to the table again.

"So the octopus has its tentacles down here in Boca, too," he growled. "How many times will this make now? Four?"

"Six," she supplied grimly.

"Six times our picture has appeared in that damned rag of hers! If photographs alone were sufficient grounds for divorce, I'd be divorced by now."

"Has Rhea been very upset by them?"

"You know Rhea, she doesn't even tell you how she feels about the goddamn weather!"

But Jonathan told Daye exactly how *he* felt about her appearing so frequently with Neil in the Town Tattler column of the *Standard* when they drove into Boynton the following evening. *Casablanca* was playing at the Imperial, and they had promised themselves that the next time the film was shown anywhere in south Florida, they would see it together.

"With all of your socializing, Daye, I'm surprised you can still find some time to work for the man." Jonathan's tone was scathing, his eyes fixed straight ahead of him, as he sat, tense and angry, behind the wheel. "But what really astounds me is the time *he* finds to follow you about while you look at swatches of fabric and paint samples."

"Are you quite through?" she demanded, her teeth clenched, her own voice frosty.

"No, as a matter of fact, I'm not. I—"

"Would you prefer me to hire someone to photograph me at my drafting table, Jonathan? I could hang a large clock on the wall behind me, and you could see for yourself just how many hours I *do* spend working, not only for *the* man, but for several other clients as well."

That seemed to finish the discussion. Neither of them spoke again, either in the car or later in the theater. Daye remained distracted throughout the entire film; Jonathan was distant and aloof. She longed for him to put his arm around her, to hold her hand or just simply rest his hand on her knee, but he didn't. From time to time, she would glance sideways at his face, see how stubbornly his jaw was still set, and yearn to stroke his cheek and feel the tense muscles relax beneath her touch. But she held herself back.

Jonathan's hands were now resting lightly on the arms of his seat. As Daye studied them, knowing so well the gentle strength they possessed, she suddenly found herself recalling how Neil's hand had felt when he had closed it so warmly over hers before the flashbulbs exploded and he had snatched it away again. She remembered, too, that she had never given him the answer he had been waiting for. She shifted in her seat and crossed her legs. What answer *would* she have given him, she wondered, if that photographer hadn't interrupted them?

She nudged Jonathan's right ankle with the toe of her shoe. He responded by immediately moving his foot away. Chagrined, she crossed her legs the other way and folded her arms over her chest. Don't shut me out, Jonathan, she silently pleaded with him. Don't play this kind of game with me. It's dangerous, and I don't want to start thinking about something I never wanted to think about again.

"Jonathan," she leaned over and whispered in his ear, "Jonathan, I'm cold."

Without looking at her, he took off his tweed jacket and draped it over her shoulders. She was raging at him inside. That wasn't what she had wanted at all! She glared at him, resisting the urge to throw his jacket to the floor and stomp on it.

When he drove her straight home after the film, Daye left him outside the door to the lobby without even saying good night. She undressed quickly and flung herself across her bed, knowing all too well that she would never be able to fall asleep. She grabbed one of her pillows and crushed it to her chest. Grinding her hips into the mattress and imagining some phantom lover lying underneath her, she tried to grind away some of the frustration she felt. If only Jonathan had relented and spoken to her. If only he had touched her. If only . . . She tried to picture him lying beside her, but she couldn't conjure up a clear image of his face. It was a blur, a disturbing combination of deep blue eyes and turquoise eyes and silver blond hair and hair the color of ebony. The features were confused, distorted, running together like a watercolor that has been hung before the paints have dried.

Oh God, she prayed as she began to cry, please don't let it start all over again.

* * *

FRANKI ROLLED over onto her back and sighed. The place beside her in bed was still warm, but he had already dressed and gone, leaving her to clean away the traces of their loving alone. It was only fair, she reasoned, he'd gotten there first today, letting himself in with the duplicate key she had had made for him, and had pulled out the bed and put the champagne on ice for them. She stretched, fluttering her hands high above her head, feeling the relaxing tingle spread all the way down to her toes. She was sated and deliciously content. God, what an incredible lover he had turned out to be. She massaged that gently throbbing place between her legs, kneading the soreness away, and recalling, with a husky trill of laughter, the three assaults it had withstood so hungrily and so well in just under two hours.

"Little Francine Dunn." She smiled as she got up to remake the bed. "The shame of it all. Who would have thought you'd actually do it one day?"

She stood naked in front of the three-way mirror in the guest bathroom as she always did before getting dressed again, and studied herself with a critical eye for several minutes. Did it show? she wondered. Did the effects of their lovemaking leave a mark on her face or on her body that she couldn't see? Did Brian even suspect? If he did, it would only be because she had finally stopped begging him to make love to her more often. The books were right, she decided; an extramarital affair definitely made the marriage easier, much easier.

As she watched her reflection in the mirror brushing out her short hair, she admitted to herself and to the mirror that she had never looked better. There was a glow about her now, a clear radiance to her skin. But more than that, there was an added ripeness to her body which convinced her that her entire being was responding to his loving like a plant awakening to the sun after a long winter's hibernation.

She dressed and slowly checked the den once more. It was immaculate. Then, as if to reassure herself that it was still there, she went into the kitchen and opened the refrigerator door. Yes, there it was, the magnum of Mumm's they had decided to buy Daye even though it was *their* anniversary. Franki hugged herself and grinned. Two glorious months already flown. God, why hadn't she thought of it sooner?"

After one final sweep of the apartment, she double-locked the door and zipped her key into the tiny mirror compartment of her purse. As she headed toward the elevators, she wished, for one foolish moment, that she had learned how to whistle. She felt like whistling right now, but she couldn't. This would be her project with Matthew, she suddenly decided, stepping into the elevator and pressing the button for the garage. She was taking Matthew and Caroline to the Red Lobster for dinner at six, and she vowed that by the time she brought them home, she would know how to whistle.

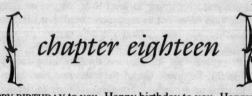

chapter eighteen

"Happy birthday to you, Happy birthday to you, Happy birthday, dear Rhea, Happy birthday to you."

Rhea smiled into the receiver. "Thank you, Daye," she murmured as a rush of tears filled her eyes. Exactly one month separated the two of them, and Daye had been phoning to sing her Happy Birthday for twenty-one years now, using the same little girl's voice as when she had first sung it to her at the age of thirteen.

"Happy thirty-fourth, Rhee!" Daye's exuberance sounded forced even to her. "Any special plans to celebrate?"

"No, not really," was Rhea's muted reply.

"Well, it certainly is comforting to have someone else around who's as old as I am."

"I suppose." Rhea shrugged.

"I considered throwing a party for myself last month, but it never materialized. Too much work, I guess. Now I'm sorry I didn't, because I keep thinking about all those presents I missed out on, not to mention—"

"Daye, is everything all right? You sound so, I don't know, so . . ."

193

"Dammit, Rhea, I miss you!" Daye's voice was quavering now. "What *is* it, what's happened between us? Was it something I did or something I should have done? Have I been too unavailable for you or too pushy? Is it because of those stupid photographs of Neil and me? Or—"

"It's not you, Daye," Rhea assured her. "It's not you at all. It's me."

"*What's* you?" Tears thickened Daye's voice as she struggled to continue. "Twenty years is too long to have a friend without putting up a fight to keep that friend. And I intend to keep you, Rhee."

"I've had things to do, Daye," she said vaguely, "things that don't involve anyone but myself."

"But are you ever going to want to be part of us again?"

Her question came out as a plaintive wail, but Rhea had no answer to it yet. She was still too confused and too preoccupied with the business of finding her own answers. How could she explain to anyone that for the first time in thirty-four years, she felt useful, far more useful than she had ever been as a friend, a wife, or a mother? For the first time in her life she was giving, giving to those who had nothing to give either to themselves or to others; knowing that in a special setting in upstate New York, some caring stranger was doing the same for her brother Steven. How could she explain that even *she* didn't know where this new discovery would ultimately lead her?

"Rhea, I'm here if you ever need me," were Daye's parting words to her.

"Daye?"

It was too late. All Rhea could hear now was the dial tone, leaving her with an unanswered question of her own. Daye, she wanted to ask, are you and Neil having an affair? The affair itself wouldn't have hurt her, because she would have expected that of Neil, but Daye's betrayal of their friendship would have devastated her. And so, for the moment, she was thankful that she didn't know.

"Rhea?"

Neil was standing in the bedroom doorway, knotting his tie and considering her with a thoughtful expression. She got up from the chaise and straightened the cushions she had been leaning on and waited for him to say whatever was on his mind.

"Are you sure you won't change your mind about dinner tonight?" he finally asked her.

She shook her head. "I'd really prefer having dinner at home."

"All right, then, I'll cancel the reservations." He buttoned his blazer and adjusted his tie. "I don't understand you anymore, Rhea. No party this year, no dinner out, not even one single charge at Saks or Gucci for all those little birthday treats you always liked to buy yourself. You sure you're the Rhea Bellon I married?"

"Is that a rhetorical question or one you'd like me to answer, Neil?"

Her retort caught him unprepared. For a moment, he simply stood there in the doorway and stared at her. Then he tossed something into the air and watched it land directly at her feet. She glanced down at the set of keys lying on the beige carpet and then gazed back up at him again.

"The Rhea Bellon I married always wanted a Mercedes. God only knows what this one wants. Happy birthday, Rhea, whoever you are."

FRANKI SIGNALED the bartender for another vodka martini and downed it in four burning gulps. Then she nibbled her way through the three tiny pimiento-stuffed olives skewered on the red plastic swizzle stick and waited for the numbness to set in. She had been a mass of vibrating nerve endings since reeling out of Dr. Stein's office an hour ago, and what she craved now was the numbing peace only the vodka could give her while she tried to get used to the idea of being pregnant.

"Congratulations, Mrs. Dunn," the young doctor had said. "You're nearly two months gone."

Gone. What an absurd term for it. But she suddenly found some humor in the remark and laughed out loud. Easy come, easy go. He had come and she was gone. She laughed again and waved her empty glass at the bartender, who gave her one of those do-you-really-think-you-should? looks. *Damned right I should!* She glared belligerently at him and dared him to refuse her. He didn't. He set another vodka martini down on the bar in front of her, took the ten dollar bill she handed him, and rang up three fifty on the register.

Of all the sleazy corners of Ft. Lauderdale, she had certainly picked the sleaziest, she decided with a baleful look around her. She didn't even know the name of the place; it just happened to have been facing the parking lot where she had left her car. And after coming from the run-down clinic where she had been just one more faceless woman in a waiting room filled with other faceless women, it had seemed the most appropriate place to go.

As she sipped on her third martini, she finally felt herself making the transition from stunned disbelief to pure, unabashed joy. When the full impact of the truth slammed home at last, she put her glass down on the bar with a thud that echoed off the peeling walls. But the sound of the cheap, thick glass hitting the wood suddenly rang in her ears like the ping of the most delicate crystal. She was pregnant! She wanted to grab the bartender by the frayed lapels of his short black jacket and shake him while she shouted to him that she was pregnant.

After all the years of waiting. After playing aunt to the children of her friends for so long. After all the time spent staring longingly after baby carriages and buying birthday gifts for other people's children. In another seven months, she, Franki Shelton, was going to become one of those luckiest of women, distinguished from other women by virtue of their being mothers. A mother! She was going to be a mother. She swallowed the rest of her drink, scooped up her change, and eased herself off the bar stool. No sooner had she wobbled to her feet than she sat right back down again.

The tennis tournament was six weeks away. Would it be safe for her to play in it? she wondered. Would she be showing by then? And Taylor. Had he already begun to notice the changes in her? She toyed with the stem of her empty glass and tried to focus on the swizzle stick with its three uneaten olives lying on the bar beside her soggy paper napkin. No one must know, at least not yet. Not until Brian knew. Brian! She began fumbling in her purse for some change. Then she pushed herself to her feet again and executed a ragged line all the way back to the pay phones in the rear of the dingy bar.

Brian agreed to meet her at home at four. That gave her less than two hours to drive back to Palm Beach and get herself into some kind of decent shape to greet him. Her legs were unsteady as she navigated her way past the bartender, the keys to the car dangling from her fingers.

"You sure you should be driving, lady?" he called after her as she began tugging at the door instead of pushing it.

"Don't you worry, my good man," she called back to him over her shoulder. "I have no intention of wrapping myself around any poles today." She gave him a wink and a wave. "Got too much going for me now. See ya."

She was waiting for Brian at the front door, wearing a long quilted-satin robe in a shade of silver-blue that brought out the silver in her hair and the blue of her eyes. Slightly sobered after a long shower and two cups of black coffee, she held out a highball glass of scotch to her husband and offered him her mouth for a hasty hello kiss.

"This had better be good, sweetness," he said, taking a sip of his drink as he followed her into the living room. "I put off my four o'clock meeting until five, so—"

"Brian, I'm pregnant, and I intend to have this baby," she blurted it out in order to get it over with quickly.

Brian's glass tipped, and half of his drink spilled, along with three ice cubes, onto the carpet. His eyes widened, and his eyebrows shot upward as his entire body stiffened and then began to shudder spasmodically.

"Oh, my God!" With a low, anguished moan, he sank into the nearest chair and let his glass drop onto the top of the coffee table. "Oh, God, God, no."

Franki came up behind him and lightly rested her hand on his shoulder.

"Brian, I—"

"No, Franki." He shook his head back and forth. "No."

"Please, Brian—"

"You can't mean it," he gulped. "You're making this up; you're just trying to hurt me. I know I haven't spent as much time with you as I should have, but whatever I've done, I've done for us. I thought you understood that, and—"

"Brian," she whispered, sliding her hand back and forth across his shoulders, "Brian, I've always understood."

"Then why?" He stared up at her miserably. "Why in the name of God did you do it?"

"I did it because a child was the one thing you could never give me." Her voice was gentle, but no matter how gently she put it, she knew that her words were going to slash right through him, and for that she was sorry, truly sorry.

His shoulders drooped, and he put his head in his hands as he started to cry.

"Brian." She tightened her grip on his shoulder only to have him shrug her off. "Brian, I'm sorry."

"You're sorry!" he barked at her from behind the protection of his hands. "You go out and find someone to knock you up, and you say you're sorry. The hell you are, you bitch, the hell you are!"

"I wanted a child, Brian," she explained, keeping her voice low in spite of the rising anger in his. "This is the one thing that's been missing from our lives all these years, and I just got tired, Brian, tired of waiting and hoping that you'd change your mind about adopting. I need this child, and in some ways, so do you."

"Some other man's kid," he snorted. "If I've never wanted some stranger's kid living in my house and passing as mine, what the hell made you think I'd feel differently about having your bastard living here?"

"Because it won't *be* a bastard. No one will ever know this child isn't ours, yours and mine."

"What about the happy father?" he spit at her. "Isn't he going to know?"

She shook her head.

"What did you do, Franki, go out and hire yourself a stud? I hear it's the in thing today among emancipated women who want a child but don't want a husband."

"I already have a husband."

"So you got some guy to give you a child for free. Now that sounds more like the Franki I know."

Her voice was icy now. "I've been having an affair, Brian, for several months now."

He picked up his glass and drained it. "Well, they always say the husband's the last to know. I suppose I should have paid more attention to all those newspaper items about the two of you. Congratulations, sweetness," he said, raising his empty glass to her, "you carried it off like the pro you are."

"Brian!" She tugged the glass from him and tried to grab hold of his hands, but he fought her off. "Brian, please try to understand!"

"Understand what?" he thundered. "Understand that I'm about to become the first sterile man in the history of medicine who miraculously knocked up his wife? You try and find someone who'll understand that!"

Franki recoiled at the sound of that hateful word. That repugnant, damning word. *Sterile.* They had known for three years that Brian was sterile, and had been ever since he had suffered a severe case of mumps as a teenager. Suspecting the truth, and both of them anxious to keep it a secret, they had returned to New York for extensive testing. They had told no one the reason for their sudden trip up north, and they had told no one about the results of the tests. Not even Franki's own gynecologist in Palm Beach. And now, as far as she was concerned, no one need ever know that the child she was carrying wasn't theirs.

"You have two choices, Brian." Her voice was under control again. "Either you agree to raise this child as yours, and I swear no one will ever know that you're . . . that you—"

"What's the matter, Franki?" he sneered. "You still can't say it, can you? The word's *sterile,* Franki, *sterile.* See, I can say it. I've gotten used to it, but obviously you never have. Your all-American dream boy came with a slight flaw, didn't he, sweetness, and that's something you still can't admit, now, can you?"

"Or you can divorce me," she continued as though she hadn't heard him. "I have enough money put away to see me through the next few years, and if you don't want to share this child with me, I'm perfectly willing to let you divorce me. I won't even ask you for a thing."

"That's damned generous of you, Franki, thank you."

She was losing her patience now. "This is no time to be snide, Brian. I've given you two choices. Let me know when you've made up your mind."

And with that, she turned and walked out of the room.

* * *

DAYE WAS anxious as she drove along the A1A toward Gorham Sound. Jonathan's phone call had been a brusque command, bristling with contained excitement. He had told her to get over to his place pronto. Pronto! If it had been that urgent, she reasoned, he could have told her what it was over the phone or traveled the ten miles to her office himself instead of making her come to him. Unless this was just his way of getting her away from her work. Nobody worked on the Fourth of July, he had insisted. She did, she had insisted right back, especially with Connie home with a strep throat, leaving her with more work than she could efficiently handle.

"Jonathan Cort," she mused out loud, easing her foot off the accelerator, "if this is another one of your clever little tricks to get me out of my office . . ." She let the thought trail off without bothering to complete it.

She suddenly had the urge to phone Rhea or Franki. She missed her long conversations with her friends, and now when she needed them the most, they had deserted her, or they had deserted each other. She still didn't know quite where the real truth lay. She needed their advice. She needed to talk to them about her relationship with Jonathan and her continuing ambivalence about it. She needed the benefit of their own experiences to help steer her through it and help her see more clearly where it was going.

It was so easy to enjoy the relationship when it was running smoothly, when there was easy laughter and exquisite lovemaking and the beauty of so many shared experiences. But she found the compromising difficult, when the bumps poked through the smoothness and the differences between them surfaced. Would it always be this way or would it get easier? she wanted to know. Did the differences ever stop mattering? Could they ever change from minuses into pluses, giving each of them the room to grow toward the other from their two very separate worlds? Would there ever be a time when neither of them kept a mental scoreboard anymore to tally up his compromise against her compromise and vice versa? But most of all, when would she stop thinking of a compromise as a sacrifice, she who had been on her own for so long without ever having to compromise for anyone?

She neared a roadside stand selling fruits, vegetables, and

freshly cut flowers, and for a moment she was tempted to stop and buy some fruit. But she didn't. And that was another thing. When was the last time Jonathan had stopped and bought her flowers at a roadside stand or given her an unusual seashell he had found washed up by the tide or written a song for her and tucked it into the white folder marked "Daye's Songs" in purple ink? She thought of all the little things he had given and done so naturally in the beginning, and she wondered, with a sinking feeling, if the courtship had already ended. Was this how it always was? As soon as a man was sure of you, did he stop courting you? She could feel the first flutter of panic. Beginnings were so beautiful. Why did they have to stop? She never wanted the courting to end. She never wanted to stop feeling excited when she knew she was going to see him, and she never wanted to stop feeling that little catch in her throat when she did. She was convinced that once the courtship died, the relationship would die with it.

She put on her flashers and turned into the gravel drive at 14 Seaside Way with a sigh of relief, her inner battle having left her feeling somewhat weakened and drained. The small stones crunching so reassuringly under the wheels of her car always made her feel that she was coming home, but she quickly reminded herself that she was *not* coming home. This was not *her* home but Jonathan's, and he had never once intimated that it might also be hers one day.

At the sight of him bounding down the steps to meet her, she felt that familiar catch in her throat and knew that everything was still all right between them. He grabbed hold of her by the waist and twirled her around and around in the air while she threw back her head and squealed with delight. When he set her down again, he thrust his hands deep into her hair and kissed her hungrily on the mouth. They were both slightly breathless by the time they broke their embrace. Daye cupped his face tenderly in both hands and lost herself in the sapphire depths of his eyes. Then she stood on tiptoes and raised her lips to his, and they began to kiss all over again.

"Why did you want me over here pronto, Jonathan?" she whispered to him, following the rim of his ear with her warm breath and feeling him shiver. "Um, tell me?"

"Because . . ."

"Because what?" She kissed the side of his neck and then kissed her way slowly along his jaw toward his chin.

"Because I missed you."

"Is that the only reason?" She traced the outline of his mouth with the tip of her tongue.

In answer to her question, he seized a handful of her hair and tugged her head back, bruising her lips with his as he put an end to her teasing. When he finally released her, his eyes were twinkling. "Do you realize that it's been three whole days?"

She was still reeling from the intensity of their last kiss. "Three whole days?" She looked up at him blankly.

"Since we've seen each other."

That brought an impish grin to her face. "And I thought only women kept track of those things."

"That shows how little you know about men, my delicious little Daye, especially this man."

"Do you mean to tell me there are still some things I don't know about you, Jonathan?" She made a playful lunge for him, but he sidestepped her and headed back up the steps to the house, taking them two at a time. "Come back here, you!"

She scampered after him, chasing him through the living room and into the dining room. They faced each other across the oval pine table, panting and laughing, as each tried to outguess the next move of the other. After a hasty peek at his watch, Jonathan suddenly held up his hand and called, "Time out!" He began inching his way toward the kitchen. "Time out for the chef to check the oven, unless, of course, you're partial to burnt *coquilles Saint-Jacques*."

"Which I'm not," replied Daye, wrinkling her nose.

"Time out then?"

"Time out."

She followed him into the kitchen and smiled when she saw Craig Claiborne's *New York Times Cook Book* propped up against a canister of flour on one of the kitchen counters.

"Yet another departure from the usual bachelor fare of that renowned playwright Jonathan Cort?" she inquired.

"Jonathan Humber Cort," he said, opening the oven door and peering inside.

"Humber? You never told me you had a middle name."

"See all the wonderful little things you're learning about me today?" he teased her, adding some more grated Parmesan cheese to the creamy seafood mixture in each of the four white scallop-shaped dishes.

"You made it up."

"Now, why would I make up a name like Humber?" he retorted, closing the oven door. "Why not something noble and distinguished like Montague or Winthrop or Norfolk or—"

"Bradley or—"

"St. James or—"

"We could go on like this all night," she said.

"You're right." He tossed his oven mitts down on the counter and opened the refrigerator door. "I almost forgot the real reason I asked you over here."

"Aha! I knew it wasn't just because you missed me." Daye grabbed him from behind and locked her arms around his waist. "Champagne!" she exclaimed when she saw what he was taking out of the refrigerator. "And all because it's the Fourth of July. How properly patriotic of you, Jonathan."

"What a sarcastic little girl you are," he clucked, squirming out of her grip. "Come, follow me."

They walked arm in arm out onto the terrace where Jonathan immediately uncorked the champagne with a loud pop and a minimum of spillage. Daye stood there silently, eagerly scanning his face, watching as he filled two glasses and handed her one of them. Setting the bottle inside the wooden ice bucket on the table, he raised his glass, clinked it against hers, and proclaimed in a deep, dramatic voice, "To *Arpeggio in Blue* and to Everett Rakwell for having the good sense to produce it!"

Daye was stunned. She said nothing while she let his words register. Then she reacted with an exultant shriek, putting her glass down and flinging her arms around Jonathan's neck. He took a startled step backward, spilling champagne on both of them.

"Oh, Jonathan, I'm so thrilled for you!" she cried, covering his face with tiny, happy kisses. "It's happening just as I knew it would. Oh, Jonathan, Jonathan, I'm so glad."

He was laughing when he finally extricated himself from her embrace. "Hold on to some of that marvelous exuberance, my darling Daye," he cautioned her. "This is only the beginning; it's a long uphill climb from here."

"Don't be such a pessimist," she chided him. Reaching down for her glass, she lifted it high in the air. "To *Arpeggio in Blue*," she said, "and to all the Tonys you can carry."

The *coquilles Saint-Jacques* were delicious, but Daye was almost too excited to enjoy the dinner. When Jonathan told her that casting for the show had already begun and that Rakwell wanted him in New York for the start of rehearsals, her appetite fled altogether. Now only the champagne could bypass the lump in her throat caused by the sudden panic the thought of his leaving had stirred up in her.

They had just started on coffee when she heard the sound of voices coming around the side of the house. A group of young men and women, all of them in T-shirts and jeans, some of them carrying bottles, others packages of paper cups, made their way along the terrace and converged on the table. Jonathan got to his feet, his arms spread wide in a gesture of welcome, and began greeting each of them in turn. Daye was slower getting to her feet. A finger of trepidation began tapping away at her insides as soon as she noticed the tall, lanky figure in the magenta blouse and magenta print skirt bringing up the rear of the ragtag procession. Her waist-length black hair was a shimmering stream of ebony in the fading rays of the sun, her wide, white smile an incandescent band in her sun-darkened face.

"Jonathan, darling!" she cried in a throaty growl. "What utterly blissful news!" She threw her arms around Jonathan's neck and planted a long, passionate kiss on his mouth. "You didn't think we'd allow you to escape without celebrating this with us tonight, did you?" She signaled to the sixteen young men and women grouped around the table, like a den mother collecting her charges. "Break out the wine, children. Our resident playwright is on his way to being restored as the toast of the Great White Way. From Gorham Sound to the Lunt-Fontanne," she sighed, pressing a hand to her heart and closing her eyes. "My God, what a masterful leap!"

With one arm around Maren's waist, Jonathan turned to Daye and winked at her, but she continued to stand in stony silence in front of them.

"You remember Daye, don't you, Maren?" he asked the woman who was returning Daye's frosty stare.

"Of course I do, darling," she purred. "How are you, pretty lady? Still decorating the homes of the filthy rich?"

Daye flushed. "It helps pay the monthly maintenance fees on the condo," she replied archly, aware of how closely Jonathan was now watching her.

"What do you think of our golden boy here?" Maren gave Jonathan a hard squeeze around the waist, and he obliged her by wincing in mock pain. "Do you think he's ready to be released to the wolves of Broadway?"

"Jonathan seems to think he is," replied Daye, "but what's more important, so does Everett Rakwell."

Maren threw back her head and laughed. "Well put, my dear, well put indeed. I can see why Jonathan finds you such delightful company. Ah, good, you have the wine open." She was now addressing her band of youthful admirers. "Well, let's pass those cups around like good boys and girls. And, oh, by the way, everyone, this enchanting creature is Daye Peters, a friend of Jonathan's." She pointed vaguely in Daye's direction. "Daye Peters, meet the members of the Gorham Sound Playhouse."

There were mumbled hellos all around, and then Daye found herself holding a paper cup of red wine and raising it obediently each time a different member of the cast proposed another toast to Jonathan and to his success. Although he was now standing beside her with his arm wrapped around her waist, Daye still felt ill at ease. She was the outsider here, the stranger, both to their world and to their ways, and as much as she loved the theater, Maren MacCaul's little playhouse had so far remained out of bounds and off limits to her. Perhaps she had hoped that by denying the playhouse's existence, she could successfully convince herself that Maren MacCaul didn't exist either. But whatever she had hoped to accomplish before, there was no denying the woman's existence now, or the possessive way she looked at Jonathan or the obvious way she brushed up against him each time she refilled his paper cup.

The cheap wine was making her dizzy, and the strain of being polite and friendly was gradually becoming too much for her. She was even considering sneaking away from the party when Maren startled her by coming over and pulling her toward the far side of the terrace.

"Tell me something, pretty lady," she began in her gravelly voice. "Just how honorable is your friend Neil Howard?"

"Neil!" In her complete surprise, his name came out sounding like a cough. "What exactly do you mean by honorable?"

"Knowing how close the two of you are, I naturally assumed that he had told you of his interest in the playhouse."

Daye cautioned herself to be wary as she answered the woman, and so she simply said, "He did mention it to me once in passing."

Jonathan sauntered over to them at that point and looped an arm around each woman's shoulders. "Is this a female conspiracy or can anyone join?" he asked, glancing from one to the other.

"Of course you can join, darling." Maren patted him on the cheek, but her eyes never once left Daye's flushed face. "You know, of course, that the Llewelyn Corporation is also interested in the playhouse, and I'd much rather sell to them, if I *do* decide to sell, than to your friend."

"I don't see what this has to do with me," said Daye.

Maren's dark eyebrows were knit together thoughtfully as she continued, "I like the sound of your friend's money, my dear, but I don't particularly care for your friend."

Daye tensed. She threw Jonathan a withering look, and the slow grin that had begun to spread across his face abruptly vanished.

"My one stipulation is that he preserve the playhouse if I agree to sell him the land," Maren explained. "At first he refused. Now he's suddenly agreeing to it."

Daye smiled in spite of herself. So he had listened to her after all. She was relieved, now more than ever, that she had never spoken to Jonathan about it as Neil had wanted her to.

"What I want to know from you, my dear Miss Peters, is whether or not I can trust him to keep his word."

Daye braced herself and said carefully, "I really don't think it would be fair of me to influence your decision one way or the other. If Neil promised you something, I assume he will keep his word. But my advice is to follow your own instincts. As you said yourself, Neil and I are close friends."

Her eyes locked with Jonathan's, but the expression in his was unreadable.

"Well, my dear," Maren said with a sigh, "I do hope he knows what a loyal friend he has in you." She gave her shoulders an exaggerated shrug. "Whatever am I to do? Jonathan, darling, what do you say? You always have such a clear head about these things."

"I'd have to agree with Daye," he told her, "and advise you to follow your own instincts, Maren."

"Men," she sniffed. "You can be such darlings when you want to be and such complete beasts the rest of the time. Especially you, my love. But I *do* adore you." She took hold of Jonathan's face with both of her strong, dark hands. Then she kissed him on the mouth again while the entire group from the playhouse hooted and clapped.

Daye began walking quickly toward her car, crumpling the paper cup in her hand as she walked. The last thing she heard as she peeled out of the driveway, spitting stones high into the air, was Jonathan shouting her name.

chapter nineteen

"WHY DID you run off like that last night?" asked Jonathan, while Daye held the receiver away from her ear to blunt the sharpness she could hear in his voice.

"I was tired, Jonathan. It had been a long day."

"And now what's the real reason?"

For a moment she said nothing, then in a small voice she admitted, "I think I just got tired of watching Maren MacCaul drape herself all over you."

"That's just Maren," he said with a laugh. "She's demonstrative and theatrical, I'll admit, but she means well."

"I'm sure she does."

"I'm sorry, Daye, I really *had* hoped to celebrate with you alone. Let me make it up to you, though. How about trying again tonight?"

"I don't think I can, Jonathan."

"Oh. Other plans?"

"Yes."

"Well, I hope they can compete with a fresh bottle of Dom Perignon and two tickets to *Dracula* at the Burt Reynolds Dinner Theater in Jupiter."

"I'm going to be working," she told him. "Neil will be back from San Francisco tomorrow, and I still haven't completed the sketches I promised him for his boardroom."

There was a slight pause, and then Jonathan said, "How can you put your work before champagne, Burt Reynolds, and me, and not necessarily in that order of importance?"

"I suppose because right now my work has to come first."

"I was half-joking, Daye."

"But I wasn't, Jonathan."

An awkward silence settled between them then, growing until neither of them knew how to break it gracefully. Finally it was Daye who said, "I'm awfully busy, Jonathan, so if you don't mind . . ."

"All right, I'll call you tomorrow, then."

She dropped the phone into its cradle and ordered herself to put him out of her mind for the rest of the day. As she was struggling to do just that, she looked down at the doodle she had been penciling around the notes she had made just before taking his call, and felt an immediate adrenaline surge rush through her. Florida Atlantic University was going to sponsor a three-day seminar on interior design, and she had been asked to participate in it. Of course Philippe Nadeau was among the other invited speakers, but she welcomed the opportunity to sit with him on the same panel to discuss their topic: Designing for an Ocean Setting: Countryscape or Cityscape. Their two opposing points of view were bound to stimulate one of the most animated debates of the entire conference. She began circling the proposed date for the seminar and felt her bubble of anticipation instantly burst. The seminar was scheduled for the second week in November. How could she give the people at FAU a definite answer now, when she wasn't sure she would still be in Florida in November?

She tossed her pencil aside and thrust the piece of paper into the top drawer of her desk. She had no time to waste dwelling on the uncertainty of her future; her immediate concern was Neil's project. Moving over to her drafting table, she unrolled her final plan for the company boardroom and got to work. Neil had been gone nearly a week, and she was grateful for every trip he took these days. It got him away from her for a while, cooling their intensifying closeness and bringing the situation between them into clearer perspective for her. It had become far too easy to enjoy being with him whenever she and Jonathan happened to be stumbling over one of the rougher spots in their own seesawing relationship, and that was the very danger she had been fighting so valiantly to avoid. She would be relieved when this project was finished. She needed to put some distance between herself and Neil before they found themselves trapped in a time warp from which neither of them could emerge unhurt.

At noon, she switched on her answering machine and left the office, swinging along South County to Worth. Turning into Via de Mario, she headed straight for number six, certain that only Troll Antiques would have what she was looking for. She needed a mirror, preferably a British antique in an ornate brass frame, to hang on a narrow wall in the main reception area of Neil's offices. It would offset the stark simplicity of the modern, brass-edged furnishings she was using in the rest of the room and provide just the dramatic contrast she was seeking.

It took her only five minutes to locate the eighteenth-century antique she wanted, but when she noticed the red Hold tag hanging from the mirror, her heart sank.

"Oh, dear," murmured the elegant and very British Myrna Sinclair who had been serving Daye, "they were to have let me know their decision on the mirror by this afternoon. Let me give them a ring, Miss Peters. It won't take a moment."

Daye continued to browse through the shop, hoping that whoever had been considering the mirror would decide against buying it and thereby simplify matters for her. She had precious little time right now to spend combing the other antique shops in Palm Beach in the hope of finding one similar to it.

"Mr. Nadeau will be over directly to have another look at the mirror, Miss Peters."

The woman coming up behind her gave Daye a start, but the name she mentioned made her grit her teeth in frustration. She would never get that mirror now. Philippe had outbid her on four separate items at two auctions in the past week, whether out of spite or out of genuine interest in the articles in question, she didn't know. Nor did it really matter. What *did* matter was that he had succeeded in topping her over and over again and that he was still managing to make her work as difficult for her as he possibly could. At the sight of him gliding through the door several minutes later, tanned to a bronze turn, his hair impeccably styled and his beige linen suit uncreased and un-wrinkled, she silently conceded defeat. Such perfection could never be bested.

"Bonjour, Daye." His lips fanned the air above both of her cheeks as he greeted her in the Continental fashion. "As en-chanting as ever, I see."

Under his appraising gaze, Daye felt herself squirm. "Phi-lippe." She accorded him a touch of a smile as she returned his greeting.

"Et maintenant." He clapped his hands together as he strode up to the mirror. "It appears you and I are forever destined to be at odds with one another, *ma chère* Daye, we both seem to have the same excellent taste."

"Only in some things, Philippe," she reminded him.

"That may very well be, *chérie,* but when we *do* agree," he rolled his eyes melodramatically, "oo-la-la!"

"Tell me, Philippe," she asked him quietly, resenting the expert way in which he was manipulating her, "do you want this mirror or don't you?"

"Do you?"

"Obviously I do, yes."

He gave his shoulders a classic Gallic shrug. "Then I am afraid I must disappoint you again, my poor Daye. Only min-utes before Madame Sinclair telephoned, Madame Barron de-cided to take the mirror after all." He motioned to the saleswoman who had been observing the entire interchange in silence, and with an imperious flick of his wrist, he said, "You may remove the red tag now, *ma chère madame,* and consider the mirror sold." He offered Daye an apologetic smile. "Perhaps next time?"

Daye returned his shrug of a moment ago. "Perhaps."

"I'm terribly sorry, Miss Peters." Mrs. Sinclair was ob-viously embarrassed as she turned from Philippe to speak to Daye again. "There are a number of mirrors quite similar to this one in the back room if you'd care to have a look at them."

Daye declined the woman's offer with a forced smile, giving her a light pat on the arm and promising to come back again.

She brushed past Philippe without another word and left the shop, glancing back over her shoulder in time to see Mrs. Sinclair pull the red tag off the mirror while Philippe nodded approvingly, wearing a smug smile of satisfaction.

FRANKI DUCKED around the side of the shop and waited for another few minutes just to be safe. She felt like a bit of a fool for hiding as her best friend walked through the courtyard of the Esplanade, but how was she supposed to explain the reason for her coming out of the Purple Turtle again with her arms full of boxes? The Purple Turtle was a children's shop, and even Rhea wouldn't believe Franki had *that* many gifts to buy, especially in July when most of the families they knew had already headed north to Newport and Martha's Vineyard.

Putting her packages down, Franki turned to study herself in the store window, trying to imagine her belly protruding, her back curved slightly from the weight, and the folds of a smocked tent dress from Lady Madonna fluttering all around her. The image made her grin, and she was still grinning when she stooped to pick up her parcels again. She had been buying gifts for her friends' children at the Purple Turtle ever since the shop first opened, and now she was finally able to shop there for her own child. Of course, no one knew that. The saleswomen simply assumed that she was just being charming Mrs. Shelton again, that devoted and oh-so-generous godmother and aunt.

She peered cautiously around the corner for some sign of Rhea, but she was gone. While every emotional chord in her being cried out for her to share her news with someone, the more rational chords were holding her enthusiasm in careful check. It was still too early—she hadn't really begun to show at all yet—and far too soon. Brian was only now plodding slowly toward an acceptance of the situation, and she couldn't hurry him. His bruises would take some time to heal, and until they did, neither of them could reveal the news to anyone. It had taken him nearly a week before he had told her that he would accept this child as his own. He loved her, he had said, and he needed her far too much to lose her now. But what he didn't say, and it was something Franki vowed she would never press him to admit, was that the main reasons for his decision were his feeling of guilt and his terrible sense of inadequacy for having failed her.

His one stipulation was that she end her affair immediately. She had agreed, but she hadn't done so yet. Although she was finally able to admit to herself that she had gone into the affair hoping to become pregnant, it had evolved into a habit far too satisfying to break. But she *would* stop it, she promised herself, as soon as she started to show, to make certain that no one could ever question the true identity of her child's father.

Making certain that no one was watching her, she leaned back, thrust her pelvis forward as far as she could and studied the effect of her pose in the window again. Then with a self-conscious little laugh, she headed for the parking lot.

THE NOTE Rhea had left Neil on his pillow explained that she had decided to treat herself to her own belated birthday gift after all by spending a few days alone in New York City, shopping and going to the theater. P.S. She had told the children that she was paying their grandparents a visit, and that was all they needed to know. When the United Airlines flight landed at La Guardia at four, Rhea picked up her rented Buick and drove directly to the town of Alindale, just south of Peekskill, New York. One mile from the Alindale Village for Special Children, she pulled over to the side of the road and stopped the car. Her body was coated with perspiration, she was hyperventilating badly, and her hands were shaking so violently that she could no longer keep a firm grip on the wheel.

She leaned forward in the driver's seat and rested her head against the steering wheel while she tried to slow her rapid breathing. She was overwhelmed once more by the enormity of what she had set out to do even though she had unconsciously been preparing herself over the past few months for the very inevitability of this visit. There could be no turning back for her now, no running away, no cowardly retreat to the safety of ignorance. She had come too far to allow her mounting anxiety to force her back into the complacency of the past.

When she had finally managed to regain some of her composure, she started the car and continued slowly up the winding, forested dirt road that led to the open stone and iron gates of the Alindale Village. It was situated in a lightly timbered clearing that covered several acres and could have passed for a small-sized children's camp. At the far end of the clearing stood two large three-story stone- and wood-trimmed buildings, their window boxes brimming with pink and white petunias, while behind them lay a basketball court, a tennis court, and a swimming pool. A dozen small white frame cottages formed a vast semicircle around the two main buildings; each had been individually landscaped with various kinds of shrubs, slender silver birches, and the occasional tall spruce.

How stark this northern retreat seemed in spite of the foliage, how austere in comparison with the ripe lushness of Florida's tropical greenery. Whereas Florida was washed in luxuriant smudges of verdant softness, here everything was punctuated by pointed spires and elongated shapes, all of them stabbing skyward like great, bristly exclamation marks. The entire setting seemed brusque, almost terse, in the unyielding harshness of its geometric design. And yet, this was home to her brother Steven. This very private place, set so far apart from the rest of the world, where nothing, no matter how well planned or well intentioned, was ever quite as orderly or quite as perfect.

Parking the car in the small, deserted lot marked Visitors Only, Rhea began walking toward the closer of the two main buildings, taking slow and carefully measured little steps. She stopped on each of the five stone stairs of the building to weigh the consequences of what she was doing against turning around and fleeing before anyone could know she was there. With one hand poised above the iron latch of the front door, she paused one final time; then she drew in a deep, steadying breath and pulled the door open.

She entered a large, carpeted reception area with a desk in the center and a number of chintz-covered sofas and chairs grouped together throughout the room with a casualness she found strangely comforting.

"May I help you?" inquired the young woman behind the desk, looking up at Rhea through a pair of tortoiseshell-framed glasses.

Rhea approached the desk with increasing trepidation, and in a tremulous voice, she stated, "I'd like to visit with Steven

Bellon, please. I'm his sister, Rhea Howard."

The young woman whose white plastic name tag identified her as Miss Kendrew said, "You've never been here before, have you, Mrs. Howard?"

A spasm of fear gripped Rhea as she replied, "No, I haven't."

"I didn't think so." Miss Kendrew smiled, a tinge of knowing sympathy warming her eyes. "It's rather unusual for someone to simply appear and ask to visit one of the patients here without first having arranged it through Dr. Donleavy's office."

"Dr. Donleavy?"

"Yes, Martha Donleavy, she's the director of Alindale."

Rhea looked down at her hands and murmured, "I had no idea whom to contact or what I would even do when I got here, Miss Kendrew. I've never met my brother, you see, and . . . and I really don't know why I'm here, except that I know I just have to see him."

Her eyes were swimming with tears as she raised her head and silently implored the young woman to find some way to help her. Miss Kendrew did not disappoint her. "Why don't you have a seat for a moment, Mrs. Howard?" she said, reaching for the phone on the desk in front of her. "Let me try to reach Dr. Donleavy. She should still be in the dining hall."

Rhea sat rigidly on the edge of a chair, winding and unwinding the strap of her beige alligator bag around her hand while she counted the number of mullioned panes in each of the room's six narrow windows. Then she stared up at the ceiling and counted the number of white acoustical tiles, forcing herself to begin again each time she lost track of them.

"Mrs. Howard?"

She leaped from her chair with a startled gasp of surprise.

"I'm Martha Donleavy." She was a handsome woman who wore her silver-white hair in a sleek pageboy and whose eyes were a clear, frosty violet. The hand she offered Rhea was as slender as the woman herself and as warm as her smile. She motioned for Rhea to sit down again while she pulled up a chair for herself and sat down with her hands loosely folded in her lap.

"Your parents have mentioned you to me quite a number of times in the four years since I've been director here," the woman said, "and I must admit to being rather pleased that the two of us are meeting at last. But tell me, Mrs. Howard, did your parents encourage you to make this trip on your own?"

"Encourage me?" Rhea laughed bitterly. "They don't even know I'm here, Dr. Donleavy. They still refuse even to talk to me about Steven."

"I see." The woman's smooth forehead puckered into a deep and thoughtful frown as she considered what Rhea had just told her. "May I ask you why you decided to come here, then, knowing how strongly your parents might have objected to it had you told them first?"

In halting tones, Rhea explained about her growing preoccupation with her brother over the years, her recurrent dreams about him, and the paintings she had been doing without even knowing what he looked like. When she talked about the books she had been reading on the subject of retardation and her volunteer work at the Boca Raton General Hospital, the expression in Dr. Donleavy's eyes changed gradually from sympathetic understanding to approving respect.

"You're a rather remarkable young woman, Mrs. Howard," was the doctor's solemn comment when Rhea had finished her story, "and quite a brave one. I can see that you've come here well equipped and somewhat prepared. However, when I take you to visit your brother, as I fully intend to do, you must be prepared to see a thirty-nine-year-old man whose mind is that of a four-year-old child. As much as he's a stranger to you, you'll be that much of a stranger to him. He recognizes your parents because they've been constants in his life, and even though he doesn't quite understand what parents are, he knows they're his friends. They bring him gifts, take him for walks, read to him, and play very simple games with him. He trusts them the way any child will trust someone who is gentle and loving and kind."

While Rhea was listening to what Dr. Donleavy was telling her, she couldn't shake off the feeling that she was walking through one of her own dreams. She was experiencing a peculiar kind of weightlessness as she sat there across from the woman, as though she were floating through a cloudless sky. And that was exactly the way she had been feeling for months now, as though her life were that cloudless sky and she was drifting through it with no signposts anywhere to provide her with a sense of direction.

"Your brother lives in a bungalow with three other young men whose mental capabilities are similar to his," the doctor was explaining to her now. "A male nurse sleeps in an adjoining room and supervises nearly every facet of their daily lives." She stood up then and signaled for Rhea to get up as well. "I suggest we walk over there now, Mrs. Howard. They should be returning momentarily from the dining hall."

Rhea rose like an obedient child and followed the woman outside. Dr. Donleavy opened the door to bungalow eight and preceded her into the small front room that served as the recreation area. It was furnished in blond wood and upholstered in a cheerful cotton print showing red and white sailboats on a navy blue background. The nurse slept to the left of the front room. There was a large tiled bathroom to the right, and the four occupants of the bungalow slept in the spacious rear room, which resembled a room in any school dormitory. The same nautical print had been used for the coverlets on the four single beds, the curtains, and the wing chairs placed in each of the four corners of the room. A pine nightstand with a lamp on it stood on one side of each bed; on the other was a simple pine dresser with a mirror above it. When Dr. Donleavy pointed out Steven's bed to her, Rhea's chest suddenly tightened, and her eyes began to mist at the sight of the three stuffed animals— a dog, a donkey, and a rabbit—clustered together on his pillow. Her parents had given her an identical black and white checked rabbit for her seventh birthday.

Leading her back to a sofa in the front room, Dr. Donleavy spent the next few minutes talking to Rhea about her brother and what she could expect from their first meeting.

"He won't understand what a sister is any more than he's been able to understand what parents are," she explained. "What you must first try to do is win his trust. The love will come later."

At the sound of footsteps on the stairs, Rhea grabbed hold of Dr. Donleavy's arm with one hand and the arm of the sofa with the other. Although the woman's pale eyes were counseling her to compose herself, Rhea found it impossible to remain calm. She stared at the door, wide-eyed and dry-mouthed, wondering if she would recognize her brother without the doctor's help. She held her breath as a casually dressed man in his early thirties wearing a baseball cap sauntered into the room and gave Dr. Donleavy an easy wave.

"That's Edward Newcomb, the nurse I was telling you about," the doctor told Rhea, returning the man's wave with a look that said, I will explain all of this to you later.

Rhea's grip on the doctor's arm tightened. She was staring at each of the four young men filing slowly into the room. She returned the smile of a plump redheaded boy who appeared to be about sixteen, and then her heart skipped a beat, flip-flopping painfully inside her chest. It was Steven. It had to be. He had her straight black hair and her soft gray eyes, except that his vacant expression lent his face an air of winsome innocence that was missing in hers. He was not much taller than she was, with the same fragile bone structure, and seeing him standing there in front of her at last gave her the features for the faceless child she had been painting for so long.

He was studying her with the same curiosity as the others when Edward began waving everyone but him into the bedroom. Then the nurse led Steven gently to the sofa. His eyes were now fixed on Dr. Donleavy's familiar face, and when she greeted him by name, he beamed at her. Sitting there so tensely and expectantly, Rhea wanted to put out her hand and touch him. She wanted to wrap her arms around him and feel his heart beating against her chest. She wanted to tell him that she was his sister and that she was sorry she had taken such a long time to come and see him. She wanted to grab back all the years that had kept them apart and start over again. But most of all, she wanted to tell her parents how wrong they had been.

"Steven." It was not Rhea but Dr. Donleavy who put out her hand to him, and like a trusting child, he took it. "Steven, I've brought someone very nice to visit you. Her name is Rhea, and she would like to become your friend."

Steven turned to look at Rhea, and he smiled shyly at her.

"Can you say Rhea?" asked the doctor.

He continued to stare at Rhea, studying her face, while she stared hopefully back at him.

"Rhea." The woman repeated it for him.

"Rhea," he said, his voice sounding surprisingly deep for someone with the face of such a beautiful child.

"That's right, Steven. Rhea." The doctor gave his hand a squeeze. "Would you like Rhea to read to you tonight before you go to sleep?"

Steven seemed to consider the question for a moment, but then he nodded several times, and his smile widened.

"Rhea read Steven?" He looked directly into Rhea's eyes as he said it.

"Yes," she whispered hoarsely, an ache so strong inside her that she could barely keep it contained. "Rhea read Steven."

When Steven was settled in the dormitory bedroom, Rhea drew one of the wing chairs up to his bed and opened his storybook to "The Three Little Pigs." Nestled beneath his covers, dressed in a pair of pale blue pajamas, and clutching all three of his stuffed animals to his chest, Steven gazed up at Rhea with a serene smile and waited for her to begin.

"When I was a little girl," she told him in a quiet voice, speaking slowly and distinctly, "I had a rabbit just like yours, Steven."

He stared at her quizzically while she repeated what she had said to him, and then he suddenly looked down at the animals he was holding. Rhea's heartbeats quickened as he finally singled out the black and white rabbit and began to nuzzle it with his chin. When he leaned toward her and held the animal up to her chin, she obediently lowered her head and nuzzled it just as he had done. This seemed to please him a great deal, because he was soon giggling happily and rubbing the top of the rabbit's head back and forth under his own chin again.

"Nice rabbit," he said, patting it on the head. "Make nice rabbit," he instructed her, holding up the rabbit so that she could dutifully pat its head a couple of times.

When he grew tired of their game, he hugged the rabbit close to his chest again and fixed his eyes on the book in Rhea's lap. She immediately picked up the book, holding it close to her eyes as she started to read to him so that he wouldn't see the tears that were coursing silently down her cheeks.

She spent another two days with Steven. She took him for long walks through the woods, she read to him from all of his favorite storybooks, and she played his favorite games with him. He especially loved his set of large wooden building blocks, and they spent hours together building houses and tunnels and castles for his collection of tiny wooden soldiers and two dozen toy cars. With Steven, Rhea discovered in herself a special kind of nurturing patience she had never had for her own children. With Steven she felt needed as she had never wanted to feel needed before. And because of Steven, she was gradually coming to know what it meant to give someone her unconditional love.

When she returned to Boca, she was exhausted, but the moment she got home, she put in a long-distance call to her parents in Manhattan. As soon as she had them both on the line, she said simply, "I've been to see Steven."

And then she waited for their reaction, expecting anything but her mother's rush of tears and the heaving sobs of her father. Battling with her own tears, she told them how she felt. "I don't know if I'll ever be able to forgive either you or myself for allowing nearly twenty-five years to slip past us this way, but I intend to make up for those years from now on. I plan to visit Steven at least once a month, just as you do," she said, "but I won't go on the weekends when you're there. I need to be alone with him, you see, just as I truly believe he needs to be alone with me."

She broke down then, sobbing openly as she remembered how he had kissed her when she had said good-bye to him and the way he had hugged her so tightly when she had promised to come back to see him very soon. And suddenly, it seemed that she was finally beginning to see a signpost somewhere in the midst of that cloudless blue sky.

chapter twenty

"WELL, NEIL, what do you think?" asked Daye as she spread *The Miami Herald* out on her desk and indicated the lengthy article and the two photographs accompanying it.

"I think you're a genius," he said, peering over her shoulder for a closer look.

She studied the photos of his newly redecorated main reception area and one of the executive suites and nodded several times in complete agreement with his assessment. She *had* done a good job. She had used a berry-toned palette for the entire office project and even in the newspaper photographs, the effect was both warm and sophisticated, its lavishness a cleverly contrived understatement. The walls of both rooms had been covered in dusty rose suede and the furniture upholstered in a startling combination of grape, mulberry, and dusty rose suedes. All of the accent pieces were in white Formica and brass-framed glass, with jewel-toned silk and suede wall hangings and the occasional area rug adding a softening burst of textured brilliance to the subtle elegance of the decor.

"You know something, Button?" Neil murmured, his breath warm on her cheek, his chest pressing against her back, and one hand covering hers as it rested on top of the desk. "You're an incredible lady, beautiful *and* talented, and that's a fairly heady combination."

"I thank you, sir," she returned lightly, trying to ease her hand out from under his and not succeeding. "Neil," she complained, her heartbeat beginning to quicken, "Neil, you're squashing me."

His lips grazed the lobe of her right ear, and she shivered. "That's not all I'd like to do to you right now."

"Stop it, silly." She bucked at him in an effort to get him to release her while her heart continued to thump even faster and harder than before.

He finally obliged her by stepping away from her, but it was only to turn her around in his arms so that she faced him. She gazed up at him and found it almost impossible to resist the obvious message being beamed at her from those remarkable turquoise-blue eyes.

"No, Neil." She shook her head, refusing even to look at him directly.

"No, Neil, what?"

"No, Neil, whatever it is you're thinking."

He laughed at that and crushed her head to his chest, hugging her against him for a moment and then releasing her with a brotherly kiss on the forehead.

"You've got a dirty mind, Daye Peters," he chided her, chucking her lightly under the chin.

She allowed the moment to pass, swinging quickly around to the opposite side of the desk and sliding into her chair. Bracing one knee against her top drawer, she made a steeple of her fingers and waited. He took his cue from her and dropped into the chair opposite her, fixing her with one of his most disarming grins.

"Can I help it if you're irresistible?" he asked her.

She rolled her eyes toward the ceiling. "My poor head will start swelling to grand proportions if you keep up this extravagant praise," she cautioned him.

His response to that was to say absolutely nothing while he continued to look at her in a way that was far more unsettling than any words could have been. Determined to defuse the situation, she sat forward with both feet on the floor again and began to gather up the scattered sections of her newspaper.

"Do you want any extra copies of this article?" she asked him as she worked busily to restore her desk to some semblance of its former order.

"I wouldn't mind a few dozen of them," he said. "I'd like to send a copy to each of my clients in Europe and South America. The more successful the Howard Development Corporation looks to them, the more secure they feel about investing in the projects we suggest."

"In that case, I should ask for a finder's fee," she said with a laugh.

"How about a hot tip on some prime real estate instead?"

She shook her head. "I couldn't afford it."

He arched one blond brow skeptically, but his voice was serious. "With the business you're building up for yourself down here, Daye, I find that a little hard to believe."

She sat back in her chair again and contemplated the ceiling. "I'll admit that I *am* doing fairly well, but it's not the way it was for me in New York. There's something missing here, that element of daring, that willingness to take a chance on something slightly beyond the safe and the traditional. I don't know, Neil," she sighed, "sometimes I get so frustrated that I find myself thinking it might be smarter of me to work exactly the way Philippe Nadeau does."

"And just how *does* he work?"

"He doesn't flout tradition. There aren't any surprises in a Philippe Nadeau concept, and unfortunately, that's exactly where my own strength lies: I surprise people. I shock them with contrasts, but I don't think contrasts and surprises go over very well in a place as traditional as Palm Beach."

"Maybe you just haven't connected with the right people yet, Daye. Not everyone's interested in preserving their hallowed past and their ancestral portraits. Give it some more time."

"Time? That's what I *have* been giving it, Neil. This is already the end of July. I've got exactly two months left in which to decide whether or not to renew my lease in New York, and the closer we get to October, the more certain I become that I should move back up north."

"Listen to me," he said, leaning forward and slapping both hands against his knees. "As soon as all of the offices are completed, we'll throw a party, an open house, to celebrate. I'll invite all of my clients, my business contacts, the people from the club, the press, everyone. What do you think of that? Think it might help?"

Her eyes were shining as she excitedly wagged her head up and down. "It might," she agreed. "Oh, Neil, I think it's a superb idea, a deliciously superb idea!"

"Good, now that we've settled that, how about my buying you lunch before I head out to the airport this afternoon?"

"Where are you off to this time?"

"Atlanta for three days." He made a face. "Feel like coming along?"

"And who'll finish your offices if I run off to Atlanta with you?"

"You will, only you'll finish them three days later, that's all."

"Don't you dare tempt me like that, Neil Howard." She laughed.

"Are you tempted, Daye?" He had lowered his voice until it was hardly more than a seductive caress. But she stared straight at him to prove to them both that she was impervious to it.

"I'm certainly not tempted to go to Atlanta," she told him airily with a disdainful wave of her hand. "Paris, perhaps, or maybe Rome. And Venice, most definitely."

"Then I'll book us a flight to Venice as soon as I get back."

"Don't be absurd," she snapped, hastily backing away from what she knew was no longer a safe little game.

"Coward," he hissed as he got to his feet and leaned across the desk to kiss her good-bye. "No lunch, then?"

She shook her head. "Too much to do."

"Okay, I'll call you as—"

"Good-bye, Neil." She cut him off, pretending to be looking for something on her desk.

"Good-bye, Daye," he replied with exaggerated politeness, giving a lock of her hair a playful tug. "You're still beautiful, you know, even when you're cranky."

She refused to look up until she heard the door to her office close. Then she reached for the phone and hurriedly dialed Jonathan's number. The only way to defend herself against

Neil nowadays was to replace his face and his voice with Jonathan's as quickly as possible. Oh, Jonathan, please be there. Please answer, she prayed, while she drummed her fingers on the top of her desk and counted fifteen rings before hanging up and dialing again. He might have been playing the piano; maybe he hadn't heard the phone. Or he might have been in the shower or taking a walk along the beach or . . . The possibilities were endless, but not her patience. After ten more frustrating rings, she slammed down the phone and tried to force her mind back to her work.

When she hadn't heard from him by four o'clock the following afternoon, she became alarmed. It wasn't like Jonathan to allow two entire days to go by without at least one call. He answered the phone on the sixth ring, and the sound of his weak and rasping voice only intensified her concern.

"I think I'm dying," he groaned. "I'd assumed that what I had was the twenty-four-hour flu, but it's hung around for nearly three days now."

"Do you have a fever?" she asked him.

"It's finally leveled off to an even one hundred," he replied with a barking cough to punctuate his words. "I've been lying in this bed for the past two days with my phone turned off, feeling very sorry for myself and wishing I were anywhere but here." He coughed again. "Damn, being sick is no fun at all."

She was smiling in spite of her worry as he continued to complain like a helpless little boy. "What you need is some tender loving company," she told him. "This office makes house calls, you know."

"Don't you dare set foot inside this place," he warned her. "I'm probably as infectious as a plague victim."

Daye laughed, but she would not be deterred. "Have you seen *The Miami Herald* lately?" she asked.

"*The Miami Herald?* I haven't even made it as far as the front door in two days."

"Then I've got something to show you that should cheer you up instantly. Stay right where you are. Dr. Peters is on her way."

As soon as she hung up, she grabbed her copy of the *Herald* and left the office at a run. She stopped at Publix and bought three tins of Campbell's Chicken Noodle Soup, a loaf of French bread, three different kinds of cheese, a jar of natural honey, a tin of herbal tea, the makings for a salad, and two bunches of yellow and white daisies before driving to his house. She scooped up the two copies of the *Standard* lying on his front porch, tucked them under her arm, and rang the bell. It was several minutes before the door finally swung open. Daye peered curiously into the foyer for some sign of her patient.

"Jonathan?"

"Behind the door," came his muffed reply.

She immediately poked her head around the door.

"Oh, for God's sake!" She burst out laughing and nearly dropped everything she was carrying. Jonathan was standing there in a royal blue terry-cloth robe wearing a World War I gas mask.

"That may be helping you, but it won't do me any good," she told him, still laughing. "Whatever it is you've got is living in every molecule of air in this house."

"Well, you can't say I didn't warn you," he said, pulling the gas mask off and covering his mouth with his hand.

"Your papers, sir," she announced, dropping them onto the coffee table in the living room on her way into the kitchen.

He padded after her and stood with his hand over his mouth at the far end of the room while she unpacked the groceries, set the flowers in a vase, and started to prepare their supper.

"You don't look as ghastly as you sounded over the phone," she remarked, glancing at him quickly while she poured the soup into a saucepan and put it on the stove.

"That makes me feel much better," he grumbled. "I only sound ghastly; I don't look ghastly."

"Jonathan," she scolded him with a shake of her head even as she was noting the faint purple smudges under his eyes, the pallor to his skin, and the cracked bottom lip that the fever had caused. He *did* look ghastly, she decided, but he was obviously much better now than he had been. "Follow me," she said, motioning to him with a crook of her index finger. "I've got something to show you."

He followed her back into the living room and stood behind her as she opened the *Herald* and pointed to the article on Neil's offices.

"Well, what do you think of your girl's first office project down here?" she asked him, leaning back against his chest while he signaled for her to hold the paper a bit higher.

He nibbled on her left ear as he hastily scanned the article. Then he planted a kiss on her neck and added a small bite for emphasis. "I think my girl's done a terrific job," he whispered. "Do you think I could afford to hire her?"

"That all depends on what you have in mind."

"What I have in mind has absolutely nothing to do with decorating."

"That sounds intriguing." She smiled. "I've never been propositioned by a dying man before."

"If this dying man were to receive some of your very special loving, my beautiful Daye, he might just pull through," he said.

Turning her around and brushing her hair back behind her ears, he began to kiss her face, starting with her high, smooth forehead and working his way slowly down to her mouth. Daye herself deepened their kiss as she responded to her own growing urgency, and as she pressed her body up against his, she was pleased to feel him stiffening beneath the folds of his loosely belted robe. With their mouths locked together and their tongues thrusting and probing, their bodies began to undulate rhythmically together until they seemed to be swaying in time to a melody only they could hear. When he lifted his mouth from hers and trailed his tongue along the slender column of her throat, she dug her fingers into his hair and threw back her head, moaning softly while he lapped at her skin.

She helped him unbutton her blouse. Then she arched her back, holding his head against her breasts and moaning again as his mouth closed around one sensitive nipple. With her own hunger now bordering on agony, she began raking his back with her nails, whispering his name over and over again and urging him on. Clinging tightly to each other, they sank slowly onto the large white flokati rug in front of the fireplace, and Daye slipped the robe from Jonathan's shoulders.

It was as though they had never made love before, so great was their mutual need. She had never known a hunger as insatiable as the hunger raging within her now when he took her. They plundered each other with an uncontrolled fury tempered only by the gentler side of their neediness; but for Daye, her release from her ecstatic tension came all too soon.

They lay together on the rug afterward, entwined in each other's arms, slick with perspiration, and breathing heavily. His head was cushioned by her breasts, and she was stroking his thick, damp hair as though she were comforting and caressing a child while a peculiar kind of restive peace stole over her. Somehow her contentment was bringing with it a disturbing uneasiness as well. It was a tiny pinprick of doubt, a shimmer of elusive pain tainting the beauty of what she and Jonathan had just shared. And suddenly, she knew why. She had not only been making love to Jonathan, she had been using his nearness and his body to fight off the persuasive pull of a memory, the elusive tug of a specter that had somehow managed to wedge itself between them.

Panic gripped her as Jonathan stirred and lifted his head to look at her. She caught hold of his face with both hands and brought his lips down closer to hers.

"Love me, Jonathan," she pleaded softly. "Make love to me again."

They made love a second time, and then they took a long, steamy shower together, with Jonathan insisting, as they toweled themselves off, that her loving ministrations had indeed saved him. He took several aspirins with the fresh orange juice she squeezed for him, and then the two of them sat down to a light supper in the kitchen, he with his soup, bread, and cheese and a mug of honey-laced herbal tea, she with a salad and a glass of white wine, both of them leafing through the newspapers she had brought in with her. At the sudden sound of him slapping his section of the *Standard* down on the kitchen table, Daye reacted as though she had just heard a gunshot.

"What's the matter?"

"And you accuse *me* of not reading the papers!" exclaimed Jonathan. "Take a look at that. Your friend Philippe has just hired himself some hot-shot designer from Chicago whose specialty happens to be—are you prepared for this?—office modernization."

"What!" Daye grabbed the paper, frowning when she noticed that the article was planted firmly in the middle of the *Standard*'s business section. "What's he doing outside the society pages?" she wondered aloud. The name Margot Thurston was unfamiliar to her, but what *was* familiar was the feeling of hopeless frustration she experienced as she read the article. Philippe was still determinedly dogging her steps, matching her stride for stride, and always managing to stay that one essential step ahead of her.

"I suppose I should be flattered," she said glumly, handing the paper back to Jonathan. "He must think I'm pretty good if he has to keep hiring specialists to help him stay on top."

"Now, that's what I'd consider having a positive attitude."

"What else *can* I have?"

"Patience."

"Patience?"

"Patience. One of these days Sybil Barron is going to get tired of his spending her money on this little game of one-upmanship and kick him out. When that happens, his expanding empire will be whittled back down to include only Philippe and the one assistant who's been working for him for the past seven years."

"Do you honestly believe that?"

"Yes, I do," Jonathan insisted. "Nothing is less permanent down here than what seems to be *most* permanent, Daye. Most of what's seen as chic and novel today will be a cliché tomorrow. Give Sybil time. She'll get bored with her pet project and find herself another one with something newer and fresher to keep her amused."

"But I don't know if I can hold out until then," said Daye. "If I don't snare one major account very soon, I'm going to be struggling down here for the rest of my life. And I'm not prepared to do that, Jonathan. I worked too hard to get to the top once to even contemplate staying small and being second best now."

"Being small doesn't have to mean being second best *or* second rate." There was a gently chiding note to Jonathan's tone. "Staying small might be exactly what you *do* need now. It's allowing you the freedom to enjoy other things, things you've been denying yourself for far too long."

"Such as?"

"Such as us."

She flushed and turned away, refusing to meet his searching gaze.

"Look at me, Daye."

She felt like a child for shaking her head no.

"Why does that bother you so much?" he asked. "Do you feel guilty for wanting something more than just your work in your life?"

She shook her head, more vehemently this time.

"What's wrong with what you and I have, Daye? Doesn't it help smooth out some of the rougher edges for you? I know it does for me."

She propped her chin up on her hand and stared directly at his chest as she answered him. "It *does* help, Jonathan; of course it does. It makes a very big difference in my life, but it doesn't change how I feel about my work. I still need the challenge I get from my work. I still want to be the best, and I just can't settle for anything less, at least not yet."

"But I don't want to settle either," he told her.

"What does that mean?"

"It means that I don't want to settle for being second in your life any more than you want to settle for being second to Philippe Nadeau."

"But how can you say that you're second in my life?" She was stunned by his accusation. "There's no one in my life right now but you."

"Isn't there?"

"Just what are you trying to say, Jonathan?"

"Don't play coy with me, Daye, when I'm trying to be honest with you. I'm talking about Neil Howard, and in a way I suppose I'm also talking about your work."

"Then I suppose I should be asking you about Maren MacCaul and *your* work."

"Come on, Daye . . ."

"Listen to me, Jonathan." She folded her arms on the table and leaned closer to him. "Neil Howard and I are good friends; you and Maren MacCaul are good friends. Subject closed. Now, as far as my work is concerned, let me turn that one around for a moment. Would you give up trying to be the best you could be in your field because the woman in your life complained about being second to your work? No, you wouldn't. No man would. No man would ever consider playing at his career on a part-time basis just to make certain that the woman he cared about didn't feel ignored. Why should a woman be expected to do that for a man? Is her career any less valid than his? We're all equally responsible for filling up the spare moments of our own lives; no one should be expected to do that for us. And if you think you're competing with my work for my attention, you're wrong, because you're not. But please don't test me, Jonathan. If I ever have to choose between devoting myself to my career in order to be the best I can be and pretending that it doesn't matter for the sake of having a relationship with someone, then I'll choose my career. It's the one thing I know I can really count on."

"You mean it's the thing you can control, don't you, Daye?"

"Is that your way of saying I'm trying to control *you?*"

"I'm saying that you're doing a fairly good job of controlling what's *between* us."

"How? By admitting that I enjoy having a life and a career of my own as much as I enjoy being with you? What's wrong with my wanting time for myself? You have time for *your*self."

"I'm not objecting to that, Daye. What I can't accept is being slotted into your timetable whenever you're through with your work and have a few hours to spare. I want to spend much more than just hand-me-down time with you, Daye. I wouldn't expect you to give up your career for me any more than I would expect you to ask me to give up mine for you. It isn't a question of giving up; it's a matter of making room for both work *and* a relationship."

"But I *am*, Jonathan," she insisted, her hurt and confusion mounting. "I *have* made room for you, more than I've ever made for any other man at any other time in my entire life."

His eyes were sad, his expression baleful as he said, "I believe you, Daye, but there's still something standing in the way, and if it isn't your work, then it has to be Neil Howard."

Daye could feel her muscles beginning to tense. "What can I say to convince you that Neil and I are only friends?"

"You can start by telling me that you were never lovers."

"Jonathan!" Her eyes were wide, and her head was starting to pound.

"You were, weren't you?"

"Neil has nothing to do with us."

"He has *every*thing to do with us, Daye."

She shook her head, and the room dipped and tilted in front of her eyes.

"Were you lovers, Daye? Are you lovers now?"

Her dinner began slithering upward into her throat. She swallowed hard, forcing the rising nausea back down again. "Why are you asking me this, Jonathan?" she whispered. "Why do you want to know?"

"Because whatever you had or are still having with Neil Howard is standing between what the two of us could have together."

Daye felt faint. The room seemed to be growing alternately brighter and fainter as though someone were playing with the light switch.

"He's not letting you go, Daye." Jonathan's voice was an insistent thrumming inside her aching head. "You're not free of him, and until you are, you'll never be able to fully share anything with anyone else. You've got to break his hold on you, Daye, or we don't have a chance."

"He has no hold on me!" she cried. Yet even as she was denying it, she could see Neil's eyes boring into hers and feel his body so close to hers that she couldn't breathe. She got up from her chair and stumbled over to the sink to turn on the cold water.

"Daye." He came up behind her and slipped his arms around her waist. His breath was warm on her neck, and his body was forcing hers up against the counter. "Daye, please."

She was suffocating. "No, Neil!" she whimpered, pushing him away from her.

She saw his eyes widen and watched as he backed away from her, his arms falling heavily to his sides. Darting past him into the living room, she picked up her purse and headed for the front door.

"Daye," he called out to her as she began fumbling with the lock, "the name's Jonathan, not Neil!"

It was only then that she realized what she had said.

chapter twenty-one

DAYE TURNED over onto her stomach in bed and watched the play of shadows on the ceiling. Sleep was impossible; even lying still seemed impossible. Her entire body was on fire, alive with a restlessness that no amount of shifting or squirming could appease. She had taken a warm bath with the lights out and sipped some brandy in the tub in an effort to relax, but that hadn't worked at all. She had taken a Valium with a glass of milk an hour later, but that hadn't helped either. It was now three in the morning, and she was still wide awake and churning inside.

She switched on one of the bedside lamps and reached for the telephone. It was no use; she simply had to call him. She had to apologize for what she had inadvertently said in a moment of extreme duress when the images inside her head had become confused and had merged into one. As she dialed his number, she thought about what she was going to say to him. Somehow nothing sounded quite right. By the fourth ring, she began hoping that he wouldn't answer. But he did.

"Jonathan," she breathed into the mouthpiece as though she were speaking directly into his ear, "Jonathan, I'm sorry if I woke you, but I just had to call."

"It's all right," he said. "I wasn't getting much sleep anyway."

"Jonathan, I want to apologize for what happened. I never meant to call you Neil."

"I shouldn't have pushed you that far, Daye. I'm very sorry that I did."

"It just slipped out because I was thinking about—"

"You don't have to explain," he told her. "I understand."

"Do you? Do you really?"

He let out a low sigh. "Yes, Daye, I think I do."

She was suddenly wary. "I don't think I like the sound of that."

"No more than I do," he said.

She sat straight up in bed as a bolt of alarm shot through her. "Jonathan, it was just a slip of the tongue. Please don't build it into something more than what it was."

"I'm not," he insisted, "but what bothers me so much is your refusal to even consider what I was saying to you."

"You're allowing your own suspicions to spoil things for us, you know."

"I don't want to spoil anything, Daye, because what we have is good, very good, and I'd hoped to see it get even better."

"Then why can't it?"

"Because you're still in love with Neil Howard."

The words were a scourge lashed across her heart, cutting her deeply and making her wince in pain. No, it wasn't true. She didn't love Neil Howard. Her passion for him had burned itself out long ago, and all that remained was the memory of what they had once shared. That and the illusion of what they might have shared had she been anyone but who she was and he had been anything but what he had become. Jonathan was wrong, and in a tremulous voice she told him so.

"Then, if I'm wrong about your career and wrong about Neil, that leaves just you and me, Daye," he said. "Maybe *we're* not working."

"That's not true," she cried. "That's not true at all. You said yourself what we have is good, and it is, we *are* good together." She was drowning, and instead of helping her, he was holding her head under the water. "Jonathan, we shouldn't be discussing this over the phone. We might say things we don't mean, things we won't be able to take back afterward. There's nothing wrong with us; we're just two people who are still trying to learn how to fit comfortably together. Can't you believe that?"

"I want to, Daye," he sighed. "I want to more than you could possibly know."

"Then believe it, Jonathan," she urged him. "Please, please believe it."

"Let's give it some time, then, okay?" he said, his voice now sounding weak and strained. "Forgive me, Daye, but I'm exhausted, and I've got to try to get some sleep."

He was cutting her off. Her rising panic kicked and clawed at her, tearing her insides to shreds while she battled to contain it.

"All right." She gave in, trying to sound brave, refusing to let him hear how defeated she felt. "Sleep well, Jonathan."

"You too, Daye."

After she put down the phone, she lay back in bed again and cursed herself for having called him. Nothing had been accomplished by it; nothing had been resolved. They hadn't gotten any further than where they had been before she had walked out after dinner. Around and around it went, always coming back again to the same thing. They were spinning on a carousel of confusion, and in the center of that confusion was Neil Howard, just as it had always been Neil Howard, standing between her and every man she had ever tried to love.

She and Jonathan saw each other only three more times during the next two weeks. They met as though they were strangers out on an arranged date, exchanging polite small talk on a variety of safe subjects in neutral surroundings where any discussion of a more personal nature was a guaranteed impossibility. The first evening they attended a performance of *The Student Prince* at the Royal Palm Dinner Theater in Boca; the second they went to the opening of an exhibit of Daumier pen and ink sketches at the Society of the Four Arts in Palm Beach; on the third evening, they went to a lecture on the Emerging Theater in Africa at FAU. After each event, Jonathan took Daye directly home, kissed her good night in the car, and then walked her only as far as the elevators in the lobby.

On her own, she used her work as a shield against her confusion and her pain, pushing herself through the days and then collapsing out of sheer fatigue late each night. As always, her work served her well, acting as the palliative she needed, but when August 15 arrived and Jonathan was scheduled to leave for New York on Eastern's morning flight to attend the first rehearsals of *Arpeggio in Blue*, she began to doubt that her work would see her through their separation. As she drove him to the airport in West Palm, she was so weighed down with despair that only the prospect of meeting Franki at Petite Marmite at one gave her the strength she needed to carry off their parting with some measure of dignity. And yet, in spite of her resolve to remain as detached as possible, just before they reached the airport, she turned to him and said, "I'm going to miss you, Jonathan."

"I'll only be gone a week or so," he reminded her.

"I know that, but I'm still going to miss you."

"Are you so sure about that?" His tone was teasing, but there was a skeptical slant to his dark eyebrows as he studied her face.

"Are you just trying to pick a fight with me so I *won't* miss you?" she asked him.

"Maybe."

"Well, don't."

"All right, I won't," he agreed, but a moment later, he added, "I'm going to miss you, too, Daye."

For the first time in two weeks, she felt a slight easing of the knot in her stomach.

"That's good," she murmured with a touch of a smile.

He was looking out the window when he said, in as nonchalant a manner as possible, "No sense in both of us missing each other. Why don't you fly up to New York with me?"

Her fingers loosened then tightened around the wheel, and her heart began to lift. "I can't," she said. "As much as I'm tempted, I just can't. I have only a few more days of work on Neil's offices, and then I'll finally be through."

"Do I detect a note of relief in your voice?" Again his look was skeptical.

"You most certainly do."

"Now, that's a refreshing change," he commented with a low chuckle.

She chose to ignore his remark. "The best part about completing the project is the party Neil's promised to throw for me," she said, feeling far more expansive now. "Who knows? It might help me to attract that one crucial account I still need."

"Well, I'd say that's a fairly persuasive reason for not wanting to come to New York with me."

"Jonathan, please don't start anything," she warned him.

"I'm sorry, Daye. I just wish I could wrench you free from that work of yours for a while. I want you to have some fun."

"But my work is fun," she argued. "You really don't have to feel sorry for me at all, you know."

"I think I'm feeling sorrier for myself right now," he muttered, slouching in his seat and folding his arms across his chest.

As she circled the crowded airport parking lot for the second time in her search for a parking space, he said, "Don't bother trying to park, Daye. Why don't you just drop me off in front of the terminal?"

"But I want to come in with you."

He glanced at his watch. "I hadn't realized we'd cut it so close. The plane should be boarding any minute now."

"There's a spot," she announced, seeing a car pull out just ahead of them. She smiled to herself as she swung into the parking space and cut the engine. Snatching the keys from the ignition and grabbing her purse from the seat beside her, she turned to Jonathan. "Ready?" she asked him.

"Ready."

To combat her growing apprehensiveness, she kept up a steady flow of chatter all the way into the Eastern terminal. They rode the escalator to the second floor where Jonathan checked in, and then she walked with him through security to the gate and waited while he chose his seat. Watching all the other passengers preparing to board their own flights made her suddenly feel envious of them. If only Neil's project were finished. Then nothing could have kept her from gladly boarding that plane with Jonathan and escaping with him for a while. She was grateful when he turned to her and pulled her into his arms, but his kiss made her wish that they were alone. She needed him to make love to her, to make her believe that they were about to be separated by nothing more fearsome than distance and a period of seven to ten days.

"Oh, Jonathan," she whispered his name into his chest as she burrowed as close to him as she could, "Jonathan, I think I already miss you."

His laugh made her cling to him even more tightly. "My sweet, beautiful Daye," he murmured, kissing her over and over again on the mouth. "Forgive me, Daye, forgive me for having been so—"

"There you are, Jonathan darling. I thought I'd missed you."

Daye froze. Her heart skidded and sank into the churning maelstrom within her stomach. So Maren had come to see him off. As she turned slowly in Jonathan's arms, steeling herself for the inevitable, her eyes suddenly widened in disbelief. The woman bounding toward them, jet earrings swinging, her long russet skirt slapping about her ankles, had a large black tote bag slung over one shoulder and an airline ticket in her hand. Without even acknowledging Daye's presence, Maren plucked Jonathan's ticket out of his hand and glanced at the seat number indicated on his boarding pass.

"Be back in a moment, love." She blew him a kiss and went off to take her place in line.

Daye stared up at Jonathan in silence and waited for some explanation.

"She's interested in a playhouse that's just been put up for sale in the Village," he explained as casually as if he were giving Daye a weather report, "and she asked me to take a look at it with her."

"How convenient."

"She knew I was leaving for New York this morning, so she thought she'd fly up for the day and—"

"I don't think I want to hear any more, thank you, Jonathan."

"Daye, I'm just doing her a favor. It's nothing more complicated than that."

"Is that why you didn't want me to come inside with you, Jonathan?" she demanded, in spite of the warning glint in his dark eyes. "I wouldn't have had to know then, would I?"

"There is absolutely nothing to know, dammit!" he hissed,

catching hold of her elbow and giving her a shake. "Time was short. I didn't think it was worth it to—"

"Oh, I'd say it was more than worth it!" She was brimming over with doubt and mistrust as she cut him off again. "Have a very pleasant trip, Jonathan." Wrenching her arm free, she started through the terminal alone.

"Daye!" he shouted. "Daye, come back here! Don't run away like that again. Daye!"

In spite of his plea, she kept on walking with her head held high and her shoulders squared while the tears collected in silent pools behind her dark glasses. And he had accused *her* of not being free. What a pair they made, the two of them.

SHE SPUN through the final days of work on Neil's project on nerves alone and very little else. Unable to sleep for more than minutes at a time, her appetite smothered by the blanket of pain lining her stomach, she was a living sore—sensitive to being touched, jumping at every sudden sound, finding even the dimmest light too bright. Jonathan hadn't called, and she had vowed that this time she wouldn't be the one to call first.

When the last painting was hung and the final cluster of flowering plants arranged in Neil's own office, Daye was near collapse. All she wanted to do now was lock herself in the condo, lose herself in some mindless evening soap on TV, and then sleep for a week. But Neil had other plans.

"You can't give out on me now, Daye," he complained when she sank into the chair behind his desk and closed her eyes. "You've earned yourself the right to a celebration for the magnificent job you've done, and I intend to see that you have one."

She opened her eyes again and tried to focus on his face. "I thought you were throwing an open house to celebrate," she said.

"I am, but I'm talking about a celebration for two in the meantime, just you and me."

"Oh, Neil, I'm exhausted. I couldn't tonight."

"Daye, it's six o'clock. We'll have one quick drink, and then, over dinner, we'll work on a guest list for the party." He came around the desk and laid his hands on her shoulders.

"Come on, Button," he urged her softly as he began kneading her shoulders in an effort to loosen the knots of tension in them, "say yes."

"O-oh, that feels so-o-o good," she sighed blissfully and closed her eyes again.

"Say yes or I'll stop."

"Neil!"

"Say yes," he repeated as he took his hands away.

"Okay," she conceded, "yes."

"Good girl." He gave her a kiss of approval on the top of her head and continued to work on her shoulders until he saw her head roll forward and her chin touch her chest. "Are you falling asleep, Daye Peters?" He gave her a light shake, and her head bobbed back up again.

"I think I'm falling asleep," she said, aiming a wobbly grin up at him.

"Oh, no, you don't."

"Neil!" she gasped in protest as he hauled her out of the chair and pointed her in the direction of the door.

"Now, march!" he commanded her, picking up her purse and then catching hold of her arm as she stumbled against a table and nearly fell. "Christ," he muttered, "and you haven't even had anything to drink yet."

Bennigan's on Federal Highway remedied that situation almost immediately. Somewhere amid the smoke, the blaring punk rock music, the staccato bleeps of four Pac-Man video games, and the animated babble of the young jean and T-shirt crowd standing three deep around the vast square bar, Daye lost track of the number of rye and gingers she had downed. Neil's face was now only slightly more clearly defined than the hanging green plants suspended above their wooden booth and the face of their handsome young waiter, who seemed to be a clone of every other Bennigan's waiter in that clean-cut, all-American way. With her head resting on Neil's shoulder, Daye was drifting high above the music, beyond the confines of their booth, past the pain and the loneliness caused by her latest confrontation with Jonathan, and heading toward an elevated plateau where all was peaceful numbness.

"The offices really do look beautiful, don't they, Neil?" she asked him for what must have been the tenth time that evening, but she had already lost track of that, too.

"Yes, Daye," he agreed, giving her a gentle pat on the cheek and then allowing his arm to remain lightly draped about her shoulder, "the offices *do* look beautiful."

"How many people did we manage to put down on the guest list?"

"About two hundred, give or take a dozen or so."

"A dozen or so what?"

"People."

"What people?"

"Daye, you're drunk!" He scowled accusingly at her and pushed her glass to the far end of the table. "Let's order something to eat before you pass out on me."

She threaded her way to the ladies' room and back twice before the food arrived, and then all she could manage to eat was a small portion of her chef's salad and the heel of a piece of French bread. It was only after drinking some of Neil's cappucino that some of the effects of the liquor began to wear off; but by the time she had finished the double cappucino he had ordered for her in spite of her protests, her head felt more like her own again.

"Feeling better now?" he asked her, and she nodded.

"Thank you," she said, giving his hand a tight squeeze.

"For what?"

"For being here, I guess."

It seemed so natural somehow, so natural and so right for the two of them to have celebrated this way after having worked so well together. She leaned her head against his shoulder again and smiled to herself when he wrapped his arms protectively around her and hugged her. She was still suspended on that gentle cloud provided for her by her own fatigue and the alcohol she had consumed, but her sense of well-being had less to do with that now than with Neil's holding her. This was how it could have been for them, she realized with a wistful sigh. The two of them—equal halves of that perfect team, meeting every challenge together and thriving on it, then cherishing each successful completion by celebrating, just as they were celebrating now.

As Neil continued to cuddle her and to gently stroke her arm, the warmth from his body began to penetrate hers, spreading across the surface of her skin like a flash fire, igniting each of her pores and every follicle of her hair. An insistent pulsing began deep inside her, and she squirmed in her seat, crossing her legs in an effort to force the feeling back down again. She nearly jumped when he put his hand on her knee and started to caress it lightly. Instead of relaxing her as she assumed he had intended it to, his touch served only to inflame her further, forcing the pulsing to quicken and pushing the intensifying heat through every open channel of her being.

"I think you'd better take me home now, Neil," she whispered as she strained to break his hold on her.

"Is that an invitation or simply a request?" he whispered back, his lips catching her on the cheek as she straightened up beside him and shook out her hair.

This brought her breasts into direct contact with his arm, and she gasped at the sharp burst of exquisite fire that streaked from each tensing nipple to her groin.

"Are you all right?" Gripping her by the chin, he forced her head around until she was facing him.

"Yes," she gulped, "yes, I'm fine."

Her lips, she knew, were parted; his were far too near, and yet she couldn't move. She couldn't widen that narrowing ribbon of space still separating them. In that one dizzying moment before their lips met, they were no longer who they were now but who they had been once, a lifetime ago, before they had made their choices and started down the paths of their separate lives. And in that kiss was everything she had had once and given up and fought against ever having with him again.

Let's leave it at that, she wanted to tell him. Let's leave it behind us where it rightfully belongs, because it can have no place in what either of us has now.

"Daye, I want you." His words were an urgent plea, a yearning command passing from his mouth to hers.

"Neil, I—"

"Daye, please, let me take you home."

She accepted the strength lent to her by his supporting arm as they left the restaurant because she no longer possessed any strength of her own. And when they stood together in the foyer of her apartment, she knew that having her own strength back wouldn't have made any difference now. She moved to turn on the lights, but he stopped her.

"Leave them off," he said, and she complied.

She led him down the hallway to her darkened bedroom, moving in a trance, only partly aware of where she was and what she was about to do. They would leave it behind them here afterward, she decided, as she lit two raspberry-colored votive candles and placed them on the bedside tables. Then she turned to him and slowly slid her hands up along his chest until she was able to twine her arms around his neck and lock them there. His mouth seized hers, and she parted her lips to accommodate his probing tongue, meeting it with hers and circling it, warily at first, and then hungrily, greedily.

While they continued to kiss, they began to undress. He turned for a moment to toss his wristwatch and his keys onto the bedside table nearest them, and then he continued with his tender exploration of her body as it was being revealed to him bit by tantalizing bit. Yielding to his mounting urgency, Daye worked quickly to release him from his shirt, longing to feel the springy warmth of the fine blond hair covering his chest against the coolness of her breasts. Freed at last from the constraints of their clothing, they began at the beginning again, remembering as they did that, although they had been lovers once, they were meeting now as strangers.

His touch was both alien to her and wonderfully familiar. The smell of him that lived in her nostrils was the smell of Neil as a boy and as a man, but the sensations he was stirring up inside her now were the sensations only the man had stirred during their few stolen times together so many years ago. With the intervening years miraculously disappearing in the intensity of the moment they were now sharing, the eternity that had separated their present from their past was a boundary she no longer recognized or felt. The very inevitability of it all propelled her forward when she still might have found the courage to pull herself back. Yet even as they narrowed the gap that had kept them safely divided for so long, she knew that all she wanted was one final glimpse of what might have been before she let go of him forever.

Where his hands had been exploring, his mouth now followed, leaving behind it a moistened path of tingling pleasure as he anointed her body from the base of her neck to the tops of her thighs. Kneeling before her on the carpet, he parted her legs, cupping her first with his hand and then with his mouth. She sighed, widening her legs for him and granting him access to her inner warmth. Burying her fingers deep in his thick blond hair and throwing back her head she began to moan softly as he penetrated her smooth silkiness with his tongue.

She stared into the flickering flame of the small votive candle and felt it mesmerizing her, while her body continued to respond with increasing fervor to his lapping tongue. Swaying above him, her back arched, the muscles in her legs stretched taut, she soared up and then plunged down again as he expertly teased her toward and then let her ease away from her climax. With her eyes now focused on the golden gleam of his watch and the silvered spread of his keys on the night table, she moaned again, louder this time, as his tongue moved faster and thrust harder to send her spiraling upward to her release at last.

Her eyes widened as she began to scream. Her screams had nothing whatsoever to do with pleasure; they were shrill howls of agonized denial and disbelief. She staggered backward, away from him, half-falling and then quickly recovering her balance.

"Daye," he choked out, "Daye, what's wrong?"

She didn't hear him. She didn't even see him. All she could hear was the sound of her own screaming, and all she could see was a key with its head painted scarlet.

"No," she sobbed, "no, no, no." She put her hands over her mouth to muffle her screams. Then she covered her eyes to block out what she had just seen.

"Daye, what is it?" Neil was on his feet and grabbing for her. "Hold still, for God's sake, and tell me what it is."

She danced away from him and flung herself across her bed. Her mind was reeling, and she doubled herself over in agony as her stomach began to pitch and heave. It couldn't be, it simply couldn't be! It was a mistake, a cruel coincidence, she told herself. But how many keys had their heads painted in Indian Red by Dior? It *was* no mistake, no cruel coincidence at all.

"Daye, please." He sounded close to tears himself as he sat down on the bed and reached for her, only to have her kick out at him with a savage snarl of pain.

Still sobbing, she raised herself up on her hands and knees and crawled across the bed until she was able to stretch out her hand and close it around his keys. Singling out the one she wanted, she sat back on her heels and dangled it in front of him, watching his eyes narrow and his dark face blanch as he looked from the key to her face and then back at the key again. In a voice hardly more than a whisper, she said, "This is my key, isn't it, Neil?"

At that, his face grew even paler.

"It is, isn't it, Neil?"

He tried to snatch the keys away from her then, but she hid both hands behind her back.

"Answer me, Neil."

"Daye, I—"

"Where did you get it, Neil?"

"Please—"

"Where did you get it?"

His shoulders sagged, and he looked down at the bed. "Franki gave it to me," he murmured.

"Franki gave it to you," she repeated, feeling her throat constrict as she said the name of her best friend, "and you and Franki have been having an affair."

It seemed that an eternity had passed before he finally nodded. "Yes."

Breathless from the pain spearing her chest, all she could manage to gasp out was, "Why? Dear God, why?"

"Why?" he echoed, his eyes suddenly blank, his face devoid of all expression.

"Yes, Neil, why?"

He spread his hands before her like a supplicant pleading for understanding and mercy. "Because she was available, that's why. She wanted it, and I guess I needed it. It was as simple as that. Taylor Mead was the perfect foil."

"My house..." Daye's voice trailed off. "You used *my* house and you both used *me*." Her voice was slowly gaining strength again, rising without her even being aware of it. "You're despicable, both of you!" she cried. "How did it feel, Neil?" she demanded. "How did it feel coming into *my* home and making love in *my* home to *my* best friend?" Her tears bubbled to the surface again and began rolling down her cheeks. All three of them had had Neil Howard now. All three. And of the three of them, only she knew the truth. "Are you pleased?" she sobbed, choking on her rage and her sense of betrayal. "Now that you've made it with all three of us, do you feel like some kind of macho hero, Neil? Do you think you've set some sort of record? Maybe they'll put you in *The Guinness Book of World Records* for this or in *Ripley's Believe It or Not* or—"

"Stop it, Daye, stop it right now!" He took her by the shoulders and started to shake her. "You're hysterical, Daye. Stop it, I said. Stop it now, please!"

His shaking served only to increase her fury. It made her strike out at him, slapping at him blindly, hitting him in the face, across the chest, in the stomach, deep in his groin. The keys flew out of her hand and landed on the carpet near the wall as they grappled with each other—he trying to calm her down, she spitting and clawing and crying.

"Get out of here, Neil!" she shrieked, slapping him one final time on the chest. "Give me back my key and then get out of my house!"

Flinging her away from him, he stumbled from the bed without another word. She seized the moment to locate a long dressing gown hanging on the back of the bathroom door and to put it on. When she came back into the bedroom again, she saw that the key was already lying on top of the bedside table next to the now guttering votive candle, and that Neil was almost dressed. As she watched him, it seemed to her that he couldn't dress quickly enough. She burned with the desire to scratch and scar every inch of his flesh, to hurl him to the floor and crush him beneath her feet, as if by doing so, she could pound into dust not only his body but all traces of her memory of him as well. She had never thought herself capable of such a towering rage, and the fact that she was, terrified her.

When he was finally dressed, he came to stand in front of her. He reached out for a strand of her hair, but she angrily pushed his hand away.

"I've never stopped wanting you, Daye," he told her, his eyes so dull with pain that she found it difficult to look at him. "I had thought that with you living down here in Florida, we'd have a chance to get back what we once had. But I was wrong. You went out and found yourself Jonathan Cort instead."

"So you used Franki to punish me."

He shook his head. "We used each other, Button, but she was never a substitute for you. I'm sorry this had to happen, Daye, because tonight we finally had that chance."

"You're wrong, Neil," she said. "Tonight would simply have put an end to that illusion once and for all."

For one lingering moment, their eyes met and held.

"Are you so sure about that, Daye?" he asked her.

Engulfed as she was by her pain, she was incapable of seeing beyond that pain and into the uncertainty of what might have been. And so she didn't even try to answer him.

"Franki has a second key," he said, in a voice that seemed to be drifting farther and farther away from her. "I'll get it back for you."

"No, you won't," she told him, "I intend to take it back from Franki myself."

"Daye—"

"Good-bye, Neil."

In her tone was a finality that kept her standing exactly where she was while it forced him to leave her there and walk away. When she heard the front door closing softly behind him, she began to tremble. Weaving on unsteady legs, she tottered into the bathroom and sank to her knees on the floor in front of the toilet. She flung back the seat just in time. Bending over the bowl, she allowed all of the pain and the guilt and the bitter regret to surge out of her aching body in one continuous, cleansing tide.

chapter twenty-two

As SOON as she heard the car pulling into the driveway, Rhea laid her book down on the table beside her bed and switched off the light. At two in the morning, the last thing she wanted was to have to listen to some involved explanation from Neil as to where he had been and with whom. Burrowing under the covers with the comforter tugged up to her chin, she stretched out her legs and wriggled her toes to relieve some of the fatigue in her leg muscles. She had worked all day on the latest in the series of twenty watercolors she had started after her first visit with Steven, and she was exhausted. But it was a happy kind of exhaustion, because she considered this newest watercolor, showing Steven sitting in a chair holding all three of his stuffed animals, to be the best she had ever done.

When she heard Neil starting up the stairs, she turned over onto her side, keeping her eyes partly closed while she trained them on the open bedroom door. As she lay there waiting, her thoughts drifted back to Steven, and she found herself beginning to smile in eager anticipation of the third trip she was about to make up to Alindale. The smile congealed on her face.

Neil was standing there in the doorway, the light from the hall behind him and his face in shadow. Tensing, she held her breath, releasing it only when he turned around and headed back down the hall. But instead of continuing on to the guest room he still occupied, he stopped just outside the door of his study, hesitating there briefly before finally entering the room and quietly closing the door behind him.

A few minutes later, the muffled sound of the telephone being slammed down made Rhea sit bolt upright in bed with a scowl on her face and her heart pounding. Whom could he have been calling at this hour? she wondered. To her astonishment, it wasn't long before he was on the phone again. She heard him raise his voice for an instant, as though he had forgotten himself, and then just as quickly drop it again. Bristling with curiosity, she glanced at the telephone next to the bed and wondered if she dared pick it up.

Before she could think better of it or even try to stop herself, she was carefully lifting the receiver from its cradle. Taking a deep breath, she held it up to her ear. But all she heard was the harsh hum of the dial tone.

DAYE PUT down the phone and slowly leaned back against her pillow. Her head was throbbing, her stomach still ached, her throat felt raw and sore, and she had a harsh metallic taste in her mouth. Covering her face with her hands, she used the tips of her fingers to massage her swollen eyelids in an effort to rub away some of their stinging soreness, but it didn't seem to help. Her sudden recollection of the very first words Franki had ever spoken to her forced a fresh gush of hot tears into her reddened eyes and only added to her discomfort. How appropriate those words were now, she thought bitterly as she blew her nose and wiped at her streaming eyes again. She had been crying over Neil then, too.

The telephone started to ring again, but this time she ignored it. She didn't want to hear him pleading with her again to forgive him, to meet with him to talk about what had happened, to try to find a way for them to remain friends, if not for their sake, then at least for Rhea's. If she had possessed the strength, she might have been able to laugh at that last bit of reasoning, but most of her strength had already been channeled into guilt and self-hatred and utter despair. Not only had he helped render her incapable of ever properly loving another man, but he had now effectively driven himself like a wedge between her two best friends and herself, and she would never forgive him for that.

It was over between them once and for all. By his own actions, he had destroyed the very thing he had hoped to preserve. His betrayal of her had finally succeeded where time and distance and other men had always failed, freeing her at last, when she had again begun to doubt her own ability ever to truly free herself.

But there was something else. He had told her tonight that he had never stopped wanting her, but he hadn't said anything about loving her. She finally had the answer to the question that had haunted her most of her life. Neil didn't love her, and he never had. Without ever knowing how it felt to be loved as a child, Neil Howard had grown up incapable of loving anyone. This last truth, more than anything else, would keep her free of him forever.

She wove in and out of a troubled sleep, her dreams alive with writhing images, deformed and ugly, all of them twisted distortions of scarlet-topped keys and Neil's parting lips, of Rhea's hurt gray eyes and Franki's happy smile, and of Daye herself standing alone on the beach while Jonathan walked away from her and the tide washed his footprints out to sea. She woke up shivering, with her teeth chattering, her skin damp, and her hair plastered against her face. Missing Jonathan, aching for Rhea, dreading her inevitable confrontation with Franki, she lay tangled up in her rumpled sheets, holding her hands to her throbbing head, wondering where she would find the energy she needed just to get out of bed.

While a thousand tiny mallets drove a thousand tiny spikes of pain into her body, she managed to take a shower and wash her hair, swallow two aspirins and drink a cup of weak herbal tea. She moved gingerly when she walked, but there was a fierceness to her movements as she tore the sheets and pillow-cases from the hide-a-bed in the den, stuffed them into a large green trash bag and shoved the bag into the garbage chute in the incinerator room. Then she went into her bathroom where she soaked several cotton balls in nail polish remover and began scrubbing at the head of her house key, making certain that no traces of Indian Red polish remained before she tossed the key into the top drawer of her dresser.

Steeling herself for what she was about to do next, she sat down on the edge of the bed and reached for the telephone. It took her several minutes before she was finally able to punch out the first digit of Franki's number. The other six were just as difficult. To her relief, the line was busy. But no sooner had she hung up than her own phone began to ring, startling her into dropping the receiver in her haste to pick it up. It was Franki.

"Daye, I've got to talk to you." Her voice sounded breathy and rushed. "Can we meet at Ta-boo at noon?"

Daye opened her mouth to reply to her, but her heart had lodged itself in her throat and she couldn't speak.

"Please, Daye, we have to talk."

Swallowing hard, Daye nodded, just managing to force out a squeaky yes before the receiver slipped out of her hands.

Even with her dark glasses on, she was grateful for the dim interior of the restaurant today as she followed the maître d' to the corner booth where Franki was already waiting, her own dark glasses firmly in place. At any other time, the two of them would have laughed at the absurdity of wearing sunglasses in a place like Ta-boo, but today neither of them could muster more than a feeble attempt at a smile for each other. Instead of sliding onto the leather banquette beside Franki as she always did, Daye hesitated for a moment and then pulled out a chair for herself and sat down, keeping her hands threaded together tightly in her lap.

"Daye, I'm so sorry," Franki blurted out almost immediately, her eyes fixed on the flickering candle in the center of the table. "I'm sorry you had to find out like that. I never meant to use you or hurt you; neither of us did. What happened between us just happened. Neil was there, and—"

"So are a lot of other people, Franki," Daye couldn't help cutting her off, "but you don't have to make lovers out of them."

"Please don't lecture me, Daye. This is hard enough—"

"I'm not lecturing you. What I'm really trying to do is sit here without screaming or clawing out the eyes of the person I thought was one of my two best friends. How could you, Franki!" she demanded. "How could you have done it, and in my home, too! If you had to have an affair with someone, why couldn't it have been Taylor Mead, why did it have to be Neil?"

Franki's eyes were still focused on the candle as she murmured, "You wouldn't understand, Daye."

"Why wouldn't I?"

"Because I'm still trying to understand all of it myself."

Taken aback by her answer, all Daye could manage was to whisper, "But I thought we were friends."

Franki met her eyes for the first time then, and her reply was anguished. "We were," she said, "and I hope we still are."

"Dear God, how *can* we be?" Daye began to blink rapidly in a vain effort to keep from crying. But all she could think of was Rhea's gentle innocence being ravaged by the duplicity of her two best friends, and she was soon sobbing openly. "How, Franki?" she asked. "Tell me how the three of us can possibly be friends now?"

She was nearly gagging on her tears and her own guilt and the sickening silence stretching out between them by the time she was able to find the strength to push herself to her feet again.

"Daye!" Franki's voice cracked and then broke completely. "Daye, please don't go. Please stay and help me find a way to keep us together. Please."

"No," she sobbed, shaking her head, "not now. I can't now." Putting out her hand, she whispered, "The key, Franki; please give me back the key."

It was cold and hard when Franki placed it in her outstretched palm, yet it burned like a vicious brand, worming its way through the surface of her skin and into her bloodstream as she closed her fingers around it. She stumbled from the restaurant, heedless of the pointed stares and the shocked expressions of the people she passed, no longer caring that she was breaking an unwritten law in Palm Beach by making a spectacle of herself in public. She walked along Worth Avenue in the steamy blaze of the noonday sun until she located a small metal trash can discreetly placed behind a low privet hedge. Lifting the lid, she dropped the key inside, watching as it disappeared under a pile of yesterday's newspapers.

FRANKI STOPPED in front of the Lilly Pulitzer shop in the Via Parigi off Worth and studied the quilted green and yellow floral baby comforter in the window. Instead of her usual excitement at having discovered something new and tempting to buy the baby, all she felt was a mild sense of curiosity. Her meeting with Daye had left her feeling deflated and depressed, both of them such alien feelings to her that she wore them now as she would a prickly wool sweater over wet and sensitive skin. What a fool she had been not to have ended her affair with Neil sooner. That way Daye would never have found out about it, and nothing would have had to change for any of them. But it was over now, and she was glad.

Glad? That was a strange word for her to be using at a time like this, she thought, as she stared bleakly at her reflection in the glass. Was she glad she had encouraged Daye to assume that she had been sleeping with Taylor Mead? Was she glad she had borrowed Rhea's husband to give her what her own husband could never give her? Was she glad she couldn't share the news of her pregnancy with anyone, especially now, when Daye might suspect the truth and tell Neil? Was she glad that as a result of her condition she had dropped out of the tennis tournament and stopped playing the one sport she truly loved and excelled in?

For the first time in her pregnancy, she suddenly began to feel nauseated. Forgetting about the comforter in the window, she started back to her car, breaking into a run and praying as she ran that she wasn't about to humiliate herself by being sick on Worth Avenue right in front of Cartier's.

DAYE TOOK the roses and stuffed them—green florist's tissue, card, maidenhair ferns, and all—into the wastebasket next to her desk. Not only had Neil been sending her flowers daily, but he was continuing to call her both at home and at the office with unrelenting regularity. He had even had the temerity to buzz her from the lobby of her building that morning, but she had refused to allow him to come up.

"No calls please, Connie." She issued the command to her assistant in the next room with a light rap on the wall for emphasis.

"Not even Neil Howard?" came the teasing response from the other side of the wall.

"Especially Neil Howard."

"What about Jonathan Cort?"

Daye had no clever reply to that one.

"Da-ye?"

"Use your own discretion."

"Oh, safe, Daye, very safe."

"Get back to work, Connie!"

"Yes, ma'am."

Daye had successfully managed to forget all about Jonathan that morning, but as soon as she heard Connie mention his name, she felt herself backsliding again. He still hadn't called, and she still refused to call him. Gritting her teeth, she picked up a pencil and began tapping the end of it against her temple. She wished she could use it to drum every thought of Jonathan Cort from her head and replace it with only thoughts that concerned the problem confronting her at the moment.

"Problem?" She startled herself by voicing that last thought aloud. It was all she could do to keep from hugging herself and dancing around the room. What confronted her now was not a problem at all, but the potential *solution* to the problem that had been haunting her ever since her arrival in Florida.

After ten frustrating months, the opportunity she had hoped for had chosen the most unlikely of times to finally present itself to her. Now when she was at her weakest and her most vulnerable, she was being challenged to garner all of her resources and to concentrate all of her creative energies on one major venture. The O'Connell-Reardon Corporation of Dallas, one of the country's largest land developers, had announced plans to begin work on a condominium complex in Palm Beach, which would back onto Lake Worth. The complex was to consist of three six-story glass towers set on landscaped grounds, two swimming pools complete with cabanas, three tennis courts, and a small private marina. They promised to be the most exclusive and opulent condominiums in all of south Florida with units beginning at 1.5 million dollars. Full-page color ads had already begun to appear in the most prestigious magazines in the United States and Europe, and three south Florida interior designers had been asked to submit their proposals for the model apartments, the cabanas, and all of the public areas in each of the three buildings. The designers selected were Philippe Nadeau, a Miami designer by the name of Bryce Lanihan, and Daye. And she was determined to be the one they ultimately chose.

What had further hardened her resolve was the telephone call she had received from Philippe as soon as the names of the three designers had been released. Although his tone had been cordial enough, the undercurrent of vitriolic hostility running through his voice had rankled.

"As they say here in America, *ma chère* Daye," he had said in concluding their brief but strained interchange, "may the best man win."

She had drawn her own very obvious conclusions from that final remark and had put down the phone with a muttered curse unbecoming the lady she still considered herself to be.

After studying the O'Connell-Reardon architectural plans very carefully, she set them aside, unrolled that first piece of white paper onto her drafting table, and tacked it down with fine metal thumbtacks. Now it was her turn. Using only her imagination and all of her decorating skills, she was to provide a color for every blank wall, a covering for each bare floor, and furnished space where only empty space existed now. With her pencil in her hand, her mind focused on a concept only she could see, she was vibrating again with the life force that the last few days had drained out of her. She was in control again, the word Jonathan had used so disparagingly to describe her that night. Perhaps he was right after all. In her work, she *was* in control. She had to be, if she was to best Philippe and establish herself here at last.

Her nights were soon indistinguishable from her days as she used every precious hour to translate her ideas first into working sketches and then into finished plans. When the telephone woke her at seven one morning, she assumed it was the alarm, only to discover, to her dismay, that she had shut off the alarm at five and fallen asleep again. Disoriented and still drugged with sleep, she wasn't able to recognize his voice. Even when he told her it was Jonathan, she didn't know whether to believe him or not.

"The password is *Arpeggio in Blue*," he said with a husky laugh that sounded vaguely familiar to her. "Now do you believe me?"

She cleared her throat, but her voice still came out sounding hoarse and subdued. "I was sleeping," she explained unnecessarily.

"That was fairly obvious," he chuckled, but then his tone became serious. "I suppose it's my turn to apologize for waking you, Daye, but I won't, because we should have spoken to each other a week ago. I'm not very good at maintaining lengthy silences, especially hurtful ones, so what I *will* apologize to you for is my part in having allowed the silence to go on for so long."

"Has it already been a whole week?" she asked, knowing full well what the answer was.

"Eleven days to be precise."

"Eleven days," she repeated. A century couldn't have felt longer.

"That's another reason for the call," he explained. "I'll probably be up here for another week."

"Oh," was all she could say.

"I miss you, Daye."

She wanted to tell him that she missed him, too, but she didn't. She didn't even want to think about what she felt for him, because missing him and wanting him had the capacity to render her incompetent and teary-eyed. And she didn't dare weaken now, not when she needed all of her resolve and all of her drive to see her through this vital project triumphant.

"Have you finished Neil's offices yet?" he asked to fill the silence.

"Yes, they're finished."

"Has he thrown that party for you yet?"

"No, he hasn't."

Shouldn't she be telling him that there would be no party now? Shouldn't she also be telling him that he had been partially right about Neil, but that Neil had been exorcised from her life, and that she was truly free at last?

"Daye, are you still there?"

"Yes, Jonathan, I'm here."

There was time enough to tell him the truth about Neil, she decided.

"I wish you were up here with me," he said.

"Do you?"

"Yes, I do. I also wish I were holding you in my arms right now."

"Don't, Jonathan," she pleaded.

"I want to make love to you, Daye," he whispered. "I miss making love to you."

"Please stop, Jonathan."

"Why don't you come up here for a few days?" he said. "If you're already through with Neil's offices, what's to keep you from flying up here and joining me now?"

"Only the new project I'm working on," she told him, in a voice that was more animated now. "Jonathan, I think this could be the one I've been waiting for."

His silence, punctuated by the sputtering crackle on the wire, was all the message she needed.

"I'm sorry, Jonathan, but this is the one time my work will just have to come first."

"The one time, Daye?" he commented dryly. "I'm afraid your one times come a little too frequently for me."

"So we're back to the same discussion, are we?" Her voice was testy, her tone sharpening as her resentment grew. "I won't apologize again, Jonathan," she said, "because I really don't think I have anything to apologize for."

"Should I apologize for wanting to spend some time with you, then?" he countered.

"No, of course not."

"Is there ever going to be time for us, Daye?" He sounded so wistful, so honestly doubting, that her rising anger instantly dissolved.

"We'll make time, Jonathan. I swear we will."

"I intend to hold you to that promise, you know, so don't say it unless you mean it."

"I mean it," she said, putting the weight of her best intentions behind her words.

"I'll call you tomorrow, then, if that's all right."

"It's more than all right." She smiled.

But she wasn't smiling when she got off the phone. Their conversation had stripped some of her guard away, and in those occasional unguarded moments, when she didn't have her work to insulate her against the pain, the ache would begin, just as it was beginning now. And the ache reminded her that her best friends had gone and that she was alone.

chapter twenty-three

ONE WEEK LATER, when Daye submitted her plans to the firm of Webb and Mallory, the Palm Beach architects on the Lake Worth project, she left their offices feeling physically limp and emotionally drained. But even in her state of complete exhaustion, a residual glow of exhilaration still remained, confirming what she had instinctively sensed all the time she had been working on the project—that this was her most inspired effort to date, the finest proposal she had ever conceived. It had come to life for her from the very beginning, breathing in the precision perfection of every line, in the artful blending of color and texture, and in the bold juxtaposition of shape and form. Everything had worked happily together to create that electrifying eclecticism for which she was noted and on which she was staking her future as a designer in south Florida.

Refusing once again to compromise her creative integrity for the sake of preserving the sanctity of tradition, she had sought to successfully combine what was both evocative of Palm Beach's past and declarative of its future. The result was a statement, powerful and yet still graceful, much like Palm Beach itself. Or *her*self. For Daye had come to view the Gold

Coast's gilded mecca as a woman, a lady, an aging patrician who thrived on the very contradictions she claimed to abhor.

She drove back to the office, found a parking space at the far end of Peruvian, and then sat with her head against the steering wheel while she tried to convince herself that it would be far from sinful to treat herself to the rest of the day off. Either she could go home and get some sleep or she could lie in the sun by the pool and pretend that for one entire afternoon she was part of the leisure set who spent *all* of their afternoons that way. Although the promise of a relaxed afternoon was extremely tempting, the prospect of spending that time alone with nothing to do but think thrust her from the car and propelled her down the street with a ferocity that astounded her.

Stopping by Connie's office to say good morning, she was greeted first with a cheerful hello and then an ivory vellum envelope being waved in the air above her assistant's curly brown head.

"A hand-delivered billet-doux," the girl explained with a saucy grin. "At least I assume it was hand-delivered. I found it under the front door when I arrived this morning."

Daye's stomach somersaulted when she looked at the hand-writing on the envelope. She would have expected a letter from Neil, but never one from Rhea. Carrying it back with her to her own office unopened, she sat down at her desk, placed the letter on the blotter in front of her, and tried to divine its contents. After preparing herself by considering every conceivable reason for Rhea's having written to her, she finally tore open the envelope and unfolded the single sheet of notepaper inside. "Daye," she had written. "Could you please stop by the house this afternoon between two and three? I have something very special to share with you. Rhea."

Daye read and reread the brief note without knowing quite how to react to its message. Once again she began to consider the various possibilities, seesawing back and forth between the hope that Rhea would have good news and the fear that it would be bad, a revelation perhaps, or even a confession. Did Rhea know about Neil and Franki? She shuddered at the very thought of it. Was it about Neil and herself? She crumpled the note in her hand and then hastily tried to smooth it out again while she read the terse message through one more time.

She chose precisely two-thirty as the time to ring Rhea's bell, but when the door opened and Rhea stood there in front of her, Daye took a shaky step backward. After so many painful weeks apart, she felt as though they would have to be introduced to each other all over again before they could even say hello. Rhea smiled, and Daye took another step back. For one ghastly moment, all she could see was Neil's face hovering between them, much like a face painted on a theater scrim, until it mercifully rose into the air and disappeared.

She locked both hands around the leather strap of her shoulder bag to disguise their trembling and followed Rhea into the house. Rhea's face appeared slightly strained and unusually pale as the two women embraced, each careful to maintain a discreet distance between them while they bent to kiss each other lightly on the cheek. It was only then that Daye noticed the change in Rhea's eyes. They seemed darker to her and brighter, too, and they were glimmering with a wonderful luminosity they had never had before.

"You look tired," Rhea said.

Daye tore her gaze away from her friend's eyes and lifted one shoulder in a half shrug. "I've just finished working on a new project."

"I saw Neil's offices. You did a marvelous job on them."

"I think he was pleased."

"Daye?" Rhea posed it as a question while she glanced nervously down at her feet and began to clasp and unclasp her hands. "Daye? Oh, God, where should I begin?" The short, embarrassed laugh she gave was softened by a lilting edge of girlish delight. "Quick, come outside with me," she said. "The best way to handle this is to simply take you to the gazebo."

Daye walked blindly by Rhea's side, her heart thumping, her mouth dry, wondering why she had chosen the gazebo when the empty house would have done just as well.

"I'm sorry if I sounded so mysterious in my note," Rhea said, taking a key from the pocket of her skirt and unlocking the door to the small white frame building with its latticework panels, "but I *did* want to surprise you." She paused with one hand on the door latch. "I wanted you to be the first to know about this, Daye. Franki will be the second."

Daye tried to swallow, but she couldn't even manage to

work up enough saliva. What about Neil, she wanted to ask, when will he know?

"Three weeks from now an exhibition of twenty of my watercolors will be opening at the Rupert Gallery on Worth Avenue," Rhea declared with such a rush of pride that Daye gasped and automatically reached out to grasp her friend's arm.

"Rhea, how wonderful!" she exclaimed, her reaction one of such startled pleasure that she was barely conscious of the relief flooding through her tensed and anguished muscles. "Oh, Rhee, I'm so proud of you, so very proud. Congratulations!"

Rhea ducked her head shyly. "You might change your mind after you see what I've done," she said. "I'm still not convinced that my work is good enough to show, but, well—have a look for yourself." She encompassed the room with a sweep of one arm. "And Daye, please be kind, you know, if—"

"If Lyle Rupert is planning to mount an exhibition of your work, Rhea, it has to be more than just good, it has to be superb."

"He *did* seem pleased," admitted Rhea, who surprised Daye by actually starting to blush, "but I'm still a bit unsure of myself."

"What does Neil think of your work?" The question slipped past Daye's lips before she could stop it.

"He hasn't seen any of it yet. No one has, except Lyle Rupert, of course."

It was with a heady feeling of responsibility that Daye finally stepped up to the first large canvas, which was leaning, as were all the others, against one of the gazebo walls. It was a portrait of a young man with straight black hair and dreamy gray eyes and an air of childlike innocence about him. He was sitting cross-legged on the grass in the middle of a tumbled garden, holding a single yellow daisy up to one cheek and gazing out at her with a beatific smile of such heartrending sweetness, that tears welled up in Daye's eyes, blurring his features into an even softer pastel wash.

"It's simply magnificent," she whispered, turning to Rhea and catching hold of both of her hands. "Oh, Rhee, there's such an exquisite sensitivity to this work, such a wonderful tenderness, that you want to reach out and pull him into your arms and protect him." While she was speaking, she scanned her friend's face for some clue as to how long this remarkable creativity had lain dormant beneath the placid façade of the undemanding friend and the pliant wife. But neither Rhea's face nor her shining eyes provided her with the answer she was seeking.

Casting a final glance at that first portrait, Daye slowly circled the room, studying each subsequent portrait with an awe bordering on reverence. And when she had seen all twenty of them once, she walked around the room a second time. Then she came back to where Rhea was standing and in a quiet voice, she said, "Who is he, Rhee?" knowing even as she waited for her response that there was little doubt as to what that response would be.

"His name is Steven," said Rhea, "and he's my brother, my thirty-nine-year-old retarded brother."

And then she told Daye the truth. As Daye listened, she was overwhelmed, not by the tragedy of Steven Bellon, but by the changes Rhea's discovery of Steven had effected in her. She was no longer the girl Daye thought she had always known as well as she knew herself. Rhea was becoming her own creation at last and in many ways a stranger as well.

"I adore him, Daye," Rhea confided to her as they walked back to the house through the garden. "Although he doesn't really know what a sister is, he *does* understand that I'm a friend and that I'm someone who cares very much about him. In just a few visits, I've grown closer to him than I've ever been to my own children. And what's more, I've grown closer to my parents as well. It's as though we were finally meeting as adults for the first time. There's no more protecting, no more dissimulating; we're equals now, three adults with a lifetime of catching up to do."

"Have you told them about the exhibition?" asked Daye.

"Oh, yes," Rhea nodded excitedly, "and they've promised to fly down for the opening. I'm afraid I'm going to shock quite a few people with this exhibit *and* with the truth about my brother."

"Have you prepared your parents for that part of it?"

"I think so," she said, and then sighed. "At least I hope so. You see, in some ways, they've had to grow up, too."

This last remark brought Daye's tears perilously close to

the surface again. She wanted to hug Rhea, to feel that fragile body crunch close to hers, so that she could tell her how happy she was for her, for her parents, and for her brother, but something held her back. She didn't want to relive the closeness the two of them had always shared if their tomorrows stopped right there at today. And so, instead of hugging her, she simply said, "I love you, Rhee, and I want you to remember that I'm still here for you if you need me."

"I *do* need you, Daye," she insisted, "but right now I'm still learning how to need just me. Will you be patient with me a little while longer?"

"You know I will," she promised, adding a smile to prove that she meant it, in spite of the terrible sinking feeling inside her.

Rhea opened the front door, but Daye hung back, not wanting to leave, yet knowing that for now the choice wasn't hers to make.

"Will you come to the opening?" asked Rhea.

Daye laughed. "Will you send me a formal invitation?"

"It's already in the mail," she admitted somewhat sheepishly. "That's why I delivered that note myself today."

They stood there looking at each other in the doorway for another moment; then they both reached out at the same time.

"Until," whispered Rhea as she let Daye go again.

But Daye waited until she had started down the steps before turning and answering with her own "Until."

Because it was such a short ride from Rhea's house to the condo, Daye hadn't even begun to absorb the full impact of their emotional meeting by the time she drove up to the front door. That would have to come gradually, she decided, as she got out of the car and left it for its weekly wash, when she was calmer, when she was alone, after she had slept for a few hours and . . . Her thoughts ended there. She stopped in the middle of the lobby, scarcely breathing, not daring to move and risk seeing the moment fragment and disintegrate. Reflected in the mirrored walls and in the faceted prisms of the crystal chandeliers were hundreds of tiny Jonathans, in thousands of glittering bits of refracted colors, all of them highlighting the black of his hair, the deep wine of his suede jacket, the pale gray of his trousers, the wine and gray stripes of his open-necked shirt.

When he glanced up and saw her standing there looking back at him, a smile broke out across his handsome face. As he got to his feet and started for her, she began moving toward him, stretching out her arms to him and calling his name at the same time that he called out hers. Time froze willingly for them in that moment when they met in an embrace that was all enclosing arms and eager lips and bodies straining to get as close to each other as two bodies could possibly be. Her fingers raked his hair, snaked up and down the length of his back, cinched his waist and pressed him into her; while his own lips and tongue and hands rediscovered what three long weeks of separation had kept from him.

"You seemed so surprised," he said, holding her away from him to look at her more closely.

"I was," she admitted with a tremulous smile, tracing the outline of his face with her fingers to prove to herself that he was really there.

"I said a week, didn't I?"

"But you also said a week or ten days when you left," she reminded him gently.

"One out of two isn't bad," he laughed. "I'm here now, though, aren't I?" he asked her as he eased her back into his arms.

"Yes," she said, clinging to him gratefully, "yes, you are."

She couldn't seem to unlock her door, so he took the key from her and opened it himself. Just as she was about to lead him down the hallway to her bedroom, she suddenly stopped and changed her mind. The specter of that treacherous interlude with Neil was like a living force, waving her away, keeping her back from the place where the memory of it was still too clear. Her need to break its hold on her drove her back into Jonathan's arms with a whimper of desperate urgency. It was an appeal for immediate appeasement, a demand for gratification then and there without the benefit of prior preparation.

They slid to the floor in the foyer. The marble was an unyielding expanse of icy smoothness against the backs of her legs as she tugged her skirt up to her waist. She needed him now, locked on top of her, thrusting, seeking entry to her whether she was ready for him or not. Reaching up to him with greedy fingers, she drew him down onto his knees. Wrapping her legs around his waist, she urged him to penetrate her and to fill all of her up now, while her need for him was so great. He met her straining need with an urgency of his own, matching her stride for scorching stride and taking her with the loving fierceness she was demanding of him.

With his arms wrapped so protectively around her, his body her shield while hers was his cushion, he was now as much a part of her as she was of him. Fused together in loving bondage, there was little space between them for a lingering memory to burrow now. And so Daye released her hold on that memory, as though it were a child's balloon, and watched it float harmlessly into the sky and vanish.

They made love again in the steamy warmth of her bathtub, among rounded banks and frothy peaks of lemon-scented bubbles. A dozen small votive candles in raspberry, lavender, and periwinkle blue dotted the vanity and the edges of the tub itself, drenching the room and the two of them in the rainbow glow of a stained-glass window. Now they took the time to nurture their mutual need, using the water and the bubbles and the languorous heat to slowly stoke their returning desire until it ignited and burst into a dizzying flame that saw them united and consumed once more.

Later when they were lying on her bed, sharing one snifter of brandy between them, she asked him about *Arpeggio in Blue*.

"All I can say is that everyone's very excited about it. And I must admit," he added with an impish grin, "so am I. It's being brought to life through these actors just the way I'd imagined it would be when I wrote it, and the songs sound a helluva lot better than they did when I was the only one singing them."

"Should I start looking for something to wear to the Tony Awards?"

"Definitely," he told her. "And while you're at it, you might as well buy two dresses, unless of course you don't mind being seen in the same outfit two years in a row."

"Oh?" Her eyebrows rose expectantly. "I do believe the

playwright is obliquely trying to tell me something. You've started another play, haven't you?"

He answered her with a casual nod, but there was no mistaking the excitement radiating across his features. "I've even chosen the title for it," he said.

"What is it?"

"*Happy Dayes,* with an *e* at the end."

"Jonathan, be serious."

"I am."

"Jonathan!"

"It's about this beautiful but headstrong young woman who drives her erstwhile suitor mad with frustration while she lives a solitary life dedicated to the pursuit of money, power, and—"

"Jonathan Cort, you're incorrigible!"

"But truthful."

"No, you're not, you're just being mean."

"Come on, Daye, it would make a great story."

"Does it at least have a happy ending?"

"I haven't gotten that far yet, but I suggest you stick around and find out for yourself."

"Have you really started on something new?"

"As a matter of fact, yes."

"But it's a secret."

"Only until I get into it a bit further," he said, his tone as serious as hers now. "I really *do* have a title for it, though. I'm calling it *Sunset Is a Sometime Thing.*"

"*Sunset Is a Sometime Thing.*" She tried it out herself. "I like it, Jonathan; it's beautiful, and really quite haunting. See, it's even given me goose bumps."

"Is that a good sign or bad?"

"Oh, good," she assured him. "If something moves me, I'll get goose bumps and start to shiver."

He edged closer to her on the bed and took the snifter out of her hands. "Do I make you shiver, Daye?" he murmured, lightly nipping the lobe of her ear. "Do I?" he repeated.

"Yes," she nodded, closing her eyes, "yes, you do."

"I missed you terribly, you know." His lips formed each word against her ear. "It took all of my willpower this last week not to fly down here to get you and take you back up north with me."

"My errant knight," she laughed softly, "how very romantic of you."

"I could be a lot more romantic," he said, as he sat up and started to tickle her, "if I had a more willing maiden to play with."

"And you don't think I'm willing!" She howled with laughter as his fingers dug into her ribs. "Stop it!" she shrieked, trying to fight him off. "Stop it, you're killing me!"

"Then submit to me, wench, or else."

"I submit, I submit," she gasped, laughing and coughing, while his fingers continued to poke away at her.

"You do?" He immediately stopped and sat back on his heels.

With a gleeful shout, she sprang up, catching him off guard, and pushed him flat onto his back. Quickly straddling him, she pinned both of his arms above his head and held them there.

"Ha-ha!" she crowed. "I lied."

"Cheat," he protested, arching his back in a feeble attempt to throw her off. "Cheat, cheat, cheat," he repeated, his voice growing fainter as he closed his eyes, turned his head to the side, and pretended to expire with one last whimpering sigh: "Cheat."

"Jon-a-than?" she crooned. "Guess what I'm going to do to you now? Jon-a-than?"

When he didn't answer her, she leaned forward and placed a warm kiss on his mouth. Then she straightened up again and contented herself with simply looking at him for a while. He was so beautiful, she thought, feeling an ache begin to build inside her as she caressed his face and his splendid body with only her eyes. There were so many things she needed to ask him, so many things she needed to tell him, but they would have to wait. Right now she didn't need to talk about anything at all.

chapter twenty-four

THE FRONT door closed, and Franki looked up with a start. Hastily folding the pale yellow crocheted sweater, she tucked it away with all the other sweaters in the third drawer of the white tallboy she had just bought for the nursery. She was still astounded by the size of a newborn's clothes, surprised that anything so small could actually fit another human being. She closed the drawer and took another quick look around her. The newly converted guest bedroom was attractive enough, furnished as it was in a cheerful yellow and green and white print, but it lacked the one element she still needed and didn't dare ask for—that special Daye Peters touch.

God, how she missed Daye. And Rhea. As she began to recall the astonishing beauty of the watercolors Rhea had shown her the week before, her eyes began to mist over. To think that Rhea, her Rhea, the consummate hostess and ultimate consumer, had developed into an artist of such depth and sensitivity. She rubbed her eyes with the heels of both hands. Damn! That was the one thing she hated about being pregnant; she was always on the verge of tears. Anything could trigger it—a commercial on TV, a song on the radio, a paragraph in a book she was reading, the smell of her own perfume. It seemed that all she ever wanted to do these days was cry.

And sleep. And that both amazed and annoyed her. She considered the fatigue that crept up on her every afternoon as something of an insult, an affront, a direct contradiction to her usual boundless energy and vigor. She had never been one to nap in the afternoon, and she had never been one to sweep about the house in a dressing gown or a duster. But now, due to her swollen breasts and her thickening waistline, she reluctantly added a dozen assorted robes, all with self-tying belts, to the collection of lace-edged nightgowns and satin peignoir sets hanging half-forgotten in her bedroom closet.

"Brian?" she called out, poking her head around the corner and wondering where he had gone. "Brian?" A moment later, the sound of the freezer door slamming shut as several ice cubes clinked into a glass told her exactly where he was and what he was doing. "Oh, Brian, Brian." She sighed sadly, switching off the light in the nursery and digging her hands into the pockets of her dressing gown as she shuffled slowly down the hallway to the kitchen.

Two highball glasses of scotch on the rocks before dinner or before going back out again had become a nightly ritual for Brian. It seemed to act as an insulator against her continued presence, or rather intrusion, in his daily life. They were hardly more than housemates now, sharing the same physical space they had always shared, but little else. While she drifted through the days warmed by the sweetness of the elusive dream that was about to come true for her, he had chosen isolation for himself, keeping away from her and maintaining an uncharacteristically cold and scowling silence between them.

"You're home early," she remarked, catching him on his way out of the kitchen.

"Am I?" He raised his glass to his lips while he concentrated on a spot somewhere behind her left shoulder.

"You look tired." She could just as easily have said he looked sad or miserable or unhappy, but he already knew how he looked.

He said nothing in response to her comment, but as soon as she tried to wrap her arms around his waist, he brushed her off with an angry "Don't, Franki!"

She backed away from him, her cheeks burning. It was "Don't, Franki" all the time now. Whenever she tried to kiss him or take his hand, whenever she reached out for him in bed or asked him to simply hold her for a while, it was always "Don't, Franki." She could feel the tears starting up again. Can you blame him? demanded that small inner voice, which repeated the same question every time she reacted badly to his pushing her away. No, she couldn't blame him; she couldn't really blame him at all.

"Do you know how it feels to get into bed with you knowing you've been making it with someone else?" he had asked her the night she told him about the baby when she had foolishly reached out for him in bed. "Well, I'll tell you exactly how it feels; it feels like shit!"

Because he had never raised his voice to her or used that kind of language on her before, his angry words had hurt her far more than if he had hauled off and hit her instead. In fact, she would have preferred a slap to the harsh sting of those words. The pain of a slap wore off after only a few minutes, but the effects of what he had said hadn't worn off yet.

"Are you staying for dinner or are you going out again?" she asked, following him into the bedroom and watching as he took off his jacket.

"I'm going out."

She lowered her head and pretended to study the bows on the slippers she was wearing. "I was hoping you might decide to stay home instead," she admitted. "I was also hoping we could talk."

"What do you think we're doing right now?"

"Please don't be sarcastic, Brian."

"That's not sarcasm, Franki. That's a simple statement of fact. We are talking."

"That isn't what I wanted to talk about," she countered.

"What *did* you want to talk about?"

"The baby."

"Well, *I* don't want to talk about the baby."

"Brian," she pleaded, "I'm already showing. We have to talk about how and when we're going to tell people."

"Why not have Sybil Barron announce it in the Town Tattler column of the *Standard?*" he sneered. "She did a fair job of reporting on all of your other social activities. Why shouldn't she have the scoop on this one, too?"

After that remark, Franki's patience finally ran out. "Do you know something, Brian?" she shouted. "You really are a shit!"

"Then you and I make the perfect couple, Franki my dear," he smirked, reaching for a tie and looping it around his neck.

"Brian?" she asked, dropping her voice to a whisper. "Brian, why are you doing this to us?"

"I'm not doing a damned thing to us. I'm just trying to live with what *you* did to us."

"You didn't have to agree to raise this child as yours," she shot back at him. "You had another option. Why didn't you take it?"

The sad expression on his face grew even sadder as he shook his head a few times and then said, "I guess it's because I'm a fool." He looked at her with eyes that were jagged with pain. "I love you, Franki, and I'm a goddamn fool for not being able to stop."

"Oh, Brian!" she cried, flinging her arms around his neck. "Brian, Brian, it's going to be all right. It will be, you'll see."

But even as she was holding him and talking to him, she could feel his body tensing, and as it continued to stiffen, she could sense him withdrawing inside himself again.

"Brian, I want to tell people now."

"Then tell them," he said as he took her arms from around his neck.

"I want us to tell them together."

"Why?" He buttoned his jacket and tossed back the last of his drink. "I had nothing to do with it. Why don't you ask the proud father to tell them with you?"

"Because *you're* the proud father, Brian."

"The hell I am, Franki!" he snorted. "I might be able to convince myself of that one of these days, but I'm having a bit of difficulty accepting it at the moment."

"You still have five more months to practice," she told him, making a desperate attempt to lighten his darkening mood.

"Yeah," he snorted, "and then we can all sit around and pretend that the kid looks just like its old man. By the way, Franki, who *is* the kid's old man?"

Staggered by his question, she could feel a spiral of nausea curling upward from her stomach toward the back of her throat.

"Anyone I know?"

This couldn't be happening! He had sworn never to ask her, and she had told him she would never tell him even if he did.

"A friend, an acquaintance, a total stranger? Tell me, Franki. I'm curious."

She shook her head. She would never tell him. She would never tell anyone. Panicked now, she suddenly thought of Rhea. If she was capable of painting such intimately revealing portraits, would she be able to just look at this child and know that Neil was its father?

"Don't tell me you're going to make me guess," continued Brian, "or should I just wait to see if it looks like anyone we know?"

Did he suspect? Franki's stomach heaved, and she grabbed one of Brian's arms for support. Neil was blond, but then so was she, and they both had blue eyes . . .

"Brian, Brian, please, you promised."

"So did you." He shook his arm free. "It went something like 'and forsaking all others . . .'"

She moved away from him as the wave of nausea rose higher and higher in her throat. Just as she reached the bathroom, she heard the front door close again, and as she dropped to her knees on the floor, she heard it lock.

JONATHAN HAD been back for six days. She knew because this was the sixth present she had bought for him since his return. Taking the small, gift-wrapped box out of its Gucci gift bag, Daye slipped it into her purse, thanked the uniformed man on the door as she glided past him and headed back down South County Road to her office. She was spoiling him, Jonathan had said, but she had also noticed that his protests weren't quite as strong as they had been at first. She enjoyed shopping for him. It had been a long time since she had shopped for a man, and this was simply her way of saying how important he was to her and how much she valued having him in her life. And she did.

While she waited for some word on the Lake Worth project,

he was being supportive and sympathetic, comforting her whenever she grew anxious, cajoling her out of the occasional mood slump she suffered, and caring for her in a way no man had ever cared for her before. He was both lover and friend to her now, that unique and magical combination she had never expected to find in a man. For her, Jonathan Cort was the embodiment of everything that had been illusory about Neil Howard.

When she walked into the office, Daye was surprised to find Connie restlessly pacing the floor of the reception area, her glasses perched high atop her curly brown head, her lips pursed in a tight scowl, and her eyebrows knitted together in a deep frown.

"Daye, where in God's name have you been?" she demanded, catching Daye so completely unprepared that all she could do was gape at her. "This was probably the most important phone call of your entire career and you had to miss it."

"W—what are you talking about?" stammered Daye, feeling her pulse beginning to quicken.

"I'm only talking about Webb and Mallory."

"Webb and . . . Oh, my God." Daye reached for the slip of paper Connie was holding out to her and bolted for her office.

"That's Martin Webb's number," Connie called out after her. Then she shouted, "Good luck, Peters!"

Flopping into her chair, Daye held on to the piece of paper with one hand and reached for the phone with the other. She punched out two incorrect digits, started again, and managed to complete all seven digits without a single mistake the second time she tried it. As soon as the phone started to ring, she decided she had to go to the bathroom. Taking a deep breath to calm herself down, she crossed her legs and squeezed them together as tightly as she could. She had to repeat her name three times before Martin Webb's secretary finally understood what she was saying, and when she was told she would be put right through, she hastily crossed the fingers of both of her hands.

A moment later, the cheerful voice of the senior partner of Webb and Mallory was booming. "Allow me to be the first to congratulate you, Miss Peters, you've been selected as the interior designer for the Lake Worth condominium project."

Daye gasped. Her fingers slowly began to uncurl themselves.

"All of us were extremely impressed with the originality of your concept, Miss Peters, and we look forward to working closely with you. You're a rather daring young woman, you know, and if you don't mind my saying so, a much needed and most welcome breath of fresh air down here."

Daye was out of her chair and dancing around the room on legs she could no longer feel. She had won! She had been awarded the project! He had said she was daring, a breath of fresh air. She had gambled one final time on being daring, and this time it had been worth it. Throwing back her head and flinging her arms wide, she emitted an ear-splitting whoop of joy that sent her assistant rushing into the room.

"Tell me what happened!" Connie shouted. "Hurry, dammit, tell me!"

When Daye flashed her the V for victory sign, Connie tugged off her glasses, flung back her head, and began shrieking, too. Suddenly remembering that she was keeping Martin Webb waiting on the line, Daye picked up the receiver again and immediately apologized to the older man for her emotional outburst.

"That's quite an understandable reaction, my dear," he assured her. "Don't ever lose that marvelous spontaneity of yours. Now my suggestion to you would be to take the rest of the day off and *really* celebrate. You've more than earned the right to do that. Then if you'll give me a call first thing tomorrow morning, we'll set up some appointments for ourselves."

She could barely find her voice in time to thank him, but she did, and then she put down the phone, threw her arms around Connie, and promptly burst into tears.

Once she was composed again, she quickly dialed Jonathan's number. To her complete dismay, there was no answer. She tried Rhea, but Chloe told her that she was at the gallery. She called the Rupert Gallery twice, but both times the line was busy. After trying Jonathan again with the same disappointing result as before, she was about to start dialing Franki's number when she stopped herself and reconsidered it. No, she decided. She just couldn't, not yet. She counted to fifty and then tried Jonathan again. There was still no answer. By this time she was nearly sobbing with frustration. She had just received the happiest bit of news imaginable, and no one was around to hear it. How absurd it seemed. Now that she had something wonderful to celebrate, there was no one to celebrate with her.

It took all of her willpower to swallow her disappointment and to put all thoughts of celebrating aside for the moment, but she did. Switching on her answering machine and turning the volume off, she sat down at her drafting table and unrolled the first of her sketches for the Lake Worth project. Now that the project was officially hers, she could begin adding all of the specific details lacking in the original plans. As she bent over her work, all that mattered to her were the lines on the paper in front of her, the shapes they formed, and the colors defining those forms. Immersed in the work she loved, she was soon at peace with herself again.

The loud rapping at the front door brought her head up sharply. Taking a hasty look at her watch as she got up from her chair, she was shocked to find that it was already nine o'clock.

"Jonathan!" she exclaimed, opening the door and seeing him standing on the steps formally dressed in a black tuxedo. "What are you doing here?"

"I might ask you the same thing."

Startled by the storm clouds gathering in his dark eyes, she could only voice a meek "I'm sorry, but I don't understand."

"Obviously," he replied, brandishing what appeared to be two tickets in front of her face.

"Oh, God, Jonathan," she gasped, "I forgot it was tonight."

Just before he left for New York, they had purchased a pair of tickets at one hundred dollars apiece to attend a gala benefit at the Breakers Hotel on behalf of the Opera Society of South Florida. The reception had been scheduled to begin at six, the dinner at seven, and a performance of selected arias from some of the world's best-known operas was to have started at nine.

"Oh, Jonathan, please forgive me. The time just slipped right by me," she said.

"Obviously," he repeated as he tucked the tickets into the breast pocket of his jacket.

Suddenly, in spite of his surliness, all of Daye's repressed excitement came bubbling up to the surface again.

"Jonathan, I have the most wonderful news," she cried. "Oh, please stop scowling. You have something to be happy about now; we both do. I got the Lake Worth project, Jonathan! Martin Webb called me this afternoon to tell me that I'd been chosen for the job. I tried to reach you, but you weren't in. Just think of it; I've actually beaten Philippe. I think I've finally been given the chance I've needed to make it down here after all."

"I'm very pleased for you, Daye," he said. "Congratulations."

She was stunned by his subdued response. The tense lines around his mouth had eased for a moment, but only for a moment, before growing taut again.

"Jonathan, you sound so cold," she told him. "It's almost as if you don't mean it, as if you don't even care."

"I *am* pleased for you, Daye, but I'm damned sorry for us."

"Jonathan!" She hurried after him as he started down the steps. "Jonathan, what did you mean by that? Please wait; don't walk away like this." She caught hold of the back of his jacket and tugged on it. Near tears, she planted herself in front of him and stared miserably up into his angry face. "I thought you understood how very important this project was to me."

"I did, and I still do."

"Then can't you forgive me for becoming so involved in my work on the project that I lost all track of time?"

"Of course I can, Daye," he replied, "but I really don't feel very forgiving right now. How would you have felt if I'd done this to you? Would you have been particularly forgiving if the positions had been reversed?"

"I think I would have understood."

"Would you?"

"Yes."

"I didn't think women were ever that understanding about being stood up. What makes you think men are any better at it?"

"I didn't stand you up," she argued. "I didn't purposely leave you sitting at home and wondering where I was while I was out with someone else. It was an oversight, nothing more. I simply got involved in my work and forgot the time."

"But your work makes it too easy for you to forget that there's a world out there, Daye, as well as a man who cares about you very, very much." He seized her by the shoulders and gave her a shake. "I want you, Daye, more than I ever thought I could want anyone, but I'm still not willing to settle. Call me possessive or old-fashioned or a male chauvinist, whatever, but you've become a very important part of my life, and I'd assumed I was just as important a part of yours. But if I'm wrong about that, Daye, I think you'd better let me know now."

She thought of the key chain she had bought him at noon and how he had been the first person she had wanted to call that afternoon after speaking to Martin Webb. Didn't that prove that he meant a great deal to her, too, that he was someone very special and very important in her life?

"Jonathan," she began uncertainly, "why don't you drive me home so that I can change, and then we'll drive back up here to the benefit? I know we'll be awfully late, but at least we'll have put in an appearance."

He shook his head at her suggestion and said, "There really isn't much point now."

"How can I make this up to you, then?" she asked him, stroking his arm and angling her body closer to his. "Oh, Jonathan, please tell me how."

He stared at her hard for a moment, and then, with a shrug of resignation, he suggested they simply go back to his place.

Her relief was almost audible. Giving him a quick peck on the mouth, she said, "Just let me lock up."

As she followed him in her own car along the A1A to Gorham Sound, she continued to brood about their latest confrontation. Her triumph had turned sour for her, and what she had hoped would be an occasion for celebrating had been more of a fiasco than anything else. Suddenly, her winning the Lake Worth project was like a lump in her throat that she could neither spit up nor swallow. To think that she had waited so long and worked so hard to win, only to be in danger of losing something else for which she had also been waiting.

When they arrived at the house, she walked silently up the stairs beside him and ducked under his arm as he held the door open for her. Flicking on the lights as he headed for the kitchen, he called back, "What would you like to eat?"

"Nothing," she answered, "but I *would* like a drink. We have something to celebrate, remember?"

"Will white wine do?"

"White wine will do perfectly," she assured him.

He came back into the living room with a chilled bottle of pouilly-fuissé and two glasses. Filling them both, he handed her one. Then he raised his own glass and said, "To you, Daye, and to your success."

They clinked glasses, and after taking their first sip of the wine, he steered her over to one of the sofas and pulled her down beside him.

"I've decided to give up my apartment in New York and to make Boca my home from now on, Jonathan," she told him. "What do you think?"

"I think it's about time."

"And I think I'm still in shock." She laughed, draining her glass. She was about to ask him to refill it for her when she suddenly changed her mind. "Jonathan!" She turned to him excitedly and set the empty glass down on the floor. "Let me make tonight up to you. Let me take you out to dinner and for a bottle of champagne so that we can really celebrate this occasion." Her voice dropped shyly. "And then, why don't we come back here and make love?"

Leaning closer to her, he said, "Can I answer yes to both questions, but switch the order around? How about making love first and *then* going out for dinner?"

"And then making love again?" she murmured.

"Greedy little girl, aren't you?"

"Uh-huh," she nodded, "very."

They made love there on the sofa with what seemed to be a new tenderness, a new awareness of each other, taking special care to protect the very precious and fragile thing they were sharing. And afterward, as he held her in his arms, her head resting on his chest, his fingers deep in her hair, Jonathan whispered up to her, "I love you, Daye."

She lay there rigid in his embrace, scarcely daring to move, hardly daring to breathe.

"I love you very, very much."

When she finally found the strength, she raised her head to look down at him and whispered back, "I love you, too, Jonathan." Her eyes filled up and quickly brimmed over. "Oh, God, how I love you."

chapter twenty-five

DAYE WAS drifting, floating in some rarefied space, unfettered by the bonds of earth. She was living alone in a beautiful, protected place with Jonathan as its only other inhabitant. He loved her, and because she felt secure in that love, she was able to return his love, feeling it soften and mellow her like no other experience before it. For the next week, she allowed him a claim on her time that no man had ever been allowed before, but when she felt her grip loosening on her work, she stiffened her spine and reached deep inside herself, drawing on the reserve of strength and determination that would rein in her obsession for him and enable her to perform as she needed to if she was to keep what she had fought so hard to win.

All of the local papers had carried the news of her triumph, and she was being flooded daily with calls from well-wishers and people suddenly interested in her work. She had arranged for the tenant subletting her New York apartment to assume the new lease, and she was delighted and relieved when the girl agreed to buy most of her furniture. After taking so long to happen, it seemed to be happening almost too quickly now, but Daye found herself slowing down from time to time just to cherish each glorious and rewarding moment of it.

Five days before Jonathan was scheduled to return to New York for the final rehearsals of *Arpeggio in Blue* before the previews, they escaped from the social flurry that had been claiming them since Webb and Mallory's announcement and had a quiet dinner together on the terrace of his house. He had made lasagna; she had tossed a salad; together they had made garlic bread; but now that they were lingering over coffee and cognac, Daye found her thoughts slipping further and further away from the two of them and focusing instead on the interior of one of the lobbies she was presently designing.

"You're off on a cloud somewhere, my love," said Jonathan, winding a long curl of her hair around his index finger.

"Hmm?"

"You're dreaming again."

She nodded absently and smiled.

"Daye, your dress is on fire."

"That's nice."

"Oh, for God's sake!"

That snapped her out of her trance immediately. "What's wrong?" she asked him.

"Nothing," he replied, staring moodily out at the ocean.

Taking a sip of her cooling coffee, she said, "Did you know that Philippe just let Margot Thurston go?"

"Go where?" he asked, deciding to be difficult.

"Back to Chicago, of course."

"No, I didn't know that."

"Do you think Sybil's finally beginning to tighten up her purse strings?"

"It would appear that way, now, wouldn't it?"

"Uh-huh." She nodded, reflecting for another moment on the wallpaper she had selected for the lobby and wondering if the pattern was too busy.

"I love you, Daye," Jonathan suddenly declared, giving her lock of hair a little tug.

She forgot all about the wallpaper and beamed at him. "And I love you," she whispered, pressing her cheek into the palm of his hand.

"Then say you'll be there for opening night."

"All I can say is that I'll try, but that it looks doubtful."

"You know I hate that answer."

"So do I, but right now it's the only one I've got."

"New York is beautiful in October," he coaxed her.

"You're talking to a native New Yorker, remember?" she replied with a laugh.

"Just picture it, Daye," he said, waving his spoon in the air as though it were a wand. "Roasted chestnuts, the colors changing in Central Park, brunch in the Crystal Room at Tavern on the Green on Sunday, the Metropolitan, a walk through Washington Square..."

"Bobby Short at the Carlyle, SoHo, lunch at the Russian Tea Room, the Guggenheim..."

"The reviews at Sardi's after the show."

She gulped. "That's the part that scares me," she admitted.

"Why do you think I want you there? I'm scared, too. I need you with me, Daye, whether it's to celebrate with all the champagne you can drink or to help me sharpen the razor blades."

"Jonathan Cort!" she exploded. "You are *not* going to need any sharpened razor blades. *Arpeggio in Blue* is going to be the smash hit of the season. The previews are already sold out, and so are the first four weeks of the show's regular run, as you well know. So there's to be absolutely no talk of wrist slashing by the esteemed playwright. Agreed?"

"Maybe."

"Besides, who'd finish *Sunset Is a Sometime Thing?*"

"Rolf could always do it."

"Wonderful idea," she groaned, rolling her eyes upward. "Now, why didn't I think of that?" She squeezed his hand hard and then planted a smacking kiss on the tip of each of his five fingers. "Please have confidence in yourself and in the play," she said. "I do and so do a lot of people who know much more about Broadway shows than I do."

"See why I need you with me?" he persisted. "You have the kind of blind faith in me that only a woman in love can have in her man. I'm being very serious, Daye, when I say I need you with me."

"I know that, Jonathan," she conceded with a heavy sigh, "but I'm just not as free as I might like to be. The O'Connell-Reardon Corporation owns a large part of my time right now, and I've got to remain as flexible as I possibly can for them."

"So you'd pass up New York in October and the opening of *Arpeggio in Blue* just to sit in on some dull meetings with a bunch of filthy-rich Texans?" He was trying to sound funny, but there was a sadness and a tinge of regret weighing down his words.

In her own poor attempt to humor him back, she said, "Now, why would I turn down a chance to be with a filthy-rich Texan when I could be with a poor but gorgeous playwright instead?"

"Uh-uh." He wagged his finger at her. "Gorgeous, well, that's debatable, but poor, never. Have I ever told you about the royalties I get from—"

"It's very rude to discuss money at the dinner table." She grabbed hold of his wagging finger and bit it gently.

"Then how would you like to discuss coming to the playhouse with me tomorrow night?"

She was instantly on her guard. "Why?" she wanted to know.

"They're doing a reading of one actor's attempts at a play, and since I'm still the resident authority on playwriting in Gorham Sound, I get to either pick it apart or praise it."

"I don't know . . ." her voice trailed off while she considered his invitation. Although she still hadn't set foot inside the famous Gorham Sound Playhouse, the prospect of spending an entire evening with Maren MacCaul was far from tempting. And so, instead of answering him directly, she said, "Tell me, has Maren made up her mind yet about whether or not to buy any of the playhouses she's seen up north?"

Jonathan shook his head and laughed. "I think she's having too good a time playing the Llewelyn Corporation off against Neil Howard. By the time the two of them are through topping each other, Maren's going to be selling one of them the most highly inflated piece of real estate in all of south Florida."

Hearing him say Neil's name so offhandedly opened the door on a half-forgotten memory, and Daye could feel herself actually beginning to blush. She pretended to be enjoying the last bit of cold coffee in her cup while she struggled to tamp the memory back down again. She had never told Jonathan the truth about Neil and herself, and as time passed, and she and Neil continued to maintain both their distance and their silence, there seemed little point in either stirring up or explaining something best left forgotten.

"I think you might enjoy the reading tomorrow night, Daye," said Jonathan as he intruded upon her thoughts and put an end to them. "There's really nothing as exciting as discovering new talent. I thrive on it, because it allows me to keep my own skills sharp while I help the newcomers hone theirs."

"We're so very similar, you and I," she mused, "except that when you talk about your career in that animated tone of voice, I can accept it as being part of you. But when I speak about my own work that way, you look positively catatonic. Can you tell me why my loving my work threatens you so much?"

"Oh, Daye, let's not go into that again," he muttered. "I'm not threatened by your work. It's one of the things I love about you, your devotion to what you do, your talent, your ambition. It's just that I still have difficulty with the way you can shut out the entire world and not even miss it when you're working."

"But you do exactly the same thing," she insisted. "If you didn't shut out the world, you wouldn't be able to lose yourself in your music. You wouldn't even be able to hear it. There's really no difference between what you and I do or how dedicated we are to what we do. I just think you men know how to handle it better because you've been doing it longer, while we women are still rather new at it. But we *are* trying to adapt, Jonathan, and so should you."

"Well, then, if adapting also means compromising," he reasoned, "why don't you and I start by compromising on how much time you can spend in New York."

Daye groaned inwardly and prepared herself for what was coming next.

"Since a week is out of the question, how about three and a half days? We'll split it right down the middle."

"I can't."

"All right, two days."

"Jonathan!"

"Opening night and the night after."

"Please, Jonathan . . ."

"Just opening night?"

"Stop looking at me that way." She scowled. "You're making this very difficult for me."

"Good, that's the whole idea. I intend to natter away at you incessantly until I manage to break down that stubborn Daye Peters resistance of yours. Come on, Daye, you can't miss the opening of my play."

"You're missing the opening of Rhea's exhibition," she countered.

"It's not the same thing."

"Why not?"

"Because I don't love Rhea, I love you."

"Some logic."

"It's no better and no worse than yours."

"God, the timing is rotten," she murmured, leaning her chin on her hand and sighing again.

George Piper, chairman of the board of the Dallas-based O'Connell-Reardon Corporation, together with a handful of company executives and Nesbit Kaylan of the Madison Avenue advertising agency of Kaylan, Dorne and Harbody, would be flying down to Palm Beach in another ten days for a series of meetings on the advancing Lake Worth project. Included on their agenda were meetings with Webb and Mallory and herself, a tour of the building site for members of the international press and a select list of potential buyers, as well as a cocktail party and dinner to be held at the Breakers on the same night that *Arpeggio in Blue* was due to open in New York.

"Do I detect a somewhat belligerent look on your face, Mr. Cort?" she asked him, trying to tease him out of his increasingly black mood, but with little success. "Jon-a-than?"

"I guess you could say it's somewhat belligerent," he agreed.

"Why, or shouldn't I ask?"

"You already know why. I want you to be with me on opening night."

"Is that statement about to be followed by 'or else'?" she asked him, all the humor gone now from her voice. "Because if it is, I think you should know that I don't like ultimatums of any kind, Jonathan."

"It's not an ultimatum, Daye," he protested, "but the success or failure of this play is going to affect both of us. This is my chance to make a comeback, my chance to make a statement on my own without sharing billing with Rolf Kerwin. It's a gamble, Daye, a gamble we should be taking together because of what it will mean to our future. But I have to know that you feel the same way about it."

His words started her heart thumping rapidly, and the night air suddenly seemed to grow colder and then warmer and then even colder again as she absorbed the meaning of those words.

"I *do* feel the same way, Jonathan," she said in earnest. "You know I do, but you *must* try to accept the fact that my career is as important to me and to our future as yours is. I'm an independent woman, Jonathan. I've been very creative and very successful, and I've been earning my own way for a long time. I don't need anyone to look after me in any other way except to love me, and I don't ever want to give up what I have or who I am on my own in order to depend on a man for all of my needs, whether it be a meal or a pair of pantyhose or a sense of self-worth. I wouldn't like myself as a dependent woman, Jonathan, and neither would you."

"But why does it have to be all or nothing?" he demanded. "I'm not asking you to give up your career *or* your independence, Daye, I'm simply asking you for one night, one bloody night!"

"But what you refuse to understand is that on the very night something major will be happening for you and your career, something equally important will be happening for mine."

"A goddamn cocktail party," he sneered.

Her immediate reaction was to ball her fists and hide them away in her lap, so fearful was she of actually reaching over and slapping him for the cavalier attitude he had.

"Did I threaten to end our relationship if you didn't stay here and take me to that party, Jonathan?" she inquired in a voice so cold that he appeared momentarily stunned.

"No," he answered her somewhat hesitantly.

"But, in effect, that's exactly what you've done to me."

When he didn't say anything she became frightened. Would he really consider ending their relationship if she wasn't with him for the opening of the play? Clammy nettles of fear rose all over her body and she was suddenly so lightheaded that she actually felt faint.

"I think I'd better go home now, Jonathan," she said, "before we spoil the few days we have left."

"That sounds awfully final."

"I wasn't the one who issued the ultimatum," she reminded him tightly.

He got up from his chair and came around to where she was sitting. Placing both of his hands on her shoulders, he rested his chin on the top of her head and whispered, "Please don't go. I swear we won't talk about it any more tonight. Why don't you come back inside with me for a while?" When she refused to move, he locked his arms around her neck and started to kiss the side of her face. "Come," he urged her, finally coaxing her out of her chair and into his arms. "Let me make love to you, Daye, my beautiful love."

They did make love, but somehow all of the sweetness had turned sour, and as she lay there in his arms, Daye felt only a wrenching sense of loss and a terrible emptiness where she had so recently felt contentment and completeness.

RHEA CLOSED the front door and picked up her suitcase again. As she started up the stairs, she wished she hadn't stopped off in the city to buy so many gifts for the children before catching the last flight out of La Guardia. She was exhausted, and she prayed that Neil was either out for the evening or happily ensconced as usual in the guest room, so that she could take a quiet bath and then crawl into bed.

"You're home rather late."

Neil's voice at the head of the stairs startled her into nearly losing her footing. Annoyed with him for having frightened her that way, she brushed right past him without even looking at him and walked down the hall to her bedroom.

"No hellos?" he asked as he followed after her.

"Hello," she responded dully.

She was so drained of energy that even speaking was an effort. It was always that way whenever she returned from one of her weekend visits with Steven. She remained floundering in a whirlpool of conflicting emotions, vacillating between elation and despair, excitement and depression. Now, as she dropped her suitcase onto her bed and turned to face her glowering husband, she could feel each one of her conflicting feelings with equal force.

"Don't the stores in Palm Beach have what you need anymore?" asked Neil, settling himself on the bed and toying with the tag on her luggage. "You know, Rhea," he continued without waiting for her to answer him, "for someone who supposedly goes up north to shop, you certainly haven't been buying very much."

"And how would you know that?" she asked. "Have you been going through my closets?"

"I'm the one who pays the bills, remember, and the monthly statements from all of your favorite New York stores have been suspiciously small."

"Think of all the money I've been saving you," she said, "by being such a careful shopper."

"I don't think you're shopping at all," he countered. "I think you're probably having an affair with a pilot."

She didn't even smile at his attempted joke. "Hardly," was all she said as she began unpacking the gifts she had bought for Matthew and Caroline.

"I'm a little confused," he tried again, but this time his voice was serious instead of bantering. "First, there are those mysterious trips up north, supposedly to shop and to see your parents, with whom you've hardly exchanged more than a Christmas card in the five years we've been living in Florida. And now, you've made this sudden decision to allow a public showing of your work, even though you've always hidden it from everyone, including your two best friends. What's going on, Rhea? I think I have a right to know."

She put down the blouse she was holding and studied him very carefully for a moment. Gazing at the clean planes of his handsome face, at the blue-green of his eyes, the golden leanness of his body, she felt nothing, absolutely nothing. His looks had once been able to weaken her, make her cling to him, cause her to need him too much. And now that she could stare at him and feel none of the emotions she had once felt for him, she wondered if she was sorry or glad.

"Is that all I'm ever going to get from you, Rhea," he demanded, "silence and then more silence?"

She blinked and hastily turned away. "Would you like to see the paintings, Neil?" she asked him.

"Now?"

"Now."

"Why not?" He shrugged, and his tone turned caustic. "Since Daye and Franki have already seen them, and the entire population of south Florida will be seeing them in a few days, I suppose I'm about due for my turn, aren't I?"

"Forget it," she snapped irritably, reaching for the blouse again.

He tugged it out of her hand. "I'm sorry," he apologized. "Let's go see your paintings."

As he slowly walked around the gazebo, straining in the room's dim lighting to study the details of each of the twenty portraits, Rhea watched the play of emotions on his face with some amusement.

"You did all of them?" he asked, somewhat incredulously, as he walked past each of them a second time.

"You seem surprised."

"I'm stunned," he admitted. "You're good, Rhea, damned good."

Once his words would have touched the softest part of her and warmed her all over, but now they reached no farther than her ears. Bracing herself, she said, "I'd like to tell you about the paintings now."

"What about them?"

"Aren't you curious to know who the subject is?"

"Don't tell me it's that pilot?" He laughed, his grin so much like the grin of the Neil she had once known that for a moment, she couldn't speak.

"No," she told him when she had recovered her voice, "it isn't that pilot. It's my brother Steven."

"You have a brother?"

"He's thirty-nine years old, and he's retarded."

"Retarded! Jesus!" He shook his head. "And you've kept it a secret all these years?"

"Yes."

"But why?"

"It's a long story," she said. "Do you have time for it, Neil?"

He didn't appear to be listening to her now; he was suddenly staring at her as though he were seeing her for the first time. "It's not hereditary, is it?" he asked her. "Something that might affect our kids?"

"No," she assured him, "it isn't hereditary."

For a moment, he looked doubtful as he combed his fingers through his hair and frowned thoughtfully. "I hope you're right," he said. "Retarded, Christ, that must have been quite a blow for your parents."

"In his own way, Steven is a very special person, Neil," she explained as patiently and as gently as she could.

Again he seemed not to have heard her. In fact, he appeared ready to bolt.

"Neil, I'd like to tell you about Steven." She tried vainly to continue.

"What?" He was completely distracted now.

"Neil—"

"Let's get out of here, Rhea," he snapped, edging toward the door. "I don't know how you can stand the place; it's so damned dismal in here."

The place or the paintings, Neil? she wanted to ask him, but she didn't, because it wouldn't have made any difference to her either way. She was actually laughing softly to herself as she followed him back to the house. How typical of Neil, she thought, refusing to countenance anything that smacked of something slightly less than perfection. How very like her own parents he was in that way; all three of them were afraid of a blight on their almighty family names.

She finished unpacking alone and then ran the water for a bath. Wondering where Neil had gone, she pulled on a robe and padded barefoot down the hall, stopping just outside Matthew's bedroom door. Neil was standing in the middle of the room, staring down at the face of his sleeping son. Just as she was about to call out to him, he tiptoed across the floor and settled himself on the edge of the bed. In a rare display of fatherly affection, he suddenly bent down and placed a gentle kiss on Matthew's forehead.

With her eyes stinging, Rhea returned to her own room and quietly closed the door. But it was only when she was safely locked inside the bathroom, with the water running to muffle the sounds, that she began to cry.

chapter twenty-six

FRANKI BLEW her nose and then wadded the Kleenex into a little ball and tossed it onto the night table beside the bed. Reaching for a fresh one, she dabbed at her eyes and blew her nose again. Never in her life had she felt more wretched than she did right now. Staring down at the Norma Kamali outfit laid out so carefully on the bed, she burst out crying all over again. How much longer would she be able to get away with blousing and poufing and tucking everything she wore in the hope that no one would notice the changes in her figure? She and Brian still hadn't told anyone that she was pregnant, and she suddenly couldn't bring herself to attend Rhea's opening tonight. She couldn't face Rhea or Daye or Neil. She simply couldn't face anyone.

As she blew her nose again, she found herself absurdly recalling the name given to her by one of her grade school teachers. Little Sunny Sunshine, the teacher had called her. Little Sunny Sunshine, ha! The nickname forced another flood of tears into her eyes. Little Sunny Sunshine, always good for a smile, good for a laugh, never down, never blue. If you see

a cloud in the sky, just send for Franki Dunn and she'll chase
it away.

"Well, who's going to chase the clouds away for me?" she
asked herself aloud, taking great heaving gulps between her
tears.

What she had once wanted to share with the world, she now
wanted to keep to herself and reveal to no one. In her desperate
bid to achieve that exalted state of motherhood, she had alien-
ated everyone who had ever meant anything to her, and what
frightened her most was knowing that the bit of life growing
inside her had been the instrument of that separation. How
would that make her feel about this child once it was born?
she wondered. Would the truth always be there, peeking out
at her from behind the well-rehearsed lies and never allowing
her to forget? Was what she had done worth it? Would she
have done it at all if she had taken the time to consider the
consequences more carefully?

"Why aren't you getting dressed?" boomed Brian's voice
from the doorway. "We're supposed to be at the gallery by
eight."

"I don't want to go," she told him, turning her head away
and sniffing into her Kleenex again.

"Why not?"

"Because I'm tired."

"Who's going to believe that?" he demanded, coming into
the room and standing over the bed. "You've never been tired
a day in your life."

"Well, I'm making up for it now."

"Get up, Franki, and get dressed. You're not going to disappoint Rhea."

Franki closed her eyes and tried to picture herself at the
opening, smiling at Rhea and trying not to feel guilty, greeting
Neil as though they were still the civil friends they had always
been, and ignoring Daye while Daye ignored her. "No," she
whimpered, covering her face with her hands. No, she couldn't
go. It was too much, simply too much. She didn't dare go to
that opening tonight.

"I feel sick," she mumbled from behind her hands, only to
have Brian rip her hands away from her face and force her to
look up at him.

"Get up and get dressed, dammit! You have a very good friend who's counting on your being there with her tonight."

"And another one who's probably hoping that I'm not."

"I don't know what happened between you and Daye, Franki, but whatever it was has nothing to do with Rhea and her exhibition."

Franki nearly choked on her tears, but Brian didn't even seem to notice.

"What Rhea's doing tonight is damned brave," he said, "and she's going to need all the support she can get."

"Spoken like a true corporate slave," she muttered. "If she weren't the boss's wife, I wonder if you'd feel the same way."

Her biting remark made him tighten his hold on her wrists. "This corporate slave is as loyal to Rhea as he is to Neil, Franki, so you'd better start getting dressed before I haul you down there in your bathrobe."

His threat only served to intensify her crying, and it wasn't long before her entire body was shaking convulsively from the force of her sobs. Brian released her hands, watching in dismay as her arms fell heavily to her sides, while she continued to weep, wretchedly and uncontrollably.

"Franki, Franki, please," he crooned, in an effort to soothe her. "Franki, please stop crying, please." Perching himself on the edge of the bed, he began to stroke her damp forehead. "I've never seen you like this before, Franki, and it worries me, so please, sweetness, please stop."

When she failed to respond to his gentle urgings, he scooped her up in his arms and started rocking her back and forth, cradling her head against his chest and pressing his mouth to one of her tear-streaked cheeks. After a while, her hands worked themselves slowly around his neck. Twining her fingers tightly together, she brought his head down closer to hers. And then, in a weak little voice, thick with tears, she whispered, "Oh, Brian, Brian, I'm so unhappy."

"I know you are, Franki," he said, his own voice catching, "but we'll find a way to work it out, I swear we will."

"Do you mean it, Brian, do you really mean it?" she cried.

"I mean it, Franki." He kissed her gently on the lips. "Now please get dressed, because I don't think all of this crying is very good for our baby."

                                   *   *   *

NEXT TO the Wally Findlay Galleries, the largest gallery on
Worth was the Rupert, yet even with its two thousand square
feet of floor space, it still seemed incapable of containing the
throng of people surging through its exhibition rooms. It seemed
as though every resident of every town ranging north from
Boca to Palm Beach had turned out to view the watercolors of
Boca's leading hostess, whose artistic talents had been so cleverly concealed for so long beneath such a perfectly manicured
façade. Every major fashion and jewelry designer in the world
was more than duly represented at the gallery tonight as many
of the names and faces featured in every social column from
Suzy to the Town Tattler showed up to be photographed sipping
champagne from Baccarat goblets and plucking wild strawberries out of Steuben bowls.

   Rhea was perched on a new pair of spike heels, which
seemed to raise her, not four inches from the slate gray carpet
of the gallery, but four miles from the earth itself. Draped in
a coral satin gown by Galanos, her throat and wrists wreathed
in pearls and coral beads, large pearl and coral drops swinging
from her ears, she was no longer a tentative presence but a
bold statement. Moving from room to room and guest to guest,
she was cloaked in such poised and confident sureness that her
whole being seemed to have been transformed from the everyday to the exquisite.

   Although she hadn't had more than a few sips of champagne,
she was flushed, heady with her success, and aglow with a
pride unmatched by even the triumph she had felt during her
most successful parties. In effect, this, too, was a party, a self-
styled coming-out party at which she was finally presenting
the real Rhea Bellon Howard to the rest of the world. What
the catalog had left out, she herself filled in, meeting curiosity
with honesty, and answering each guarded question with the
open truth. To her surprise and delight, she found that because
she had dared to admit that she was more than just a wind-up
doll who could dress up and play at life, many of the other
women were eager to admit as much to her. After brief glimpses
into their own vulnerability, Rhea quickly realized that behind

so many polished performances lay stories as heart-breaking as her own.

"Well, Rhea, you've certainly thrown this town for a loop," Neil remarked, as he came up behind her and handed her a fresh glass of champagne. "The tongues might never stop wagging."

"Does that bother you, Neil?" she asked him.

"Bother me? No, of course not."

"Is it making you uncomfortable, then?"

"Don't be ridiculous," he snapped irritably. "It's *your* show, and it's *your* brother."

"That's exactly why I asked if you were uncomfortable."

"Why should I be? It has nothing to do with me."

"Precisely."

Neil's eyes narrowed. "This is more than just an exhibition to you, isn't it, Rhea?"

"How very perceptive of you, Neil." Her smile was enigmatic as she squared off against him in public for the first time.

"What exactly is it then?"

After a moment's consideration, she replied, "Perhaps it's simply Rhea Howard's version of the Declaration of Independence."

"Independence from what?" he ground out. "I was the one who gave you the independence you wanted, Rhea. You wouldn't know what to do with any other kind. You never have."

"That's where you're wrong, Neil," she retorted, her dark eyes blazing. "These past few months have given me more than our thirteen years together have given me, and I've learned more about me and more about us than you could ever hope to know."

On that note, she turned her back on him and walked into the adjoining exhibition room. She tried to locate her parents in the crush of people around her, but it was impossible. When they flew back up north over the weekend, she would be going with them. Then the three of them would visit Steven together for the first time. She had asked Neil to come with them, but he had refused, which hadn't surprised her and therefore didn't disappoint her at all. In a way, she was relieved, because sharing Steven with her parents for the first time would be enough of an emotional experience in itself without some stranger looking on.

She continued to walk about by herself for a while, but as soon as she caught sight of Daye coming through the door, she hurried over to her.

"Rhee, you look spectacular," said Daye as she greeted her friend, "and the exhibition, what little I've seen so far, has been mounted extremely effectively. God, I'm proud of you!"

"I'm sorry Jonathan couldn't be here tonight," Rhea told her, giving her a light peck on the cheek and then peering more closely at the faint purple smudges beneath her large, gold-flecked eyes. "Are you all right?" she asked.

Daye's smile faltered somewhat, but she replied gamely, "I'm fine, although Jonathan and I didn't exactly part on the best of terms. And don't you dare tell me how tired I look, because I already know that."

"The Lake Worth project?"

"Eighteen hours a day and loving every minute of it." As she listened to the sound of her own words, even *she* could hear the strain in them.

"You miss him, don't you, Daye?"

"Of course I miss him, but I've been so busy that—"

"I think you'd better try to convince yourself of that before you try convincing me," Rhea interrupted quietly.

Daye began to fidget with the rope of onyx beads she was wearing. "All right, Rhee," she sighed, "what gave it away?"

"Your eyes."

Daye instinctively dropped her lashes.

"They looked the same way when you got off the plane last November."

"How did they look?"

"Sad," replied Rhea, "sad and scared."

Daye thought about what Rhea was saying, and she couldn't help frowning. Why would she be scared when her future in Florida was brighter now than it had ever been? And sad. What reason could she possibly have for being sad? Jonathan loved her, and she loved him, and they weren't being kept apart by anything more threatening than distance . . . and poor timing . . . and the demands of her career . . . and . . . She glanced up at Rhea, wanting to tell her how wrong she was, that she wasn't sad or scared at all, when she suddenly noticed Franki and Brian coming into the gallery. Brian gave her a friendly wave, but just as he was starting toward her, Franki laid a restraining hand on his arm and held him back. Daye bit down hard on her bottom lip as she watched Rhea turn her head and smile and then excuse herself to go over to them, leaving Daye to stand there all alone.

She meandered into the adjoining room, feeling strangely dejected and isolated, and tried to concentrate on a portrait of Steven sitting on a swing. But all she could see was Franki's radiant face, and she couldn't stop herself from wondering if her luminous glow was the result of her having found another lover.

"How are you, Daye?"

The sound of his voice rooted her to the spot.

"Aren't you even going to say hello to an old friend?"

She wanted to laugh at his use of the word *friend*.

When he touched her arm, she flinched, and when she slowly turned around to look at him, she found herself staring up into the face of a stranger.

"Hello, Neil," she said softly to the stranger.

"You look beautiful tonight, Daye."

Your wife just told me that I look sad, she thought, but she thanked him for the compliment anyway.

"Where's your friend Jonathan?" he asked her.

"He's in New York," she answered matter-of-factly. "His play opens on Broadway the day after tomorrow."

"So I understand. One of my friends is backing it; I hope he doesn't lose his shirt."

"He won't." There was a fierceness in Daye's tone as she rose to Jonathan's defense. *"Arpeggio in Blue* is bound to be the smash hit of the season."

"So it's love after all, is it, Button?" His smile was almost wistful as he studied her flushed face. "You remind me of a mountain lioness protecting her young from attack."

"Aren't I?" she retaliated.

"Touché." He raised his glass to her and then drained it.

She turned away from the bruised look she saw in his eyes and busied herself by glancing about the room and picking out familiar faces. She was surprised to recognize one of them as Philippe Nadeau's, but what surprised her even more was the fact that he was alone. When he noticed her standing there with Neil, he started across the floor, advancing on her with his arms dramatically extended and a broad smile fixed on his dark face. She studied him suspiciously through half-veiled eyes as he pecked at the air near both of her cheeks, but then, instead of addressing himself to her, he turned to Neil with a courtly half bow and said, "My congratulations, monsieur. Your wife displays a unique gift for capturing the elusiveness of innocence. I greatly admire her ability."

As Neil accepted the Frenchman's compliment with a slight inclination of his head and a twist of a smile, Philippe trained the full force of his charms on Daye.

"It would seem that the better man has indeed won the golden prize, *ma belle* Daye. May I offer you my felicitations?"

She was so taken aback by his effusiveness that her reply was hardly more than an awkwardly mumbled thank you.

"And where is the charming Sybil this evening?" interjected Neil in a voice laden with sarcasm.

Philippe responded to Neil's query with an expressive shrug, accompanied by a heavy sigh. "Alas, the lovely Sybil and I have suffered what you might call a parting of the ways. She has decided to turn to art for her pleasure now and is at present considering opening a gallery in the Royal Poinciana Plaza. She has this divine new partner. Perhaps you might know him . . ."

His spirited voice continued to give them the details of Sybil Barron's latest venture, but Daye was no longer listening. Jonathan had been right. As Philippe carried on with his elaborate charade, all Daye could do was stare at him and pity him for the game a man such as himself was continually forced to play.

"Tell me, *ma chère* Daye," Philippe was directing himself to her once again, "have you as yet submitted your proposal for that marvelous new yachting community on Stuart?"

"No, I haven't," she admitted frankly, "have you?"

"But of course."

"I didn't know you were interested in sailing or golfing developments, Philippe," she said.

Again that Gallic shrug. "Business is business, is it not, *chérie?*"

She was still smiling thoughtfully at the irony of it all when he slipped off to speak to Rhea, but the parting glimmer in his deep brown eyes warned her that the rivalry between them was far from over.

"It looks as though you've made yourself a friendly enemy for life, Button," commented Neil with a wry chuckle.

"It must be my night for it," she replied, excusing herself and leaving him staring after her.

Her head was pounding as she worked her way slowly through the exhibition, not as much from the champagne, the noise, and the occasional bit of clever conversation she was forced to indulge in as from the nagging feeling that something was missing. When she caught Rhea's eye over the heads of several strangers, she realized how right her friend's perceptions had been. She *did* miss Jonathan, much more than she had ever expected she would.

Without him, all of the arguments she had been using in defense of her work and her independence had begun to disintegrate, breaking apart into phrases, then words, and finally, into syllables, which had sounds but no meaning. He had spoken of compromise, but she had seen it only as capitulation on her part. He had talked of sharing, but she had thought of it as an attempt to convince her to surrender the rights she had fought so hard to win in a competitive world dominated by men. It was true that she still had her work to occupy her time, but where there had always been satisfaction before, there was now a peculiarly unsatisfying hollowness to everything she did. And tonight, as she stood back and watched so many couples drifting past her, she was finally able to admit to herself that she really didn't want to be alone anymore. Her heart fluttered anxiously in response to what she was thinking, but she couldn't stop the flow of her thoughts. If Jonathan was willing to take a chance on the two of them, then she was, too.

Jonathan. Simply saying his name warmed that deepest part of her that she kept reserved only for him. Repeating his name to herself made her think of the message he had left for her five days ago on her answering machine.

"Hi!" he had said. "Just called to tell you that I love you and miss you very much. New York may be only a few hours away from Florida, but it might as well be the moon. I need you, Daye, so get up here as fast as you can, because there's a very lonely man up here who wants to put his arms around you."

She had been playing it continuously through the days, just as she was playing it over again in her mind now, feeling it smooth away some of the roughness created by his absence and fill up some of the emptiness his absence had created. But the taped message was just a substitute for him and a rather inadequate one at that, and her missing him had become an obsession. During her vital meetings with the O'Connell-Reardon people, Martin Webb, and Nesbit Kaylan, she had found herself too easily distracted, and as well prepared as she had thought she was, she had considered her various presentations to be frighteningly unprofessional. When she should have been concentrating on the discussion taking place around her, she was busy doodling, writing her name and Jonathan's across the notes she had finally stopped jotting down, and then bordering their two names with an assortment of hearts, ribbons, and flowers.

Glancing at her watch, she wondered what he was doing at that very moment. Was he having dinner with some of the members of the cast at Elaine's or Joe Allen? Or was he perhaps attending a performance of some other Broadway show? Was he taking a leisurely stroll through the Village or along Broadway, stopping to browse through the record stores that seemed to stay open all night? Or was he already back in his suite at the Plaza, missing her as much as she was missing him?

Suddenly, she found herself battling the impulse to grab hold of the woman standing nearest her and shout that she was in love with a man named Jonathan Cort. She not only loved him, she also needed him. That she was finally able to acknowledge her need for him sent a heady rush of relief surging through her, filling her with a glorious feeling she wished she could have shared with everyone around her. But right now, the only person she wanted to share that feeling with was Jonathan. She needed to talk to him, to hear his voice caressing her as softly and as lovingly as his hands would have caressed her had they been together. Would Rhea think she was being terribly rude if she left now? she wondered, anxiously scanning the crowded room for some sign of her friend. Relieved when she finally located her standing near the front door of the gallery, she hesitated before going over to her, searching her addled brain for some apology to cushion the abruptness of her departure.

But she needn't have been so concerned. No sooner had she walked over to her friend than Rhea herself pulled her toward the door with an urgent whisper. "Let's go outside for a moment, Daye. There's something I'd like to ask you."

Before she could respond, Daye found she was following Rhea down the steps and onto the sidewalk and then stopping under the old-fashioned street lamp just in front of the gallery.

"Daye, the reason you and Franki haven't been speaking to each other lately," Rhea began, her hands fluttering in sudden agitation to her throat, "is it because . . . were you and Neil . . ." She looked directly at Daye and cleared her throat, and then she said, "Were you and Neil having an affair?"

Daye sucked in a bit of air to fill her burning lungs and then expelled it in a long, shaky whoosh. "No, Rhea," she said, "Neil and I were *not* having an affair." Yet even as she denied it, she could still see Neil on his knees before her, while she . . .

"Franki found out about it and—"

"No, Rhea!" Daye repeated, denying it again with a vehement shake of her head. "Neil and I were only working together, I swear it."

Rhea held Daye's eyes with hers for another long moment, and then she slowly released them as she looked away. "I'm sorry," she apologized, "but I simply had to know."

"I promise you, Rhee," Daye's voice was fierce even though her legs were threatening to give way beneath her, "that there was nothing between us, nothing at all." But knowing that there could have been made her writhe inside.

An eternity seemed to pass before Rhea solemnly nodded her head and murmured, "I guess I'd better go back inside now." Giving Daye a hug, she whispered "Thank you" before turning and walking back toward the gallery.

Her strength gave way, and Daye slumped against the lamppost while a pair of tears trickled slowly down her cheeks. The agony breathed inside her all the way back to the condo, tarnishing the joy she had felt only moments ago and paralyzing her. She didn't call Jonathan as she had intended. Instead, she took the phone off the hook in her bedroom and spent the rest of the night lying fully clothed on top of her bed with the sound of the dial tone ringing in her ear.

WHEN HER meetings on the Lake Worth project were concluded the following afternoon, she left Martin Webb's office with her head spinning and her ears ringing with the extravagant praise lavished on her by George Piper. In spite of her disappointment in herself, the chairman of the board of the O'Connell-Reardon Corporation had obviously been impressed with her, and that was far more important than her own critical appraisal of her performance. Driving home along the A1A, with the ocean on her left and the lush foliage and the mansions of the wealthy on her right, she imagined herself in a cab instead, being driven through the narrow, clangorous streets of Manhattan, crowded, dirty, autumn-faded Manhattan, and up to the doors of the Plaza. But she quickly shook the image from her mind to focus instead on the upcoming cocktail party and press banquet at the Breakers.

She saw herself sweeping alone into the party as she had swept alone into so many other parties. She saw heads turning, saw the admiration in the eyes of the men she passed and the tightening of the lips on the women with them. She watched as she tossed her head and smiled, holding a glass in her left hand while she used her right to shake the hands of the various people being brought over to meet her. She saw herself sparkling brilliantly as she discussed her plans for the Lake Worth condominiums, while dozens of flashbulbs went off in her face and recorded her triumph for yet another social page in yet another publication.

But all she could think of as she ransacked her closets for something especially smashing to wear was that she didn't want to go to that party alone. Five dresses, two evening gowns, and one cocktail suit soon littered her bed, and still nothing pleased her. Any one of them would have been appropriate for the party, but none seemed appropriate for the opening night of a Broadway show. Her sudden intake of breath took her by surprise. The whole time she had been looking for something to wear to the party, what she had really wanted to look for was something to wear to the opening of Jonathan's play.

Her heart was thumping loudly as she lunged for the telephone next to her bed. She called the Lunt-Fontanne, and when the management couldn't locate him, she tried the Plaza. He wasn't there, either. She saw him standing under a lighted marquee with the name *Arpeggio in Blue* splashed across it in bold, black letters, while a tall, rangy woman with cascading ebony hair stood beside him, preening and smiling proudly, as she tucked her arm through his.

"No," she cried, reaching for her address book and opening it to the letter *A*. Finding the number for American Airlines, she punched it out, repeating the word "no" over and over to herself. If they didn't have a flight for her, she would try Delta, then Eastern, and then . . .

The woman's bland voice at the other end confirmed her on the flight to La Guardia at nine the following morning. Without pausing to even think about what she was doing, she quickly dialed Connie's number and told her that she was about to be designated the official representative of Daye Peters and Associates at the cocktail party and press banquet at the Breakers.

"But I've got nothing to wear," wailed Connie, "and my hair, Daye, I'll have to do something with my hair, not to mention my nails—"

Daye was laughing as she cut into her assistant's excited babble. "Close the office, take the entire day to do whatever you have to do, and consider this as a bonus for having worked so hard for so long without a raise. Shop anywhere but Martha, and I'll reimburse you as soon as I get back."

Just as she was about to phone New York again and leave messages for Jonathan both at the theater and at the hotel, she stopped herself. She would surprise him, she decided with an exultant grin, clapping her hands together delightedly. Instead of sweeping into the Breakers, she would sweep grandly into the Plaza and into his waiting arms. Hugging herself, she began dancing slowly around the room, imagining that he was holding her, that his breath was fanning her cheek, and that his husky voice was whispering in her ear how much he loved her.

"Oh, Jonathan, my darling Jonathan," she murmured, as she continued to move in a slow, gentle rhythm as the melody from his ballad "How You Loved Me" played on inside her head. "You were right, Jonathan, it *is* only a party. Wait for me, my precious love, I'll be there with you soon just as you wanted me to be." But even as she spoke, a small part of her was praying that she wasn't too late.

When the doorbell rang, Daye froze in the middle of a turn. Scampering into the foyer, she looked through the peephole, but she couldn't see anyone out there. The bell rang again, and she realized that whoever it was was either crouching or standing off to the side and therefore out of view. Annoyed, she called out, "Yes, who is it?"

Silence.

Again she asked who it was, and a moment later, she heard a sobbing voice say, "It's Franki."

She threw open the door and caught her friend as she collapsed weeping into her arms.

{ *chapter twenty-seven* }

THEY SAT across from each other on the pair of matching sofas in the living room, much as adversaries might sit—each perched awkwardly on the edge of her seat, each with her hands clasped tightly in her lap. Daye glanced from Franki's unhappy, tear-lined face down to her own hands and then back up at Franki's face again. A hint of that wonderful luminosity was still there, but at such close range, Franki's face also seemed fuller than usual. In fact, she seemed to have put on some of the weight she had spent most of her life battling to keep off.

"What I have to say is probably going to shock you, Daye," Franki began uncertainly, clenching and unclenching her fingers as she spoke, "but please don't interrupt me or try to stop me, because if you do, I know I won't have the nerve to finish what I came here to tell you."

"All right, Franki," she agreed, mentally bracing herself for what was to follow.

Franki drew in a deep breath, and as her eyes began to fill again, she stared up at the ceiling and said in a quavering voice, "I'm nothing but a pathetic imitation of you and Rhea."

Daye automatically opened her mouth to contradict her and then just as quickly closed it again.

"You were the ones who had it all, and I was the one who was always trying to catch up. You had the looks and the talent and this incredible ambition, and Rhea had the ability to attract champions without so much as lifting a finger. She just glided through life while someone else held the door open for her. And me?" She gave a harsh little laugh. "I was the outsider. Oh, none of you ever knew it, but I was."

"Franki—"

"Don't, Daye."

She immediately fell silent again.

"My parents taught me how to lie, and I was the perfect pupil. They were working-class people, and yet they moved us into this prestigious East Side apartment building where we still lived like paupers, but"—and she held up a finger for emphasis—"we had the chance to pretend that we were part of the upper crust. They told me that if I acted rich, I could marry rich, so I put on a good act and found myself Brian Shelton, the ideal catch, with good looks, good breeding, and good potential." At this point, she stopped to wipe her eyes and blow her nose. "Unfortunately, my golden catch came with a slightly less than golden medical history. He couldn't give me children. He's . . . he can't . . . Dammit all, he's sterile!" she spit out the word and then hastily covered her face with her hands while Daye just sat there, watching her with a rising sense of helplessness and trepidation.

A moment later, Franki continued, and her voice was a rasping vise of pain as she said, "I'm pregnant, Daye, and the baby is Neil's."

Daye gasped and grabbed the arm of the sofa for support.

"I used Neil Howard to get what Brian could never give me," she admitted, "and I think I only used him because he was Rhea's."

Daye's heart flip-flopped painfully inside her chest, and she reached up with one hand to massage the spot where a terrible ache was beginning.

"I've always wanted children, Daye, always, but it seemed I was destined to be the outsider in this area, too. Oh, I could be everyone's favorite aunt and act as everyone's substitute mother, whenever their *real* mothers were either too busy or too tired or too bored to spend any time with them, but I could never be a real mother myself. My two sisters had children, Rhea had children and couldn't have cared less about them, and I had none." She shredded the Kleenex she was holding, and her voice was bitter as she said, "Brian refused to adopt a child, so I finally did the only thing a substitute mother *could* do: I found myself a substitute father."

"My God, Franki, why are you telling me this?" Daye blurted out without thinking. "How could you take a chance on telling me?"

"I suppose it's because I just can't handle it alone anymore. It's not turning out the way I thought it would, and—"

"Then Brian doesn't know who the real father is?"

"No."

"Does anyone else know?"

Franki shook her head. "Only you."

Daye groaned. Now part of the responsibility for this continuing masquerade of Franki's was hers, and it was a burden she neither wanted nor appreciated. And yet, as she looked at her friend's stricken face, she wondered what other choice she had. The next few minutes ticked by in uncomfortable silence. Then Franki got up, came to sit on the sofa next to Daye, and reached for both of her hands.

"I always wanted to be like you, Daye," she confided, "because you were independent and successful, but I also wanted to be like Rhea, with children and a man who could give me everything. In my own way, I've managed to achieve all of those things to a greater or lesser degree, and yet, somehow, I still feel like the outsider, the imitator, the fraud. I know I have no right to be asking you this, but I'm going to ask it of you anyway. Please try to forgive me. Forgive me for wanting to be like the two of you and for botching it up so badly."

After that, she had nothing left to say. Pushing herself to her feet, she wiped away her tears with the back of her hand and turned to leave.

Daye's voice stopped her. Standing up, with her hands shoved into the pockets of the slacks she was wearing and her head bowed, Daye said in a gentle voice, "We knew all about your family, Franki, but it didn't matter. We loved and accepted you for exactly who you were, not for the person you were pretending to be."

"You knew!" Franki's eyes were wide, the expression in them wild and disbelieving.

Daye nodded. "Yes, we did."

"You knew, and all the time I thought I was getting away with it!"

"What mattered was the kind of person Franki Dunn was," Daye repeated. "What counted was her warmth and her sense of humor, her intelligence and her loyalty as a friend. The fact that her family owned a couple of drugstores in Queens never mattered one damned bit. But"—and she shook her head as she continued—"what Franki Dunn Shelton did because she wanted a child is something I don't think I can ever accept."

Franki started walking toward the door, and this time Daye didn't hold her back. With her hand resting on the doorknob, she turned and whispered, "I loved you, too, Daye, I've always loved both of you."

As the door closed behind her, Daye sank back onto the sofa again with her head in her hands, too sick at heart to cry.

FRANKI SAT slumped against the steering wheel with her head resting on her arms. They knew! And they had always known. The words and the realization of what those words meant spun around and around inside her head like frenzied bats, blind and out of control. When she lifted her head, it was to gaze up at the lighted windows of the condo seven stories above the ground, where she had played out her dangerous game with Neil in the hope of finally having it all at last. She swallowed hard, and for the first time she noticed the terrible taste in her mouth. It was the taste of blood and salt and bile. And it was also the bitter taste of defeat.

She had it all now, and yet she still had nothing. What her father had begun, she had simply perfected. In twenty-five years, the small lie had grown into a monumental lie, and in using Neil to give her a child, she had only perpetuated that lie. Having Rhea's husband hadn't made her Rhea, excelling in sports and squirreling away a small fortune hadn't made her Daye. She was still Francine Dunn, the girl from Queens, sleeping with her two sisters in one small room, while her parents slept on the hide-a-bed in the living room of their otherwise unfurnished apartment with the smart address, high above Manhattan.

As she drove north along the A1A toward Palm Beach, she suddenly realized that she had taken Brian's Mercedes instead of her wagon. How natural it had seemed to visit Daye in the Mercedes. All three of them had a Mercedes now. All three of them. That made her smile. The three of them, the best of friends. She made no attempt to stanch the flow of her tears as they continued coursing down her cheeks, but she *did* turn up the volume on the radio as far as it could go.

That way, when she accelerated as she approached the abrupt bend in the A1A known as Sloan's Curve, she didn't hear the screeching of the tires or the high pitch of her own screams or the sound of crunching metal as the Mercedes slammed head-on into one of the stone retaining walls that held back the sea.

THE JANGLING of the telephone jarred Daye from her troubled sleep. She fumbled for the receiver, knocked it to the floor, and then used the coiled plastic cord to pull it up.

"Daye, it's Brian," announced the quavering voice before she could even say hello. "There's been an accident. Franki . . . she's in the hospital, and she's asking for you."

Daye sat straight up in bed and raked the hair out of her eyes. Then she had him repeat what he had just said.

"She's at Good Samaritan Hospital in West Palm," he continued between sobs, "in Intensive Care. They've operated on her, but it . . . they . . . they don't think she's going to make it."

"Oh, my God," Daye gasped. She stretched out her hand and switched on the bedside lamp. "Oh, my God," she repeated over and over again, blinking in the bright glare of the light and peering at the time. It was only six o'clock. "I'll get dressed right away, and I'll be there as soon as I can," she promised him.

"Thank you, Daye," he murmured hoarsely. "I'm going to call Rhea now."

She streaked north along I-95 to Good Samaritan on Flagler, stopping at only three of the eight red lights she encountered on the way. She careened into the parking lot and ran into the main building of the large hospital, and it was only as she sagged panting against the wall of the elevator that she suddenly realized how spontaneously and automatically she had responded to Brian's call. One of her best friends was in trouble, and she had reacted as only another best friend could. She had forgotten about what had happened between them and had come running.

A nurse with a solemn young face showed Daye to the first in a series of glass-partitioned cubicles, and as she stood outside the window, staring at what remained of her friend, all she could see was a thirteen-year-old girl, her short blond hair blowing like feathers in the breeze, bounding toward her with a tennis racquet in one hand and her schoolbooks in the other. And as usual, she was smiling. Franki Dunn was always smiling. Through a blaze of tears, Daye began to smile herself. Little Sunny Sunshine, that was the nickname Franki had been given once, a name she insisted she had always hated. Little Sunny Sunshine. How long ago that all seemed now.

She jumped as someone touched her shoulder lightly. Turning, she saw that it was Brian, and she felt her heart break into a thousand agonized pieces. His face was ashen, his eyes were red and swollen from weeping, and his voice trembled as he said, "If anyone asks, pretend that you're her sister. They won't let anyone in but family right now."

Daye gave his hand a squeeze and then walked slowly into the glass-enclosed room. As she cautiously approached the bed, she saw that the bandaged figure lying in it looked less like a human being than she did a giant white-wrapped puppet dangling from a series of wires and tubes and pipes, like so many dancing strings. Daye choked down a wave of nausea and edged closer to the bed with its raised metal sides. It was a crib for an adult, she thought bitterly, designed to confine her movements, to keep her still, to protect her from falling out and hurting herself. As if she could hurt herself any more than she already had.

Franki's face was cut and bruised, but it was fully exposed, unlike the rest of her head, which was completely bandaged, and both arms, which were set in plaster casts. A white sheet covered the rest of her body, while every part of her seemed to have been wired to one of a number of overhead machines, which blinked and beeped and charted and gave some credence to the fact that Francine Shelton was still marginally alive. Wondering whether she was awake or asleep, Daye bent down and touched Franki lightly on the cheek. A moment later, Franki's eyelids fluttered open, and a semblance of a smile flickered across her face.

"Hi," came the cracked whisper.

"Hi," Daye whispered back to her.

"I did a good job, didn't I?" She said it so softly that Daye had to bend even closer to hear her. "Not quite good enough, though."

"Ssh, Franki, don't talk that way."

Franki tried to laugh, but it came out more like a husky gasp. "I lost the baby, Daye," she whimpered, "but *I'm* still alive. Don't you think that's funny?"

"Oh, Franki," moaned Daye, unable to stop herself from touching the few strands of blond hair escaping from the bandages wrapped around her head. "I'm so sorry. I'm so sorry about everything."

"So am I." Franki coughed as she tried to raise her voice. "So am I." Moving her head slightly, she appeared to be looking around the room for something. "Rhea?" she asked weakly. "Where's Rhea?"

"Brian called her just after he phoned me," replied Daye. "She should be here soon."

As Franki closed her eyes again, she whispered, "She'd better hurry."

Blinking back her tears, Daye looked up from the bed and tried to focus her attention on one of the machines. In the flashing lights she saw three girls huddled together on the sofa in Rhea's den, watching Lon Chaney in *The Wolfman* on TV and eating out of the same giant bowl of popcorn. She saw Franki bending down to tie both Daye's and Rhea's ice skates, because neither of them could ever tie the laces tightly enough, and then holding each of them by the hand while they skated together around the rink at Rockefeller Center. She saw Franki as the second bridesmaid at Rhea's wedding, the two of them wearing identical yellow and white dotted-swiss gowns and walking down the carpeted aisle together, side by side in perfect step. She saw Franki mugging for the camera in twelve different European cities, as Brian proudly showed her the movies he had taken of their honeymoon. She saw Franki with Rhea's children . . . Franki with Neil . . . Franki . . . so many Frankis, so many images, all of them tumbling and mixing together . . .

"Daye?"

Rhea was standing there, her hands twisting nervously in front of her, her eyes dull, her mouth pulled down into an unhappy grimace of pain and confusion.

"Rhee?" It was a fading gasp from the bed behind them.

Together Daye and Rhea turned and went over to the bed, peering down through stricken eyes at Franki's battered face.

"Rhee, don't blame Daye," whispered Franki. "It was me. Neil and me, never Daye."

Even without turning her head, Daye could feel Rhea's eyes searching out hers.

"You, Franki!" Rhea was incredulous. "But why?"

"Because he was yours, and I wanted to be you."

Rhea's face was now as white as Franki's. "Daye," she pleaded, "what is she saying? What does she mean?"

"Later," Daye cautioned her, holding a warning finger to her lips, "I'll explain it all to you later."

Just then, a nurse strode into the room, all brusqueness and efficiency, pointing first to Rhea and Daye and then to the door.

"Neither of you should be in here, you know. Now out, please."

"But we're her sis—" began Daye, only to have the woman cut her off with a knowing, but sympathetic smile.

"Even if you were," she said, "I'd still have to ask you to leave. I'm very sorry."

"They're my best friends," protested Franki, coughing violently as she tried to raise her head. "Please . . ."

As Daye hung back, the nurse began escorting her toward the door by the elbow.

"Daye . . . Rhea . . ."

"We'll be right outside, Franki," Daye promised the anguished figure on the bed.

"Please, Daye . . . I love you . . . both of you . . . I swear . . ."

The door closed quietly behind them, and Daye and Rhea

exchanged shattered glances. As soon as they reached the waiting room, they collapsed together onto a Leatherette couch and
fell into each other's arms, sobbing.

"She's going to die, isn't she, Daye?" wept Rhea.

"I don't know, Rhee. I honestly don't know."

"I thought we were friends," she sobbed.

Daye shuddered at the sound of her own words coming back
to haunt her. "We were, Rhea," she told her, "and we still
are."

"But something happened to us," she insisted, "something
we had the power to stop and never did. We lost touch with
one another and forgot what it meant to *really* be good friends.
Look at us now, Daye, and you'll see that I'm right." She
reached into her purse for a handkerchief and frowned when
she couldn't find one.

"Will a Kleenex do?" offered Daye with a hint of a smile.

As Rhea put out her hand, she was actually giggling through
her tears. "I think a Kleenex will do very nicely, thank you."
Then after giving her nose several delicate blows, she said to
Daye, "Now please tell me what Franki meant."

So Daye did, and when she was through, she added, "I had
a crush on Neil when I was a kid, and somewhere in the back
of my mind I had the idea that when we grew up, he and I
would make a spectacular team." She would dissemble, she
told herself, for the whole truth would serve no useful purpose
now. "I thought I'd never get over it when he married you—
my best friend—but I did, because I loved you far more than
I'd ever cared for him."

Rhea was slowly crumpling the Kleenex in her hand while
she considered what Daye had been telling her. Then, in a
thoughtful voice, she said, "I always suspected that there had
been something between the two of you, but I never really
wanted to find out. And after a while, it no longer mattered."
Then, giving her head a sorrowful shake, she murmured, "Poor
Franki. To think that she never considered herself good enough.
Were we awful snobs, Daye, to have made her feel that way?"

"What troubled Franki had very little to do with us, Rhee,"
Daye told her sadly. "It had started long before we even met her."

"You know, as much as I feel sorry for her and what she did
because she so desperately wanted a child, knowing that she used

Neil and that the two of them had an affair doesn't hurt me now the way it might have hurt me once. In fact, I really don't feel anything at all."

As Daye followed Rhea's eyes down to her hands, she noticed that for the first time in thirteen years, Rhea wasn't wearing her diamond wedding band.

"I've decided to leave him, Daye," she said.

"Leave Neil?" Daye's eyes were wide.

"I don't need him anymore, at least not the way I needed him when I married him. Everything's changed for me, Daye, and I'm finally prepared to do what I should have done years ago. I've already found myself an apartment in Boca, and I've enrolled at FAU to get my degree in special education. My parents are helping me financially, but I intend to keep on painting and selling my work, to supplement my income when I start classes full-time in January." Her eyes were bright again, glowing with that luminosity which had only been temporarily dulled by her grief. "Once I have my degree, I'll be qualified to teach children just like Steven in a remedial setting of some sort, but while I'm working toward my degree, I intend to work on myself as well, trying to find out more about who Rhea Howard is and what she ultimately wants for herself. One day I might even want Neil again, but the fact that I might not no longer frightens me." She looked down at the floor for a moment, and when she raised her eyes again, some of their former pain was back. "I haven't been a very good mother," she said. "Franki was always much better with my children than I was. I hope that in time I'll be able to make it up to them, but right now, I need that time for me."

"My little Rhea," murmured Daye, using both of her hands to stroke the sides of her friend's small, thin face, "I don't know whether to applaud or cry."

"Just be happy for me, that's all," she said, wrapping her arms around Daye's neck and hugging her. "I'm sorry I ever doubted you, my dearest friend, but I'm here for you now, the way I wish I could have been all these years."

They were still holding on to each other when Brian came over to them to say, "I'm being allowed back in to see Franki for another five minutes, but there's no sense in your hanging around, because they won't let anyone else see her today."

Daye waited until he had gone before turning to Rhea again. "Jonathan's play is opening tonight on Broadway, and I'd planned to fly up there this morning and surprise him." Rummaging through her purse for change, she said, "I'll be back in a minute. Just let me cancel my flight and call Jonathan to let him know what's happened."

"Don't you dare!" Rhea snatched the quarter out of Daye's hand and pulled her down beside her again.

"Rhea!"

"You're *not* canceling that flight."

"But how can I go now while . . ." Her voice trailed off as she glanced down the corridor toward that row of glass-enclosed rooms. "I can't leave, Rhea; I just can't."

"Oh, yes you can, and you will," she insisted. "Brian just told you that no one else is going to be allowed in to see Franki today, so there really *is* no point in your being here. Jonathan needs you with him tonight, Daye, much more than Franki needs you now, so don't let him down, not if you love him."

Daye slumped forward in her seat with her elbows on her knees and her head in her hands, torn between wanting to leave and needing to stay; needing to be with the man she loved and wanting to be with the friend she might never see again. She thought of New York in October and Broadway on opening night and a man standing there with his arms open and empty, waiting for her to come and fill them. And she thought of twenty-one years of friendship, of a bond tighter than the bond of sisterhood, and she saw it fading, loosening its hold on her even as she fought to keep it strong and taut and . . . forever.

"Brian said we couldn't see her," she mumbled, turning her head just enough to look at Rhea's face, "but no one said we couldn't wait here, did they?"

"No, they didn't."

"Then we'll wait."

And so they sat together on the couch, neither of them ever farther away from the other than the tips of their fingers, with some part of their bodies always touching, as the hours ticked by and Brian slipped in and out of Franki's room for five minutes at a time and then returned to his chair in a corner of the waiting room to weep alone. At one, Rhea poked Daye and said, "You'd better leave now if you plan to make that three o'clock flight."

"I haven't even packed yet," she sighed, stretching out her legs and staring balefully at her wrinkled trousers.

"Then please go home right away and pack."

"Do you think I should call Jonathan and tell him—"

"I thought you wanted it to be a surprise."

"I did, but now—"

"Then keep it a surprise."

Daye sighed again. "All right," she conceded, "I will." She gave her friend a grateful hug and then kissed her warmly on both cheeks. "I love you, Rhea Bellon Howard," she declared fiercely.

"And I love you, Daye Peters." She patted her on the back and then gave her a friendly shove. "Now, go!"

Daye rose obediently and snapped her a mock salute. "I'm going, Rhee," she told her. "I'm going."

She stopped and spoke to Brian for a moment, and then she walked back down the corridor to the Intensive Care Unit. Staring bleakly through the glass at the pale, bandaged figure on the bed, she willed Franki to open her eyes and look at her one last time. She waited and waited, but Franki's eyes remained closed, and it was only because Rhea came over to her and steered her away from the window that Daye was finally able to leave.

"And you promise that you'll try to speak to her?" Daye asked one final time as they walked together to the elevators.

"I promise."

"She needs to know that you understand, Rhee, and that we both forgive her."

"I know, Daye." Rhea gently squeezed her friend's cold hand. "I know." A moment later, the elevator arrived and they said their goodbyes all over again.

It was as Daye was swinging through the revolving door on her way to the parking lot that she saw him. He was coming toward her, his stride hurried, his head bowed against the brisk fall wind, which forced his thick, blond hair straight back from his forehead. Although he was moving with that same energetic purposefulness that had always powered his steps, when he got closer to her, she could see that something terrible had happened to his face. It was as though some primeval hand had reshaped his features, turning the handsomeness ugly and his youngness old. Suddenly, Neil Howard was an old man, whose long life was chronicled in the lines and shadows of his face.

It was creased inside each furrow on his forehead, etched into the web of fine lines radiating outward from the corners of his eyes, and tracked in twin arcs from his nose to his tugged-down mouth. Under his eyes were deep smudges of sooty gray, while his eyes themselves stared out at her like the gaunt, faded hollows of a death's head. Putting out his hand to hold her back, he called out to her with the crumbling voice of a withering spirit. But she stepped aside and hurried past him, feeling the tips of his fingers travel down the length of her arm as his hand fell away from her.

"Daye!"

Once more she heard her name being called, but she no longer knew if it was Neil or the wind through the trees or the faint whisper of a memory.

{ *chapter twenty-eight* }

SHE LEANED as far back as she could in the aisle seat, with her seat belt loosely buckled around her waist and her eyes closed. Adjusting the volume on the headset she was using, she turned toward the window and the empty seat beside her when the achingly beautiful Barbra Streisand and Neil Diamond hit "You Don't Bring Me Flowers" started to play. She could feel her eyelids beginning to sting—the three of them had decided that the song was one of their all-time favorites—and just as she was about to switch to another music channel, the flight attendant touched her on the shoulder and asked her if she wanted anything to drink. She ordered a double rye and ginger.

Pouring the contents of both miniature bottles of rye and a touch of the ginger ale over the single ice cube in her plastic glass, she proceeded to administer the stiff drink to herself as though it were cough syrup. Before swallowing each mouthful, she would hold it in her mouth until it began to burn her throat, and then she would gulp it down quickly. It was a trick Franki had taught her—how to achieve a maximum effect with a minimum amount of alcohol—and it always worked.

It wasn't long before that familiar tingling began spreading through her body, fanning outward to the tips of her fingers, and then reaching all the way down to her toes. When she was able to touch the tip of her nose with her index finger and feel it growing numb, she knew that once again the remedy for alleviating all pain and all caring had worked. By the time her plastic glass was empty, she was floating upward toward a gentler place where, elevated above her agony, she became a painless part of the air itself.

But the images were still alive behind her closed eyes. Images much like those on *Movietone News*, the black and white newsreel highlighting the major events of the day, which had been run before every film she had seen as a child. Now, instead of a news story, she was viewing her own story and the stories of her two best friends. Some of the images were in black and white, others were in full color, while still others had been softened by a sepia wash into faded daguerreotypes.

The past flared brightly for one final moment, and then in an incandescent burst of flame, it was gone, much the way a single frame of film footage that has jammed in the projector flares and then disintegrates because of the intense heat of the bulb in back of it. Wavering images of the present soon took the place of those from the past, and a freshly sharpened nail of painful awareness began scratching away at the protective layers the alcohol had wrapped around her.

"Look at us now," Rhea had urged her, and so she did. And what she saw was a photograph of the three of them as it was slowly splitting into three separate parts. Rhea had said that somewhere along the way they had lost touch, forgotten how to really be friends. But what if she was wrong? What if they had *never* been real friends? Because after twenty-one years of knowing each other, it seemed they hadn't really known one another at all.

She shifted about in her seat, looking for a more comfortable position for her restless, aching body, as she continued to search for the answers to some of the questions invading her numbed mind. There were just too many questions, she decided wearily, questions about the three of them, about Jonathan and herself, about her career . . . She squirmed and shifted and fidgeted and then squirmed some more. Too many questions . . . too few answers . . . It was impossible to get comfortable at all . . . simply impossible . . .

"Daye, darling, what a delightful surprise!"

The headset had been lifted, the protection of the music was gone, and nothing could prevent the sound of that familiar, throaty growl of a voice from reaching her ears and piercing her skull. Hackles rose on the back of Daye's neck, and a droplet of icy fear began trickling its way down the entire length of her spine. She turned her head slightly and trained disbelieving eyes on the shadow darkening the aisle next to her seat, traveling upward from the tooled leather boots and the long fringed and beaded forest green suede skirt and matching jacket to the sun-bronzed face framed by its spill of sleek jet hair. Turning her head to the side again, Daye closed her eyes and willed the specter with the smiling slash of a mouth to vanish and leave her dreams undisturbed.

But Maren MacCaul didn't go away. In fact, for one heart-stopping moment, Daye was afraid the woman was about to settle herself in the empty seat beside her.

"Don't look so surprised, pretty lady," came that gravelly purr again, much to Daye's dismay. "You didn't think I could possibly allow *Arpeggio in Blue* to open without my being there, now did you?" Without waiting for Daye to reply, she continued. "Jonathan was a complete darling, of course, sending me six complimentary tickets for the opening, but no one else in my little company could scrape together the necessary funds for the air fare"—this was emphasized by a deep, dramatic sigh—"and so, naturally, it's been left to Maren to see that the Gorham Sound Playhouse is adequately represented there this evening."

"Naturally," agreed Daye with a forced smile.

"You know, of course, that I've decided to sell the playhouse and move up-north."

Daye was instantly alert, her eyes wide, her heart thumping.

"Oh, yes, darling, the sun has this ghastly tendency to turn the brain to mush after a while, and mine is definitely starting to go on me. I'm bored with the tropics now, and besides, I've always found that one functions far more effectively in a colder clime. So, pretty lady, bid me a fond farewell and wish me luck, because within the month, I shall be the proud proprietor of the most divine little shack in the entire East Village."

Daye's words were suddenly tumbling all over themselves

in their rush to get out, as she asked, "Did you sell the playhouse to the Llewelyn Corporation or to Neil Howard?"

"Neil Howard?" The woman threw back her head and roared with laughter. "Even if he *is* a dear friend of yours, he's still an opportunist, and I simply detest opportunists. No, darling, I sold it to the Llewelyn Corporation. They apparently are quite sincere in their intentions to preserve rather than destroy things of beauty and significance. In spite of your loyalty, my dear, to the dashing Mr. Howard, you *do* approve of my decision, don't you?"

To her complete surprise, Daye found herself actually nodding. "Yes, Maren," she told the woman, "I *do* approve."

"Well, then," Maren tossed off the words with a clap of her hands, "no doubt we shall see each other this evening to toast our champion's triumphant return?"

Daye steeled herself and met the woman's challenging gaze straight on. "No doubt," she answered with a finality in her tone she hoped might signal an end to their discussion.

Dipping her head as if in acquiescence, Maren declared, "Until tonight, then."

And with a dramatic twirl of one large-boned wrist, she swept down the aisle toward the rear of the plane.

Daye slipped the headset back into place, but the mood was gone, the spell broken. She no longer needed the music as a cushion for her weightless body and drifting thoughts, but she wanted it as a diversion to block out all of the questions that Maren's presence on that aircraft had sent skittering across her mind like so many hard-edged metal jacks. Was her decision to purchase a playhouse in the Village based on Jonathan's return to Broadway? Would he be dividing his time as well as his affections between the two of them now? Maren in New York whenever he was in New York; Daye in Florida when he happened to be in residence in Gorham Sound . . . A sick feeling of dread rose up inside her and closed her throat. At that moment, if she had been aboard a bus, she would have pulled the cord or pressed the button and gotten off at the very next stop.

But she wasn't on a bus; she was on a plane, thirty-five thousand feet above the earth. And instead of soaring with it and enjoying the freedom of the flight, she was being dragged down and bound to the ground by the weight of her fear.

When the plane landed at La Guardia, Daye remained in her seat, her seat belt still fastened, her arms hanging limp by her sides. As the cabin gradually emptied out and Maren brushed past her without so much as a backward glance or a hasty smile, Daye turned her head and looked out of the window again. How bleak and gray and forbidding it seemed out there, with no dot of color, no touch of softness to brighten and gentle the harsh somberness of the asphalt landscape as it stretched farther than her eye could see. She shivered in the cold that was filtering through the cabin and thought of the languid warmth and the shimmering haze of the seashore she had just left behind, and she missed and needed its gentle balminess and its restorative peace.

"Are you all right, miss?"

Daye glanced up at the flight attendant bending over her so solicitously and offered her a faint, apologetic smile.

"We seem to have gone through this once before," she said in her low-pitched voice, watching as the young woman bent even closer to catch what she was saying.

"I beg your pardon?" There was a hint of confusion and suspicion in the flight attendant's pale blue eyes.

"Never mind. I was just thinking out loud," murmured Daye, dismissing the subject with a distracted wave of her hand.

"Have you any personal belongings up front or—"

"Yes, a garment bag," Daye interrupted softly.

It was only as Daye neared the open door of the plane, her tote bag slung over one shoulder, her body finally braced and ready to leave, that the flight attendant folded the blue vinyl dress bag over her arm and gave her a professional parting smile. Daye returned her smile and kept it fixed on her face all the way through the terminal. At one point, she caught sight of Maren up ahead of her, and she immediately slowed her pace, holding back in order to keep the safety of distance between them. As she continued walking, she couldn't help remembering another flight and another long walk, away from the cold and into the warmth, away from the past and toward the future, and into the waiting arms of her two best friends.

Was she doing it all in reverse now? she asked herself, as she approached one of the luggage carousels and kept on walking. And then, suddenly, there was no further room for thought. *It couldn't be!* She stopped in her tracks, and the man striding along just behind her narrowly avoided slamming right into her. It couldn't be, but it was. He was standing directly in front of one of the red exit signs, his eyes darting this way and that as he scanned the scores of passengers pouring into the terminal.

Her heart rose, only to sink again almost immediately. He was obviously there to meet Maren, not her. He was expecting Maren and not her. He didn't even know she was coming. She felt the tears begin as she stood there, rooted to the spot, unable to move either forward or back.

"Daye!"

She was only vaguely aware of someone calling her name.

"Daye, over here!"

She looked up. And it was then that she saw him coming toward her, brushing past all of the people standing in his way as he fought to get to her. She looked around for some sign of Maren, but the woman was nowhere to be seen. And then she looked straight into the marvelous face of the man reaching out for her, and her heart began to soar all over again.

"Jonathan," she sighed as she fell into his arms.

He kissed her over and over again, and when both of them were laughing and gasping for breath, he said, "Rhea phoned and told me you were coming. Oh, Daye, my precious, beautiful Daye, I love you, I love you."

"I love you too, my Jonathan," she whispered, knowing she was truly home at last.